DEDICA

This book is dedicated to my mot
gentlest and caring of mothers, w .... my
great Aunt Maryanne O'Rourke, who, in 1903, weathered the
harsh journey across the Atlantic to follow her dream.

ACKNOWLEDGEMENTS

Jean Chapman
Romantic Novelist's Association
Rosemary Hoggard
Leicester Writers' Club
Lutterworth Writers' Group

My daughter Samantha for her insight and help with revision.
My husband Dennis for giving me space to write.
My lovely family and grandchildren for their support.

My publisher: Peter and Kemberlee Shortland; my grateful thanks.

My editor, Christine McPherson, for her keen observations in spotting errors.

A huge thank you to cover artist, Amanda Stephanie, for the amazing book covers.

CHAPTER ONE

Dublin City 1917

Jo Kingsley awoke from a troubled sleep. Her eyes flickered open, and her gaze rested on the thick velvet curtains, partly drawn across the bedroom window. The street lamp shone through, casting shadows on the ceiling. She glanced at the holy pictures on the wall that had always been a source of comfort to her. But tonight the Virgin Mary did not appear to be smiling down on thirteen-year-old Jo. A distant scream reverberated around the room. She felt a stab of fear and reached across the bed to her grandmother.

'Grandma. Grandma, please wake up.' With trembling fingers, she traced the outline of her grandmother's face. It was cold. Startled and distressed, she drew back in the clear knowledge that the wailing sound was none other than the Banshee.

Jo scrambled from the bed, hurried down the stairs, grabbed her black woollen coat from the hallstand, and ran barefoot from the house. Her long fair hair flew out behind her as she raced down the street to her mother's cottage. The Dublin streets were dark and dimly lit, and the frosty pavement made her feet tingle as she hammered on the door. Her stepfather, Tom, wheezing and gasping for breath, finally opened it. She stepped inside.

'Ma! Ma! Come quickly, something's happened to Grandma.'

Kate, a thin woman in her early forties, appeared in the doorway of the bedroom, rubbing the sleep from her eyes. 'What in the name of God brings you out at this time of the night, girl?'

'I think me grandma's dead,' Jo cried. 'I...I heard the Banshee.'

Kate sprang into action. 'You look after things here, Jo-Jo.

1

Sleep on the couch for now.' In minutes, her mother was dressed and rushing up the street.

Five-year-old Liam cried out in his sleep, and Tom handed her a cover before going back into the bedroom and closing the door behind him. Jo held the thin well-worn blanket close to her shivering body. She didn't want to be here. A dull ache gripped her. How could her grandma be dead? She'd been all right when they'd bid each other good night. Powerless to stem the tears that trickled down her cold face, she sat in the darkness. What would happen to her now? She bit her nails, digging into the tops of her fingers until they hurt.

The room smelt damp and Jo had no recollection of ever living here. Now, whenever she had cause to visit her mother, it was a sharp reminder of how lucky she was to have been brought up by her grandmother. She curled up on the couch, but couldn't sleep.

She heard coughing, and a shaft of light appeared in the doorway. Tom shuffled into the room clearing his throat, carrying the twins. Jo swung her feet from the couch onto the cold floor. 'Is there anything I can do?'

He shook his head, too breathless to speak, and placed the whimpering babies down next to her. He lit the lamp on the table and turned up the wick. The light threw shadows across the room, the wallpaper peeling from the walls. Jo looked down at the children's thin frames and spindly legs, and covered them with her blanket. Innocent eyes looked up at her, the same blue as hers, except theirs were hollow and lacked lustre. She shivered and wrapped her arms around herself to keep warm. The reality of her mother's life hit her and brought a lump to her throat. She felt sorry for the children, who, in spite of the cold, had fallen asleep.

Feeling wretched and helpless, she made a fire from the turf piled up in the corner by the hearth, hoping it would take the chill from the room. She glanced across to where Tom was lying with his head down on the table, his bald patch visible and a blanket pulled across his thin shoulders. There was no sound apart from his laboured breathing as he dozed, and the sparks from the fire as the turf ignited. She filled the black kettle and hung it on one of the hooks over the fire.

The cupboard was bare apart from a packet of oats, and she wondered if her mother was drinking again! She made the porridge. It was tasteless, watery with little substance, unlike her grandmother's creamy porridge. Her poor grandma! She had looked after her for as far back as Jo could remember.

Tom stirred and looked across at the sleeping babies, yawned and stretched his long thin arms. The kettle hissed and spouted water, almost extinguishing the fire. Jo got up and made a fresh pot of tea. She poured Tom a mugful and placed it on the table next to him. He was coughing again, beating his chest with his clenched fist. His consumption seemed worse and she pitied him. 'Tis always worse at night,' he told her.

'The porridge is a bit thin, but it's the best I could do.'

'Aye! It's grand.'

When at last daylight seeped through the thin curtains, her mother hadn't returned.

The room depressed her and she wanted to go home to her grandma's.

'I'm going back now, will you be all right?'

'Aye. Thanks,' he managed between a fit of coughing, calling out to her when she reached the door. 'Sorry...for your trouble, Jo.'

* * *

The curtains were closed at her grandmother's. Kate had worked through the night and had, by now, washed and habited the corpse of her ex-mother-in-law. Jo found her in the kitchen standing on a chair, her thin bare legs visible beneath the hem of her skirt. She was reaching up searching the cupboards. 'Jo-Jo!' she called, when she saw her in the doorway. 'Where did she keep the porter?'

'Grandma never drank it! But there's a decanter of sherry in the dining room sideboard, shall I fetch it?' Jo hoped to appease her.

'A lot of good that is!' she said, clicking her tongue. 'Oh, get it out anyway. The neighbours will drink it when they call. You can fetch me a jug o' porter later on.'

Thoughts of her grandmother lying dead upstairs brought fresh tears as she carried in the sherry.

'There's no point in you getting upset,' Kate chided. 'She was an old woman. She couldn't live forever.'

Jo wished she could, as she placed the decanter with a glass on the table.

'We can't have her brought down until the men come with the coffin. It won't be long now.' Kate poured herself a glass of sherry and settled down in the armchair. After a couple of glasses, she began to yawn. Jo sat on a hard chair, her hands clasped in front of her. In the silence, the ticking clock appeared louder.

When her mother nodded off, Jo slipped upstairs. The smell of death and candle wax met her as she entered the room. She held onto the brass bedpost to steady herself and looked down at her grandmother's body. Kate had taken care of everything, down to the last detail, ensuring that Mary Kingsley was ready for her last public appearance.

Jo was glad to have this time alone with her grandmother before folk came to mourn her passing. Word of death – no matter whose it was – spread quickly. There was a peaceful expression on her waxy white face, lips tightly closed. Her long grey hair, that had cascaded around her shoulders at bedtime, was now neatly encased in a hairnet on top of her head. Her hands were joined as if in prayer, and her rosary beads circled her fingers.

A white linen cloth covered the small table, on which a container of holy water had been placed. On either side of the crucifix, a lighted candle flickered in the draughty room. Melted wax trickled down and set, giving the candles a distorted appearance.

Jo was no stranger to death; for her it was part of everyday life. She had seen the corpses of neighbours, and stillborn babies who had never seen the light of day. But this was a new experience, the feeling in the pit of her stomach; an ache, she felt, would never go away. Bending, she kissed the colourless cheek, gazed at the lifeless body before her, no longer capable of showing love. Her beloved grandmother, who had loved her always and encouraged her to play the piano, was now gone. Jo's life was on the verge of change and, instinctively, she knew it would never be the same again.

'Oh, Grandma. Grandma, what am I to do without you?' Grief stricken, she dropped down by the side of the bed and sobbed.

CHAPTER TWO

The following morning, thick frost coated the rooftops, and a bitter wind blew down from the Dublin Mountains. Jo returned from the shop with a packet of Lyons tea and a jug of milk. Children played skipping and hopscotch in the street to keep warm. She wanted to join them, but her mother had insisted she was to come straight back.

She walked down the street towards her grandmother's, where the wake was to take place. It was the only home she had ever known, and she felt a deep sadness at the thought of having to leave it. The ivy covering the walls seemed to be clinging tighter today. And a few red berries were beginning to appear on the holly bush. A sign of a hard winter, her grandmother had always said. She passed the row of run-down cottages, and in particular, the one her mother lived in with her second family; the contrast was startling. Her grandmother had given them the cottage rent-free when Tom became too ill to work, and regularly sent down provisions. Jo helped out whenever she was asked to, in spite of the fact that her mother had never shown her any love, not the way her grandmother had. Right now, she had no idea where she was going to live and her future looked bleak.

Outside the house, she took a deep breath before going in. Voices could be heard coming from the dining room. The door was ajar and she could see the piano, with her sheet music untouched since her last lesson. The metronome that helped her keep time, perched where she'd left it days ago, would now be silent for a while.

Fearful of intruding, she knocked before entering. A young

woman was sitting at the table, a basket laden with seasonal fruit and vegetables at her feet. In her hand she was delicately balancing a bone china teacup and saucer, while Kate poured tea.

'Ah! There you are, Jo-Jo. What kept you so long? Come over here, and say hello!' Hesitant, Jo placed the milk and tea on the table. The young woman stood up to face her. Her fully rounded figure showed no lack of nourishment. Her long flowing skirt rustled as she moved. And her white frilly blouse, set against her dark hair, gave her a regal look. 'Don't you recognise your big sister then, Jo?'

'Cissy, is it really you?' Crying, she rushed into the young woman's arms.

'You stay and help your sister prepare for the wake, Jo-Jo.' Then, picking up her coat, Kate seized the opportunity to leave them alone.

'I nearly didn't come, you know,' Cissy said, and brushed Jo aside. 'But we'll talk about that after we've done the baking.' She walked towards the kitchen, tying back her hair, while Jo struggled behind with the basket of produce. Cissy unhooked one of their grandmother's aprons and got to work. Soon delicious smells of homemade bread and fruit pies filled the kitchen. For a moment Jo felt as if her grandmother was back. Fascinated, she watched her sister's nimble fingers as together they peeled and chopped vegetables in preparation for the broth. That done, Cissy said, 'Keep a gentle stir on that pot, Jo, while I see to the oven.'

Jo admired the orderly way in which her sister worked. She let nothing distract her until everything was cooked, covered, and put away for the wake.

They were sipping their tea and eating homemade scones, when Cissy declared her feelings. 'I've never forgiven me grandma for sending me away, and I vowed never to come back.' True to her word, she had made no visits home and, apart from the odd letter, they had heard nothing from her.

'It wasn't Grandma's fault. She did her best.'

'Not for me she didn't.' Bitterness crept into Cissy's voice. 'But then, Ma didn't want me. She didn't want any of us.'

7

'Why?'

'Of course, you were only a toddler when we were left on me grandmother's doorstep. I was old enough to know what was going on.' She brushed the crumbs from her skirt, anger hardening her green eyes. 'She needed room for her new man and those two beanpole daughters of his. An odd pair they were!' She shook her head slowly.

Cissy reminded Jo of their mother when she got cross, but Jo thought better than to say it. 'I don't remember them, but Grandma said they went to England.'

'Huh! Well, good riddance. They never did a stroke to help me ma, lazy lumps they were.'

'Did Ma really leave us on the doorstep? Grandma never spoke of it.'

'Aye! After Da died, she told Grandma that we were her son's kids, so she could look after us. Da would have turned in his grave, if he'd known.' She sighed and sat down again. 'I remember standing with Ned, crying me eyes out, when Grandma told her she wasn't fit to be a mother. Ma got on with her lot and never bothered with us. And she never cared when me grandma sent me into service. I was much younger than you are now.'

'What's it like, working, I mean?'

'I hated being a scullery maid, scrubbing and cleaning 'til me hands were raw. Well! I'm a parlour maid now.' Cissy stood up. 'I can afford to treat meself to some of the latest fashions.' She did a twirl.

'I'd love a skirt like that when I'm older.' Jo lifted the hem of her sister's skirt, revealing her petticoat.

'Don't be cheeky.' Cissy ran her hand down her skirt. 'I'm only here because me employer insisted. Besides, it's an opportunity to show Ma I've done well for meself without her.' She moved across the room. 'Has there been any word from Ned?'

'No. Not yet.'

'I take it he's been told?' She placed her hands on her hips and stretched her back.

'A telegram got sent on the day Grandma died,' Jo replied.

'It'll be weeks before he gets here. Tell him I want to see him, will you? He might decide to sell up, him being left everything and living in America, like.'

Jo's face dropped. 'But…'

'Oh, you needn't worry, me ma'll take you in. You won't be sent away to work with strangers like I was.' Turning, she walked out of the kitchen.

* * *

The sky in February was overcast and a sprinkling of snow covered the ground. A small group stood by the open grave, as Jo's grandmother was laid to rest. She shuddered, stifling a sob, which appeared to catch the back of her throat. The tops of her fingernails were red where she had bitten them down to the quick. Pushing her hands inside her muffler, her shoulders sagged and her head dropped forward. She could hear the priest chanting in the eerie silence of the graveyard, and the mumblings of those around her joining in, but Jo couldn't pray. The words wouldn't form on her tongue, and she trembled while struggling to keep her grief from spilling over.

She felt the spray of the holy water as her grandmother's remains were lowered into the earth. The thud, as clumps of earth landed on the oak coffin, made her flinch. She swayed, but managed to stay upright where she stood, sandwiched between Cissy and her mother.

'I'll pray for Mrs. Kingsley's soul,' the priest said, moving aside. She heard someone thank him. In sombre mood, they walked back towards the cemetery gates.

'Well,' her mother said, 'that's that over with, thank God.' Jo burst into tears. Cissy put an arm around her and guided her to where the hansom cab awaited them.

Back at the house, Jo sensed her mother's agitation, knowing she had only attended the funeral for appearances' sake. Cissy reheated the vegetable soup. They ate in silence, letting the thick broth soothe their aching limbs.

Once the neighbours knew they were back, they called in to

offer their condolences. Aggie Murphy, a constant visitor to her mother's, helped with the food and then helped herself. 'Pour a drop o' that porter in there now, Jo-Jo,' she said, pointing to her empty glass, her plump fingers reaching for a slice of corned beef, cooked to a turn by Cissy. 'Your mother could do with Ned being here today. When's he due, Jo?'

'I don't know, Mrs. Murphy.' America was a long, way away, that was as much as she knew. Each time she thought about her grandma, a funny feeling came over her. So she kept herself busy putting food on the table, brought in by kindly neighbours, while Cissy mingled amongst the mourners with glasses of sherry, and bottles of porter for the men.

Before long, the house was packed. Jo observed the genuine mourners – men with black diamond patches neatly stitched to their jacket sleeve, the women in black. Neighbours came from nearby streets to join in the traditional wake of music and dancing. Some were strangers, moochers, lured in by free drink, snuff and tobacco. She remembered her grandmother saying that nobody was allowed to depart this world without a party to send them on their way. The sound of feet tapping could be heard on the tiled floor, as the fiddlers played on.

Jo knew from experience that as long as the alcohol flowed, the wake, too, would go on and on. The smell of tobacco smoke and fumes from the gas lamps filled the room. In need of fresh air, she went out into the hallway. The front door was always a draughty spot, especially in winter; she stood letting the cold breeze revive her. She was chewing her fingernails when her mother walked through.

'When are you going to give up that disgusting habit?' Her words slurred, she slapped Jo's hand down from her mouth.

'Where's Cissy?'

'I don't know.' Jo guessed she'd gone outside with some of the older boys and girls, bored with the wake.

'We need more glasses.'

Jo hurried towards the kitchen.

'And bring out more food while you're in there.'

* * *

Dawn was breaking when Jo finally got into bed. Exhausted, she fell into a deep sleep. She dreamt she saw her grandmother floating towards her, as if she had no feet. She was smiling down. Jo reached out to her. There was so much she wanted to tell her. But she couldn't get close. An invisible barrier kept them apart. She woke upset. Why had her grandmother not comforted her, or told her what was going to happen to her? Didn't she care about her anymore?

'You've been dreaming,' Cissy said, glancing towards the bed. She was already up, pinning the last strands of hair neatly on top of her head. A small attaché case was lying open on the bed, her nightclothes folded inside.

'*Please*, don't go, Cissy! Stay another day?'

'I can't.'

'Weren't you even going to say goodbye?' Jo threw back the covers.

'You'd had a restless night. I didn't want to disturb you.'

'Can I come as far as the tram with you, *please*?'

'You'll have to be quick. I don't want to be late back.' Cissy snapped her case shut, and carried it downstairs.

Jo hastily dressed in her beige woollen dress with the Peter Pan collar and wide pleated skirt. She brushed her hair and ran down the stairs after her sister. Cissy was by the front door, struggling with her case and parcels. Kate came into the hallway as Jo was pulling on her coat.

'Where do you think you're going?' she bellowed.

'She's walking to the tram with me.'

Their mother's eyes narrowed and she glared at Cissy. 'Where were you last night? If it hadn't been for Aggie Murphy, this place woulda bee' a pigsty this morning.'

'I have to go.' Cissy edged her way out of the door onto the pavement.

'Mind you come straight back, Jo-Jo. Do you hear me? There's plenty of chores to do, and you won't need your fancy clothes on to do them.' Her voice echoed as the door closed behind them.

Frost from the previous day clung to the rooftops, as the girls walked in silence towards the trams. Jo dug her hands inside her pockets, balancing one of Cissy's parcels under her arm. 'Where did you go last night?'

'Where do you think? I had to get out of there.' Cissy's words did nothing to instill confidence. Her grandmother had once told her that Cissy was insolent and unmanageable, and putting her into service was the best thing for her. But when Ned went to work on the ships, her grandmother had been inconsolable. When his ship docked in New York harbour, he left his plumbing job on board ship for one on shore.

They reached the city and Jo glanced around her. The excitement she had experienced on her last shopping expedition with her grandmother had all but disappeared. It was now over a year since the Rebellion, and the city was still recovering. Some of the Georgian buildings along Sackville Street were blackened and partly damaged. People walked with purpose, intent on catching their tram to their place of work. A few trams were already lined up alongside Nelson's Pillar. As she waited with Cissy, she wished they were boarding the tram to Killiney beach, or Blackrock, places their grandmother had taken them before Cissy and Ned went away.

'Me grandmother loved you best, you know!' Cissy broke the silence.

'That's not true, Cissy.'

'Why'd she send me away then?'

'I don't know, but I wish she wasn't dead, Cissy.'

'Yeah, well! Happen she did me a favour; otherwise, I'd still be at home looking after me ma's snotty-nosed kids.' Her tram pulled up alongside, and her mood changed. 'Look,

I've got to go.' Jo reached out to embrace her, and was surprised when Cissy kissed her on the cheek. 'Don't worry! You'll be grand.' She picked up her case. Jo handed her the rest of her belongings, and she boarded the tram. 'I'll write.'

'Me, too!'

As the tram moved away, Jo waved goodbye to her sister.

Thoughts of living permanently with her mother filled her with dread. She remembered her brother making her laugh before he went away. Now she couldn't wait to see him, because she felt sure she'd never see her sister again.

CHAPTER THREE

Life at her mother's was hard. At night, Jo was kept awake by the sound of her stepfather struggling to breathe, the rattling noises coming from his chest so desperate it frightened her. She could hear him muttering apologies, and in the darkness see the outline of her mother administering his medicine. When at last Tom's breathing eased, the twins began to whimper, and Jo wondered how anyone ever slept in such close proximity. After weeks of sharing a bed with the younger children, her shins were covered in bruises. Most mornings she woke early shivering, with no alternative but to get up.

Things would be different once her brother got here, she told herself. At the very least, there'd be more food on the table. Ned would insist she went back to school, because her mother showed no interest in the fact that she'd been off for weeks.

Once she was up, Jo lit the lamp, and cleaned out the ashes as quietly as she could. In place of kindling, she used rolled-up newspaper, twisting it tightly. Putting a match to it, she placed small pieces of turf on top. A few days ago, she had crossed her fingers, but now she felt more confident, unhooking the bellows and gently pumping until the flames were roaring up the chimney. She filled the kettle from the water bucket and hung it over the fire. Then she sat down to wait.

As the kettle boiled, and steam gushed from its spout, her mother appeared bleary-eyed in the doorway. 'Aye! You're a good girl, Jo-Jo.' She reached for the large enamel teapot. Warming it, she scooped in three teaspoons of tea before pouring the boiling water on top. It was the first time she'd been alone with her mother since the wake, and her words of praise encouraged Jo.

'Ma...I...I'm missing school.'

'Can yeh pass me the oats?'

After that, Jo lost her nerve. While the porridge cooked, they drank their tea in silence. The sound of Tom's hacking cough alerted her mother and she pushed back her chair, making a scraping noise on the stone floor. She half filled a mug with tea, poured milk in, then lots of sugar before stirring it.

'I'll take this into Tom, he'll be parched.' When she came back, Jo was spooning out the porridge. Kate drew back the flimsy curtains. Ice had formed on the inside of the window. Rubbing hard with her fist, she made a circle big enough to peer outside. She shivered; pulled her jaded shawl tighter around her thin shoulders. 'It's a bitter morn. The childer will need their porridge inside them today.' The fire sparked and crackled and Jo felt the crackling of tension building up inside her.

Liam came from the bedroom, crying and trailing his trousers on the floor. Jo put a bowl of porridge in front of him. 'Don't want to go to school.' He continued to cry, spluttering into his food. At five years old, he had not yet become accustomed to school life.

'You're not stopping home, Liam,' she said. 'So you'd better get used to it.'

Jo sat him on her knee and got him dressed. Kate snatched his shabby coat with holes in the elbows from the back of the door, and pushed him into it.

'I'll take him, Ma.' Jo picked up her coat. She felt stifled. And this was an opportunity to get outside and maybe visit the library on the way back.

'No! He'll be fine. Besides, the school inspector might spot you and start asking questions.' Laying her hands on Liam's shoulders, she took him to the door. Other children were making their way up the street towards the school, their teeth chattering. Kate shoved him along with them and closed the door.

'I should be getting back to school, Ma! I'll help you when I come home,' she said boldly, feeling her stomach tighten. She could see the disapproval etched on her mother's face.

'What! At your age? Don't be silly, girl,' she sneered. 'You've had all the learning you're likely to get. Besides, I need yeh here.' And she left the room.

Jo stamped her foot and dug her nails into her palms. Her education had always been important to her. Without it, how was she going to find employment? A feeling of hopelessness flooded through her. If only she could escape back to her grandmother's, but Kate had locked it up, telling her to stay away until Ned arrived.

Her mother returned with the twins and sat them on a rug on the floor. They were so under-nourished and, at two years old, looked half their age. Jo filled two baby bottles with warm sugary tea and passed them one each. Her dejected look didn't go unnoticed.

'Look! It's time we had a talk.' Kate pulled a chair out from the table and beckoned her to sit. 'Things won't get much better when Ned comes home.' She rubbed the back of her neck.

This wasn't what Jo wanted to hear and she dropped her gaze. 'Surely it'll be better.'

'Listen to me, Jo-Jo. Your grandmother was good giving me the cottage rent-free. But Ned may have other plans, might want to sell up, move back to America. I'm his mother, but I don't know how he feels about me.' She glanced down at her hands. 'After all, I did abandon him. He may want me to pay rent. But for Tom's sake, I pray it won't come to that.'

Before Jo could speak, Kate stood up, alerted by the sound of her husband knocking on the bedpost. 'He's expected tomorrow, I thought you should know.'

* * *

Jo spent the following morning helping prepare for Ned's homecoming. Excited about seeing him, she plaited her hair and changed into her green dress. And for once her mother didn't disapprove. She could tell Kate was happy, too, because she was wearing her best Sunday dress and lilting the tune, *Come back to Erin*, even though she'd had another sleepless night. Her dark hair showing signs of grey around the temples, neatly piled on top of her head, gave her a girlish look. When she smiled, the tiredness that had previously creased her face disappeared, and she glanced out of the small casement window more than once.

Ned had lived with his mother until he was eight, so Jo guessed there might be some closeness between them. Jo paced up and down, then she pulled on her coat and stood in the doorway, her neck craned watching for her brother. The midday sun struggled to get through another bitterly cold day, and the neighbours – anxious for a glimpse of their new landlord – waited with an exuberance of curiosity and apprehension. Some hovered in the doorway, bucket and brush in hand, each with a sudden urge to scrub their doorstep in spite of the frost coating the pavements. Some stayed indoors for fear of eviction.

When Jo caught sight of her brother, her heart lurched. He had a confident swagger as he entered the street, raising his cap to the ladies in their doorways. His dark curly hair bounced down over his forehead. Jo watched him as he drew closer, carrying a suitcase, a haversack slung over his shoulder. His clothes were new and he wore them well. At nineteen years old, he appeared strong and capable.

'There's a young man who knows where he's going.' Aggie Murphy nudged her daughter, standing behind her in the doorway. 'Nice to see yeh home, Ned.'

'Nice to be home, Mrs. Murphy.' He lifted his cap.

'Handsome looking lad, so he is. He'll break a few hearts,' Aggie muttered.

Ned stopped in his tracks when he saw Jo at his mother's door; on impulse, she rushed down the street to meet him. Ned immediately put down his suitcase and swung her up into the air with such ease.

'How's my baby sister?' he roared, placing her down on the pavement, and kissing the top of her head. Jo felt her cheeks burn and embraced him warmly.

'I'm grown up now, don't forget!' she said.

'So I see, and what a beauty of a sister I have.' He twirled her round, placing his arm around her shoulders. 'Let's go inside, I'm parched.'

Jo smiled up at her brother, who kept his arm around her until they were inside her mother's cottage. Kate came forward.

'How are yeh, Ma?'

'Much the same, you know, what with Tom being ill.'

'What's the doctors say?'

'We've no money for doctors, Ned, and damp rooms don't help.'

'I'm sorry about Tom, Ma, but look.' He sat down. 'I could murder a cup of tea.'

Jo saw a smile creep round the corner of her mother's mouth as she poured the tea. 'We've been expecting yeh for weeks. How was your journey?'

'Long, Ma! I spent most of the time drinking and sleeping and being sea sick, but I'm here now.' The table was already set awaiting his arrival, and Jo cut him a large piece of apple pie, freshly baked by her mother.

'Ah! This is what I've missed,' he said, biting into the pie. 'Sorry I missed the wake, Ma!' He looked up at her. 'How'd it go?'

'Oh, you know. We could have done with you here to get rid of the blackguards that came at the smell o' the drink; there was more strange faces than we knew.'

'I've been making arrangements since receiving your telegram. It takes time, Ma. I was lucky to get a passage, there's a war on, yeh know?'

'I know, son. The bloody Germans sunk the Lusitania; all them poor people. It was the talk in Dublin for many a month.' She sighed.

'I read about it in the New York newspapers. Many more lives will be lost before this war's over.'

Kate nodded 'We're lucky to have you back safe then.' She placed the tea down next to him, and glanced over to where Jo was playing with the children. Then she pulled her chair closer. 'What are your plans, Ned?'

'Pour us a drop of that good old Irish porter, and I'll tell yeh.'

Kate poured while she listened to her son, his Irish brogue tainted with the New York accent. Jo watched the hard lines on her mother's face soften when she heard they would be moving into their grandmother's house.

'Thanks, Ned.' Kate wiped a tear from the corner of her eye. 'I don't deserve your loyalty.'

'That's in the past now. You're still me ma, and I won't see you go without. Besides, this place is damp. I'll give the house the once over before you move up there, but it should be pretty sound.' He turned and smiled at Jo, who was digesting all of this slowly.

'You're not selling up then?' her blue eyes widened.

Puzzled, Ned shook his head.

'Thanks be to God,' his mother said.

'What gave yeh that idea, Ma? I'm assuming that in a few years time the cottages will be condemned. I'll just make what I can out of them until then.'

'Oh, it's just something Cissy said.'

'By the way, how is Cissy? Did she come to the wake?'

'Oh, she came all right. I was as surprised to see her as anyone,' Kate said.

'Cissy wants to see you, Ned,' Jo said.

'She does, does she?' Ned reached out and pulled one of Jo's pigtails. 'I'll look forward to it, pet.'

'You've taken a load off me mind, son. You're a good boy.' Then, with a spring in her step, Kate got up to attend to her husband.

When her mother left the room, Jo went over and sat next to her brother. 'Does this mean I can go back to school and practise playing the piano again? I've really missed it.' A smile brightened her face.

'You play the piano?' Ned joked. 'So you're not pleased to see me at all, just so long as you can play your piano.' This was the Ned she remembered, always joking. Their laughter became infectious, making the children giggle, their faces smeared with chocolate all the way from America.

CHAPTER FOUR

The transfer to her grandmother's house was relatively easy, their possessions few. The biggest obstacle they encountered was moving Tom. Ned pushed him up the street in the twins' go-kart, and gently carried him upstairs, laying him down on the bed Jo had made ready. She pitied him when he waved a hand in thanks.

Back in familiar surroundings, she soon had a cosy fire burning in the hearth. Ned helped with the heavy stuff, leaving Jo and Kate to sort out sleeping arrangements. Later, he went out, saying he'd be late back. He had lots of loose ends to tie up regarding his grandmother's estate. As soon as he'd gone, Kate put on her new American shower-proof, running her fingers over the material, feeling the cosiness of the fur lining. She pulled it snugly around her thin frame and buckled the belt. Looking into the mirror, she secured the navy hat Tom had bought her some time ago on top of her head.

'A good match, don't you think?'

Astounded, Jo stood staring at her.

'Yeh can take that face off yeh, if you know what's good for yeh. I haven't felt this good in ages, and I don't need you spoiling it.'

'Don't go out, Ma! Sure, there's a still a load to do.'

'You can manage to look in on Tom, feed the kids, and sort out the beds. I won't belong.' She walked towards the dresser and pick up her purse.

'*But, Ma!* I want to go to the library before it closes.'

'Ungrateful brat! If you're not careful, you'll find yourself out on the streets,' she said, and slammed the door behind her.

20

Stunned, Jo's eyes filled with tears. Kate had never had a kind word for her – the reason her grandmother had insisted she had as little as possible to do with her. But now her grandmother was gone, her mother could treat her how she liked. It wasn't fair! She stamped her foot and flounced into the parlour. Her grandmother used to sit and listen to her playing the piano in here. She raised the lid and ran her fingers over the keys. After weeks of standing idle, some of the notes were sticking. When she turned round, the twins had followed her and she smiled when they clapped their hands.

Later she brought Tom up his meal of scrambled egg. And by the time she had fed the children, organised sleeping arrangements, and quelled squabbles, she felt weary. She made herself a mug of Bovril and curled up in her favourite armchair, watching the glow of the embers dying in the grate. She heard Ned come in and go straight upstairs, and she guessed he was tired after his long voyage. Jo was still awake when Kate stumbled into the kitchen smelling of alcohol. She pretended to be asleep.

* * *

A few days later, Jo was delighted when Ned asked her to accompany him to see Cissy. Kate, determined to have her own way, found excuses to keep her from going. But Jo quickly retaliated, crossing her arms in front of her. 'It'll have to wait til I get back. I'm going with Ned,' she said, standing next to him.

'You'll do as you're bid, girl!'

'For goodness sake, Ma, give the girl a break,' Ned said, throwing up his hands. And Jo rushed upstairs to get her coat. When she came down, Kate was subdued, and her glare left no doubt that she was none too pleased. She had discouraged Jo's school friends, telling them that she had no time for childish games; well, she wasn't going to stop her going with her brother to see their sister. She quickly stepped outside on her brother's arm, grateful for the opportunity to get out of the house.

She was sure her sister would be as anxious to see Ned as she had been, and as they neared their destination, Jo kept a look out for

Cissy. When she spotted her walking briskly towards the bridge to meet them, Jo could barely contain her excitement. Cissy's initial greeting was cool, and she showed little interest when Jo told her about the changes Ned had made.

'Well!' she said, looking at Ned. 'I haven't got all day. Can we go somewhere private?'

'What's the hurry? It's your day off. Why don't we catch the tram to Blackrock?' Ned said cheerfully, rubbing his hands together. What do you say?' He looked from one sister to the other. Jo's face lit up at the prospect, while Cissy's remained cold and detached.

'Like I said, I haven't got all day.' She turned and walked towards the park.

Ned pursed his lips. 'It's a bit cold for strolling through the park.' But he followed her anyway. They paused halfway along the icy path, and Cissy glanced at Jo. 'I thought you'd be alone, Ned.'

'Can you give us a minute, pet?'

Jo walked away, feeling the cold work its way through the thin soles of her boots. She had no idea what she'd said wrong! But Cissy wasn't happy – not even to see Ned. When she turned around, they were sitting on a park bench talking. She wondered what they were saying. Why had Cissy been offhand with Ned? Anxious not to return too soon, she walked across to the pond. A few ducks fluttered their wings on the centre island, none brave enough to swim on the partly frozen water. She pulled her woolly hat down over her ears and walked back slowly. Cissy was standing up, her face red like she'd sat against the fire. She was flexing her gloved fingers and pulling her red scarf tighter around her shoulders.

'What's going on?' Jo asked, her teeth chattering.

Cissy didn't answer, but glared at Ned. 'You haven't heard the last of this, Ned Kingsley.'

Ned stood up, his arms outstretched, shaking his head from side to side. Cissy, without a word of goodbye, turned on her heel and walked out through the park gates.

Ned looked down at Jo; saw a flicker of confusion cross her face. 'Don't you worry about your sister, pet.' He took her cold hand in his and pushed it inside the pocket of his overcoat, and they walked in silence out of the park and across the road to the tram stop.

* * *

That night, Jo hardly slept. She couldn't relax until she knew what was going on with Cissy. Why wasn't she happy to see Ned after his years in America? And her behaviour had bothered Ned, because he hardly spoke all the way home.

Early the next morning, Jo took him in a mug of freshly brewed tea, hoping to lift his spirits. He was sitting on the side of the bed, rubbing the stubble on his chin.

'Ma said you wouldn't be up yet, but I knew you would.' Smiling, she placed the tea on the small table next to him.

'Sit down, Jo.' He patted the bed. He looked down at her and she wondered if he had any idea how much she needed him in her life.

'Is there something wrong? Is it Cissy?' She bit her thumbnail, something she hadn't done since her grandmother's funeral, then she quickly hid her hands in the pockets of her pinafore.

'No,' he smiled. 'Nothing for you to worry about, and as for Cissy, she'll come round. She wants Grandma's rings and I've given them to Ma! I didn't know that Grandma had promised them to Cissy.'

'So that's why she was in a huff?'

'Grandma left her ten pounds. I thought she'd have been thrilled to bits.' He smiled. 'And guess what, pet? She left you the princely sum of twenty pounds, and her piano. What do you think of that?'

'Oh, really! That's wonderful, Ned.' She smothered a gasp of delight. 'I didn't know me grandma had any savings! Why didn't she use it to repair the cottages?'

'I guess she wanted you and Cissy to have a good start in life.' He reached inside his pocket and handed her a form. 'Here! I want you to sign this so the money can be paid into the post office for you. You'll need it when you move away from here.'

'Move away!' Jo could hardly believe her ears. 'Where to, Ned?'

'New York, of course, but not just yet.'

'New York! Oh Ned, I can't wait. What about Ma?'

'Don't you worry your pretty head. Ma'll be well looked after.'

Her hand trembling, she signed her full name, Josephine Mary Kingsley. Ideas of going to New York with Ned swirled around in her head. It would all be possible now. Sooner than she had expected, her life was going to change. Thank you, Grandma, she murmured. Deliberately ignoring her mother's call for her to come down, she said, 'Ned, tell me about America?'

'It's the land of opportunities, Jo, but…'

'Jo-Jo! Where are yeh, girl?'

Ned placed his arm around her shoulders and winked. 'Go on down, pet, before she starts shouting again.'

CHAPTER FIVE

The next few weeks were hectic, as Tom's health deteriorated. Jo didn't have a minute to herself and there was little time for her to dwell on her inheritance. She walked into the kitchen as Ned and Kate were discussing strategies for extracting the weekly rents. She felt sure that her brother hadn't been prepared for the tales of woe.

'You've got to make a stand, Ned, or none of us will survive,' Kate was saying.

He stroked his chin. 'I'm thinking, Ma, I'm thinking!'

Jo had put the twins down for a nap, and Kate had left carrots and potatoes, courtesy of Ned, on the table for her to prepare. She longed to be included in their discussion, and prodded the fire to ease her resentment. She hated being treated like a child; after all, she was thirteen. She prepared the vegetables, making a loud chopping noise on the wooden table. Neither of them took any notice.

'Yes. You're right,' Ned was saying. 'I've spent more on repairs than I've accrued in rent.'

'Holy Mother o' God, Ned, what will you do?'

He lifted his cap and scratched his head, then stood up, paced a little and sat down again.

'I hate to do this, Ma, and we won't be popular, but they've left me no choice. Except for the widow in number five, the bad payers will have to go!'

'It's a sad state of affairs, so it is, son.'

'I'll have new tenants in before I return to the States.'

Jo's ears perked up at the mention of the States, and she waited to hear more, hoping Ned would take her with him.

'How much longer can you stay, Ned?' Kate asked, pouring their tea.

'I'll stay as long as I have to.'

'God bless yeh, Ned, what would we do without yeh?' She stifled a sob.

Jo watched her brother strike through names on his sheet.

Although Jo didn't envy her mother's constant anxiety over Tom's worsening tuberculosis, she wondered if she was overreacting. Surely, with Ned's generosity, things couldn't be that bad.

Kate stood up and straightened her shoulders as Aggie Murphy came through the door. 'How's Tom today?'

'He's much the same, Aggie, much the same! He hardly has the strength to cough.' She gave a deep sigh as the two women mounted the stairs.

Ned looked over at Jo. 'I want everything to be in order for Ma when I leave, so I've a hard task ahead of me, pet. Perhaps you should come with me?'

Jo, delighted to be part in whatever her brother was planning, left what she was doing and followed him. As they walked down the street, she swallowed when one of the women hurried inside and bolted the door. But Ned stood his ground and continued knocking until she finally opened the door. Two small children peeped out from behind her skirts.

'I'm…I'm…sorry, Mr. Kingsley. If yeh give me a few more hours, His Lordship will be home then.'

Jo felt sorry for the women, who were always left to make excuses.

'Wasn't it your husband that got work on the docks a week ago?'

'Yes, Mr. Kingsley, but…'

'No more *buts*, Mrs. I'm not prepared to wait until he's squandered the lot. In fact, I'm sure I saw him earlier on waiting for Mooney's to open. If I don't get the rent in full today, I hereby give you notice to quit the property a week today.'

'You're a hard man, mister. You've no pity; no pity a' tall,' the woman said, and banged the door in their faces.

'Oh, Ned.' Jo's hand flew to her mouth. 'Her husband never comes home once he'd been paid. Does that mean she'll have to go?' Jo looked sad.

'I'm afraid so.' With a determined look on his face, he moved on to the next house and the next, delivering the same shattering news. When they came to number five, Ned said, 'We'll leave the widow be, she needs time to grieve, poor woman.'

Curtains twitched as they walked back up the street. Inside the house, Ned pulled a chair to the table and sat down. Jo brought him a glass of porter and sat down next to him. His brow wrinkled.

'In spite of what you might think, Jo, I found that difficult. These feckless men fail to provide for their families and they'll carry on in the same vein if they're allowed to get away with it. Grandma was too soft. Too much kindness won't put food on the table.' He took a long drink from his glass and wiped his mouth on his sleeve. 'No-one ever diddled me grandpa out of his rents and, by God, they won't do it to me.'

'Are things that bad, Ned?'

'What do you think? And it will only get worse when I'm not around. Those four haven't paid a penny in six months, Jo. I thought you'd have known that!'

She understood only too well Ned's frustration, remembering how her grandma felt, and she hoped that the outcome to her brother's plan would be a success.

Just then, Kate rushed into the kitchen and they both looked up. The tired, jaded look that had paled her face for days made her appear older than her forty-two years.

'Ned, quick, fetch Father Kelly, Tom wants to make his last confession. And Jo-Jo, bring a bucket of fresh water upstairs.'

Ned hurried out the back, jumped on Tom's bike and sped off. Jo picked up the wooden pail and went out into the street, to the shared water tap. A neighbour was filling her bucket when Jo reached the pump.

'How's your stepfather, Jo? Your poor mother must be kilt with worry.' She dragged her heavy bucket away, so that Jo could put hers underneath. Jo's weak smile told her all was not well. At the far end of the street, a small group of women congregated on the pavement.

'Yous won't have much luck!' screamed one, shaking her fist at Jo.

'After what your brother's done to us poor families, he ought to be ashamed of himself,' another yelled.

Jo didn't answer; weary from it all, she just wanted to get back inside. She finished filling her pail and water splashed out onto the cobbles as she struggled under its weight.

Inside, Aggie was coming down the stairs sniffing. She beckoned for Jo to take the water up. When Jo entered the bedroom, she heard the soft shallow breathing of a dying man.

She wrung out the cloth in the fresh water and handed it to Kate, who gently dabbed the beads of sweat on her husband's brow. He turned his face towards her, his eyes stark.

The curtains were drawn, making it oppressive as Jo tidied the room in readiness for the priest. Kate appeared numb and, with only the candle burning on the bedside table, they sat in silent vigil.

Jo was sitting at the foot of the bed when the piercing screech of the Banshee penetrated the walls, sending a shudder through her body. She glanced up just as Tom's hand fell limply by his side. Kate called out his name, and paced the floor raining down curses on the evil fiend.

* * *

Jo was pleased when Ned stayed on an extra week. Her mother was distraught, and Jo worried about the children still so young. The day after the funeral, Jo was alone with Ned, giving her the opportunity she was waiting for.

'When are we leaving, Ned?' she asked.

'Sit down, Jo. I want to talk to you about the collections. The cottages will hardly make us a fortune, but I want you to carry on collecting the rents, like you did for Grandma. Give half the money to Ma. I've arranged with the post office to forward the rest to me.'

For a moment she was speechless. 'But…but I won't be here, will I?'

Sighing, he ran a hand across his brow.

'Ah, Ned, don't leave me here!'

He reached for her hand. 'I'm sorry, Jo.'

Frightened of the responsibilities that lay ahead, Jo had practically begged Ned to take her with him.

'Listen, Jo.' He put his arm around her shoulder.

She shrugged him off and stood up. 'Go then! I thought you were my friend, but you don't care, just like *her*.'

'That's not true, Jo; I do care, but she needs you. Don't you see that? It won't be for long.' He smiled, and made a funny face trying to cheer her up.

'But I need you, Ned, please don't leave me.' Tears almost choked her.

'Look, Jo! You've a lot of growing up to do yet. And it has to be done here.' He reached inside his coat pocket and handed her a post office savings book. 'Put this in a safe place. You have no need to use any of it until you leave here.'

'Why can't I come with you?' She threw the savings book to the floor and stamped on it. Ned picked it up and put it into her pinafore pocket.

'Jo, please don't be like this…I can't take you with me. I'm sorry if you misunderstood.'

She sobbed into her hands. She knew she should be grateful, but with her only chance of escape gone, it felt like the end of the world.

'I know it's hard on you, Jo, but life is hard. When you're older you'll understand.' He smiled down at her, tilted her chin and looked into her blue eyes. 'You know what has to be done. Good girl!' He hugged her warmly. Trembling, she clung to him until he had to un-wrap her arms from around his waist. He cleared his throat, and she saw a tear glisten the corner of his eye. He straightened his cap, picked up his case from behind the door, threw his bag over his shoulder and swept out of the house.

Jo ran after him and watched him walk down the street,

whistling the tune, *In Dublin's fair city, where the girls...*

'May God go with you, Ned,' Aggie Murphy called from her door. 'Say hello to me cousin Eileen, if you see her.'

Jo was amazed that some folk really had no idea how big America was. She stood on the pavement crying, fighting the urge to chase after him, until he was out of sight. How would she survive without the antics and good humour of her brother?

Kate, who had said her goodbye in private, watched the proceedings through the bedroom window.

'There's another light gone out of our lives, Jo-Jo,' she said, when she came back down, then she reached for her jug.

CHAPTER SIX

The hopelessness of Jo's life seemed intolerable without Ned. She'd lost count of the times she wanted to run away to America, even though she had no idea how to get there. Her brother's generosity did nothing but fuel her mother's addiction. Feeding the family became less of a priority to her, and Jo was left frantically trying to make ends meet.

'If you don't care about me, at least think of the little ones,' Jo dared to say, a sickening fear in her stomach.

'Who the *bloody hell* do you think you are, telling me what's good for me own kids?' Kate yelled. 'Nobody asked your opinion.'

The pattern was always the same, with Jo on the receiving end of her caustic tongue, her mother's tears, and then a promise to curb her drinking. But it never lasted, and it was left to Jo to cope when the children were fretting and missing their father's presence in the house. She comforted them, told them that he was in heaven with Jesus and the angels, like she had been taught at school. And each time Liam wet the bed, she dragged the limp mattress to the open window to dry.

Her birthday came and went without a mention. Her grandmother had always baked a cake and bought her different coloured ribbons for her hair. But Jo had never received a word of greeting from her mother, and it still hurt to know that she wasn't important to her.

As summer approached, doors were flung open and fresh air gushed in, eliminating the fusty smell that had clung to the walls during the winter months. Blankets were given an airing, and washing, only attempted at this time of the year, and billowed in

31

the breeze. Liam played outside with the twins, and they rarely showed their faces until their bellies rumbled. This gave Jo the opportunity she craved for – a few precious moments to play her piano. Flexing her slender fingers, she let them glide over the keys, humming to herself, letting the notes play around in her head. The instrument needed tuning, but nevertheless, these were treasured moments.

Deprived of her education, she lived for her visits to the library. It was weeks since she'd been there, and the first thing she noticed was the new lady librarian behind the counter, her chestnut hair catching the sunlight that filtered in through the tall windows. A few people were reading and it was quiet and peaceful. Fear of breaking any rules, Jo walked as if on eggshells, tiptoeing around the bookshelves like she was in church.

'If you need any help, don't hesitate to ask,' the librarian whispered. It made a pleasant change from the grumpy old man who complained at the slightest sound. Her manner was pleasant and Jo, smiling, nodded her thanks.

Plucking a Beatrix Potter from the children's section and a history book on America for herself, she took them across to the lady, who opened the front covers, stamped them and handed them back. Her smile was warm and it aroused a response from Jo.

As she left the library, the sun's rays beamed down on her, making her hot. Her grandmother had always insisted she wore a straw hat to shade her fair skin, but that was such a long time ago now. Back in the street, she could see three-year-old Hubert sitting by the open door, his twin James by his side and Liam comforting them both.

As she drew closer, Hubert was crying and she heard the familiar wheezing coming from his chest.

'Where's Ma?'

'Don't know,' Liam replied.

Handing Liam the library books, she lifted Hubert and took him inside, soothing him until he calmed down. Then she gave him his medicine. Liam helped her to carry the sick child upstairs and place him on the bed. James stayed close and refused to play out again. He climbed up beside his twin. Jo sat on the side of the bed stroking Hubert's fair hair. It felt soft, like her own when she had the time to wash it.

James picked up the book. 'Wead story, Jo?'

She began reading the tale of Jemima Puddle-Duck, pausing to show them the colourful pictures. Hubert was smiling, but before she'd finished, they were both asleep. Leaving the book on the bed, she crept from the room.

Downstairs, she wandered aimlessly into the kitchen. Kate's jug was missing. An anxious feeling churned her insides and she prayed that Hubert wouldn't get any worse.

When Liam came back in, he was frowning and there was a hole in the seat of his pants. Jo sighed. She didn't want him to become anxious so close to bedtime. Kate hadn't bought them anything new for months and she'd had to cut the toes out of six-year-old Liam's shoes.

'I'll put a stitch in them before Ma sees them.'

His face brightened and he sat next to her on the couch. 'Is Hubert going to be all right?'

She reassured him that with rest, he'd be fine. Jo had become fond of the children and she couldn't abandon them to Kate's selfish neglect.

Later, Liam helped her set the table for their meal of bread and dripping, and she wondered what Ned would say if he knew.

She heard Hubert coughing and went upstairs. James was awake and the book lay open on the bed, a page ripped from its folds.

Horrified, she asked. 'Did you do this, James?'

'For Ubert!'

'Oh, no! You *bold gossoon!*' She immediately regretted her words when James howled, waking Hubert, who was clutching the missing page in his small fist. A lump formed in her throat. 'There! There! Don't take on so.' she said. 'It'll be grand.' She put the book on a shelf out of reach and then placed her arms around them both. But for the rest of the evening, she worried about returning the book in its present state.

* * *

On Saturday morning, Jo arrived at the library – the busiest day of the week. She wandered around for ages, unsure what to do. She wanted to explain to the lady, but would she ever let her take home a book again? What if she asked her to pay for the damage? And worse still, would she tell her never to come into the library again. The longer she thought about it, the more nervous she became.

The librarian was busy answering queries and no-one noticed her slip the book beneath a pile waiting to be checked in. She tried to put the torn book out of her mind, but her conscience pricked her all the way home.

* * *

A week later, Jo came downstairs, surprised to see Kate already sitting at the table, and the kettle boiling.

'You're up early,' she said.

Her mother jerked round, her eyes red. 'It's Hubert! The damn consumption! Poor wee mite, sure I couldn't bear it if…' She covered her face with her hands.

'He's not well, Ma. He needs a doctor. I'll go.'

'Hold on! I've no money for doctors,' she sniffed. 'He's easier now. I'll keep me eye on him.'

Jo knew that he'd get worse later on, and she also knew the consequences of disobeying her mother. She made two strong cups of tea and sat down next to her.

'You must let me go for the doctor, Ma. I'll pay for him.'

Kate glared at her. 'What do they know? They did nothing for Tom. I'll get Aggie to look in on him later.' She picked up her tea and went back to bed. After a night's drinking, Jo doubted the sincerity of her mother's tears. And Jo was adamant that Hubert would see a doctor, sooner rather than later. Because, God forbid should anything happen to Hubert, it would push them both to the brink.

CHAPTER SEVEN

Jo was mopping the floor when Kate walked in holding a letter. She pulled out a chair and sat down. 'There's a letter here from Cissy.'

'Oh! How is she?' Jo quickly stopped what she was doing and sat down. 'Is she coming home?'

'She's getting married.'

'Well that's great, Ma, best news ever. Can I read it?'

Kate closed her fist over the letter and pressed it into her apron pocket. 'It's time she settled down, that one. It'll be a brave man that takes her on!'

'What's his name, did she say his name?' Jo was bobbing up and down on her chair, unable to contain her excitement.

'Calm down, girl! His name's Larry Kenny, from Baggot Street. I've not heard of him. He's good looking, according to your sister.'

'Did she say anything about the wedding?'

'No! No, she didn't,' Kate snapped.

'So, she's not coming then.' Jo stood up and picked up her mop, wondering what else was in the letter her mother was so keen to hide from her.

'Listen, Jo-Jo. Your sister's still hankering on about your grandmother's rings. If you ask me, she's the cheek o' the devil, that one. The truth is, I had to pawn them, except for this one on me finger, and you know how things have been.'

Only too well, Jo thought. And as Kate rattled on, Jo stopped listening. She wanted to dwell on the happy news of her sister's wedding.

'Everything's gone up, Jo-Jo. I can't make ends meet.'

Jo knew how much money her mother had; sure, didn't she collect the rents herself? Half went to Ned, leaving her mother with fifteen shillings. It was enough to keep them in comfort. And yet, Jo still had to scrimp to put food on the table. It was shameful and she gritted her teeth, felt the heat rise to her face.

'What are we to do, Ma? You heard what the doctor said. We need a leg of mutton to make proper soup for Hubert.' She sat down again. 'I could get a job at the biscuit factory. I'm old enough. I'd bring home a good wage.'

'Haven't I told yeh before? I need you *here*. What I want is...'

Jo felt her patience snap. 'If you won't agree, I'm going to take my money and leave. I mean it! I've had enough!' she cried. 'Do you hear me, Ma?' Resting her head on her arm she sobbed bitter tears.

Kate straightened. Astonished by her daughter's outburst, she reached out her hand then drew back. 'Ah, sure...don't do that, Jo-Jo, at least not yet. The...the kids would miss yeh.' She sighed. 'But there is something you can do for me.'

Jo lifted her head, wiping her tears with the back of her hand. 'Do for you! The kid's are yours, Ma, not mine.' There, she'd said it. But instead of the usual torrent of abuse, Kate's tone softened.

'I promise, Jo-Jo, things will change. Just hear me out and later we can talk about you getting a job.' Kate leant both elbows on the table and cupped her face.

Hoping Kate had taken her seriously, she listened.

'What I was going to ask,' Kate continued. 'can yeh give me a few shillin' to tide me over for when Cissy comes, otherwise I don't know what we're going to do.'

'So, she's coming! Why didn't you say?'

'Yeh didn't give me a chance.' Kate clicked her tongue, placed her hands palms down on the table, and waited.

Her mother always managed to back her into a corner, make her feel guilty if she refused. She thought about what Ned had said about not touching her inheritance.

'You shouldn't need my money. Ned looks after you well,' she blurted, and from the disdainful look on Kate's face, she knew she'd overstepped the mark, but it was too late. Her mother's face hardened, and Jo slunk back into her chair. Kate leaned over and slapped Jo hard across the face, knocking her sideways. She cried out, pressing her hand to her cheek to ease the sting that penetrated her ear. Moving closer, Kate's eyes narrowed.

'You watch your tongue, girl. Where would you be if I hadn't put a roof over your head?' She prodded Jo with her finger. 'If you don't care about putting on a good table for your sister and her young man, I'll tell her not to come,' she said, and swept out of the room.

* * *

Barely able to contain herself, Jo checked several times to see if the dining room table was set properly. The silver cutlery her grandmother had used for special occasions sparkled. The red serviettes she'd made from crepe paper saved from last Christmas gave the table a festive look. Outside in the neglected back garden, pink roses, entwined with stinging nettles, clung to the wall. She cut them free and brought them inside and popped them in a vase for the centre of the table. Then she stood back to admire her efforts.

Cissy was such a fusspot, and Jo wanted the occasion to be just so! She had a few cooking tips under her belt since her sister's visit almost two years ago. The vegetable soup was made, and she could smell the bacon and cabbage simmering away nicely with large floury potatoes in the pot. Her fingers crossed that nothing would spoil. She had made ample, so the boys were assured of a good dinner later on.

Jo was flicking dust off the back of one of the dining chairs, when her mother walked in, an agitated expression on her face. 'Oh, stop your fussing! It's only Cissy, and he's nobody important.'

'Oh, I know, Ma! But it's exciting, isn't it?' Jo said, undeterred by Kate's somewhat jittery mood.

'We'll see!' she said. 'The twins are asleep, I won't be long.'

'What about Cissy? You promised,' Jo called after her, as the door closed behind her. Jo's happy mood changed to despair. How was she going to entertain Cissy and a man she had never met before, without her mother to help her? Oh, why did she have to disappear at a time like this?

When Kate didn't return, Jo paced the room and looked out of the window several times. 'How could she do this to me?' she said aloud, wringing her hands. A loud hissing and a strong smell of bacon and cabbage sent her dashing to the kitchen, where she lifted the large cooking pot from its hook. The dinner was cooked and ready to be served. Deflated, Jo dropped down onto her grandmother's stool and, clasping her hands in her lap, lowered her head. This time Kate had gone too far. What would Cissy say? How would she react to their mother not being here? When she looked up, Cissy and Larry were standing in the doorway.

The two sisters smiled and greeted each other. 'Jo, this is Larry, my fiancé,' Cissy beamed.

'Pleased to meet you,' Jo said. Then, turning to her sister she said, 'You look grand, Cissy.' She was wearing a yellow dress and navy jacket and her cheeks were glowing. Jo felt shabby in comparison.

'You look all grown up yourself,' Cissy said.

'Um…that smells good,' Larry said.

'Please go through.' Jo pointed towards the dining room.

Larry was skillfully balancing a cake in one hand. Removing it from the box, he placed it carefully on the table.

'I hope you like lemon cake,' he said. 'Oh, and we brought some fig rolls for the children.'

'Thanks, that's kind of you,' Jo said, feeling a flush to her face.

Cissy pulled out a chair from the table and sat down, telling Larry to do likewise.

'I've always loved this room,' she smiled. 'Where's Ma?'

'Oh! She won't be long. You must be hungry. I'll bring in the food.' Jo hurried back to the kitchen, followed by Cissy, a quizzical expression on her face.

'I thought she'd be here, Jo? Will she be long?'

'I'm sure she won't be.' Jo placed the bowls of hot vegetable soup on a tray and Cissy carried it through to the dining room.

'I can wait,' she said. 'We're in no rush.' Something in her tone unnerved Jo as they settled round the table.

Picking up a plate of freshly-cut bread, Jo offered some to the guests before helping herself.

'Larry works at the bakery, so we won't go short of bread when we're married.' Cissy linked her arm through his, giving it a squeeze.

'I hope not, sweetheart,' he said, looking adoringly at Cissy. 'You never know what could trigger off a bread strike, for instance, if the troubles blow up again?'

'Oh! Do you think it will?' Jo frowned.

'Don't exaggerate!' Cissy said.

'I'm telling you!' Larry said. 'There's something brewing again in the city, haven't you seen the papers? Sure, there are riots in Belfast.'

Jo hadn't read a newspaper in days. 'Well, let's hope they won't start down here.' And her sister reassured her it would come to nothing.

Halfway through their dinner, they heard Kate coming down the hall and go straight to the kitchen. Jo excused herself, and Larry touched her arm.

'That was the best bacon and cabbage I've had in ages,' he said.

'Really!' She felt herself blush and began to fidget with her hands.

'Credit where it's due!' her sister said. 'You stay and talk to Larry.' She pressed Jo to sit back down. 'I want to talk to Ma!'

Jo felt hot again; what would she talk about to a man like Larry? Nervously, she curled a lock of her hair between her finger and thumb. She had washed it, especially for the occasion, and was sure it must smell of cabbage. Larry seemed to notice her discomfort and broke the ice.

'You know, I remember feeling nervous the first time I asked Cissy if she'd walk out with me.' He gave Jo a wry smile. 'I took her to the Volta picture house in Mary Street.' He laughed. 'I can't even remember what was showing.' He leaned back in his chair and unbuttoned his jacket, and took a deep breath. 'I've eaten too much. But that's down to your splendid cooking, Jo.' He patted his stomach and, with his easy manner, Jo began to relax. She envied her sister's good luck in finding such a nice man. At twenty-six, he was just two years older than Cissy.

'What do you intend doing with your life, Jo?' Larry asked.

'I'd like to follow Cissy into service, or travel, maybe see a bit of the world, but…' she shrugged, "tis only a dream.'

'Hold on to your dream, Jo, and it will happen one day.' His words were reassuring and she wanted so much to believe him. Talking to Larry hadn't been so bad after all, and the few minutes flew by until her sister's abrupt reappearance brought their conversation to a halt. Kate was right behind her.

'Well! That takes the biscuit, yeh cheeky hussy,' Kate was shouting.

'I only want what's rightfully mine,' Cissy said, keeping her voice as dignified as possible in front of her fiancé.

Her mother pulled the sapphire ring from her finger and threw it at her. 'Here! Take it, if it makes yeh happy.'

Cissy scrambled to pick it up from the floor.

Jo got to her feet. She couldn't believe what was happening. Disgusted with her mother – who smelt like a brewery – and embarrassed for Cissy, she glanced towards Larry who was looking somewhat bewildered.

'Now go!' Kate screamed, waving her arms. 'And take your fancy man with you. I never want to see you again.'

CHAPTER EIGHT

Jo gazed out of her bedroom window. The September sun had set and the Dublin streets were grey and colourless except for the distant view of the Wicklow Mountains. On a clear day, rolling shades of green, mingled with purple of the heather, could be seen across the hills, now clouded in mist. They represented Ireland's changeable climate, and reminded Jo of her unsettled life and changing moods.

Later that evening, she was lying on the bed reading when her mother called her. It was a pattern she was well used to; but tonight she was slow to respond, until thoughts of the children downstairs alone, forced her into action. She rolled off her bed and, in listless mood, went down. To prove she was no longer obedient to her mother's call, she entered the room deliberately tardy, her face showing resentment. Kate, without a word, grabbed her shawl and left the house.

When the children were asleep, Jo sorted through their clothes. Liam's were the worst for wear as he was the healthiest of the three. All their clothes, including her own, had holes and needed patching, but tonight she couldn't be bothered. Instead, she picked up Jonathan Swift's *Gulliver's Travels*. Reading was her only escape to places she only dreamt of. She had read a shelf of books by Irish authors and some on American history.

But the loneliness she felt never left her. With only two pounds left of her inheritance, her dreams of America were dwindling. Apart from the girl at the library who always had a kind word for her, she had no grown ups to talk to.

Later, she went to check on the children. Liam's bed was

littered with crumbs, making her smile. He had fallen asleep happy, after munching through the biscuits Larry had brought. James was sleeping soundly next to his brother. Hubert seemed to be coughing less and his breathing was slow and easy. She pitied him. He opened his eyes and looked up at her. Gently lifting his head, she raised his pillow, which sometimes helped. Stroking his hair, she kissed him lightly on the forehead.

'Good boy,' she murmured, a lump forming in her throat. He was such a lovable little chap who didn't deserve Kate for a mother. She decided to sit with him for a while, at least until he fell asleep again. She must have dozed, for when she woke up the lamp had gone out. The stillness hit her immediately.

Lifting Hubert's hand, she was relieved to find a weak pulse. Leaving him lying next to James, she rushed down the stairs and out into the street to find her mother.

She didn't have to look far – and located her in Aggie Murphy's, singing and pouring drinks from her jug. 'Send down for another jug, Aggie. I'll pay this time.'

Jo stood in the doorway, tears streaming down her white face. 'Ma, you've got to come home!'

'What's the matter, girl?' They all stopped singing and looked towards Jo.

'It's…it's Hubert. He's barely breathing!'

Kate's shawl slipped from her shoulders as she hurried towards the door.

'I'll come with you, Kate!' Aggie followed her out. And the two women ran; Kate the thinner of the two reached the house first.

Jo, drained of energy, paused to relieve a stitch in her side when the piercing screams of the Banshee invaded the space around her and she covered her ears to block the keening of the *evil one*. Then she ran, chased by the screeching menace, towards her grandmother's house. Her breath coming in gasps, she raced upstairs. Before she entered the room, the whiff of alcohol made her want to heave. Her mother was cradling Hubert in her arms.

'Why? Oh, why? God Almighty! Why?'

'Ma, did you hear the Banshee?'

'No! Be quiet, Jo-Jo. I heard nothing.'

'There's still a weak pulse,' Aggie said. 'Keep him warm while I go home and warm some broth.'

But the soup had no effect. Within the hour, Hubert died in his mother's arms.

Jo knelt down beside him, stroking his hair. And her eyes filled at what had almost mirrored her grandmother's death.

'I know he was an ailing babe, but I shouldn't have left him,' Kate moaned.

'There was nothing you could have done,' Aggie told her. 'Sometimes things happen that don't make sense at all. It was God's will.'

Four-year-old James cried out for Hubert, and Liam looked on bewildered. Jo, struggling with her own emotions, placed her arms around both boys and took them into her own bedroom, leaving their mother rocking and crooning to Hubert. Aggie stayed in the room with her friend, to offer support and do what was necessary.

* * *

For months after Hubert's death, Kate stayed in and resumed her motherly role. Her jug of porter was now consumed at home with the help of Aggie, who called in of an evening to keep her company. Jo felt a weight lifted off her shoulders, confident that sooner or later Kate would agree to her finding work. Jo was beginning to warm towards Aggie, although at times she felt that she encouraged her mother to drink and wallow in grief.

One evening, as Jo returned from the library, she overheard the two women talking as she passed down the hall. The fact that they mentioned her name made her stop to listen.

'I dare say they'd take Jo-Jo on,' Aggie was saying. 'They're looking for young ones right now.'

'Not for *her*, Aggie, for me.'

'Ah sure, it's more suited to young ones, Kate. Take a look at me hands, raw and sore from filling the packets with soap powder. If it wasn't for me long service, they'd have let me go by now.'

There was a pause, then Kate said, 'Aye! Happen you're right, but I can't cope with the kids, Aggie. Young Liam's a handful and Jo-Jo's got the patience of a saint.'

'Aye! She's a good girl, that one! And if yeh don't cut her some slack, she'll go anyway.'

Jo waited, but her mother didn't respond. When she heard the clinking of glasses, she placed her books on the hall table and went in. Kate had James on her knee. The boy glanced towards Jo.

'Shall I put him to bed, Ma?'

'Aye, yeh can, he's about ready. Liam's out in the street somewhere. Aggie will chase him home when she goes.'

The child scrambled down and ran to Jo and, as she took the boy upstairs, a glimmer of hope swept through her. At least now she knew that her mother had taken her threat to leave seriously.

* * *

Jo's visits to the library became more frequent, and she looked forward to seeing the librarian, whom she now knew as Annie O'Toole. With Annie's help, Jo found the books she wanted quickly. She also discovered that they both had dreams of going to America. Kate barely noticed her absence these days, and with Annie, Jo didn't feel so lonely.

She began to stay longer at the library, lingering over the books, reading in the peace and quiet, a welcome respite from the labours and worries at home. In time, a trusting friendship developed between the two girls.

At first, Annie had reminded Jo of her sister, Cissy, but after months of getting to know her, she realised there was little resemblance between the two. Annie was twenty and Jo could hardly believe her luck that the older girl with a shock of chestnut hair had befriended her. Their five year age difference was of little importance and when Annie asked her if she'd like to visit the cinema sometime, Jo found a new world had opened up to her.

Returning home one evening after a night out with Annie, Jo was surprised to see a man talking to her mother on the doorstep. As she drew nearer, she saw her mother was upset, her apron held up against her face. The man was waving his arms and displaying aggressive behaviour. Something about him unnerved Jo and she ran the rest of the way. He kicked the door as her mother tried to close it.

'You've got till Friday...' he grinned menacingly. 'My boss isn't happy, *missus*, and it brasses me off...'

'Who are you? And what do you want?' Ignoring Jo, he had Kate by the scruff of her neck, lifting her off her feet. 'Do you understand me, lady? Next time I won't be so nice.'

Kate nodded.

Doors opened and neighbours gathered on the pavement.

'What's this all about, Ma?'

'Perhaps you'd better enlighten the young lady,' he said, and stalked off.

Jo hurried her mother inside and closed the door. Kate was shaking, and as Jo sat her down she began to sob. 'There's something I have to tell you.'

Jo sat opposite her, a worried expression on her face. 'Where are the boys?'

'They're all right. They're with Aggie.'

'Why was that man threatening you?'

'I owe money to Big Tom. He wants three pounds, ten shillings by next Friday.'

'God, Ma! How could you?' Jo swallowed. Everyone knew what Big Tom was like. If he didn't get his money, he'd send his bullyboys to collect it for him, sometimes with disastrous results. 'What were you thinking of to go borrowing from a man like that?' Jo buried her face in her hands.

'I'm sorry, Jo-Jo. I only borrowed a couple of pounds to tide me over. Now he's added interest. Oh, what am I to do, Jo-Jo?' For an instant Jo felt like the parent, exasperated with a defiant child. She would have to take charge of the situation or heaven knew what debts her mother might run up. She stood up and placed her hand on her mother's shoulder.

'You can have what's left of my inheritance. You'll have to put Friday's rent money to it.'

'We'll have nothing for food.'

Jo had been dipping into her savings to put food on the table most weeks, and this was the last straw. 'Just promise me you won't go near big Tom again.'

Kate nodded. 'I'll make it up to you, Jo-Jo. I'll get work,' she said, drying her eyes.

'It won't be easy, Ma! Annie says that most vacancies want young girls. That way they don't have to pay a full wage.' Jo picked up the paper, more determined than ever to find a job.

'There's more ways to skin a cat, my girl! I'm not completely useless, you know. I was a seamstress when I met your father.'

Kate had never mentioned Jo's father before, and it came as a surprise to hear that she had once been a seamstress. Holding down a job wasn't something her mother could do right now, and besides, extra money in her purse would be a temptation sure to drive her out of the home. This was Jo's opportunity and she jumped in with both feet.

'Listen to me, Ma. I'm the one who is going to get a job! I'll go down to the biscuit factory first thing in the morning.' She moved away expecting a reaction, but instead the lines on Kate's face relaxed.

'Okay, Jo-Jo. What other choice do I have?'

'None! Promise you'll look after the boys?'

'I will. I'll do my best.'

That night, for the first time since Jo was forced to live with her mother, an understanding developed between them.

CHAPTER NINE

1921

No longer the scrawny girl in pigtails that Ned had left behind four years ago, Josephine Kingsley could be seen most days walking with purpose, her head held high. Her eyes were no longer sad, but brightened by prospects to secure her own future.

Unprepared to lose her, or the financial security she was hoping the girl would bring her, Kate had agreed to her daughter's wishes. Jo had quickly found work at the biscuit factory, but now they were on short time she was forced to look elsewhere. She applied for shop work, but the shopkeeper's wife told her, "You're too pretty, and my husband has a wandering eye."

Determined not to give up, she continued to look down the situations vacant in the evening newspaper, until she spotted an unusual advertisement that got her excited.

Smart young lady wanted as French lady's maid.
Live in, or out. Must like parrots!
Write in the first instance.
To Box Number 5634

Annie looked over her letter of application and gave her a character reference before she sent it off. When the reply came back, Jo opened it with trembling fingers. The letter asked her to attend an interview at 10am the following morning. She was to ask for the housekeeper, Miss O'Breen. The address printed on the top of the page read:

Chateau Colbert,
21 Laburnum Avenue,
Rathgar

A smile spread across Jo's face, and that evening she could hardly wait to tell Annie the good news.

'I'm pleased for you, Jo. I'll say a prayer.' Her friend gestured with her hands. 'Call in on your way home, I'll be itching to know how you got on!'

'Thanks, Annie. Ma thinks it's out of my class and that I won't stand a chance of getting it,' Jo sighed.

'Well, I don't agree. You can do better than a biscuit factory, Jo. Just remember, don't fidget, keep your shoulders back, be polite, and only speak if invited to.' And before they parted company, Annie offered a few tips on how to dress for the interview.

Jo woke to April sunshine that streamed in through the window. A mixture of excitement and anxiety gripped her as she got ready. She wore a hyacinth blue dress that buttoned to the waist and fell in gentle folds six inches below the knee, a white belt emphasizing her small waist. She stood in front of the cracked mirror and took a deep breath, wondering if a skirt and jacket would have been more appropriate.

'Jo-Jo, can yeh run to the shop for a loaf of bread afore yeh go?' Kate called up to her.

Jo continued to brush her long hair. She had learnt when to pander to Kate's wishes and when not to. Her mother had been against any job that took Jo away from the city limits and this was a ploy to make her late and discredit her. But Jo was having none of it. She knew how suitable this position might prove should she be lucky enough to get it.

After one last glimpse in the mirror, she placed her straw hat on her head. The blue ribbon trailed down her back. She slipped on a pair of white gloves that Annie said would put the finishing touches to any outfit. Then, picking up her purse with the letter inside, she called cheerio and quickly left the house.

* * *

Half an hour later, Jo found herself looking down an avenue where laburnum trees lined both sides of the pavement, their branches laden with buds, some already open to reveal flashes of yellow. She inhaled, letting the scent linger in her nostrils. As she walked, she glanced at the beautiful houses.

Halfway along, the road curved and Jo found herself staring up at a magnificent mansion. She stood transfixed. Could this be the place she was looking for? Black railings surrounded the grounds. The three-storey house had white sash windows, and white pillars flanked the imposing front door. A brass plaque secured to the gatepost, suitably inscribed with the words *Chateau Colbert*, left her in no doubt. It was now that she wished she'd used the privy before she left home.

Straightening her shoulders, she took a deep breath and pushed open the heavy gate.

Her boots made a crunching noise on the gravelled driveway. She gripped the iron railings and walked up the curved steps, lifted the shiny knocker, and waited.

The door opened, revealing the friendly face of a tall gentleman, his hairline receding, and his dress immaculate.

'My...my name is Josephine Kingsley, and...'

'And mine is Foster the butler.' He raised his eyebrows and smiled down at her. 'Please use the servants' entrance, Miss O'Breen is expecting you.' He pointed round to the side of the house. Mumbling her apology, she hurried back down.

A maid with a surly expression opened the side door and, without speaking, stood back and allowed her in. Jo was surprised by the girl's lack of manners. Hair escaped from underneath her cap and her apron was stained and wet. She beckoned and Jo followed her along the passage, the sensations in her tummy worsened by the maid's attitude. The girl flung open a door.

'Wait in here,' she said, then closed the door behind her.

The smell of beeswax polish was strangely comforting and reminded her of her grandmother. The ornate clock on the mantle shelf chimed out the hour, and Jo was pleased to have arrived at the appointed time. It was a charming room, fresh and airy. The sun shone through the large windows, accentuating the order of the arranged pieces in the room. She couldn't see a speck of dust. Too nervous to sit, she remained standing, noting the elegance of the furniture, the likes of which she had never seen before.

Her confidence ebbed. What was she thinking, standing here amidst such grandeur? How would she fit into a place like this? She wondered what Miss O'Breen would be like. If she was as frosty as the maid, Jo would have no option but to suffer the embarrassment of asking for the toilet.

She swallowed as the housekeeper bounced into the room. She was a woman in her forties. Her curly hair, streaked with grey, was swept up at the back, so that the curls on top of her head danced when she walked. Her uniform was freshly starched. She smiled, offering an outstretched hand.

'You must be Josephine Kingsley!' she said, looking at her notes.

'That's right, Miss O'Breen.' Unable to stop her knees from knocking, she handed her the letter.

'How old are you?'

'Seventeen…but I'll be eighteen soon, Miss O'Breen.'

'Firstly, I'd like to know what experience you've had, and look at a reference from your last employer. Then we shall see if Madame Colbert will see you. She, of course, will have the final say.' She beckoned Jo to sit on one of the high-backed chairs and sat down next to her.

'I'm…sorry, Miss O'Breen. I've…I've never worked in service before. I worked at the biscuit factory for nearly two years. We're on short time at the moment.' She entwined her gloved fingers. 'But I have a character reference from the librarian near where I live.' She opened her bag and handed it to the housekeeper.

'I see!' She read the reference, then looked up. 'So you have no experience, child?' She twirled her pencil between her long slender fingers. 'How would you look after and entertain an intellectual elderly lady?'

Jo swallowed and cleared her throat. 'Well…Miss O'Breen, I can cook and clean, read newspapers and books. I have been to see many of the latest plays, I can also play the piano, and I'm…I'm very willing to please.' Relieved the words came rushing out and didn't stick in her throat, Jo cast her eyes down to her hands and fought the urge to fidget.

'I see,' the housekeeper said, after a long pause. 'I'll check if Madame will see you!'

'Thank you, Miss O'Breen.' She went away for a few minutes, and when she returned she took Jo upstairs.

Madame Colbert put aside her embroidery and looked up when they entered the room.

'This is Josephine Kingsley, Madame.'

'Thank you, Miss O'Breen. I'll ring when we've finished.'

When the housekeeper left, Jo's nerves began to bite again, and she took a deep breath.

'Please sit down, my dear. No, no! Not there, dear, over here where I can get a good look at you!'

Jo was struck dumb by the elegance of this lady and everything that surrounded her. She did as she was instructed, resting her hands in her lap. She had removed one glove and was twisting it tightly in her hands.

'You are very beautiful, my dear, and will break some young man's heart one day.'

'I'm sorry, Mad–' Jo began nervously.

'Don't be, my dear, don't be,' Madame Colbert laughed, and Jo immediately warmed towards her and relaxed a little.

'I mean thank you, Madame Colbert,' Jo returned more confidently.

'I believe you play the piano?' She pointed with a manicured fingernail towards the baby grand by the French window. Her gown was navy in crushed velvet, with a white collar set off by a string of pearls. She stood up and walked towards the window and Jo noticed the French knot that held her white hair neatly in place.

'Yes, Madame.'

'Would you play for me, my dear? I would really like that.' She had one of those lingering smiles that lit up her face and didn't immediately vanish.

Jo's heart raced and her cheeks flushed. This was the last thing she had expected. Slightly hesitant, and trying to stay focused, she moved across the room to where Madame Colbert had already raised the lid of the piano, revealing the smooth black and ivory keys. Jo sat down on the red velvet piano stool, pulling it in under her until she felt comfortable. Aware of being watched intently, she played one of her compositions to warm up. The piano was tuned to perfection. Then, as she played one of Moore's melodies, the sudden squawking sound of the bird made her jump and her fingers hit all the wrong keys.

'I'm sorry, Madame.'

'Don't worry, Miss Kingsley. Lulu hates to be excluded. Do you like parrots, my dear?'

'Yes, of course.'

'Who's there? Who's there?' the parrot mimicked in a voice so human it made Jo smile.

'Come and meet Lulu, Miss Kingsley.' Madame Colbert walked to a corner of the room and lifted the cover from the golden cage. The bird looked sideways at Jo and ruffled its red feathers.

'What a lovely bird. Is it friendly?' Jo edged closer to the cage.

'She's very tame, my dear, loves to hear herself talk.'

Feeling much more relaxed, Jo almost forgot she was having an interview.

'Would you still like to work here, Miss Kingsley?'

'Oh yes, indeed I would, Madame Colbert.'

'Very well then,' she said, walking back across the room. She tugged on the tasselled cord, hanging by the large marbled fireplace. 'Miss O'Breen will discuss terms of employment and instruct you as to your duties. Goodbye for now, Miss Kingsley.'

'Goodbye, Madame Colbert, and thank you.'

CHAPTER TEN

Unsure at first in her new role, Jo, as well as keeping her elderly employer entertained, was expected to undertake light domestic duties on her behalf. Her introduction to the kitchen staff was brief. She shook hands with Molly, the sour-faced maid who had admitted her for her interview, and received only a cursory glance from Rosie, the parlour maid. The cook, Mrs. Quigley – smelling of flour and yeast, her cheeks glowing with health – flapped around in a state of confusion, then wiped her hands on a tea cloth.

'It's nice to meet yeh, miss.' She shook Jo's hand warmly and then yelled at Molly to get some pots washed.

Miss O'Breen handed Jo a white frilly pinafore and matching cap. 'Cook will find you something to do in the kitchen when Madame Colbert has her afternoon rest,' she said. 'If you have any problems, I'll not be far away.' Then she bounced out, leaving behind the smell of lavender and freshly starched linen.

Ensuring her hair was neatly tucked up underneath her cap, Jo proceeded upstairs with the morning tray towards Madame Colbert's quarters on the first floor. She knocked before entering, and placed the tray with poached eggs and freshly baked croissants on the bedside table. The rooms were bright and colourful. Beautiful French tapestry hung on the walls. She recognised the Champs-Elysees and the Eiffel Tower from a book she had seen at the library. A lavishly decorated screen, depicting peacocks in vivid kingfisher blues and greens, concealed a washstand in the corner of the bedroom. Jo's instructions were to leave out fresh laundry every day, then take away the basket for washing when

Madame had finished dressing.

'Good morning, Madame.'

'Good morning, my dear. Can you take my tray to the table by the window?'

Jo did as instructed, placing the morning newspaper next to it. She could see why Madame preferred to sit by the French window. It was light and sunny, with a glorious view of the garden.

Later that morning as she carried out her chores, she'd forgotten about the parrot until it called out to her as she was cleaning the cheval mirror.

Madame Colbert glanced up from her newspaper. She stood up and walked towards the cage and lifted the cover. '*Ma petite*, this is Jo.' And she repeated Jo's name over and over to the bird, until Jo found herself giggling at the performance.

'Jo is an easy name for her to remember. But this cover must go on in the evenings,' she said, folding it and placing it next to the cage. 'Otherwise, Lulu would talk all night long, and I'd get no sleep.'

'I'll see to it, Madame.'

After that, whenever Jo came within earshot of the parrot, it called out her name. And when she brought in the tray each morning, the bird called, 'Ere, a bit for Lulu.' This continued until Madame fed Lulu one of her special almonds. The parrot intrigued Jo and she looked forward to listening to its repertoire. And when she played the piano, it hummed and danced up and down on its perch.

'Lulu is very special to me, *chérie*. My grandson, Jean-Pierre, brought her here from Paris a few years ago. He's a dear boy, so kind to me.' Her eyes misted and she looked across to the mantle shelf, pointing to his photograph. 'Can you pass it down to me, my dear?'

Jo reached up and carefully took down the silver-framed photograph of Jean-Pierre and handed it to her. Madame brushed her hand lovingly over it. 'This was taken a few years ago. He is so like his father, François, who died with his wife in a tragic skiing accident when Jean-Pierre was just sixteen.'

'I'm sorry, Madame.'

'That's life. I learnt to cope with it a long time ago. Pierre is my life now.' She handed the photograph back and Jo replaced it on the mantel, noticing the young man's striking resemblance to his grandmother. He had her slender fingers and tall, upright posture. And as Jo busied herself polishing and dusting, careful not to break anything, Jean-Pierre's dark eyes seemed to follow her around the room.

* * *

Working at Chateau Colbert, it was easy to blot out the threat of a civil war. And as the pattern of her days became firmly established, Jo couldn't help sharing her joy with Annie when they met for tea.

'It's like I've died and gone to heaven,' she claimed, her eyes looking upwards. 'And I'm getting paid for the privilege.'

'I couldn't be happier for you, Jo. But be careful coming home at night. You've read the newspapers. There's unrest everywhere, and who knows where it will end?'

'I know, Annie, but we have to carry on.'

'Just be careful.'

Annie had taught her so much; her guidance had helped secure the position she now held, and she blessed the day they had become friends.

When Jo received her first month's pay, she took it home to Kate – an arrangement she had agreed to in return for her freedom. Another stipulation was that she came home every evening to help with the chores, unaware at the time the hardship it would entail. Kate, in return, gave her back a few shillings for her own personal use, most of which got swallowed up in tram fares. Although her mother never borrowed from Big Tom again, she couldn't help running up debts. With Jo out working, Kate collected the rents, and at times her brain was so befuddled she forgot to sign the rent books and couldn't remember who had paid and who hadn't. When Jo became frustrated with her, she was reminded of her own stupidity in allowing her inheritance to slip through her fingers.

But she had a lot to be grateful for. A nourishing meal everyday had put the colour back into her cheeks, and Mrs. Quigley often slipped her some of the leftovers to take home to the family. The young ones rushed to meet her when they saw her coming down the street. All was fine, until one evening she returned to find that James was far from well.

That wheezing sound she had hoped never to hear again was back to haunt them. Alarmed, Jo called in the doctor. Knowing the family's history of TB, he suggested a spell in a sanatorium for children with consumption. Kate was reluctant to let him go.

'Unless you want to lose him, I recommend you listen to your daughter here,' he said tersely. 'I'll arrange for an ambulance to pick him up in a few hours.'

Jo burst into tears, then she went upstairs and carried James down. Kate was rocking him on her knee when Aggie called in. 'Oh, Aggie,' she cried. 'The doctor says he's sending an ambulance. I'm frightened to let him go.'

'You've got to, Kate! What can yeh gain by keeping him here? Them's good places, I hear,' she said, her plump arms resting under her bust.

'Do yeh think so, Aggie?'

Within a few hours, James was taken to a sanatorium. In spite of her own doubts, Jo stayed up half the night to reassure her mother.

It was almost dawn when Kate drifted off, allowing Jo a few hours sleep before she had to get up. It was not surprising she arrived late for work.

Miss O'Breen was waiting. 'We don't tolerate poor time keeping.' Her voice had an edge Jo hadn't experienced before. She tried to apologise, but before she could finish, the housekeeper handed her Madame's tray and briskly walked away.

Close to tears at not being allowed to explain her lateness, Jo rushed out with the tray. Outside the door, she took a deep breath, knocked and entered. She placed the tray down, her hands trembling.

'I'm sorry…I'm late Madame…but…'

'You're upset, my dear? Sit down and tell me what troubles you.'

Jo remained standing. She shouldn't have been late and she felt bad about it. 'My young brother, James, was taken to the sanatorium late last night. I overslept. It won't happen again. I'll make up the time.'

'I'm sorry to hear that. How distressing for you. You must go home when you finish your chores.'

'No, really…Madame, I…there's no need.'

'I insist!'

Later, when Jo came down to the kitchen, Mrs. Quigley informed her that Madame Colbert had instructed Miss O'Breen to order a basket of fresh fruit from the local fruit shop for James. Jo, unaccustomed to such generosity, had to bite back tears.

'Sure, she's always pitied the unfortunate,' Cook said, handing Jo the basket of fruit.

* * *

That evening, Jo found James at the end of a long row of beds, propped up chatting with other children who were there for observation and suspected TB. James smiled up at her, and a hint of colour had returned to his sickly white face. Every window was flung open and the ward was chilly – Jo felt cold in her summer jacket. Some patients were outside on the veranda and she felt pleased that it hadn't been deemed necessary to put James out there.

'Fresh air helps to clear the lungs,' the nurse said, when she saw Jo tuck the bed covers around James, fearing he'd catch cold.

'Yes, of course! It seems rather strange.'

'It is at first, but patients soon realise it's for their own good; with fresh air in their lungs, it's surprising how quickly they start to improve.'

'What have you brought me, Jo?' James tugged at her bag.

She lifted the basket of fruit onto the bed, and untied the red satin ribbon, revealing an abundance of colourful fruits. James had never seen fruit like it and his eyes widened. He reached out to touch the oranges, but he was hesitant to eat one.

'It's all right, James. It's from my employer, Madame Colbert.

It's good for you.' And she peeled the fruit, breaking off segments for him to taste, and laughing when juice ran down his chin. She offered some to the other children. Before long, James was tucking in and had eaten an apple down to the core before the nurse returned.

'Judging by your appetite, young man,' she smiled, taking the basket of fruit away, 'you'll be out of here in no time.'

'That's good to hear.' Jo smiled, hoping her prayers would be answered and that James, unlike his twin, Hubert, would make a complete recovery. Towards the end of visiting time, Jo noticed James's bottom lip begin to quiver. She stuck a paper windmill she had bought for him, on the side of his bed. 'I'll see you in a few days.' And, quickly kissing him, she moved towards the door.

When she looked back, James was smiling and touching the windmill as it whirled round violently next to the open window.

CHAPTER ELEVEN

As Christmas approached, it did nothing to quell the fear of unrest that had settled over the city, and the whole of Ireland. With news filtering through of random raids on homes and shootings taking place in and around Dublin, Jo wasn't surprised to find the library quieter than usual, and she wondered what 1922 had in store for them.

Annie was reading the evening newspaper spread out on the counter. She glanced up when she saw Jo. 'I can see a civil war brewing up here,' she sighed, closing the newspaper. 'It's getting worse.'

'I don't know what to believe any more,' Jo said.

'I don't know myself,' Annie confessed. 'I'd love peace, but I still want a republic. Whether I'm willing to die for it is another thing.' She sighed and gave Jo a wry smile. 'It's a complicated business.'

'Madame Colbert wants me to consider living in. I'd like to, Annie, but Ma doesn't always cope well without me.'

'You should take your employer's advice. Start saving for your future; if there is one after they've blown the city to bits. Besides, it's not safe for a young girl travelling about at night.' Annie shook her head. 'And I fear when I read of innocent civilians getting injured in the crossfire.'

'Don't worry about me, Annie! I'll talk to Ma over Christmas.'

'I can't help it, Jo. Your mother's there to look after things, isn't she? I'm sorry, I shouldn't have said that. I know how hard you work and, well, it's unfair.' She shrugged. 'But you have to decide.'

'It's easier said than done.'

'Well, until you see sense, you can borrow my bicycle. The trams are unpredictable at the moment.'

'Are you sure? How will you get to the library?'

'Oh, I'll be grand. It'll only take me an extra ten minutes to walk. Here's that book you wanted. Still interested in American politics, I see.'

'Well, yes. It makes a change from what's going on here.'

'Come on. I'd better lock up. There's an eerie feeling hanging about.'

They went around to the back of the library where Annie's black bicycle was secured to the railings. 'Why don't you ride it home?' she said, pushing it towards Jo. 'The dynamo's a bit wonky. You might have to buy a new lamp.'

Apart from a small tricycle that her grandmother had bought her when she was little, Jo had never ridden a bike. Placing her feet firmly on the pedals, she practised riding it up and down on the pavement, wobbling from side to side. She fell off a couple of times, grazing her knee, but she got back on until she got the hang of it.

'Thanks, Annie, it feels like Christmas already.'

'Do you still think about emigrating?' Annie asked, as they walked to the corner of the street.

'Get off, Annie. Sure, that was only a dream.'

'Well, dreams do come true. I'm leaving as soon as I've saved enough money. Maybe we'll go together and meet two dishy men!' Annie arched her eyebrows and they both fell around laughing. It took her a while to cycle home and on the way, she saw graffiti splashed across walls – even the school wall had the slogan, *No Surrender* painted in white, the paint still dripping.

* * *

Kate looked surprised when Jo wheeled the bicycle into the hall. 'Whatever do you want that thing for?' she frowned.

'It's Annie's. She's let me borrow it. I can dodge down the back streets, keeping away from the city altogether until the troubles die down.' She leant it against the wall as Kate pondered, then agreed that it might be a good idea, as long as she came home each evening,

Just then, Aggie Murphy came in. Her cardigan sleeves, rolled halfway up her arms, were digging into the folds of fat. She was carrying a recipe book. The two women, who had been swapping recipes for weeks, made their Christmas puddings with whatever ingredients they could afford between them.

'Oh hello, Jo,' she said, when she saw her in the hall. 'Still enjoying working for the gentry, are yeh?'

'Yes, I am, Aggie. I've just been telling Ma, I'm going to ride to work on the bike.' Jo jingled the bell.

'Umm…our Joan has one of them contraptions, but she only goes as far as the soap factory. You be careful and keep away from the city – it's not safe.' She wagged a fat finger. Smiling, Jo went upstairs, leaving the women to their chatter.

* * *

Madame Colbert went to stay with friends for Christmas and Mrs. Quigley gave the maids food parcels to take home for the holiday. There was enough good food to last them for days.

'At least they give generously to the poor at that posh place where yeh work, Jo-Jo,' Her mother unwrapped the food and stored it away in the cupboards.

On Christmas morning, Jo walked into the kitchen to the sound of breakfast sizzling in the pan; the appetizing smell made her ravenous. 'That smells good, Ma. Anything I can do?'

'No,' she said, looking round at Jo. 'Sit yerself down.' Kate finished cooking the breakfast and brought it to the table. She could not remember her mother ever serving her with a cooked breakfast and it felt good. Liam sat next to her, elbows on the table, holding his knife and fork ready to tuck in. They ate heartily, and nothing remained.

'No-one round these parts has money for food like this, Jo-Jo.' Kate poured their tea and then warmed her hands on the mug. 'I'll give Aggie a bit of that lovely dripping yeh brought home last week.'

'Has there been any word from Cissy?' Jo asked.

'No, and why would there be? But there's a Christmas card from Ned.' She pointed to the drawer in the dresser. 'I meant to put it on the mantelpiece.'

Jo got up and took out the card. Ned wished them all seasons greetings and had enclosed money to buy presents for the children and hoped they were coping in these troubled times. She still missed him. She placed the card on the shelf over the fireplace alongside the others and returned to the table. 'What happened to the money?'

'I spent it on the kids. Here yeh are, Liam,' she said, passing him his unwrapped gift.

'Thanks, Ma. Look, Jo.' He slung the red woollen scarf around his neck, and pulled the matching hat down over his ears.

Jo looked across at Kate, surprised that she had knit a set for both the boys. 'Why, they're lovely, Ma.' She fingered the soft wool. The colours were bright and cheerful, made with great care.

Kate folded James's blue set, putting them to one side for when she went up to see him.

'Must have taken you ages to knit them,' Jo said.

'Well, yeh know. I did a bit each day when the boys were at school. I miss James. He should be here with us now,' she sniffed.

'He'll be having a great time where he is, Ma, and besides, he'll be home soon. Didn't the nurse say so? I'll take him his presents later on if you like, now I've got the bicycle.'

'Oh, that would be grand, Jo-Jo, he'd like that. Tell him I'll be in to see him when the trams are running back to normal. Aggie says that Santa Claus goes round the wards,' she said, ripping the red paper from the small gift Jo had bought her.

'Right grand it is, Jo-Jo.' She pinned the sparkling brooch, in the shape of a bow, to her frock collar. Liam was gazing at his shiny new shilling.

'Thanks, Jo.'

'Here,' her mother said awkwardly, thrusting a small parcel at Jo. 'This is for you.'

Jo tore the paper away and discovered a box with a black shiny bicycle lamp inside. It was so unexpected, she felt overcome; she would always remember it as the first present her mother had ever given her. She wanted to reach out and embrace her, but Kate quickly pushed back her chair, lifted the dirty plates, and carried them to the sink.

CHAPTER TWELVE

By spring, Republican discontent simmered and the city was perilous. A small majority supported Michael Collins and the Anglo-Irish treaty, with the opposition leaning towards de Valera. Although the treaty did not bring about the desired effect, the majority of people prayed for lasting peace and an end to the civil war.

Maria Colbert didn't pray like the rest of the community, but her concerns were the same. Having come to reside at Chateau Colbert forty-five years before, as the young bride of Louis Colbert, there was little – if anything – she didn't know about the Irish situation. And tonight, she worried about the fate of the country. She could see a great divide and had almost given up trying to work out what went on in the minds of politicians.

She sat at her dressing table un-plaiting her locks, thinking of her young maid. So far Jo's mother had won and she continued to race home each evening without a thought for her own safety. Maria sighed and picked up her hairbrush, gently brushing the long wavy strands, casting her mind back to a time when the same locks had been honey blonde. How Louis had loved her hair, loved to slide his hand down its shiny length after her maid had finished brushing it.

Those heady days when they were first married. She had loved him with a passion, and he her. 'Dear Louis,' she murmured, 'is it really that long ago?' He had been a diplomatic correspondent in the French foreign office, before being sent to Dublin as a temporary replacement. But he fell in love with the country and bought the beautiful 'Grand Chateau' renaming the property

'Chateau Colbert' after the family name.

Green fields and rolling hills had surrounded the house then. At first she had felt isolated and lonely, but in time she'd grown to love the place, and its people. Both she and Louis had always been forthright in showing compassion to the less fortunate, while they enjoyed a dualistic prosperous married life. Although she attended fewer functions these days, she still supported her many charities.

Removing the pearls her beloved Louis had given her, she thoughtfully fingered the beads. His sudden death from a heart complaint had left her with a great sense of loss. The fact that her husband had been buried in a nearby cemetery had influenced her decision to stay in Ireland. She'd sold part of the surrounding land to persistent housing developers, feeling it would create jobs for the needy.

She sighed. Now, their grandson, Jean-Pierre, was her only successor; she adored the boy, and loved it when he came to stay.

A car backfiring jolted her from her thoughts. What was she doing? She chided herself. It wasn't often she let her mind wander like this. But lately she had found the evenings long once Jo had gone home. She did so admire the girl's dedication to her family.

She rose, walked across to the window, and glanced up at the darkening sky. Now that spring was here she was looking forward to sitting in the garden again. She went back toward the bed. Rosie would be up soon to see to her needs. She shouldn't make comparisons, but the girl irritated her with her sloppy attitude, and she wondered why Miss O'Breen hadn't noticed. If only Jo would reconsider living in. But she mustn't rush her; she must let her make up her own mind. Maria could see herself in the young Jo, with the same hopes and dreams. Aware of her own privileged status, she wanted to help Jo to realise her potential, and felt that she deserved better. There was something about her that she'd not seen in any other maid she'd employed. She had observed Jo closely, her passion for reading and learning. And there was her musical ability, a talent that had barely scratched the surface. As far as she was concerned, Jo would have that opportunity.

* * *

For Jo, life at Chateau Colbert sharply contrasted with her dull life at home. The uncertainty of a civil war brewing affected her mood until she was back at work.

When Jo went up with Madame's breakfast, the sun shone through the French window. Madame Colbert was already dressed and sitting at the reading table. She looked up and smiled as Jo placed the tray of fresh coffee and warm toast down on the table.

'Good morning, Madame. I trust you slept well?'

'I'm afraid not, *ma chérie*, but I expect it occurs as one gets older.' She folded the newspaper, putting it to one side.

Jo took the small vase of fresh flowers from the tray and arranged them on the table by the window.

'*Merci*. I love the smell of spring flowers. Are these daffodils from the garden?' She inhaled their scent.

'Yes, the gardener cut them this morning, Madame.'

'How are your family?'

'Oh they're grand, thank you, Madame. James will be home soon from the sanatorium.' She continued to set out the breakfast.

'Good, one thing less for you to worry about. Take a moment, my dear. Sit down.' She nibbled on her toast. 'What with the country in the state it's in,' she shook her head.

'What do you think will happen now, Madame?'

Maria picked up the folded newspaper and handed it to Jo. 'Read this, it's important you keep abreast of what is going on out there on the streets.' She moved her half-eaten toast to one side.

Jo opened the newspaper with a picture of Michael Collins on the front page. How handsome he was, she thought, before reading the main issues. Maria picked up her French newspaper, giving Jo time to absorb the news that might affect them all.

'Well. What do you think of the Anglo-Irish treaty, my dear?'

One of the things Jo loved was the way her employer challenged her to think for herself.

'I want peace, like the majority, Madame. Michael Collins seems to want that, too. I agree that twenty-six counties is better than nothing. He says he can negotiate for the other six later on.

Surely that's good, isn't it?'

Maria folded her newspaper and put it aside. 'Peace is priceless, I would agree with that.' She straightened her shoulders. 'But what if the treaty achieved is unfair, Jo, and the country is still divided? That will not bring peace to those who believe that Ireland should be whole.'

'Do you think that possible, Madame?'

'I wish I could see that far ahead, Jo, but you are young; you have an enquiring mind. I always find it best to look carefully at both sides, before making up one's mind.' She stood up and moved away.

Jo followed her into the bedroom. Madame Colbert sat down at her dressing table. Jo began to brush and then plait her employer's long hair to the nape of her neck, then gently curl the remaining strands into a tight bun, encasing it in a silver hairnet.

'Even so, Madame, it's not easy to decide,' Jo continued, while stripping the bed and gathering up the washing.

'Eamonn de Valera still holds out for a united Ireland, and the majority of the working classes are behind him. Is he right, my dear?'

As Jo worked, they continued their discussion until Maria leaned back in her wicker chair and closed her eyes.

'You're tired, Madame. Forgive me, the time has flown. Can I get you anything before I go downstairs? Another cup of coffee perhaps?'

'No, thank you, my dear, but now I would like to forget the outside world for a while. Put that beautiful song, *Macushla*, onto the gramophone and leave an old lady to her dreams.'

Jo selected the record, placed it on, and gently brought down the needle. As the sentimental tones of John McCormack echoed through the house, Jo slipped from the room.

CHAPTER THIRTEEN

A few days later, it was Rosie's day off and it was late when Jo finished upstairs. Downstairs in the kitchen, Molly, the scullery maid, was crying. 'We'll all be shot in our beds.' She was pacing the floor holding her head. 'The Black and Tans are here.'

'Oh, do control yourself, girl,' Miss O'Breen said, continuing to check the stock cupboards as though nothing else mattered.

'Has something happened?' Jo glanced towards Mrs. Quigley, who shook her head and sighed. 'The paper boy has told Molly that fighting has broken out in the city, and that people were being moved to safety.'

Jo walked over to Molly, who was still whimpering. 'The Black and Tans have gone, Molly,' Jo explained, but even so, just the thought of them and the terrible things they had done made Jo shiver. She felt sorry for Molly, who was finding it difficult to cope with the unrest in the city. Jo had read about the siege at the Four Courts, and inner city families being evacuated and taken to safety. 'Your family will be grand, Molly,' Jo reassured, placing her hand on her shoulder.

'Get off, you!' Molly scowled.

In spite of Jo trying to befriend the girl, Molly continued her hostility towards her.

Cook rolled her eyes. 'Now, can you please get some pots washed, Molly?' Mrs. Quigley, who was kneading the dough with her stubby hands, turned to Jo. 'You ought to stay tonight, if what the paper boy says is true.' She rolled out the bread until it looked like a round cake, then made the shape of a cross on the top.

'I can't abandon my family, not now.' Jo frowned. Their house was on the fringe of the city and she hoped they would be all right. She knew how nervous Liam was, and with James due home, she wondered what she should do.

Mrs. Quigley brushed back strands of loose hair, leaving traces of flour on her rosy cheeks and on the tip of her nose. 'Look, dearie. Your mother's at home, isn't she? They'll be fine.'

The butler walked in, and after a few hushed words with the cook, he said, 'In view of the situation, those with families in the city can return home to check on them.'

Molly dropped the large pot she was scrubbing, making a loud clatter, and soapy water splashed out onto the floor. Cook threw up her arms, but Molly paid her no heed and dashed for the door. Jo mopped up the mess, then she looked at Cook.

'I'm sorry, Mrs. Quigley. I'll be back as soon as I can.' She grabbed her coat and scarf, jumped on Annie's bicycle, and rode like the devil towards her home.

* * *

Although it was a mild evening in July, Jo felt a shiver pass through her as she approached the city; there was a smoky smell that she couldn't identify. Then she heard the sound of gunshots, horns hooting, and people shouting. Thinking she was about to ride into trouble, she turned down a side street and found herself caught up with a mass of angry protesters heading for the city centre. She struggled, desperate to push her way through, but it was hopeless. The crowd surged forward. They were mostly working class men in caps, and some women carrying banners. One man carried a placard with the slogan, *Home Rule Bill*. Men were running, some rode bicycles, young men clung to automobiles, shouting and waving their arms. Frightened for her life, she had no choice but to race along with them.

When they reached Carlisle Bridge, a murky mist had settled over the city. Soldiers blocked their path, their uniforms stark and intimidating, enhanced only by the sparkle of the brass buttons on their jackets.

'Stay back, don't come any further,' one shouted to the angry crowd.

Jo felt herself sway and gripped her bicycle for support; there was no reasoning with anyone. She was terrified and annoyed that she had not acted quicker to avoid the situation she now found herself in. The mood of the crowd was explosive; some protesters moved back. Cars and bikes were abandoned. The crowd split, some scurried down side alleys, giving Jo the opportunity to break away.

She pedalled as fast as she could down one side of the Liffey, past McBirney's department store. She heard shouts for her to go back, but she carried on, looking for somewhere to dart out of harm's way. Ahead, another angry crowd blocked the bridge leading to the Four Courts, smoke billowing from its rooftop. She could smell the stink of the smoke seeping into her mouth. Glad of her scarf, she wrapped it around the lower part of her face. Her eyes streaming, it was difficult to see where she was going. She felt terror as shots rang out. Panic seized her. Her heart almost stopped as a Free State soldier ran towards her brandishing a gun.

'Halt or I'll shoot!' he roared. 'This area is unsafe to civilians. Are you trying to get yourself shot?' He was waving a rifle at her. Her bicycle wheel caught in the tram track and, unable to save herself, she fell to the ground. It lay on its side, the back wheel spinning. When she came round, she felt woozy. A *Cumann Na mBan*, was reviving her with a hot drink from a flask. Jo, shaking from shock, thought the world had gone mad as she watched an injured civilian with blood streaming down his face, helped by a soldier towards an ambulance.

'This area is restricted, you shouldn't be here!' the woman said.

'I…I was trying to get home, when I got caught up in the crowd.' Blood began to trickle down her face.

'You have a nasty cut there.'

Jo raised her hand and felt the gash to her head. She winced and looked down at her fingers covered in blood.

'Where do you live?'

'Over Pearse Street way. I never meant to come this far – can I get back?'

'I doubt that. Go down as far as Bolton Street, and back around that way. You'll be all right if you stick to the back lanes. I'll clean you up first.' She opened her First Aid bag. Jo's head throbbed. 'You're lucky you weren't shot,' the woman said, and helped her to her feet.

Anxious to get home, Jo rode away, her legs shaking. The front wheel of the bike wobbled, slowing her down. On the way, she saw a priest carrying a Red Cross flag leading a group of women and children to a safe shelter, and she wondered what she might find when she reached her mother's. She passed a public house; people were shouting and jeering. A drunken man chased after her. She cycled faster, but her legs felt like lead and she prayed they wouldn't give way, not now.

Weary from her ordeal, she arrived home and found her grandmother's house deserted. An eerie silence enveloped the street. Her heart thumping, she hurried down to Aggie Murphy's and banged on her door. Never closed, tonight it was barred and bolted. Aggie looked through the window before letting Jo in.

'God be praised, Jo, you're late. We were getting worried.'

'Oh, Aggie, I…I thought I was going to get shot!' Jo pressed her hand against her chest to catch her breath. Her mother, Liam and James heard the commotion and came in from the scullery. The neighbours had gathered in small groups for protection and reassurance. The house was in darkness apart from the glow in the fire grate, which Aggie had lit to cheer them.

'What's happened, Jo-Jo?' her mother asked.

'Sit her near the fire, she's shivering,' Aggie instructed. 'Why didn't you stay at work when you heard there was trouble in the city? There was a warning in the newspaper telling people to stay indoors.'

Jo, still suffering from shock, was too emotional to speak. When James and Liam placed their arms around her, tears spilled down her face and she wept.

'Get her a drop of that whiskey, Aggie,' Kate said, 'she's done in.'

Jo sipped, spluttered and coughed, screwed up her face and handed the glass back to Aggie.

'Get it down you, girl,' her mother insisted. 'It'll stop yeh from shaking.' Reluctantly, she drank some more before the glow from the fire lit up one side of her head. 'What in God's name happened to you, Jo-Jo?' Kate turned Jo's face round to get a better look.

'Let the girl catch her breath,' Aggie said. And as the whiskey began to take effect, Jo told them all about her harrowing journey across the city.

It was past midnight when they walked back up to the house. 'You won't be going back there now, Jo-Jo, you're better off staying at home,' her mother said, before going upstairs with the boys.

Jo didn't go to bed. She took something to ease her headache then she sat at the table and wrote a letter to her mother. She intended to return to Chateau Colbert, and this time she planned to stay.

CHAPTER FOURTEEN

When Jo arrived at Chateau Colbert, she hung up her coat and pulled on her working cap, hoping to hide the injury to her head before turning round.

'What's happened to you?' Cook wiped her hands on her apron and came over to get a better look.

'You wouldn't believe me if I told you, Mrs. Quigley.'

Miss O'Breen bounced in. 'Ah, you're back, Jo. I trust you found your…What have you done to your head, child?' Blood was beginning to seep through the white dressing.

'It's a long story, Miss O'Breen, have we time?' Jo glanced up at the clock.

'Of course, sit down.' She indicated a chair.

Struggling with her emotions, Jo relived the vivid memory of the previous evening. Miss O'Breen was speechless, and Cook stood at the table, one hand clapped across her mouth. In the other, she held a hot drink, then placed it in front of Jo.

'Madame Colbert will be saddened to hear of this,' the housekeeper said, turning towards Mrs. Quigley. 'I guess there's no word of Molly yet?'

'No, Miss O'Breen. Sure, living in the city, God knows what she found when she got home.' She started making pastry for her meat pies.

Miss O'Breen turned back to Jo. 'Rosie's upstairs. She can help out in here until Molly arrives. You come with me, child.'

Jo followed her up the back stairs to the third floor. The housekeeper's room smelt of lavender. It was homely and inviting with the essentials to make it comfortable. The single iron bedstead was in the centre of the room, covered with a white silk eiderdown; a white nightgown neatly folded on top of the pillow. A carved oak chest rested on the floor at the foot of the bed. Jo guessed it was where Miss O'Breen kept her treasured possessions. A washstand and basin stood in the corner of the room, with a matching blue and white ceramic jug.

'Do sit down.'

Jo sat on the chair next to a single wardrobe, noticing the many silver-framed photographs that lined the mantelpiece.

The housekeeper poured water from the jug into a small basin, opened her First Aid box, and proceeded to remove Jo's dressing, carefully washing the wound with soft cotton wool. She smeared on a small amount of lanolin ointment before covering it with a clean piece of lint.

'Thank you. That feels much better.'

'Good,' she said, handing Jo the ointment. 'Please keep it. Use it every day. It will help it to heal.' She opened a drawer by her bed and took out a small bottle of witch hazel. 'My dear mother swore by it. Apply it morning and night on the bruising.'

It was a long time since anyone had cared for her needs and, thanking her again, Jo rose to leave.

'Sit down a moment, Jo.' The housekeeper sat opposite her in the armchair by the empty grate, her small feet resting on the round footstool in front of her. 'Madame has requested many times that you live in. In view of what has happened, you'd be wise to give it serious thought.'

'I already have, Miss O'Breen. I've brought a bag with a few of my belongings and will collect the rest on my day off.'

'Good! That's settled then.' Smiling, she got to her feet. 'Now if you feel up to it, you can take Madame her morning tray, and inform her of your decision.'

* * *

When Madame Colbert heard Jo's news, her eyes lit up and she clapped her hands like an excited child. 'No more chasing across the city, my dear, you'll be safe here and well cared for.'

'Thank you, Madame, you're most kind.'

The large windows had a panoramic view of the back garden, and as Jo carried out her duties, she could smell the scent of the rose bush that trailed up the wall to the open window. Most of the shrubs were in full bloom, displaying pinks and yellows, and it made her feel good to be alive. Humming to herself, she lifted Lulu's cover.

'Is that you, Jo?' the parrot repeated over and over, dancing up and down on the perch.

Jo, now familiar with Lulu's chirrupy chatter, called back, 'Yes, it's me, Lulu. How are you?'

'How are you?' it mimicked.

Jo found herself talking to the bird as if it were human. 'Come on, out you come while I clean your cage.' She lifted the bird onto her shoulder where it stayed obediently.

'We're going to have to watch our p's and q's,' Madame Colbert said, laughing out loud when Lulu repeated her words.

'What a clever girl you are, Lulu,' Jo said, cleaning the bird's mirror and placing her back inside.

'She'll be asking for extra nuts next.' Maria, still smiling, went over to sit by the window and leant back on her cushions. 'I haven't laughed so much in ages.' Her eyes came alive when she laughed and Jo could well imagine how beautiful she must have been as a young woman. Jo gave the parrot a nut and she settled down while Jo finished her chores.

'Hasn't the paper arrived this morning?'

'I'm afraid not, Madame.'

'Disruptions are inevitable. Maybe you could read to me a while, my dear?'

'I'd be delighted.' Jo welcomed the opportunity, especially as Madame Colbert had such a wide range of books. Since working here, her knowledge of world affairs had increased in all directions.

'I've got a wonderful novel that I'm sure you'll enjoy as much as I.' She gestured towards a small parcel wrapped in brown paper on her writing desk. 'Would you open it, my dear, and bring it to me? Jean-Pierre sent it from Paris. He's such a dear boy!'

Jo removed the wrapping and read the book's title. '*Madame Bovary* by Gus...Gus...' She still struggled with the French language.

'Gustave Flaubert,' Madame Colbert helped her, and Jo loved the natural way it rolled off her tongue. 'According to Pierre, he is considered the father of realism, and has a large

following. The story portrays the tragic life of a woman whose drab everyday existence brutally conflicts with her romantic dreams.' After the brief introduction, Jo could hardly wait to start reading it. Halfway through the third chapter, Madame Colbert fell asleep. Jo, so engaged in the story, carried on to the end of the chapter before placing the bookmark inside.

Descending the stairs, she crossed the hall towards the kitchen, hoping Molly had returned safely. If not, there would be vegetables to wash and potatoes to peel.

'Jo,' Miss O'Breen called from across the hall. 'Has Madame said anything about your sleeping arrangements?'

'No, Miss O'Breen.'

'Come back upstairs, child,' she said, leading the way. When they reached the first floor, Miss O'Breen opened up one of the bedrooms and looked inside. 'This is where you'll sleep. It should be big enough for your needs and close to Madame should she need you for anything,' she said. 'But she rarely ever rings in the night.'

She walked in and drew back the long velvet curtains; sunlight bathed the room. When she turned round, Jo was running her hand over the pink silky eiderdown.

'Is it suitable? If not, there is another bedroom I cou–'

'No, thank you, it's lovely.'

'Very well then, if you're happy. Mrs. Quigley would appreciate your help in the kitchen.' And she left her alone. Jo stood for a moment. It was more than she had expected. She had imagined herself sharing with one of the other maids; a room of her own had never crossed her mind. The bed reminded her of a pretty pink pincushion. On the corners of the bed linen, the words *Chateau Colbert* were embroidered in fine silks of deep blue. Jo wondered if Madame had embroidered them herself at some time.

She looked out onto a green lawn that bordered both sides of the house. Well-established trees and conifers screened the high wall. Jo had loved the garden ever since she had first sat out in it with Madame Colbert. Now she could watch it blossom through her very own window. She could hear the birds singing, and it made her want to sing, too; she felt so happy. Turning away, she walked over and sat on the bed. A smile crept over her face and she bounced up and down a few times on the soft mattress, before making her way downstairs.

'Molly's brother's been to say she won't be in today,' Mrs. Quigley informed her as soon as she walked into the kitchen.

'Is she all right?' Jo asked, changing out of her frilly apron and cap, and putting on a waterproof apron.

'They were moved out during the night,' Cook said, handing Jo a white hat to cover her hair. 'Her brother said they were all grand, though, and that Molly would be back to-morrow.'

Rosie, who never had much to say at the best of times, gave a loud sigh from the scullery where she was scrubbing the pots. Mrs. Quigley rolled her eyes and she placed more vegetables into the sink. 'Can you finish washing and preparing these, Jo? Miss O'Breen is partial to a drop o' leek and asparagus soup.'

'I'm sure it tastes lovely. I've never had asparagus. Is it nice?' Jo asked, scrubbing the leeks clean.

'Well, you can taste it yourself later. Oh, I almost forgot,' she said, rushing towards the stove to gently remove the French bread she baked every two days especially for Madame Colbert. After testing it was cooked, she busied herself with the rest of her bread-making. She threw flour onto a hot griddle, marked her soda bread, then opened the oven door and pushed it inside. 'Foster says there's talk of surrender.'

Jo, who was chopping the vegetables and putting them into a large saucepan, glanced up. 'Is it true then?'

'Is what true?'

'Talk of surrender.'

'Oh. I don't know, Jo.' She filled the kettle. 'But it's time for a cuppa before we start the lunches.'

How can Cook be so sketchy about surrender? Just because she lived in at Chateau Colbert didn't make her immune. Jo placed the saucepan on the hob and sat down. She was desperate to know more. 'Did Foster say where he heard about it?'

Mrs. Quigley poured their tea and sat opposite her. 'I suppose it could be true. Foster usually hears important news like that first hand.' She paused. 'He has a cousin works in The Daíl. But don't get your hopes up. There's many a rumour flying around at the moment.'

CHAPTER FIFTEEN

Jo settled down to life at the Chateau, and the country's troubles became less of a threat to her. She heard nothing more about a truce, but rumours of something simmering beneath the surface left the majority of law-abiding citizens with a feeling of unease.

In August, a letter arrived from Ned. It was just what Jo needed to take her mind off the unrest. Ned was returning from the States. As she read on she was surprised to feel a twinge of jealousy that he had met a woman he clearly admired. Would he bring her with him, and if so, would it alter her close relationship with her brother? In another month she would be eighteen, and with so much to tell him, she could hardly wait for him to get home.

The following morning, Jo was in jubilant mood as she swept in with Madame's tray. Thoughts of seeing Ned again after four years made her want to sing. Her employer was already sitting at the morning table reading the newspaper.

'How are you this morning, Madame?' Jo asked, smiling. She rested the tray of poached eggs and coffee with Madame's favourite croissants on the table. But before she could divulge her exciting news, Madame Colbert frowned.

'You haven't heard, have you my dear?' She lowered the newspaper. 'Michael Collins has been shot dead in Cork.'

Jo felt the colour drain from her face.

'Oh, my dear! Are you all right?'

Jo sat down. She could scarcely take it in – after all he had done. 'He can't be! Is it…is it true, Madame?' Tears of disbelief welled in her eyes.

'I'm afraid it is, my dear. This war makes no sense, no sense at all,' she murmured.

'Why would anyone…' Jo bit down on her bottom lip.

'It's very disturbing. My dear Jo, I should have realised that Michael Collins was a hero to most young girls, and you would be no exception.'

Yes, he was her hero. He was going to bring peace to Ireland. Now she felt foolish that Madame had guessed her infatuation. Rising from her sitting position, she poured coffee and handed it to her employer and sat down again.

'Thank you, dear. Will you be all right?'

'I'm fine, Madame. It's just a shock. But, I suppose anything's possible, the times we're living in.' She traced the rim of the coffee cup with her finger.

'That's true. It is a sad state of affairs and there's sure to be a public outcry for such a man.'

Jo felt as if the bottom had dropped out of her world and, forcing a smile, she carried on with her duties.

* * *

Downstairs, the kitchen was buzzing with the assassination of Michael Collins.

'Well,' Rosie said, 'I'm glad it was him and not de Valera.'

'How can you say that, Rosie? Neither of them deserves to die.' Jo glared at her.

'Killing is wrong. Always will be,' Mrs. Quigley said. 'Now can we get on with the lunches and leave politics out of my kitchen?' She plodded across to where Jo was standing by the sink and thrust a large head of cabbage into her arms. 'This won't wash itself.'

It was noon when Jo went back upstairs with Madame's lunch, consisting of smoked salmon, tea with French toast. She smiled when she heard her talking to Lulu.

'Lulu sounds more human with every day,' Maria said, coming to sit at the table. Jo nodded her agreement but Michael Collin's death still baffled her.

'Who do you suppose organised the ambush, Madame?' she asked, while they ate their lunch.

'I think that is going to be pretty hard to prove.' Maria Colbert sighed 'As things stand, it could have been a number of people, unfortunately there are many who would have wanted him dead, unhappy about the treaty settlement. Try not to dwell on it, my dear, as it will only unsettle you.'

It had unsettled her, and she was aware that if a military figure like Michael Collins could be shot down, there would be revenge attacks and the war would rage on. But Madame was right; she mustn't let it interfere with her duties.

'I'm sorry. I'll clear away the dishes, and if you wish, I'll read you some more of *Madame Bovary*.'

'Oh! That would be lovely, my dear, lovely. But leave the dishes, Rosie can see to them.' She tugged on the bell cord. 'Come! Let us sit over here.' And when she was settled in her armchair, Jo sat opposite her and had just started reading when Rosie knocked and entered.

'Please thank Mrs. Quigley for lunch,' Madame Colbert said. Rosie didn't reply. She placed the empty dishes noisily onto the tray and fixed Jo with a disapproving stare before leaving.

Madame Colbert sighed. 'That girl is sullen. I must have words with Miss O'Breen.'

'I think the news of Michael Collin's death has unsettled us all, Madame,' Jo said in Rosie's defence. 'Shall I read on?'

'No. I'd like you to tell me what it was that first drew you to Michael Collins?'

The question was so unexpected that she felt a flush to her face. Turning away, she placed the book on the table next to her.

'Well. The first time I saw him, he was standing on a platform in the city, giving a speech on behalf of his party. My friend, Annie, and I were on our way to the Theatre Royal. The power in his voice penetrated the crowds, and we felt forced to stop, pushing our way through to the front. He had great presence, and I was determined to shake his hand. Oh, Madame, he was so handsome. I thought I'd die there and then, and told Annie I'd never wash my hand again.' She lowered her eyes. 'From then onwards I believed in his policies.'

'And now?'

'I don't know, Madame. Ireland has lost a great man. I don't believe the perpetrators have any idea what they've done.'

Her employer smiled. 'Ireland will always have great men, Jo. Did I ever tell you about my first love, Jo dear?'

'No, Madame. Do you mean your late husband, Louis?'

'Oh no! Louis wasn't my first love.' Her eyes lit up mischievously. 'His name was Andrea. I was just fifteen, he sixteen. We were only children, never together un-chaperoned you know. But I loved him, and thought my young heart would break when his family moved from Paris to Toulouse. We promised to write, pledged undying love for one another. He kissed my hand and my mother wondered why I refused to wash for dinner.' She looked across at Jo who was listening intently to the love story. 'We wrote letters, but young love doesn't last my dear, but it leaves a lifelong impression.'

'Oh! How sad, Madame Colbert.'

'It happens to most of us; few rarely, if ever, marry their first love, and perhaps Michael Collins was yours.'

Later, when Jo came downstairs, Rosie and Molly snubbed her. And when Jo looked towards Mrs. Quigley for an explanation, she shook her head and rolled her eyes towards heaven.

* * *

The following day was Jo's day off. Tired of Rosie and Molly's vendetta, she was pleased to get away from their snide whispering. The day was fine and she was looking forward to visiting her sister. She picked up a newspaper which she read on the tram. The death of Michael Collins filled the pages and it saddened her. When she arrived, Cissy, prone to bad moods, welcomed her with a smile. Her dark hair, usually scraped up, bounced around on her shoulders. 'Grand you could come, Jo. Come on in.'

'Have you seen today's paper?' She placed it on the table.

'No. I don't bother with one every day. Sure it's all doom and gloom. I trust de Valera will get things sorted.'

Jo didn't agree. The civil war still raged. But today wasn't a day to talk politics. Cissy took her coat. 'How do you like married life?' Jo said, sitting at the table. Smiling, Cissy placed tea on the table, alongside homemade sponge cake.

'Larry's working overtime at the bakery. We need the extra money now I'm in the family way.'

'Oh, Cissy, that's wonderful! I knew there was something different about you. I'm delighted,' Jo beamed. 'I'll be an aunty.'

'Well, to tell the truth,' Cissy began, 'I'd hoped it'd be a while before we started a family.' Then her eyes softened. 'Larry's thrilled; thinks he's having a son – picking names already,' she laughed. And it did Jo a power of good to see Cissy so happy.

'Does Kate know?'

At the mention of Kate, Cissy's expression changed. 'No! And I don't want her to. You've got to promise me you won't tell her, Jo! *Promise!*

'Okay! But why? Surely it would bridge the gap between you?'

'Don't mention her again. She's not part of my life any more.'

Sorry now to have uttered her mother's name, Jo quickly changed the subject. 'I've had a letter from Ned. He's coming home.' Opening her bag she passed the letter to her.

Cissy scanned it. 'I hope he knows what he's doing!'

Having spent a couple of hours with her sister, Jo called on Kate. She wasn't looking forward to it, but she needed to pick up the rest of her belongings.

Kate gave her a hard time about leaving home to live in, telling her that she was forgetting her responsibilities. Jo didn't reply as she didn't want to leave on a sour note. But Kate tried her patience, following Jo around the house as she packed more of her stuff. And if it hadn't been that she was longing to see the boys, she'd have left sooner.

Jo sat at the table sipping her tea, while her mother continued to blame her for everything. At times her eyes bore into Jo's and it felt like she knew Jo was keeping a secret from her.

CHAPTER SIXTEEN

A few days later, Miss O'Breen informed the staff that Madame Colbert's grandson, Jean Pierre, would be arriving within the week. At the same time she was checking the food cupboards.

'Let me know if there's anything else you need, Mrs. Quigley. I'll order extra provisions to include Jean-Pierre's extravagant tastes. Rosie's preparing the bedrooms. And, Jo, could you accompany me on an inspection of the linen cupboards?'

The next few days were extra busy for everyone. The garden was made even more attractive, windows sparkled, mirrors shone and brass doorknobs and knockers polished until you could see your face. To Jo, the air of expectation was a bit like preparing for Christmas, only on a grand scale.

That afternoon, Jo found Madame in the garden chatting to James the gardener; he was giving her a grand tour, pointing out the new shrubs and trees recently planted. She was taking a great interest in how he had rearranged the flowerbeds. At this time of year the garden had lots of colour and as Jo walked towards them, she breathed in the scent of the roses and the strong honey fragrance of the buddleia. James had a knack of providing colour each month throughout the year.

'Thank you, James. Keep up the splendid work,' Madame said, as Jo arrived at her side. The gardener raised his cap before walking across a stretch of lush green lawn and disappearing into the spinney at the far end of the garden.

'I'd like to spend a while in the garden, my dear. Will you join me? It's such a lovely afternoon.'

'Yes, it is, Madame.' And they walked with companionable ease towards the summerhouse where Maria often sat for afternoon tea during the summer months.

'Won't you join me in a glass of lemonade, Jo?'

'Thank you, Madame.' Jo lifted the jug and poured their drinks. From where they sat, she could hear the humming of bees collecting nectar.

'When is Jean-Pierre due to arrive in Dublin, Madame?'

'According to his letter, he should arrive at the weekend. I'm so looking forward to seeing him, the dear boy.' Her face glowing with anticipation, she said, 'It will be lovely to have him close again; he will have so many amusing stories to tell.'

'Will he be staying long?'

'He's on a month's leave, my dear. He's a tutor at the Lycee Condorcet College in Paris.' She sighed. 'A month is never long enough, especially when he brings his society friends with him. I can never get him to myself. But I mustn't grumble, my dear.' Smiling, she turned towards Jo. 'It would be lovely if you would dine with us one evening, Jo. Just the three of us.'

Taken aback by the unexpectedness of the invitation, Jo hesitated, then she accepted graciously. Although she had had lunch occasionally with Madame, this was completely unexpected. How would this go down with the rest of the staff? It was bound to cause a stir. She felt confused. She was fond of Madame Colbert, felt privileged to be in her service, but what this was leading to concerned her. She stood up. 'Perhaps you'd like some tea, Madame. I'll…'

'Don't trouble yourself, *chèrie*.' She placed her hand on Jo's arm. 'I've arranged with Mrs. Quigley to have tea sent out about now.'

It was Molly who carried the tea tray with homemade scones to the summerhouse, giving Jo a disapproving glare. Why was Madame doing this? Couldn't she see the impossible situation she was putting her in?

* * *

On the day of Jean-Pierre's arrival, the kitchen staff started earlier than usual as there was so much to do. The weather was humid.

Even with the large windows pulled down, it did nothing to alleviate the heat generated by the range. Cook's face was rosier than ever as she frantically rushed about sliding batches of bread into the oven. Jo was measuring flour into a bowl for the next lot. Molly was mopping the floor, deliberately wetting Jo's shoes and ankles.

'Eh up, Molly. What did you do that for?'

'Look here! I've enough on me plate without you two starting.' Mrs. Quigley, who was washing the fruit under running water, turned round to glare at Molly. 'You're about as much use as a wet rag today. Had another fall out with that young feller of yours, have yeh?' Cook shook her head despairingly, while Molly scoured the pots in slow motion. When they were eventually washed, wiped and hanging on their hooks, Mrs. Quigley said, 'Thanks b' to God that lot's cleared. I don't know what's got into you, Molly, today of all days.'

Miss O'Breen rushed in, her face flushed. 'When Rosie's finished putting the washing through the mangle, she'll be in to help. And if you like I can arrange for temporary kitchen help, Mrs. Quigley.' But Cook insisted they would only get under her feet.

'As you wish, but let me know immediately if you change your mind.' Then addressing Jo she said, 'As soon as Rosie appears you'd better see to Madame.'

'Until then, where can I be of most help?' Jo asked. Cook looked up, pushing a strand of her hair under her bonnet.

'Can you make a start on the punch? I've put everything out ready.'

The cooked food was covered with a muslin cloth on one table and on another the meat and vegetables to be prepared. Jo had never seen so much food in her life, and as she peeled the fruit for the punch she was reminded of a time when she had queued outside Boland's Bakery for the previous day's bread to feed the family.

Mrs. Quigley had boned and was stuffing the fowl ready for cooking, and the smell of newly-baked bread wafted through the kitchen. Molly was peeling the potatoes, a furious expression on her face.

'Me fella's thrown me over for someone else,' she blurted.

Jo made no comment. Whatever she said would be the wrong thing.

'You're better off without him,' Mrs. Quigley said. 'Most of them aren't worth the tears wasted on them.' Her remark sent Molly rushing out in tears. Cook threw up her arms, saying if the girl didn't buck up her ideas she would have to have words with Miss O'Breen about a replacement.

Later, her head bowed and red-eyed, Molly returned. Cook pointed to the silver on the kitchen table to be cleaned.

* * *

Before the guests arrived, Jo was upstairs arranging Madame's hair. From the first time Jo styled her hair, no-one else had the privilege. She enjoyed piling the soft strands into large looped curls for special occasions, pinning each one in place on top of her head. The silver clasp Jo fastened at the back of her head contrasted with her hair. She wore little jewellery, apart from a string of pearls around her neck that complimented her silk dress – a peacock blue, with matching comfortable court shoes. Jo had seen photographs of her as a young woman and found her beauty still astonishing.

'Bon ton. What do you think, my dear?' She was inspecting her hair in the three-way mirror. 'Will I do?'

'You look grand, really grand, Madame.'

'It's all down to you, *ma petite*. I wouldn't want Jean-Pierre to think I'd let things slide.'

When Foster arrived back from the city docks with Jean-Pierre and his guests, the staff lined up to greet them. Jean Pierre fingered his neat moustache, then glanced along the row of staff.

Introducing his friends simply by name, he said, 'This is Madeleine and Ricardo DuPont, my good friends, and Maurice Bonnet, composer and musician.'

'You are most welcome,' Miss O'Breen said.

Jo felt a flush to her face as he bent his tall, slender form to shake her hand and she curtsied accordingly.

Miss O'Breen asked Rosie to show the guests upstairs, knowing that they would be tired after their journey. 'There are refreshments in your rooms,' she said.

A short time later, Foster instructed Jo to take up the finest claret that Madame Colbert had said was Jean-Pierre's favourite.

As she entered the room, it was quiet and she guessed Madame had left Lulu in the boudoir. She walked across the room and put the drinks tray down by the French window. Jean-Pierre stood with his arm around his grandmother, tenderly glancing down at her. She held him at arm's length, gripping both his hands.

'Let me look at you, *mon chérie*' she said, smiling. 'A little more weight perhaps.' Jean Pierre kissed the back of her hand and they walked across to where Jo was pouring the claret.

'I'll come back later, Madame.' She smiled, placing her hands together in front of her. 'Before I go, is there anything else?'

'No thank you, my dear. Can you leave Lulu's cover on for a while longer, otherwise she'll be joining in our conversation?'

'Fair enough, Madame.' And as Jo turned to go, she felt Jean-Pierre's dark eyes follow her.

'Before you go, Jo dear, let me introduce you two properly. Jean-Pierre, this is Jo, the young lady I spoke of in my letters! Jo, this is my only grandson, Jean Pierre.'

He put down his glass and shook her hand warmly, holding onto it longer than was necessary. 'Jo, it's a pleasure to meet you at last.' His voice was soft and lyrical and Jo was surprised at the way it made her feel.

'You too, sir,' she curtsied.

'Please, call me Jean-Pierre, my grandmama tells me you are *en famille*.'

She lowered her head, and for the third time that morning she felt a glow to her face. The revelation that she was considered to be one of the family shook her. She could think of nothing to say except, 'I'll leave you now. You must have lots to talk about.'

'*Merci*, my dear.'

And as Jo retreated, Jean-Pierre reached the door first and held it open. '*Au revoir, Jo.*'

'*Au revoir, Monsieur,*' she said, looking up into his soft dark eyes.

Outside on the landing, she took a deep breath. It was indeed an extraordinary day.

Downstairs, Foster was unloading the remaining luggage from the carriage and Jo noticed the colourful hotel stickers on the guests' suitcases. Mrs. Quigley was sorting through an array of French produce and crates of the finest wines.

'There's no fear of us running short for the next month,' she said. 'Now where have I put my French recipes?' She went to the drawer and pulled out an assortment.

By the end of the day, Jo, although exhausted, couldn't sleep. She went over the French phrases that Madame Colbert had taught her in case she might need them. Then she wrote a letter to Annie, telling her all about Jean-Pierre.

CHAPTER SEVENTEEN

When Jo went up to Madame the following morning, her eyes were drawn to the picture hanging on the wall in the room.

'You like it?'

'It's stunning, Madame. Such vibrant colours!'

'Jean-Pierre knows my tastes so well.'

And as Jo continued to admire the painting of a young couple on the dance floor, she attempted to read the title. '*La Danse à la Ville* by Pierre Auguste Renoir.'

'Well done, my dear. Your French is improving.' Smiling, she went behind the screen to dress and Jo carried on with her duties, scooping up the linen for washing and placing it in the basket.

Later that morning, Madame Colbert handed her a piece of music. 'Will you play for me, my dear? It will be good practice.'

'"*April Showers*",' Jo said. 'Is this one of the latest?'

There was a light tap on the door and Jean-Pierre entered. '*Bonjour, Grandmère.*'

'*Bonjour*, my dear boy. I trust you are well rested.'

'Yes, indeed I am.' He kissed both her cheeks. 'And you, *Grandmère?*'

'With you here, I slept soundly, dear boy!'

'Maurice and I are going to the city. Is there anything you require?'

'I have all I need, *chérie*.' Then a frown creased her brow. 'You will take care, Jean-Pierre. The country is at war and atrocities are still…'

'*Grandmere!*' He took her hands in his. 'If my being here is going to cause you concern–' He smiled warmly. 'I'll be careful.'

He kissed her hand and moved away.

'Of course! Don't be late, *chérie*. We're dining at home tonight.'

'I look forward to it.' He glanced across at Jo standing by the piano, her eyes fixed on the music in her hand. '*Au revoir*, Jo.'

She glanced up. '*Au revoir, Monsieur*.' As he closed the door behind him, she glimpsed him straighten his cravat.

'Now where were we, my dear?'

After a blissful hour in the company of her employer and the amusing tricks of Lulu, it was lunch time. She was about to leave when Madame said, 'Jo, you've heard Jean-Pierre mention Monsieur Bonnet. He can be,' she paused, 'a little playful, but harmless.' She smiled. 'I have spoken to him about your budding talent, my dear, and he is looking forward to hearing you play. Would you be happy to play for him this afternoon?'

'Yes, of course, Madame. Thank you.' Although the prospect unnerved her, she couldn't possibly miss such an opportunity. She trusted Madame Colbert, knew whatever she suggested was for her advancement, and felt a depth of gratitude towards her.

As she picked up the basket of linen to take downstairs, Madame Colbert said, 'Don't forget to remind Cook that they will have to manage without you this afternoon.'

Downstairs, she placed the washing in the tub at the side of the kitchen, and for the next hour her head was full with musical notes. To be asked to play in front of a talented composer was daunting, and she felt indeed fortunate. This was a huge step forward and nothing was going to stand in her way now, not even the resentment of the maids.

* * *

Maurice Bonnet removed his hat as he entered the room. His action revealed a bald head, and Jo guessed he was in his middle forties. He had broad shoulders and his long jacket gave him a squat appearance, but his outfit was faultless. And he had a habit of fingering his short ginger beard.

Madame Colbert greeted him. '*Bonjour, Maurice, comment allez-vous?*'

'*Bonjour, Madame, très bien, merci.*'

He turned towards Jo and held out his hand. 'You must be Mademoiselle Kingsley.' His eyes bored into her.

She stood up with a nervous smile. 'I'm pleased to meet you, Monsieur Bonnet.'

Bonnet lifted the back of his jacket and sat down. He gestured with a circular movement of his wrist and Jo commenced playing. He closed his eyes. His face, at first relaxed, gradually creased as though in pain. Jo stopped playing, swallowing nervously, but he motioned for her to continue to the end. When she had finished, he sat in silence, then he asked her to play it again. His eyes still closed, he stroked his beard.

At the end of the piece she waited for his comments, but he remained silent. It made her nervous. A man like Bonnet, what was he thinking? Her offering made her feel inferior.

She glanced towards Madame as her confidence ebbed. But her employer's smile encouraged her to stay calm. Rosie knocked and entered carrying a tray of coffee and biscuits, breaking the silence. Before she left, the girl glared across at Jo. But Jo was concentrating too intently on the French man to pay her much heed.

Then, as though coming out of a trance, Bonnet slipped his hand inside his coat pocket. He removed a notebook and pen and began to make notes, and after a few moments he got to his feet and moved towards her. He tore a couple of pages from his book and handed them to her. 'These will help you with your technique. Study them carefully and often. You've got potential, young lady, but real success is achieved through practice,' he paused. 'You must practise, practise and practise.' He made a fist of his hand and tapped three times on the top of the piano.

'Yes, thank you, Monsieur Bonnet!'

He went on to tell her how he started his career in a music hall, working long hours for the love of his art, before becoming a successful composer. Then, without warning, he perched himself down next to her on the piano stool. She could feel his hot breath on the side of her neck. Smiling, he leaned across her, spreading his fingers over the keys.

Self-conscious, she stood up. Madame Colbert patted the sofa next to her and Jo joined her. And for the next hour Maurice enthralled the ladies with his repertoire. He played French songs about love, '*Parlez-moi d'amour*' which Jo hadn't heard before, and then just for her he sang it in English, making her blush. Then he played '*Toot, Toot, Tootsie, Good-bye*' and 'Basin Street Blue', along with a selection of jazz and razzmatazz, making Jo giggle and Madame laugh out loud. Jo was amazed at how versatile he was and thanked him for giving up his time.

He kissed her hand. 'I wish you good luck with your music, Mademoiselle Jo.'

'*Merci, Monsieur!*'

He turned to Madame Colbert. '*À tout à l'heure, Madame.*'

'Until later, Maurice.'

When they were alone, Maria Colbert glanced at Jo, her face flushed. 'I must congratulate you, *chérie*. You did well. I am proud of you.'

'Thank you, Madame. I was so nervous.'

'Well, it didn't show, my dear. Practise, practise, and practise,' she said in mock tones of Maurice Bonnet, and they both laughed.

At first, Jo had felt out of her depth, but the experience had delighted her, so much so that she almost forgot her duties.

'Oh, do forgive me, Madame. I'll fetch you some fresh coffee?'

'No, my dear,' she patted Jo's arm. 'Ring for Molly. You have more important things to concentrate on now.'

* * *

The following morning when Jo went down to the kitchen, both Rosie and Molly gave her the cold shoulder. She expected as much, but it still hurt. 'What should I do, Mrs. Quigley?' Jo asked, when they were alone.

'Take no notice.'

'How can I? I've tried talking to them, but they won't listen.'

'Jo, you know I don't have time for tittle-tattle.' She dried her hands on a tea cloth. 'But now you've asked. Two years ago, when

Madame's maid of twenty years took sick and had to leave, Rosie thought she was next in line,' she chuckled. 'Well, you've seen her; she hasn't the personality or the patience, for a start.'

'That explains it then, but what's wrong with Molly?'

'Take no notice o' that one. She and Rosie are thick as thieves at the moment. It won't last. Anyway, a bit of extra work won't kill either of them. Now, you'll have to excuse me pet, sure I'm rushed off me feet.'

Jo picked up the tray, and as she passed along the hall towards the stairs, she bumped into Molly. 'Getting tick with them upstairs, aren't yeh?' Molly smirked.

'Molly Connor! I'm only doing my job.'

'Who'd you think you're coddin'?' Her eyes narrowed. 'Next, you'll be having her grandson's babby. That's what usually happens, and he won't marry yeh, yeh'll see.' Her voice rose in pitch.

Jo glared at her, feeling her hands shake beneath the tray. 'Oh and your sort would know about that kind of thing, wouldn't you?'

Miss O'Breen, hearing the commotion, appeared before them. 'Are you forgetting that we have guests?' Her eyes blazed furiously. 'Jo, take Madame's tray up. I'll speak to you later. And you! Miss Connor, get in my office at once.' And she marched Molly along the corridor.

No matter how she tried to forget Molly's outburst, the cruel words had upset her deeply, making it difficult for her to concentrate. When tears welled in her eyes, Madame Colbert became concerned, asking if she was feeling unwell. Jo longed to discuss her situation with her, but fear of being the cause of Molly possibly losing her job would play on her conscience.

'It's just a headache, I'll be grand,' she said.

Later on, Jo went to the drawing room where Miss O'Breen waited. She related her side of the story. 'I was stunned, Miss O'Breen, I've done nothing wrong, and nothing to be ashamed of.' A worried expression crossed her face.

'Molly is given to exaggeration and jealousy, and I expected you to rise above it, Jo. You must learn to ignore her.'

'But...Miss O'Breen. The things she said! Why does she hate me so much?'

'Look, Jo.' The housekeeper's eyes softened. 'It's obvious that Madame is fond of you, she told me so herself.' She paused. 'You may not be aware of it, child, but in the two years you've been here, you've blossomed into a beautiful young woman, and you may not also be aware that jealousy is usually prevalent amongst the maids, especially when one is favoured.'

'*Favoured*. But...'

'You've nothing to worry about. Both Rosie and Molly have been warned about their behaviour. If you encounter any more unpleasantness, come to me at once. Put it out of your mind. Now, if you'll excuse me, we've both got work to do.'

Her chat with the housekeeper hadn't helped. There were things Jo wanted to discuss with her. She hated to think she was the cause of the maid's jealousy, and she must seem like teacher's pet to Molly. But what was she supposed to do?

For the rest of the day she avoided Molly. She knew the girl was a little naive, now she had discovered that she had a vindictive streak as well.

CHAPTER EIGHTEEN

Jo was preparing Madame's breakfast tray when Foster walked in. 'Good morning, Miss Kingsley. Could you inform Madame that the car will be outside in one hour?'

'Yes, thank you, Foster.' She hadn't been aware that Madame Colbert was going out. It would mean more work in the kitchen and confrontation with Molly. But when Jo arrived upstairs, Madame Colbert was already dressed.

'I hope I haven't delayed you, Madame?' Jo placed the tray down, glancing towards the ornate clock.

'No. Not in the least, my dear. I wanted to surprise you. We're going to the city today. Life does go on, war or no war. Jean-Pierre has made me see that.'

Jo's eyes widened. 'You want *me* to accompany you?' She hadn't been shopping in the city for ages.

'Well, of course, my dear. There's no-one else I'd rather take.'

Excitement bubbling, Jo delivered Foster's message.

'Wonderful,' Maria said, clipping on her earrings. 'I want to buy some new gowns, Jo. Having you around has made me feel alive again.'

'Thank you, Madame.' If doing her job made her employer happy, then it pleased her, too. She sighed. It was bound to cause another rift below stairs. But a car ride to the city, how could she refuse?

'You mean more to me than just a paid servant, Jo. You have talent, and I'd like to nurture that by pointing you in the right direction, if you'll let me.'

What could she say to this woman who had just offered her the world? 'You've given me so much already, Madame.'

'Oh, I know all this must seem rather strange, *ma chérie*. Do forgive me. I'm an old lady with no-one here to spoil. It would make me happy if you would allow me to treat you from time to time.' She raised her eyebrows. 'Now, off you go, dear, and get ready.' She glanced at her watch. 'You have half an hour.'

Excited, Jo hurried to her room. With little time to decide what to wear, she got dressed. Wearing a pink floral dress, white cardigan and matching accessories, she walked back towards Madame's room. Rosie passed her on the landing.

'Oooh,' she grinned. 'Miss La-di-dah! We are moving up in the world.'

Jo paused; each day she was finding it harder to rise above it, as Miss O'Breen had advised. But right now, she didn't have much choice.

* * *

Madame Colbert was slipping on her blue lightweight jacket when Jo walked in.

'Are we ready, my dear?'

Smiling, Jo picked up the tray.

'Leave that for Rosie or Molly and we can leave for the city straight away.'

When they went out front, Foster was waiting. It was amazing weather for early September, and he rolled back the top before helping them into the car. As they set off, Jo glimpsed Molly and Rosie peering through the drawing room curtains. But she refused to let them dampen her spirits, not today.

Soon they were in the midst of familiar sounds, smells and sights, with evidence that prosperity was slowly returning to the city. With few cars as yet on the streets, people waved and gentlemen raised their hats in the direction of Madame Colbert's chauffeur driven-limousine; more so today with Jo by her side. Maria Colbert smiled across at her young companion, the sun catching her hair turning it a golden blonde.

Foster dropped them outside Brett's clothing shop in Talbot

Street, and Pim Bros. in South Gt. George's Street. Jo fingered the exquisite silk garments, the likes of which she had never seen before.

'You must choose something, Jo,' Madame Colbert said, when she saw her glance at the price tags. 'Do not worry about the cost, my dear. It will be my treat.' Maria passed a yellow satin dress to the assistant, her arm already laden with colourful evening gowns. 'Isn't this wonderful?' she said, excitement showing in her eyes. Then she wandered off to another section of the store, leaving Jo awestruck. This had to be a dream, but if it was she didn't want to wake up.

The assistant slipped a cream blouse from the rail, the lace so delicate Jo was frightened to finger it. 'This would suit you very well.' She held the blouse close to Jo's face. 'If you come this way, Miss, I can show you a lemon yellow skirt that will go with this.'

Jo couldn't speak. Following her, she swallowed hard. The skirt was made of sheer silk and had a white underskirt that swished against her legs when she tried it on.

'Madame would like you to choose two more outfits, Miss,' the assistant said. Clothes Jo had only seen on models in magazines now belonged to her. Doors were opened and closed behind them as they left the store with their many packages.

Outside, Foster loaded the boxes and packages onto the back seat of the car, while they took a break from their shopping spree at one of the restaurants in Sycamore Alley, relaxing and chatting over their coffee.

Later, when the two excited women settled into the car for the return trip home, Foster raised his eyebrows and smiled. It wasn't his job to make comments, but he looked pleased to see his elderly employer embracing life again. Her grey eyes sparkled as he placed the rug across her knees.

'I don't know when I've enjoyed myself more, Foster,' she said. 'I feel ten years younger.'

'I'm glad you found the experience a pleasant one, Madame.'

'How about you, my dear?'

'Oh yes, thank you, Madame. It was amazing.' She couldn't

help herself peering over her shoulder at the boxes piled high on the back seat. 'I can't wait to try them on again later.'

'Of course,' Maria laughed. 'Me, too!'

Back in her room, Jo twirled in front of her wardrobe mirror. This was sheer indulgence, she told herself, but she liked the feel of pure silk and satin against her skin. It was the kind of thing most girls dreamt about, but this was real. Her life was changing fast. She had come from nowhere special – and now this. She flopped down onto the bed, wondering where this turn of events would take her.

* * *

When Jo went upstairs, she observed Madeleine, her dark hair cut low on her brow. Ricardo was escorting her towards Madame Colbert's quarters, his arm around her slim waist, his left hand tugging at his waistcoat riding up over his bulging abdomen. Jean-Pierre walked behind with Maurice Bonnet, wearing a white dinner jacket, his dark hair falling over his forehead. He wished Jo a good evening.

Madame had promised her that she would dine with them before Jean-Pierre returned to Paris, and she wondered how she might fit in with their elegant grandeur and society chit chat. She wished she could have her hair cut in a modern style like Madeleine. As it was, she would have to pile it on top of her head and make it as pretty as she could with some artificial flowers. But she didn't have long to wonder, for the following evening Madame Colbert invited her to dine with her and her guests in the dining room downstairs. She accepted gracefully, recalling when she'd stood in the same room waiting to be interviewed. So much had changed since that day and at such a rate she could hardly keep pace. But she was also aware of how it would appear to the other maids. What was she to do; throw it all away? She had grown fond of her employer, and her life at Chateau Colbert was beyond anything she'd ever dreamed of. Pushing negative thoughts from her mind, she got ready.

That evening, Jo hesitated before slipping into the dining

room; the light was on over the well polished table and six places had been set. Madame Colbert moved toward her. 'Come in, my dear. You look lovely.' And she drew her into their circle, simply introducing Jo as a devoted companion. Jean-Pierre greeted her warmly, as did the DuPonts. She was wearing a black and white full-skirted dress with a boat-shaped neckline, showing off the tops of her slender shoulders. Maurice Bonnet's eyes bored into her, and made her feel uneasy.

She lowered her gaze. Then he placed his hands on her bare shoulders and kissed both her cheeks. 'You are lovely, *Mademoiselle* Jo.'

She smiled politely, feeling a flush to her face. Jean-Pierre switched on the wireless and the quiet melody that played in the background suited the mood and relaxed her. The butler poured the guests an aperitif as they chatted. Jo sipped hers, unsure if she liked the taste. When Madame took her place at the head of the oval table, Jo found herself seated next to Madeleine and opposite Bonnet. Jean-Pierre sat at the far end and, when they were all seated, the delicious smells of French cooking wafted up the hall. A few moments later Rosie and Molly carried in the food. Both of them were smirking at Jo behind the guests' backs and Jo wondered how they dare risk such childish behaviour. The butler took charge of the wine.

'How are you getting along with your music, Jo?' Bonnet asked, as the maids left the room. 'Are you practising?' He passed her the meat.

'Oh, yes, I am thank you, *Monsieur.*' She helped herself to the lamb and passed the dish to Madeleine. She was watching intently to see what the others did with all the implements on the table. 'And how are you enjoying your stay in Ireland, *Monsieur* Bonnet,' she asked.

'It's a charming city.' He helped himself to the asparagus tips.

'And you, Jean-Pierre?' She turned her head to glance towards him. 'Apart from the ongoing war, that is.' She smiled.

'I'm enjoying every minute, Jo. Disputes can be tiresome the longer they go on, but things will calm down eventually. I'm sure of it.' He was helping himself to the breast of chicken and Waldorf salad with mayonnaise.

Madeleine and Ricardo, recently married, only had eyes for each other, while Maurice spent the remainder of the meal discussing the realms of music with Jo, as Jean-Pierre paid a great deal of attention to his grandmother. When the meal was over, the guests – relaxed and smiling – retired across the hall to the salon as Rosie and Molly came in to clear the table.

Molly discreetly inched close to Jo. 'Underneath that posh frock you're still a paid servant,' she whispered.

Trying not to show her discomfort, Jo swallowed hard. Miss O'Breen's advice was not going to be easy and she worried how long she would be able to hold her tongue.

* * *

Later, Maurice Bonnet entertained them with songs. They all laughed at his amusing verse, and Jo blushed shyly at the cheeky ones. Jean-Pierre placed a record on the gramophone and Madeleine and Ricardo danced to the fast tempo of the Charleston. Jean-Pierre said it was all the rage in Europe, and Jo watched fascinated. After that it was a romantic waltz by Strauss and she was surprised to find Jean-Pierre at her side; he bowed with one arm behind his back. '*Voulez-vous danser?*'

Bonnet was chatting to Madame and the DuPonts were already smooching to the music. Jo hesitated. She had never danced with a man before. What if she made a fool of herself? Madame Colbert's warm smile encouraged her, and she stepped forward. And when Jean-Pierre swept her round the room, his arm holding her firmly, Jo felt the first flush of romance.

Later, Jo was sitting on the *chaise-longue* when Foster returned with more chilled wine. He refilled their glasses, extending the same courtesy to Jo as to the other guests, and left. Bonnet quickly joined her. He unbuttoned his jacket, crossed his legs and lit a cigar.

'Tell me a bit about yourself, *ma chérie*! Apart from your musical talent, I know nothing about you.'

Jo felt her heart pound. What did he want to know? Her background was the last thing she wanted to discuss, but it would be rude of her not to answer.

'Have you ever been abroad, Jo?' He inched closer, whispering endearments in her ear, his eyes moving down across her shoulders.

'Well, no. I haven't.' She felt his hot whisky breath on her neck and inched away. Madame Colbert's eyes were closed as she listened to another waltz by Strauss, and Jean-Pierre was engaged in conversation with Ricardo and Madeleine.

'Are you free tomorrow evening?' Bonnet placed his arm around her shoulder. She shifted in her seat, then stood up.

'I'm afraid I'm busy, Monsieur Bonnet.'

Jean-Pierre walked towards them. '*Excusez-moi*, Maurice,' he said, smiling at Jo.

'Ah, Jean-Pierre.' Maurice clapped his back as though only seeing him for the first time that evening. Then he turned towards Jo. 'Pardon me one moment, *Mademoiselle*.'

And as Maurice Bonnet followed Jean-Pierre outside onto the open veranda, Jo sighed and glanced outside to where the two men were taking in the fresh air and smoking cigars.

When the record stopped, Madame Colbert stood up and Jo went towards her. 'Jo, my dear, would you be so kind as to help me to my bed, I'm afraid the wine has gone to my head.'

'Certainly, Madame.' Jo took her elbow and they walked towards the door.

Madame thanked her guests and wished them goodnight in French, and when they were out of earshot, she said, 'You're looking a bit bewildered, my dear. Are you all right?'

'Yes, thank you, Madame. I hope I didn't offend Monsieur Bonnet. He was well…I told him I was busy tomorrow evening.'

'Excellent, my dear.' She smiled. 'His pride will be dented but you mustn't let men intimidate you.' She patted Jo's hand. 'I asked Jean-Pierre to bring him along for the sake of your music, not for his obnoxious habits.' And they both laughed.

The evening appeared to have tired her mistress. Jo made her comfortable then, before leaving, she said, 'Thank you for a wonderful evening, Madame Colbert.'

As she walked towards her room, Jean-Pierre was coming upstairs. 'I hope Maurice didn't upset you. He can be a little amorous. I trust it didn't spoil your evening?'

'Oh no. I had a lovely time, thank you. Goodnight, Jean-Pierre.'

'Jo, before you go.' He fingered his moustache. 'Would you dine with me tomorrow? I'll clear it with Grandmama.'

'Oh, I…' She frowned. It was so unexpected she didn't reply, wondering if she'd heard him correctly.

'Forgive me, I should not have asked,' he said. 'I thought it would be an opportunity to get to know the young lady who is caring for my grandmother.' He turned to go.

'Jean-Pierre,' she called. 'It's my day off tomorrow. I'm going to see my brother, he's home from America. Perhaps another day!'

CHAPTER NINETEEN

Jo woke early, excited about seeing Ned and meeting his new wife, Beanie. She'd missed him so much. It was five long years since she'd set eyes on him, and now he was home, she hoped he would never go away again. It had only been a month since her last visit home, but in that time her life at Chateau Colbert had climbed to new heights. Cissy's baby was due any day now; for all she knew, she might already be an aunty.

She rode on the tram, her basket stuffed with sweet cake and biscuits, a couple of fowl legs, a bowl of dripping with the jelly congealed at the bottom, and French sweets for the boys from Jean-Pierre. Mrs. Quigley treated her no differently to the other maids, giving her plenty of food to take home to the family.

Jo wasn't keen to see her mother as Kate was never satisfied, no matter what she did to appease her. And she was sure to go on at her for wearing face powder and lipstick. But she couldn't dent her confidence, not now. Her clothes were more refined and she had money to spend, but she was still the same person.

Excitement churned her stomach as she walked down the street towards Ned's. She wondered if he had changed much and what his wife was like. As she approached the house, a ginger-haired woman with a slender figure was deep in conversation with Aggie Murphy on the doorstep. From the way they were talking, they looked serious and Jo paused for a moment pondering what could be wrong. Was that Ned's wife talking to Aggie? Had something happened to Ned? A feeling of dread rose in her stomach.

Aggie spotted her first. 'Jo-Jo, Cissy's had a baby son. Your mother and Ned have been at the hospital all night. She had a difficult birth, and her husband sent for your mother, that's all I know.'

Jo dropped her basket at Beanie's feet and her hand flew to her mouth. 'Is Cissy all right, and what about the baby?'

'We don't know, Jo-Jo,' Aggie said.

'Oh, I'm sorry,' Beanie said. 'Pleased to meet you, Jo. Sorry it's a bad time.' She reached out and shook her hand warmly. 'I recognise you from your photograph.' Anxiety creased her face. 'Ned wants you to meet him outside Holles Street Hospital.'

'I'll go there straight away.'

As she hurried towards the hospital, all she could think about was how bad her sister must be to allow their mother anywhere near her. What would she say once she discovered she had known about the pregnancy all along?

When she arrived, Ned was in the doorway of the hospital, finishing a cigarette. She had never seen him smoke before.

'Ned!' She ran towards him and wrapped her arms around him, tears of joy and sadness tumbling down her face.

'Let me look at you.' He held her at arm's length. 'You're a proper young lady. I've missed you, sis. Have you met Beanie?'

'Only briefly, Ned.'

'When this worry is over, we'll have time to catch up.'

'What's happened, Ned? How are they?'

He lowered his head. 'Cissy had to have an operation to remove the babby. Larry was worried and sent for Ma.'

'Is the baby all right?'

'He's bonny, but Larry's beside himself with worry over Cissy. We all are. Come on, let's go in, perhaps you can console him.' He ushered her inside.

When they joined her mother and Larry in the waiting room, her mother looked surprised. 'With all the goings on, I forgot you were coming. Wipe that powder stuff off yer face. And them clothes are a bit fancy for round here!'

'Ma,' Ned glared. 'This is neither the time nor the place.'

Used to her mother's snide remarks, Jo turned her attentions to Larry, who was pacing the floor, anxiety etched across his face. She touched him gently on the shoulder. 'How are they?'

'The nurse is looking after the babby, he's all right. It's Cissy I'm worried about, Jo.' He sighed. 'I wish to God we'd…if anything happens to her…I'll never forgive myself.' Larry sat down and buried his face in his hands.

'This is a nice how do yeh do, isn't it? Me daughter giving birth, and her own mother knowing nothin' about it,' Kate moaned. 'If it hadn't been for the fact that she nearly died, I'd still be none the wiser.'

'Oh, for God's sake, woman, shut up.' Larry's outburst was so out of character that everyone went quiet and Jo placed her hand on Larry's arm. Kate would upset a saint.

Ned glared at Kate then took her to one side. 'Ma, you're upsetting Larry. The main thing now is that Cissy gets well.' He passed her his handkerchief, and she blew into it. Ned went to see if he could persuade one of the nurses to make them another pot of tea.

Her mother looked at Jo. 'This must have come as a shock to you, too? Who told yeh? Was it Aggie?'

Jo nodded. That way she wasn't telling any lies. She sat down heavily next to her mother and looked across at Larry. She pitied him. Ned returned with a tray of tea and biscuits.

'I don't know how yeh do it, Ned Kingsley,' his mother said, when he handed her a fresh cup of tea, milked and sugared just how she liked it.

'Ah, it's me charm, Ma, with the hint of the American accent does it every time,' he grinned.

'Get away with you,' his mother said, before giving way to a yawn.

'Look!' Jo said. 'You two go home after you've had your tea. I'll stay here with Larry.' Jo promised to run home and let them know if there was any change, and her offer was gratefully accepted.

But just before they left, a nurse informed them that they could see the baby. Jo saw a smile curl the corner of her mother's mouth, but Larry never looked up. He sat rubbing his temples up and down with his forefingers. 'I've seen him earlier. You go, Jo.'

Jo felt a lump form in her throat. The baby was big – eight pounds, the nurse said; perfect, with jet-black hair, the image of Larry.

When Ned and Kate had left, Jo wanted to put her arms around Larry, tell him everything would be okay. He looked so forlorn.

'If anything happens to Cissy, I don't know what I'll do.' He began to fidget with his signet ring, twisting it one way then the other.

'Cissy's going to get well! She's a fighter, not one to give up easily.'

'You're right about one thing, Jo. She won't give up without a fight,' Larry agreed.

It was an age and many cups of tea later before a nurse finally walked towards them.

'Mr. Kenny, you can see your wife now. Only for five minutes mind, she needs rest.' Larry jumped to his feet and followed the nurse out of the waiting room and down the long corridor. Relieved, Jo sat back down and buried her head in her hands. She prayed for Cissy and her baby son, and wondered what they would call him.

Pleased with the outcome of Cissy, her mother and the baby, Jo would have to wait a while before she could congratulate her sister. The day had been an eventful one, a day to celebrate a new life. Cissy's baby had changed all of their lives in some way. Jo didn't get to talk to Ned, at least, not in the way she'd hoped. But this wasn't the time for her to unburden herself to him; well, not today anyway.

CHAPTER TWENTY

It was late when Jo returned to Chateau Colbert. She crept upstairs so as not to disturb the guests. Jean-Pierre passed her on the landing and enquired about her day.

'Today I became an aunty,' she whispered, feeling a flush to her face. It happened each time she was standing close to him.

'Congratulations! Aunty Jo,' he said in soft French tones. 'I will never be an uncle. It's one of the drawbacks of being an only child.' He smiled good-humouredly. 'Are you free tomorrow evening, Jo?'

'I…well…I mean, I would have to check with Madame Colbert.' She hadn't expected him to ask her out so soon, and she felt butterflies in her stomach.

'Of course, I'll speak to Grandmama. I could book a table at Premier's,' he paused. 'But if you'd prefer…'

'Premier's sounds wonderful. Thank you. If Madame approves, I shall look forward to it,' she said, unlocking the door to her room.

The following evening, determined to look her best, Jo took time getting ready. She was nervous. She had never dined out with a man before, and especially one as sophisticated as Jean-Pierre. In an effort to stop her hands from shaking, she reminded herself that she knew enough about the upper classes to get by and she could hold an intelligent conversation. And if Jean-Pierre was anything like his grandmother, he wouldn't deride her background.

Wearing a sky blue close-fitting hat, with a narrow brim that matched her blue suit – one of the outfits bought for her by Madame Colbert – she couldn't resist seeking her approval.

Maria Colbert looked up and smiled appreciatively as though she was seeing her daughter off to her first dance. 'You look *bon ton*, Jo,' she said. 'One moment, dear!' And before Jo knew what was happening, Madame was pinning a sparkling brooch to the lapel of her suit. Then she stood back to admire the girl in front of her. 'Have a wonderful evening, my dear Jo, you deserve it.'

Jean-Pierre watched her descend the staircase, making her blush. He looked handsome in a dark dinner suit and bow tie. Foster was waiting with the car, and he assisted them inside with a smile. As the car moved away, the curtains twitched. Molly and Rosie again, she thought. This would give them something to talk about for sure.

The evening had turned chilly, as Foster dropped them outside Premiers, and Jean-Pierre said they would take a cab home. They were greeted at the restaurant by the doorman and escorted upstairs to the busy dining area. Jo gazed around at the plush surroundings as they were seated at a candlelit table for two. The silver cutlery glistened against the sparkling glasses, and dimmed chandeliers allowed the soft glow of candlelight to create a feeling of intimacy.

As the music drifted up from the dance area below, Jo turned her head, taking in the colourful scenes of Paris that decorated the walls, her nervousness receding.

'Oh, Jean-Pierre, isn't it wonderful!' she said looking at him.

'I'm so glad you like it. Would you like some wine?' His voice was soft.

She was unsure whether she should refuse and ask for a soda. She had liked the sophisticated taste of the wine the other night when she had dined with Madame and the guests, so she nodded and Jean-Pierre called the waiter over. The man presented a bottle to Jean-Pierre for approval and drew out the cork. It popped, making her jump. Then, as the waiter poured the wine into their glasses, they both laughed.

Jean-Pierre asked for the menu. Jo had never seen a French menu before. Observing the lady at the next table eating a prawn cocktail, she asked for the same, while Jean-Pierre chose crab with a sweet dressing. As they ate, she noticed the fashion worn by the young women. She was *bon ton*, Madame Colbert had told her so. The wine relaxed her further and, while they waited for their main course, Jean-Pierre asked her to dance.

'I'd love to. *Merci!*' It felt surreal as he took her hand and guided her down the staircase to the floor below. As the quartet played a quickstep, Jean-Pierre swept her off her feet. Aware of his hand pressing into the small of her back, she was overcome with unfamiliar emotions. Struggling to keep up with the tempo and avoid stepping on his shoes, Jo felt a flush to her face when the music stopped.

'You dance very well,' he told her.

'Thank you.' Jean-Pierre was the first man she had ever danced with, and if she hadn't had an ear for music she would never have attempted to try. As the band struck up again, he twirled her round underneath his arm and before long she was following his steps like a professional. Anyone looking at them would assume they had danced together for years. They returned to their table and enjoyed the French cuisine.

'The food is out of this world,' she remarked, dabbing the corners of her mouth with her napkin.

'French food can only be cooked to perfection by a French chef,' he said, quickly adding, 'no disrespect to Mrs. Quigley. Please don't tell. She'll only get grumpy and refuse to cook any more of my favourite food.' A mischievous grin lit up his face. While they finished their wine, Jean-Pierre answered Jo's many questions about Paris and the Eiffel Tower.

'Some still think it's a monstrosity, but,' he added, 'they will grow to love it as I do. I gather you've not been to Paris, Jo?'

She sighed. 'No. Perhaps one day.'

He told her about *L'Arc de Triomphe*, built to glorify Napoleon Bonaparte. About the *Louvre* and avant-garde art galleries, restaurants promoting romantic songs, situated on tree-lined boulevards. She was spellbound, captivated by the eloquent tones as he spoke. She could have listened to him all night.

'It all sounds wonderful. I once dreamed of going to America when my brother Ned first went there.'

'And now?'

'I rarely think about it. My friend Annie is emigrating soon.'

'Won't you miss her?

'Very much.'

'Tell me about you, Jo? How did you come to work for Grandmama?'

'It was Annie who told me about the advertisement in the press. I was determined to make something of my life and your grandmother gave me that opportunity. Otherwise, I'd still...' she paused. She told him about Ned and Cissy and her own grandmother, but she never mentioned her mother, Kate.

Jean-Pierre talked about his work at the Lycee Condorcet College in Paris.

'My pupils will return next week.' He looked pensive. 'I will miss *Grandmère* and you, too, Jo.' His face brightened. 'If I write, will you reply?'

'Yes, of course.' She blushed at her boldness. They chatted on; Jo felt comfortable in his company, and it was late when they left the restaurant. Jean-Pierre had been a perfect gentleman and made no attempts to flirt with her. If he had done, she had no idea how she might have reacted and it would have spoiled their friendship. In a few days he would be back in Paris and she would resume her life as it was, before his visit.

They parted company at the top of the stairway. 'Goodnight, Jean-Pierre.' And smiling, she thanked him for the most romantic evening of her life.

* * *

After the visitors' departure, the place seemed quiet and Jo missed the comings and goings of the guests. She had felt special when she had dined with them, and when Jean-Pierre had taken her to Premiers. Now, only when Madame Colbert brought his name into their conversation, did she think about him. He had sent a letter to his grandmother, but not to her. Maybe French men were not to be trusted after all.

111

With Jean-Pierre back in Paris, she felt no real urgency to speak with Ned, as her life at the Chateau was returning to normal.

Madame Colbert looked particularly vulnerable without her grandson around, and Jo made an extra effort to entertain her, playing her favourite songs on the piano, reading to her, and sitting with her sometimes until she fell asleep. 'I do miss him, the dear boy.'

'Don't be sad, Madame. He'll be back again soon.'

She patted Jo's hand. 'You are right, my dear Jo.'

Apart from her own grandmother, Madame Colbert was the kindest person Jo had ever known and she was sad to see her looking so drained when only a few weeks ago she had been full of life. 'If tomorrow's fine, would you like to sit out in the garden, Madame? The fresh air might do you good.'

'Tomorrow you and I are going to the city again, my dear,' she said, forcing a smile to her tired face.

'If you're sure you feel up to it, Madame. I'll look forward to it.'

Madame nodded. 'I'm so glad we have each other, my dear.'

'Well, of course Madame. If you need me, I won't be far away.' Jo had had no idea that Jean-Pierre's departure would leave his grandmother so low. 'Is there anything more I can do for you tonight?'

'Perhaps a soothing melody and a small glass of wine will send me to sleep.'

Jo brought the wine and put the record on the turntable before sitting down next to the bed, where she stayed deep in thought. Once Madame Colbert was asleep, she slipped quietly from the room.

CHAPTER TWENTY-ONE

Some weeks later, when Jo went up with afternoon tea she found her employer clutching an envelope, a cheerful expression on her face. 'Come and sit down, my dear, I want to read you a telegram from Jean-Pierre.'

Jo put the tray down and Maria translated the message in English.

'The dear boy wants me to come to Paris in October. It's not too hot then. He says it would be an opportunity to see us both again. He will make all the necessary arrangements. What do you say, Jo, shall we go?'

Speechless, Jo's hand covered her lips. How many young women of her class were offered an opportunity like this, days before their nineteenth birthday?

'I'm…I'm sorry, Madame, but it's all…'

'I know. You need time to take it in, my dear.' She smiled, placing the telegram back inside the little brown envelope. 'I need you with me, my dear. Besides, Jean-Pierre will be disappointed if we don't come.'

'How long would we be away?'

'At least four weeks. There are sights to see, shops to visit, music recitals, concert halls, artists and musicians to meet.' Excitement lifted her voice. 'Such an opportunity should not be missed. You will love it, dear Jo.' She joined her slender fingers together, and rested them underneath her chin.

'Yes of course, Madame.' Jo's pulse raced. 'I'd be honoured to accompany you,' she said at last.

'Wonderful! I'll ask Foster to send a cable today. Now I can eat.' In the excitement, the tea had gone cold. Jo quickly offered to replace it, but Maria tugged the bell cord and soon Molly came into the room.

'Can I have the same again, Molly, please?' The girl removed the tray, wearing her usual scowl. 'Does that girl ever smile?' Maria asked, as the maid closed the door behind her, but Jo was in a daze, her mind still coming to terms with this latest surprise.

* * *

Jo was delighted when Ned and Beanie decided to settle in Ireland, and she felt the urgent need to tell them her exciting news. A free trip to Paris was beyond her wildest dreams and she couldn't help the enthusiasm building up inside her. After spending a few hours with her friend Annie, Jo arrived at Ned's early. Beanie opened the door, her face flushed.

'I'm sorry I'm a bit early.'

'That's okay, Jo,' Beanie said cheerfully. 'Come in! Ned's not home yet, but your mother's here.'

She stepped into the kitchen, detecting a familiar smell. Her mother was sitting at the table, glasses and a half empty jug of porter in front of her. Realising she'd interrupted an afternoon of drinking, Jo apologised.

'Oh, it's you!' Kate, who was slumped in the chair, sat upright.

'I've come to see Ned.'

'You'll have a drop, now you're here?' Kate lifted the jug, but Jo waved her hand surprised to find Beanie drinking with her so early.

'Your mother's a bit low and she asked me to share a glass with her.' Beanie drained her glass and took it to the sink.

Kate would always find an excuse to drink and right now she looked like she'd had quite enough. Jo's good news would have to wait until later. Her mother would spoil it all in seconds with some derogatory remark. If only she would go home, or fall asleep, before Ned arrived.

Beanie rinsed her glass and turned towards the stove. 'I'll put the kettle on. I'm sure you'd like a cup of tea, Jo.'

'That would be lovely, thanks.' She took off her coat and sat down.

'Too good to drink with your mother, are yeh?' Kate started. 'Coming here with airs and graces. You're forgettin' who yeh are since rubbin' noses with the gentry,' she slurred.

'You know I've never liked the stuff, Ma.' Jo picked up yesterday's newspaper determined not to be goaded into an argument. There was a ripple of tension in the air. Beanie, looking anxious, glanced out of the window several times and Jo wished that she hadn't arrived so early.

A short time later, Kate yawned and stood up. 'I'm away home to me bed for a lie down.' And Jo was glad to see the back of her.

'Take no notice, Jo,' Beanie turned to look at her. 'It'll be the drink talking.'

With hindsight, Jo knew that was true. And she guessed her mother wasn't about to change now. In no time at all the appetising smell of Irish stew was wafting round the kitchen, when the door burst open and Jo's half brothers, Liam and James, rushed in. 'Hello, Jo.'

And greeting her with a hug, they turned to Beanie. 'Can we stay for dinner?' Liam cried. 'We can smell it from outside.'

'Of course you can. Sit yourselves down. It won't be long.'

With Ned and Beanie around, Jo worried less about the boys.

When Ned walked in through the door, Jo greeted him. 'Oh, it's good to see you, Ned.'

'Good to see you, too, sis! Just let me have a quick wash, otherwise I might spoil your nice clothes.' He held up his hands covered in putty and white dust and went to the sink under the window, letting the water run freely over his face and hands until they were clean, then drying them. He kissed Beanie. 'Ma's been here then?' he asked, glancing at the glasses on the draining board. 'How was she?'

'Oh, the usual.'

Ned ruffled the boys' hair, kissed Jo on the cheek, and sat down next to her. 'Well, anything strange or wonderful to impart?'

Jo was smiling. 'Ned! You'll never guess. Madame Colbert has asked me to go to Paris with her for a whole month. I can't believe it!'

Ned's mouth fell open; the boys glanced up, but soon became engrossed in the food Beanie was setting down before them. 'Aren't you the lucky one?' Beanie smiled towards her.

'My, you do lead an exciting life, Jo.' Beanie placed a mug of tea down next to Ned. He drank thirstily and listened while Jo told them about her employer lavishing gifts on her and her romantic evening at Premiers French restaurant, before he spoke.

'Your employer appreciates what you do for her. It's not unheard of for rich ladies to bestow gifts on their servants.'

'It feels so strange.'

'Don't read too much into it.'

The boys got up from the table and thanked Beanie before going outside again.

She brought the warm stew to the table and they tucked in.

'What I want to know is,' Ned asked, 'do you have feelings for this French man?'

'*Feelings!* I don't think so. I'm caught up in a whirlwind, but I have to admit it feels grand.' She didn't tell him how she blushed whenever Jean-Pierre came close, and how she had put it down to nerves.

'A rich Frenchman and an Irish colleen,' he joked. 'Stranger things have happened.' He ran his hand over his face. 'You don't think it could be part of Madame Colbert's plan, do you?' She knew he was teasing her, and she wanted him to be serious.

'Come on, Ned.'

'Well!' He took a deep breath. 'I think you should stop worrying. You have in Madame Colbert a trusting counsellor.'

'I think Ned's right, Jo.' Beanie placed a chunky carrot into her mouth and wiped up her plate with bread.

'And, Jo.' Ned winked. 'Don't take Jean-Pierre too seriously.'

'Of course not.'

'Well, I think you'll have a wonderful time in Paris.' Beanie stood up and took the dirty plates to the sink then sat back down. 'Is your friend Annie still going to America?'

'She talks about it all the time. You two don't regret coming back, do you?'

'Not a bit.' Beanie smiled.

Ned reached out and patted his wife's hand. 'As for me, well, I found my pot of gold.' Then he pushed back his plate and stood up. 'Come on.' He pulled Jo to her feet. 'It's getting late. I'll walk you to the tram.'

CHAPTER TWENTY-TWO

The October day was bright and sunny, but a biting wind swept across the deck when Jo and her employer crossed the channel to Cherbourg. Travelling first class, they dined in style and later sat on deck, muffled against the sea breeze, fortified with hot broth.

'You make a good sailor, Jo.'

'Thank you, Madame. My grandmother took me and my brother to the Isle of Man once. I remember the sea was rough, but it didn't affect me. Jean-Pierre mentioned that you are a seasoned sea traveller yourself, Madame.'

'Oh, that was a long time ago, my dear. Of course I've been on many beautiful ships, and travelled to many distant lands. Dear Louis booked a surprise trip on the Mauritania.' She sighed. 'It has such style. One walked in sheer luxury; a floating hotel. We dined and danced to a live band. Everything you would expect from the Ritz and more. Oh, listen to me.' She removed the rug that lay across her legs. 'Shall we go inside, my dear? It's getting cold.' She stood up, handing Jo her binoculars, and retired to her cabin, insisting that Jo return and enjoy the sea breeze.

The journey wasn't as long as Jo had expected, and before long people were piling on deck to watch as the ship approached Cherbourg. Jo, her eyes bright with expectation, hurried back inside to alert Madame Colbert, and found her peering through the porthole.

'I'm sorry, Madame, I should have come back sooner, but I got carried away looking out at the port with white, blue and red fishing boats. It looks so peaceful and reminds me of Kinsale in Cork.'

Madame Colbert smiled as a porter arrived to take their baggage. Up on deck, people were moving in readiness for disembarkation. Jo watched with rising interest as the ship slowly and steadily manoeuvred towards protected anchorage. She listened to the chatter of passengers eager to be off the ship and on their way.

Madame Colbert and Jo were escorted towards the waiting train. For their onward journey they boarded a Pullman express to Paris, while attendants saw to their luggage.

Although it was mid-afternoon when they settled into one of the carriages, Madame Colbert closed her eyes. Jo, too excited to sleep, read the magazine she'd picked up at the station. Soon they would see Jean-Pierre. It had only been weeks since his visit to Dublin. She was looking forward to seeing him again and, for the first time, the splendour of Paris.

As the train approached the city, Madame Colbert began to stir; the sea voyage had put a glow on her delicate complexion. The way her grey eyes sprung into life when she wakened, as if she had never expected to do so again, intrigued Jo.

'I've not been much company, Jo. The journey is tiring. Did you sleep?'

'I'm too excited, Madame. The short rest will have done you good.'

'I'm feeling better now the sea trip is behind us. October can be changeable at sea.'

The train stopped and Jo pulled down the window. People were moving towards the train. The soft melodious tones of the French accent resounded everywhere as passengers were greeted by friends and lovers. At first she couldn't see Jean-Pierre. Then she spotted him, his tall slender figure moving to and fro, searching for a glimpse of them, his black silky hair falling across his forehead He was wearing a grey silk cravat. Dear Jean-Pierre, she thought.

'He's here, Madame. Jean-Pierre's here.' She waved to him through the open window, excited to be here at last.

'Welcome to Paris.' Extending his hand, he helped his grandmother, then Jo, to step from the train. '*Grandmère.*' He kissed both her cheeks. To Jo he extended a light kiss on the hand.

'I'm happy to see you, Jo.'

'Thank you. I'm very happy to be here.'

He picked up their luggage and they followed him to the carriage. Strong smells of cigars and perfume wafted past them as people made their way out of the busy station. Soon they were being whisked across Paris, and Jo's head was full of the sights. The smells of the city were powerful through the open window of the carriage: horse dung, coffee, mixed with the perfume of flowers for sale along the pavement. Jean-Pierre pointed out his apartment that overlooked the Champs-Elysees, lined with chestnut trees, where elegantly dressed Parisian ladies wore colourful hats balanced on upswept coiffures – making hers look quite dated – and gentlemen wore bowlers and wing-collar shirts.

Jo pointed towards the giant Ferris wheel as it rotated slowly, its passengers pointing out various landmarks. But the romance for Jo was Paris itself, the high buildings with wrought-iron balconies. Jean-Pierre slowed down from time to time so that she could see the Eiffel Tower and many more famous landmarks on the way to their hotel.

The carriage stopped outside the Grand Hotel where they were to stay. Lost for words, Jo gasped in amazement. Jean-Pierre left them to settle in, saying he would call the following day when they were rested.

* * *

The rooms were adjoining, and Jo was awestruck by her lavish surroundings. Madame Colbert expected nothing less. Cream walls and high ceilings, with crystal chandeliers blended tastefully with the soft gold of the rugs. Heavy gold drapes hung on the long windows. Madame laughed girlishly when Jo said she would never sleep in such luxury.

Over the next few days, while Madame caught up with old friends, Jean-Pierre escorted Jo around Paris. She insisted on walking to see everything close up, to feel the atmosphere, take in the different aromas of coffee that filtered through the opening of every restaurant. And each time a Parisian lady passed them by, she tried to detect the names of the different perfumes that filled her senses. Jean-Pierre took her into a *parfumerie* and bought her all four brands when she could not make up her mind which she liked best.

In spite of the many cars whizzing past, Jo loved the horse-drawn carriages and the clop of hoofs; even the smell of horse dung reminded her of home. They walked along in companionable silence, Jean-Pierre hands behind his back, aware of the admiring glances coming their way.

'I never expected to see so many tourists in October, Jean-Pierre.'

'This is nothing.' He smiled down at her. 'From May through to July, the city was packed for the summer Olympics.'

'That must have been exciting.' She stopped to watch an artist sketching a barge on the River Seine. She loved the movement on the water as barges and steamers sailed up and down.

'Ah yes, it was. I didn't attend any of the games myself. I was busy working on exam papers at the college and then organising my trip to Dublin.' He sighed. 'It was for me a memorable time.'

'So memorable that you forgot to write?' She said it without thinking. They were walking close to the water's edge.

'I wrote many times, Jo. And because I...' He paused, looking out towards the boats. 'I was a coward. I discarded them.' He glanced down at her.

What could she say? She had only spoken in jest. What reason would he have for keeping up an acquaintance with the girl who was a servant to his grandmother?

'I wanted to see you again, Jo. I knew *Grandmère* loved Paris at this time of the year, so I used my spare time arranging the trip for you both. Some things are best said face-to-face.' His dark eyes clouded and Jo lowered her gaze. She recalled Ned telling her not to take all this seriously. She didn't know how to answer him. He seemed sincere, but she didn't want their friendship to end.

'What do you mean, Jean-Pierre?'

He didn't answer and, taking her hand, he pulled her after him up the bank. 'I know a place north of here where we can row on the river.' Before she could protest, he hailed a carriage. Soon they were sailing out across the cool water and Jo leaned back, relaxed. She reached out to touch the water as it rippled between her fingers, aware of Jean-Pierre watching her as he rowed. They were the only couple on the river that day.

'I think I'm falling in love with you.' He stopped rowing and on impulse, reached across and kissed her cheek. The boat swayed.

'Don't be silly, Jean-Pierre.' She laughed to cover her embarrassment.

'You don't think that's possible?'

'You can't love someone like me! It's not the way of things.'

'Someone like you is perfect. My feelings are sincere, Jo.'

No-one had ever said they loved her, not like this. And she had no idea what to say. His grandmother had always told her to follow her heart.

'I'm sorry, Jean-Pierre. We hardly know each other.' Smiling, she touched his hand. 'I think we should go back now.'

He looked disappointed. 'I've upset you. Please forgive me?'

'There's nothing to forgive.' How strange, she thought, how a few simple words of love can change things. She liked him very much, enjoyed his company. And in spite of blushing when he was near and, feeling flattered by his attentions, she had never been in love, so had nothing to compare it with. All she knew about men was what she had read in books; how fickle they could be. So when Jean-Pierre said he thought he was falling in love with her, maybe he didn't mean it.

* * *

That evening Jo dined with Madame Colbert and Jean-Pierre. She took particular notice of what Parisian ladies were wearing and, in particular, the French hairstyles. The main topic of conversation round the dinner table was the international monetary situation, abstract paintings and astronomy which fascinated her. She was always at ease when the conversation turned to music.

It was after one such evening that Jo decided to have her hair cut in the French style, finding her own long hair tedious and outdated. She chose a short bob with a fringe, as opposed to the ribbed wavy look that was all the rage. Madame told her she looked *chic*.

'I'm astounded by the amount of mascara women are wearing,' Jo remarked. 'And they pluck their eyebrows.'

'This is Paris, I suppose anything goes,' Maria smiled. 'They even wear false eyelashes, did you notice?'

A few evenings later, Jean-Pierre invited her to accompany him to the opera. Jo had fallen in love with the Paris fashions and treated herself to a white satin halter-neck gown; a white cardigan covered her bare shoulders. She carried a clutch handbag covered with sequins, and her necklace hung low round her slender neck. Jean-Pierre smiled when he saw her.

Most of the performance was in French, but it didn't spoil her enjoyment of the story. During the interval, they danced the foxtrot in the theatre foyer with the other patrons. Some of the ladies held long thin cigarette holders to their lips.

'Are they really smoking those?' Jo whispered to Jean-Pierre, as he twirled her round on the dance floor.

'Some do, some just hold them to be fashionable.' He was smiling down at her. 'Are you enjoying yourself, Jo?'

'Yes, thank you. I'm having the time of my life. Your grandmother will dispense of me if I carry on neglecting her.' She smiled.

'She's enjoying herself far too much to notice.'

The music stopped and they walked back to their theatre seats.

* * *

The weeks flew past and during that time Jean-Pierre remained the perfect gentleman, never again mentioning his feelings for her. Jo began to enjoy his company more and more. And Madame was right about there being so much to see and do.

Before they were due to leave, Madame Colbert noticed a poster announcing Maurice Chevalier's comeback at the Paris Empire, to sing his love songs. 'We must see him before we leave, my dears,' she said.

It was a perfect round-up to a wonderful holiday. Maurice Chevalier's songs were full of frivolity and reminded her of Maurice Bonnet. But Chavalier's dashing good looks, his cheeky grin, personality and presence on stage, showed no resemblance to Bonnet. When Maria introduced her to him at the end of the show, Jo almost went weak at the knees.

After a glorious month, it was time for them to leave; time for Maria Colbert to say a tearful goodbye to her grandson. It brought a tear to Jo's eye. She glanced down at her suitcase – a little heavier than when she'd arrived – before it was hoisted on board the train. She had many theatre and concert programmes to take home to show Annie.

'I will remember this trip forever,' she told Jean-Pierre.

'*Au revoir, chérie.*' He lifted her hand to his lips. 'I will miss you.'

She would miss him, too, but refrained from saying so. She thanked him again and noticed his shoulders sag as he waved them off from the platform.

The train journey had a hypnotic effect on Jean-Pierre's grandmother. Jo closed her eyes, but she couldn't sleep; She had too much to think about. When they boarded the ship, her employer retired to her cabin. 'It's hard to stay still in Paris, Jo. I've slightly overdone things. I'll perk up once we're home.' Jo left her to rest for the remainder of the journey.

Foster collected them at the dockside. At the Chateau. They were greeted warmly by Miss O'Breen and Mrs. Quigley.

'It's lovely to have you back, Madame Colbert,' Miss O'Breen told her. 'You, too, Jo.' She smiled. 'Your bed is aired and ready, Madame. Would you like something to eat or drink?'

'No thank you, Miss O'Breen, I think sleep is all I need.' Her voice was flat and jaded. Jo guided her fatigued mistress towards the small lift that took her to her quarters. Her tiredness was to be expected, after the miles they had travelled. Jo met her at the top of the stairs and gently led her down the corridor to her rooms.

In Paris it was so easy to forget that her employer was an elderly lady, by the way she embraced life. Jo helped her undress and saw to her comforts, before she returned to the kitchen where Mrs. Quigley was waiting to hear all about her travels.

CHAPTER TWENTY-THREE

When Jo met Annie, she held her spellbound for the entire evening with tales about the trip to Paris. She described her nights out with Jean-Pierre and the wonderful time he had shown her.

'You make my going to America seem mundane, Jo. It certainly won't be anything as luxurious as your trip to Paris with Madame Colbert.'

'I know, but Paris was a once-in-a-lifetime opportunity. Going to America is something else.'

'I suppose so. But you'd better be careful with Jean-Pierre, especially as you say you don't have feelings for him. Why is it that I never get to dance with a Frenchman? Or any man for that matter.' She laughed.

'Oh, he was only being polite,' Jo said nonchalantly.

'You don't really believe that, do you?'

Jo shrugged. 'I don't know.'

Annie looked pensive. 'I can't believe I'll be in America in a few months.'

'Oh, Annie, I'll miss you so much.'

'I wish you were coming with me, Jo.' She raised her eyebrows. 'Is there any chance?'

Jo had always thought she would, but now, with so much going on in her life, she rarely thought about it. She would miss Annie more than she dared to say. Annie had always been there for her, and now she might never see her again. Her tone was light-hearted when she replied. 'I'll follow you over there one day, Annie. Would you like me to ask Ned for the address of a suitable lodging house? He got to know a few people while he was in New York.'

'Father O'Leary's given me the address of a Catholic family. But it can't hurt to have another option.'

* * *

Madame Colbert took two days to recover from the effects of the sea travel. By the third day she appeared to be her usual self, laughing and discussing the trip. A couple of days later when the post arrived at the Chateau, it was Rosie who brought it upstairs.

'Some letters from Paris, Madame,' she said, and retreated towards the door.

'Thank you, dear.' Madame Colbert flicked through the post. 'Oh look, Jo. There's one for you.' She smiled. 'There's a letter opener on the desk. Can you pass it to me, my dear?'

Jo felt her face colour. She hadn't said anything to Madame about Jean-Pierre, but somehow she had this strange feeling that the older woman knew something. Jo wanted to take the letter to her room and read it in private, but when Maria slit open her envelope and slipped the letter out, she handed the opener for Jo to do the same.

While Marie read her letter from Jean-Pierre, a smile lit up her face.

Jo opened her letter and read:

Dear Jo,

Sometimes it is difficult to write with the words that are inside one's heart. I hope you will understand and forgive me when I say I had no wish to upset you. Now there are autumn nights and a fire burns in my room, but my heart is cold. The summer was ended on the day that you returned to Dublin.

Grandmère looked so tired when she waited for the train. Mes apologies for asking this, but I am hoping you will write with news of her health and that she has recovered from her journey.

Yours,

Jean-Pierre

Moved by his letter, Jo was anxious to reply, but she would

have to wait until later when she was off duty.

Madame Colbert folded her letter and placed it back in the envelope. 'The dear boy is lonely and it will take him a while to settle again now that we're back.' She smiled, but she didn't attempt to ask Jo what was in her letter. And besides, Jo was miles away, her mind on how she should phrase her letter to Jean-Pierre.

'What is it, *ma petite*?' Marie reached out and gently touched Jo's arm, a frown creasing her face.

'I was thinking about Paris, Madame, and the wonderful time I had there with Jean-Pierre,' Jo admitted, rubbing her hand across her brow.

'Yes, my dear Jo. I think the boy's in love with you. Who would blame him? It was obvious in Paris,' she said, looking at Jo. 'But you don't feel the same way, do you?'

Jo's eyebrows shot upwards. 'How…how did you know, Madame? Has Jean-Pierre spoken of–'

'No. But you have a troubled look.'

'I'm so confused, Madame Colbert. I'm very fond of Jean-Pierre.' She bit her lip. 'He is so attractive, charming and…' She paused, not sure how her words would be received.

'Love is confusing at your age.' Madame sighed. 'I must admit that I did have a secret longing that the two of you would…well… Our destiny's in the stars.'

'Aren't you worried what people might say, Madame?'

'I'm not a snob, Jo, and we're not royalty. I want my grandson to be happy. Besides, I felt that you and he were ideally suited. But let's speak no more of it.'

'I appreciate your being so understanding, Madame.' Then, as Maria's eyelids began to droop, Jo secured a rug around her thin frame, drew across the heavy velvet curtains and left the room.

* * *

Later when Jo read Jean-Pierre's letter again, she felt the urge to write back to him. She opened her drawer and took out writing paper and a fountain pen and began to compose a letter, but the words didn't come easily.

Dear Jean-Pierre,
It was lovely to hear from you.

She paused, ripped the page from the pad, crumpled it into her fist and threw it into her wastebasket, and began again.

Dear Jean-Pierre,
The days have flown by since our return.

She struck a line through that. She couldn't say what she really wanted to. After all, she was more than fond of him, and could easily grow to love him. At twenty-nine, he had seen more of life than she had, and in spite of their class divide, she felt quite at ease in his company. With so much to consider, she wasn't going to get carried away by his words; words that could easily be misconstrued.

Dear Jean-Pierre,
Thank you for a wonderful time in Paris. It is something I will never forget. I value your friendship and I'm pleased we can still remain friends.

Your grandmother is well rested after her travels and we are still discussing our trip. Although she appears to grow tired easily, that could be due to the change in the weather. I will finish now as it is time for me to check on her.

With kindest regards,
Jo

She used a piece of blotting paper to dry the ink, quickly addressed the envelope, folded the letter, and sealed it inside before she could change her mind again.

* * *

January brought bitter winds sweeping down from the Dublin Mountains. Madame Colbert showed little interest in going out or entertaining her friends who enquired after her health. She preferred to stay indoors by the cosy fire made up by Rosie, and kept going throughout the day by Jo to maintain the room's temperature.

'Go out for a while, my dear,' Maria Colbert said, when she noticed her still in the room, doing little jobs to keep busy. 'Visit the art gallery. Go to the theatre with Annie,' she insisted, giving her a weak smile.

'But I don't want to leave you,' Jo said, tucking the rug snugly round her employer's knees. 'Besides, it's much too cold to go out,' she told her, and settled down in the chair next to Maria, a small bundle of sewing on her lap.

'You mustn't worry about me, Jo. It's just old age, it comes to us all.' She gave a little chuckle, and Jo saw a sparkle return to her eyes. Jo offered to get her another warm drink, but she shook her head and tapped her fingers irritably on the arm of her chair. 'Run along now. Go into Brown Thomas, buy yourself something cosy and warm. Charge it to my account.'

'Thank you, Madame. That's very kind of you.'

'It'll snow soon,' Maria said, turning her head towards the window.

The mention of snow excited Jo. She stretched her long legs and crossed to the window. The sky was overcast, the trees were bare and spindly and the garden looked bleak; apart from the evergreens, a flush of red berries clung to the holly bush, giving the garden a splash of colour.

'Yes! You could be right, Madame. The sky is laden.' Jo turned back into the room. Maria Colbert had fallen asleep. Jo picked up her lily-white hand and placed it underneath her rug, then glanced lovingly at the woman who now meant so much to her. 'I love you,' she murmured, before leaving the room.

* * *

Annie's preparations for emigrating were under way and took up most of her spare time. Jo went with her to the various societies who advised Irish women before they finally made up their minds to leave Ireland. Annie told Jo she'd answered an advertisement from a businessman living in the Bronx, as a live-in nanny to his two young children.

'It is just what I'm looking for, Jo.' They were drinking coffee and munching through a selection of sandwiches in Grafton Street.

Jo stopped eating and glanced up. 'Well, in that case, I'm sure you're just the person for the job. How soon will you know?'

'It could be weeks before I hear anything. I'd prefer to have a job to go to.'

'Yes, I agree. But what if you don't like your employer when you get there?'

'It'll be grand. I've got to stay positive.'

'Of course. By the way, Ned's given me the name of a boarding house in the Bronx.' When Jo handed over the piece of paper with the address, the realisation that her friend would soon be gone out her life, hit her. 'Oh my God, Annie. Will I ever see you again?'

'Of, course you will. Don't be sad! I'll write often, and who knows, you might follow me over. I'll pester you until you do.' Annie bit her bottom lip. 'I want to get away from Ireland, make a new start you know, find a husband before I'm too old.'

'Twenty-five's not old.'

'What about you, have you heard from Jean-Pierre yet?'

She had been trying to forget Jean-Pierre's letter, but couldn't now that Annie had mentioned his name. 'Yes I have, and I think he likes me more than he should.'

'Do you love him? And what's more, do you believe him?' Annie's directness made Jo's colour rise.

'I don't know. But then I've never been in love.' She stirred the remains of her coffee.

'Have you told him how you feel?'

'Yes, and no. I've kept my reply friendly.'

'Well then. There's still time for you to come to America with me! I'm not going until May. I'd wait if I thought you'd change your mind,' Annie said optimistically.

'Don't tempt me, Annie. I'd love to, but,' she heaved a sigh, 'this isn't about Jean-Pierre. Madame Colbert needs me now more than ever. But I'll admit going to Paris has given me the urge to travel.' She sipped the remainder of her coffee. 'You will keep in touch?'

'I promise.' Annie got to her feet. 'Have you seen the time?'

'Oh look!' Jo exclaimed, staring out of the window. 'It's snowing.' They both rushed outside, pulling their collars up against the falling snow. 'Madame Colbert was right. She said it was going to snow.' Jo looked down at the ground as the white flakes settled beneath their feet.

CHAPTER TWENTY-FOUR

As the months passed and spring arrived, Madame Colbert appeared less lethargic. Jo was encouraged to see her entertaining her society friends again. So it was with a happy heart that she went upstairs to check on her arrangements for lunch. She found her employer frantically searching the drawers of her dressing table, a puzzled expression on her face.

'Can I help, Madame Colbert?'

'My pearls are missing, dear! Did you place them back in the case?'

'Yes, Madame, I put them in the black case right here!' She picked it up and found it empty. Thinking her employer may have absentmindedly placed the pearls in another jewellery pouch, Jo searched among the rest of the precious gems but it wasn't there either. Jo pondered, her hand covering one side of her face. 'How very strange, Madame. It's some time now since you last wore them.'

Madame Colbert sat with her hands in her lap. 'Where are they? They were a present from my dear Louis. They must be found.' Her brow creased into a frown, and her grey eyes clouded.

'I really can't think what could have happened to them, Madame.' Jo immediately felt under suspicion, as she was the only person who handled them apart from her employer. 'Would Foster have taken them for cleaning?' Jo asked. Her employer shook her head.

'I gather you're lunching out today, Madame?'

Another nod of her head was the reply, leaving Jo feeling uneasy. Then she said, 'They may have slipped down the back of your dressing table. Please don't worry.'

Madame's slender neck looked elongated without the pearls. She wore a blue woollen suit, an outfit she was never seen to wear without her pearls. She stood up, worry etched on her face. 'I've already looked.' Her dismissive tone left Jo feeling worse. 'Would you inform Foster that I must speak with him immediately?'

'Straight away, Madame.' Jo hurried out, her face hot and her eyes teary. She felt responsible. Her position in the household was one of trust, and she would never jeopardise that. How could she prove that she hadn't taken the precious pearls? She had access to them and other valuables every day. The more she thought about it, the worse she felt. Overwhelmed with guilt, she went to deliver the message to the butler. Madame Colbert was bound to blame her – everyone would. How had she not noticed the pearls were missing?

Jo kept going over in her mind the last time she had seen them. But was that the last time Madame had worn them? Now she was having doubts.

* * *

When the butler rapped the door and walked in, Madame Colbert's head jerked round, a solemn expression on her face. 'You wanted to see me, Madame?' He came closer to where Maria Colbert was perched on the *chaise longue*. She was wearing a double row of white beads around her neck.

'Yes, Foster.'

It was unusual for her to summon him; Miss O'Breen dealt with any domestic situations that arose.

'What is it, Madame, has something happened?'

'It's rather a delicate matter, Foster. My precious pearls have gone missing.' She sighed.

'This is indeed serious, Madame. Do you want me to call in the Garda, or do you wish me to deal with it?'

'This is very unpleasant, Foster, and distressing to think that someone has been amongst my personal possessions. Check our security. And then you must question the staff.' She stood up and eased her black leather gloves onto her slender hands. 'I'm lunching out, Foster. Can I leave you to deal with this sensitively?'

'Leave everything to me, Madame. Please don't distress yourself, I'll get to the bottom of it.'

'Thank you, Foster,'

'Madame Colbert,' he said, turning back to face her. 'Once I question the staff, I must include Jo, otherwise…' He was looking straight at her, observing her reaction.

She took a deep breath. 'Unfortunately, I suppose you must.'

* * *

Later that day, the butler and housekeeper walked into the kitchen. 'Miss Kingsley,' the butler said, 'can you come with us to the drawing room.'

Jo's heart thumped as she followed along behind them. She was under suspicion and it made her feel ill and frightened for her future.

By late evening, everyone had been questioned. When Jo came down to the kitchen, Mrs. Quigley was ranting on about the length of service she had done, and in all that time she had never taken so much as a loaf of bread without first clearing it with Madame. 'I don't take kindly to being mistrusted,' she said, snivelling into her handkerchief.

Jo placed an arm around the older woman, who had shown her kindness ever since she arrived in the house. 'Has someone said something to upset you, Mrs. Quigley?' Jo asked.

'Foster is sure it is one of us. Miss O'Breen has searched the maids' rooms and is searching mine right now. Can you believe it, Jo? I haven't climbed those stairs in years. Me poor old legs wouldn't be able.'

'Why, that's unfair.' Jo sat the older woman down.

'It's her room that should be searched,' screeched Rosie, pointing a finger at Jo.

'Yeah!' Molly agreed. 'She works upstairs, not us. It's not fair, why should she get away with it?'

Foster was passing the kitchen and heard Molly's outburst.

'Hold your tongue, girl. Any more talk like that and I'll be forced to call in the Garda.' He glared at Molly. 'Now get on with your work.' Straightening his shoulders, he walked away.

Frustration and anger eating away at her, Jo rushed from her accusers in time to see the butler walk briskly along the landing towards Madame Colbert's rooms. She wanted her room searched; she had nothing to hide. It was understandable that Rosie and Molly should suspect her. She was in an intolerable situation.

* * *

The butler stood by the open bedroom door, his arms folded. Jo stood next to him biting back tears of frustration as Miss O'Breen searched her room. Mistrusted and humiliated, Jo felt her colour rise as her personal belongings were searched, her undergarments flung onto the floor, her trinket box turned out. The leather music case – a recent gift from her employer – was shaken out vigorously and thrown onto her bed. Tears of anger stung her eyes.

Without speaking, the housekeeper pulled across a chair, allowing her access to the top of the wardrobe. Jo hadn't looked up there in months. The housekeeper stretched her arm and reached back as far as she could.

'You're wasting your time. I haven't taken the pearls,' Jo said, sobs catching the back of her throat.

'*Be quiet*,' the butler said. 'At least until the search is completed.' In the seconds that followed, Jo bit down hard on her lip. And when Miss O'Breen drew out something wrapped in a sheet of newspaper, Jo gasped. Throwing aside the paper, the housekeeper held up the precious pearls. Jo felt her body sway and she gripped the doorpost.

'I don't suppose you know anything about this?' Her tone sharp and accusing, the housekeeper stepped down from the chair.

'No, I don't. *I don't*. I've no idea how they got there.'

Foster gave her a suspicious glare. Humiliated to the core, Jo instinctively rushed into Madame's sitting room.

The bewildered woman glanced up. 'What is it?'

'I didn't take them, Madame Colbert. I would never steal from you.' Her face ashen, Jo shook with anger as Miss O'Breen entered.

'The pearls were found in Miss Kingsley's room, Madame.' The housekeeper held them up.

Madame Colbert's eyes glazed. She reached out and took the pearls, examining them for possible damage.

'I would never do such a thing,' Jo told her accusers.

Madame Colbert gripped the arms of her chair.

'What are your instructions, Madame?' Foster asked.

'I'd like you to leave us now,' she said in a low voice. 'I'll let you know my decision later.'

The housekeeper frowned. Foster coughed and straightened his shoulders, then he and Miss O'Breen left the room.

'Madame, I care too much about you to steal from you…I…'

'Please sit down, my dear. How do you think the pearls got into your room?'

Jo shook her head. Molly and Rosie had disliked her from the first day she'd come here. Had Molly done this? If so, how could she prove it? 'Someone must have planted them in my room, Madame; someone who obviously hates me very much.'

'To give you the benefit of any doubt, I must insist that Foster involve the police.'

* * *

Jo had no intentions of taking the blame, her good name blackened for something she didn't do. Her anger building, she entered the kitchen. Molly was pushing the wet sheets through the mangle and Rosie had her head in a cupboard.

'The sooner this business is cleared up the better,' Mrs. Quigley said. 'It does my heart no good at all, at all.'

'Oh, it will be.' Jo glanced towards the two maids, their heads close in conspiratorial whispers. 'If either of you had anything to do with this…' She paused. 'I'll see to it that you never work in service again. Madame Colbert is calling in the Garda, and the real culprit will be found.'

CHAPTER TWENTY-FIVE

The following day Foster was again summoned by Madame Colbert. As he made his way upstairs, he tried to make sense of the unfortunate business of the pearls. Miss Kingsley was a refined sort of girl, or so he'd thought, but her background was as impoverished as the other two maids and yet Madame insisted on protecting her. He decided to keep his own counsel for the time being.

He knocked and entered to find Madame warming her hands by the open fire. 'Oh, there you are, Foster!' She turned to face him. 'Have you called in the police?'

He stood before her, his hands clasped in front of him. 'No, Madame.'

'Why not?' Her fingers played with the beads around her neck. 'I want this cleared up immediately. I don't believe that Miss Kingsley hid my pearls in her room. It's preposterous.'

The butler cleared his throat. 'If I may suggest, Madame, as the pearls have been recovered undamaged, it might be best to deal with this internally.' He waited, noting her frown. 'If you believe Miss Kingsley is innocent, that's good enough for me.'

'How do you propose to deal with this, Foster?'

'In my experience, Madame, these things usually leak out sooner or later.'

'Do you have any suspicions as to who it might be?'

'Not yet, Madame.'

'I'm not happy, Foster. If you are no nearer to the truth in a couple of days, I will insist you let the police deal with it.'

'As you wish, Madame.'

* * *

When Jo went in to help Madame retire for the night, she couldn't help noticing how tired she looked. This business with the pearls had upset her as much as it had Jo. Molly and Rosie knew something, Jo felt sure of it. And unless she could prove it, she would remain a suspect forever.

With Madame Colbert settled, Jo went to her room, but sleep eluded her. She got up, took out her notepad and pen, and began to write; first to Ned, then changed her mind. He would only make a fuss on her behalf and make matters worse, so she wrote to Annie, pouring out everything in a long letter. It proved therapeutic and she slept.

When Jo went up with breakfast, Madame showed little interest. Her eyes were closed, her hair cascading over the white silk pillowcase.

'Won't you try a little something, Madame?' Jo gestured towards the lightly buttered toast cut into fingers.

She shook her head. 'Just a glass of water, dear.' And Jo helped ease her into a sitting position, placing an extra pillow behind her head. She poured water from the jug and handed it to her. After a few sips, Madame lay back down. Jo's concerns over her health increased. She placed an extra blanket over the bed.

'Would you like me to call the doctor, Madame?'

'No thank you, Jo. Can you see to it that my letter to Jean-Pierre is posted, and then can you ask Miss O'Breen to come up, please?'

'Yes, Madame.' Jo picked up the letter from the writing desk. She wondered if Madame Colbert had told her grandson about the pearls, and what he would make of it all. She hadn't written to him for a couple of weeks and owed him a letter.

It wasn't until later that afternoon, when she saw Madame Colbert's physician enter her room with Miss O'Breen, that Jo became concerned. When Jo questioned the housekeeper, she was told that the doctor had suggested a full time nurse to take care of Madame's needs.

'Does this mean I'm no longer needed?' Jo asked, a frown creasing her forehead.

'I couldn't say,' was the curt reply. 'You'll have to ask Madame Colbert.'

* * *

Hurt and puzzled as to why Madame had not confided in her, Jo placed a hot water jar in her bed. 'If there is anything else you need, you will ring, won't you, Madame?'

'Come here, *ma chérie!*' She patted the bed.

Jo perched on the end. 'No, come closer, dear. I spoke to Miss O'Breen because I didn't want to worry you. You're young and I don't want you to end up looking after an old lady.' It was as though she had read Jo's mind.

'But…but, Madame. I…' Tears filled her eyes.

'My dear, don't upset yourself.' She placed her hand over Jo's. 'It's nothing to do with you, or the pearls.' She forced a smile to her pale face.

'But I can look after you, Madame. You'll soon feel better.'

'I need medical help now, dear. My illness is not life-threatening, just old age. I've been feeling tired this long while.'

'Oh, Madame, I don't want to leave you. Please…please don't send me away.'

'You can stay here as long as you wish.'

'That's most kind of you. How would I occupy my time if I'm not looking after you?'

'Miss O'Breen will sort something out. Please don't worry!' She squeezed her eyes shut as if in deep pain, and lay back on her pillow. Jo leaned across the bed and kissed her forehead.

'Can I get you anything, Madame?'

She shook her head. 'I want to sleep now.'

Choking back tears, Jo left the room.

The following day, Jo in a despondent mood read a letter from Annie:

Dear Jo,

I was furious when I received your letter. Don't they realise that you would never do such a thing? You have nothing to fear. Your employer believes you and the others will realise that and apologise. If it was me, I'd get a solicitor to clear my name. Whoever did this might never own up and where will that leave you?

Let me know if there is anything I can do to help and when this is cleared up, come to America with me.

Yours, Annie

Jo smiled. Annie had never given up on her dream to go to America; with all this business of the pearls, Jo was tempted. She already had a valid passport from her trip to Paris. But how could she contemplate leaving the country when some people believed her to be a thief?

* * *

Until the nurse arrived, Jo continued to take Madame up her breakfast. She was up and dressed sitting by the fire, a thick rug around her thin frame. She had a letter in her hand and she smiled up at Jo. 'Jean Pierre sends his love,' she said, as though it was the most natural thing in the world. Jo wasn't sure how she should respond. 'Sit closer to the fire, my dear.'

'You look well. Are you feeling better?' Jo enquired cheerfully.

'It's just got better, my dear.'

The parrot called out Jo's name and made her smile. She went across and gave Lulu a nut and the bird settled down on her perch. 'Before I sit, I'll tidy your bedroom and then I'll come and read to you, Madame.' Jo picked up her dusters and proceeded towards the bedroom. She had just started to clean the cheval mirror when her employer called to her.

'I have something to ask you, Jo. Leave that and come here.'

Jo swallowed, fearful that the discussion might have something to do with Jean-Pierre; she still had no idea how she felt about him.

'Your friend, Annie! Has she gone to the States yet?'

It was the last thing Jo had expected her to say. 'She's due to leave next month, Madame.'

'Good! Now I want you to listen carefully to what I'm going to say. You've been like a daughter to me, and that's how I feel about you.' Tears glistened in her eyes. Jo opened her mouth to speak. 'Don't interrupt.' She patted Jo's hand. 'Go to America with Annie. Follow your dream and become a musician, fall in love and be happy. You can't do that stuck here looking after me.'

'But…but I love looking after you.' Tears welled in Jo's eyes.

'I only want what's best for you, Jo. Say you will, and make a sick old woman happy.'

'I can't go anywhere while I'm suspected of being a thief.'

'Your name will be cleared, have no fear of that, my dear. Promise me you'll do as I ask?'

How could she refuse? As tears welled in her eyes, she said in a quiet voice, 'I promise.'

'Good. Now leave me, my dear. Miss O'Breen will find you something to do.'

* * *

When Jo passed Foster in the corridor, he avoided her gaze and she hesitated to ask him when he intended to call in the Garda. Although Madame believed she hadn't hidden the pearls in her room, she felt disappointed that nothing was being done to clear her name. Jo couldn't concentrate on anything other than how she was going to bring the culprit to heel. If she carried out what was on her mind, she would surely get the sack and have to leave without a reference. But she was determined to prove her innocence.

By evening, her mind was in turmoil. Madame Colbert's illness concerned her greatly, particularly as she intended to employ a nurse. How ill was she? Jo wasn't sure if Mrs. Quigley knew any more than she did herself, and Madame's health wasn't discussed below stairs. If she couldn't look after her employer, Jo felt no inclination to work in any other capacity, with mealy-mouthed maids and staff who – without saying anything – still branded her as a thief.

Her employer had shown her more consideration than her mother ever had. Right now she felt upset, confused and vulnerable, afloat like a ship at sea, and she wished she hadn't promised Madame she would go to America.

That night, as Foster checked the premises before retiring, he saw Molly and Rosie giggling on the landing above him. They were so engrossed in their tittle-tattle that they didn't see him approach.

'That'll teach her to think she's better than us,' Molly was saying.

'I still don't think you should have…' Rosie said.

'You want 'er to go, don't ye?' Molly stopped abruptly as Foster approached them.

'And who, may I ask, are you referring to?'

'Oh, we're just gossiping about a neighbour, Mr. Foster,' Rosie said.

'Why aren't you in bed?'

'We're…we're just going, Foster,' Molly said.

'I'll see you both in my office first thing in the morning. Is that understood?'

'Yes, sir,' Molly muttered.

Glaring at them both, he said, 'Get to your beds.'

* * *

The next day, Jo, tired from lack of sleep, was putting the finishing touches to her hair when she heard a knock on her door. Opening it, her heart skipped a beat when she saw Miss O'Breen standing before her. The image flashed across her mind of the last time the housekeeper had stood in her room, when she had accused her of hiding Madame's pearls. Was she about to accuse her again?

'What is it, Miss O'Breen? Is…is Madame unwell?'

'No. I believe she's quite well.' The woman's face was flushed and Jo wasn't sure if she was angry or upset. 'Foster would like you to come to Madame's sitting room straight away.'

Jo's heart sank and she swallowed as she closed her door

and followed the housekeeper along the corridor to Madame Colbert's quarters.

Foster and Madame were seated and Molly and Rosie were standing, their hands together in front of them, eyes downcast.

'What is this all about?' Jo asked.

'Come,' Madame said, 'sit here, *ma petite*.' Jo felt her legs shake as if she was on trial. 'Continue, please, Foster,' Madame said.

The butler cleared his throat. 'As you all know, allegations have been made against Miss Kingsley, and we are all here to get at the truth. Now these two maids here have something to confess, isn't that right, Rosie and Molly?'

Jo felt her stomach start to relax.

'This has nothing to do with me,' Rosie retorted. 'Ask her.' She turned towards Molly.

'She made me do it. She said Jo would get the sack and–' She began to bawl.

'That's not true. You're a liar, Molly Connor.'

'Hold your tongue, Rosie. We'll have no name calling here.'

Jo let out a huge sigh. So she had been right all along. Anger coursed through her at the callousness of the pair.

Madame Colbert's knuckles whitened as she gripped her walking cane.

'Come here, both of you. Now which one of you went through my personal possessions, took my pearls, and then hid them in Miss Kingsley's room?'

'I had nothing to do with that, Madame,' Rosie insisted.

'You laughed when I told you. You said it served her right for taking your job!' Molly sneered.

'What you did was despicable,' Madame continued. 'You tried to ruin a decent young woman's character, and you both ought to be ashamed of yourselves.' She paused and closed her eyes. 'I want you to leave my employ as from today.'

'But, Madame...' Rosie, a defiant look on her face, glared at Molly. 'You're not going to believe her, are you?'

'Collect your things and leave immediately,' the butler said, and ushered them both from the room.

Miss O'Breen placed her hands over her face. 'I'm so sorry about this, Madame, and my sincere apologies, Miss Kingsley.'

Jo swallowed back tears. As far as she was concerned, she would never have the same respect for Miss O'Breen or, for that matter, for the butler.

CHAPTER TWENTY-SIX

A thin waif of a girl replaced Molly as scullery maid, and Mrs. Quigley said she did twice as much work as her predecessor. Rosie's replacement was a housemaid with six years experience who had been forced to leave her employment when her mistress died. After a week, things settled down. But, despite the apologies, Jo couldn't forget that terrible day nor the repulsive glare of the butler and the mistrust in the housekeeper's eyes.

Jo wasn't sure how she felt about Nurse Cooney, who wore a blue and white starched uniform and liked her eggs hard boiled. But she was forced to admit that within days of her arrival, the woman's professional care had brought about a marked improvement in the elderly lady. With Madame's nurse in constant attendance, Jo felt bereft. She longed for the afternoons when Nurse Cooney took a break and she could sit and read to Madame for an hour.

With only two weeks left before Annie was due to sail, Madame Colbert urged Jo to buy her ticket. Realising her days at the beautiful Chateau Colbert were coming to an end, Jo's mind was made up. Overcome with sadness, she said goodbye in private to the woman she had grown to love.

'Let me know how you get on, my dear.' Madame Colbert held out a hand. 'Keep in touch.'

Jo, determined to stay in control of her emotions, felt a lump form at the back of her throat. 'I'll never forget you, Madame.' She forced a smile and, bending down, she kissed her tenderly on the cheek.

Later, alone in her room, Jo gave way to her pent-up emotions.

* * *

The task ahead of her wouldn't be easy, she knew that, but the sooner she got it over with the better. Cissy was her first port of call. Her sister opened the door to her with baby Patrick in her arms, trying to get him to stop crying.

'Have I picked an awkward time?' Jo said. But the sweet smell of baking made her feel she was expected.

'You're early, that's all. And Larry's on the late shift.'

'I've decided to go to America and I couldn't wait to tell you,' Jo explained, taking the baby from Cissy. Jo rocked him gently and he stopped crying.

'You can't be serious. America, my eye,' Cissy laughed.

'Why not? I've saved enough money. Besides, I'm going with Annie.' She placed baby Patrick against her shoulder and he sucked his thumb.

'You're mad, you know! And that Annie O'Toole needs her head looking at, dragging you halfway across the world.' She shook her head. 'Ned can put a stop to this, at least until you're twenty-one,' Cissy said, pushing herself up out of the chair. She put the kettle on and placed cups on the table.

'Ned's happy for me. Why can't you be?'

'I'm sorry, Jo, but it's such a long way. I'll miss you, especially with another babby on the way.'

'Oh, Cissy!' Jo placed the now sleeping child down in his pram. 'You must be pleased. How's Larry taken it?'

'He doesn't know. I've only just found out.' Cissy pursed her lips. 'If he's not working late, he spends his time at the public house. Some days he doesn't see Patrick at all.'

'Have you two had a falling out?' And when her sister shrugged, it confirmed Jo's suspicions. She was well aware of Cissy's volatile temperament.

As the child slept, the women chatted over tea and homemade scones. 'Does Ma know you're emigrating?'

'Yes, but I guess there'll be hell to pay before I sail. Can I stay here tonight, Cissy?'

'You don't need to ask. Sorry, we haven't a spare bed.'

'I'll be grand here on the couch.'

* * *

Cissy had gone to bed when Jo heard Larry coughing as he came in the back door and went upstairs to bed. Larry's cough was just like her stepfather's when he had TB. She prayed that Larry would be okay for Cissy's sake, especially now with a new bairn on the way.

Jo slept surprisingly well and only woke to the sound of Larry's cough as he passed up the lane to work. She doubted he'd had anything to eat, and felt guilty that he'd gone without his breakfast because he hadn't wanted to disturb her.

'Did you sleep well?' Cissy asked, when she came into the room, yawning as she ambled over to the stove.

'Grand, thanks!' Pleased to see her sister in a happier mood, she asked, 'Is Patrick still asleep? I never heard a peep out of him all night.'

'Yeah, he's a good babby. He'll sleep for another hour,' Cissy replied, pouring them both a mug of tea.

'How long has Larry had that cough?'

'It's only come on him this past week. I'll get him some cough mixture today.' She sat down next to Jo.

'Have you told him about the baby?' Jo asked, sipping her tea.

'Yeah,' Cissy chuckled. 'He's delighted at the news. Picking out names already he is.'

Jo smiled, pleased to see the spark return to her sister's eyes. 'Well, I've got to go. I'm meeting Annie in town.' She kissed her sister's cheek and stood up.

'Are you really going ahead with this idea, Jo?' Cissy placed her elbows on the table.

'Yes. And try not to worry. It'll be grand.'

'I doubt that. I doubt that very much,' Cissy muttered.

* * *

Jo arranged to meet Annie in the city to go to the ticket office. She couldn't eat with excitement, and her tummy kept doing somersaults as she made her way across town. But when she saw her friend outside Cleary's department store, a huge smile lit up her delicate features, and any remaining doubts vanished from her mind.

'Well, are you all set to get that ticket?' Annie asked. 'I hope we can still get you a passage on the same day.' Linking arms, they walked towards the ticket office.

'My God, Annie!' Jo exclaimed. 'I can't believe I'm doing this. Apart from Ned, I'm not getting much encouragement from the rest of the family.' She sighed.

'Mine were just the same at first,' Annie assured her. 'But they'll get used to it by the time we sail. Come on,' she urged. 'Fingers crossed you're not too late.'

As they moved along the queue, Jo felt a fluttering in her stomach, and when at last she finally secured a third-class ticket on the same passage as Annie, she felt elated. It was due to depart from Cobh in Cork on the first of May.

'I've done it now, Annie,' she cried excitedly, kissing her ticket. Madame Colbert and Jean-Pierre pushed to the far corners of her mind, Jo's thoughts were full of her new life in America. Their heads in the clouds, the two friends rushed off to Bewley's to celebrate and discuss their plans.

* * *

Back at Ned's, Jo rushed in full of excitement. 'Ned! Ned! Where are you?' she called. Her mother's disgruntled face met her in the kitchen doorway, stopping her in her tracks. 'Isn't Ned home yet?'

Beanie nodded. 'He won't be long.'

'You can forget this business of America, Jo-Jo.' Her mother waved her arms dismissively.

'Too late, Ma, I've bought my ticket.' She held it up. Beanie smiled, shaking her head, and carried on peeling vegetables.

'I won't give my permission. Do you hear me?' Kate's voice rose.

Jo sat down and looked her mother in the eye. 'I don't need your permission, Ma. I'll be twenty-one in a few months; I can make my own mind up.' She knew Kate would be missing her wages from the Chateau, but she couldn't go on supporting her forever.

The slap was unexpected and sharp across Jo's face. 'Deserting your family, giving up a perfectly good job, and for what?' Kate snarled. Stunned, the excitement drained from Jo's face. But before she could answer, Ned walked through the door, his face furious.

'That's enough, Ma! I could hear you in the hall. Leave the girl alone. It's proud of her you should be, not berating her every chance you get.' He removed his cap and banged it down on the table, then plodded across to wash his hands at the sink.

'That's right, side with her,' their mother hissed. 'Well, I won't sign any consent form.'

Jo swallowed the lump in her throat. Ned went over to where his mother was still standing glaring at Jo. 'You won't need to, Mother, I'll do the signing.' And he sat down next to Jo.

'She'll never come back, and it'll be your fault, Ned Kingsley. It's not fitting for two women on their own to go traipsing across the world.'

'I came back, didn't I?' Then he muttered, 'Although God knows why.'

'Well, she won't be welcome back here,' Kate ranted.

Ned got to his feet and ushered his mother out of the kitchen.

Beanie came over and joined Jo at the table. 'Look, Jo. I don't agree with your mother,' she said, pressing a cold flannel to Jo's face. 'But it's a hard journey crossing the Atlantic, and I went with my family,' she said, lifting the flannel to look at the girl's burning face.

'Ouch!' Jo winced, as her face began to sting. 'I'll be grand. I'm not going alone, Annie will be with me.'

Ned came back minus his mother. 'I know you're excited, pet, and I guess if you're going, you may as well go with Annie.' He smiled. 'Show us that ticket.' Taking it from Jo, he frowned. 'This is a third-class!' he exclaimed. 'Why didn't you buy a second-class ticket, I would have helped you.'

'I was lucky to get one at all. Annie purchased her ticket ages ago, and we want to be together. Why?'

'Well, it's just that the journey is long and debilitating. And the inspection at Ellis Island can be humiliating, especially for women.' He rubbed the stubble on his chin. 'But don't worry, you and Annie have a clean bill of health, so you shouldn't encounter any real problems.' His smile reassured her, and she smiled in spite of the pain in her face.

* * *

The day before they were due to depart on their Atlantic crossing, Ned and Beanie threw a party to give Jo and Annie the send off they felt they deserved. In spite of her misgivings about her sister leaving, Cissy attended with Larry and baby Patrick.

Kate, still begrudging Jo her freedom, came along with Aggie and most of the neighbours joined them. Ned, who could never resist dancing whenever he heard Irish music, danced with Jo and Annie in turn, swinging them around until they were dizzy, falling onto the sofa in fits of laughter.

Beanie, pregnant with their first child, was called on several times to sing and was finally persuaded by Aggie.

'Give us a burst there, Beanie,' she called. 'Wheesht, pray silence now. Give the girl a bit of room!' Aggie shouted. Ned winked at his wife and put an encouraging arm around her shoulders. Looking up at him, she took a deep breath and began to sing.

'If you loved me half as much as I love you
You wouldn't worry me half as much as you do.
You're nice to me when there's no-one else around
You only build me up to let me down...'

Beanie had a lovely singing voice, and she entertained everyone by wagging her finger at Ned as she sang, and finished to a rapturous applause. For Jo and Annie it had been an enjoyable evening. Kate had said nothing to upset them, because she had fallen into a drunken stupor in a corner of the room.

The two boys, James and Liam – now ten and twelve – threw their arms around Jo and she promised them she'd keep in touch. They were staying more and more with Ned and Beanie, and Jo was glad of that. Soon they would want to leave home, and she didn't blame them.

It had been a strange night of tears and goodbyes, with friendly advice from neighbours. Tears filled Jo's eyes as she kissed her sleeping mother, whom she felt had never really loved her. Ned noticed her distress and hurried to her side. 'Don't worry about Ma, Jo. I'll see she's okay.'

'I know you will, dearest Ned,' she said, falling into his outstretched arms. 'I've left your address with Madame Colbert, Ned. Will you keep me informed on how she is until I get settled?'

'Course I will. I might even pay the old dear a visit.'

'And, Ned, will you do one more thing for me?'

'Name it!'

'Please send me a piece of shamrock on St. Patrick's Day.' She wept as he held her tightly, kissing the top of her head.

'You can always come back if things don't work out,' he said, and tugged a strand of her short stylish hair. 'You have Mrs. Miller's address? She'll look after you and tell you where to find work.'

'Thanks, Ned. I'll miss you,' she cried. 'You'll write, won't you? Promise?'

'I'll write, but you, young lady, will be too busy seeing the wonders of New York to write back.'

'No I won't, Ned Kingsley.' She nudged him with her elbow. They clung together in a last embrace before he broke away.

They spent the following night at Annie's, giving her family the opportunity to say farewell to the two women; so brave, they said, crossing the Atlantic Ocean on their own. Annie had been as tearful as Jo had been, parting from her family for the first time. Annie's mother cried bitter tears as they left.

When they arrived at Kingsbridge Station for the train to Cobh, Jo was still overcome with emotion. 'Oh Annie, will we ever see them again?'

'Of course we will, now come on,' Annie said, putting on a brave face.

CHAPTER TWENTY-SEVEN

May 1925

The two girls arrived in Cobh, Cork, and made their way down to the ship. It was warm with an overcast sky. Small groups of people had already formed on the quayside to bid farewell to loved ones.

'I never realised so many were still leaving Ireland.' Jo scanned the faces in the crowd. 'I'm glad Ned didn't come to see us off, Annie, it would turn me over having to say goodbye again.'

'Me an' all.' They joined the end of a long queue. 'We're not a minority; look at the number of women going on board.'

'They've got husbands, Annie.'

'Well, there's bound to be some women like us. Besides, it's a well-known fact that the Irish were emigrating long before the famine.' They shuffled along the never-ending queue in floral summer dresses and warm cardigans, lugging their large suitcases, coats slung over their arm. 'Aren't you at all worried, Annie?'

'No more than anyone else. Cheer up, we'll soon be on board.' And they heaved their way up the gangplank. They moved along narrow passages packed with people, clambered over baggage, and stepped between people cramming the stairways, until they finally located the baggage compartment. Relieved of their luggage, they made their way back on deck for a last glimpse of the land they were leaving behind. People were still coming on board and the ship was heaving. They watched the poignant reactions of the men and women around them waving, cheering and weeping at the same time.

Jo and Annie waved goodbye to Ireland, their emotions

heightening until tears trickled down both their faces. Annie put a comforting arm around her friend's shoulder, both of them too choked to speak. They stayed on deck until they were completely surrounded by the ocean and Cobh and Ireland had vanished from view, then battled their way down below deck to the women's dormitories. Galvanised buckets were scattered between the wooden bunks. Down in the bowels of the ship, it was stifling and the lighting was poor; nothing like the luxury she had experienced when she had travelled to Paris with Madame Colbert.

Two hours into the voyage, they were all awakened by the storm sending high waves lashing the sides of the ship. The large pipes above them creaked and groaned as the ship tossed from side to side. A feeling of being propelled upwards and then down was making Jo feel sick. Women around them were throwing up, and before long Jo was vomiting along with Annie.

The ship lurched and Jo slipped off her bunk. She lay on the floor next to Annie, her arms outstretched, while sick and slime from overturned buckets seeped around their legs

and the hems of their dresses. Jo didn't care; she just wanted to die. Some of the women began to pray, but Jo couldn't summon up the energy. The sound of heavy objects crashing and rolling across the deck above them was frightening.

At times, terrified for their lives, Jo and Annie huddled together. The stench all around them made Jo feel worse, and the sour bile left a taste in her mouth.

Annie sat upright, her back against the wall; the movement made her heave. 'This is my fault for talking you into coming with me.'

'I wanted to come.' Jo's voice quivered. 'But, in case we should drown, I've a confession to make.'

'I'm not going looking for a priest! Just say an act of contrition.'

'No, you don't understand. Years ago, I returned a library book damaged by my little brother. I concealed it with some other books and never told you.'

'I don't remember,' Annie said. 'It doesn't matter now.'

'I was frightened I'd lose my membership at the library,' Jo went on, 'just like I'm frightened now, Annie.' She moved closer. 'Surely to God this storm can't last much longer.'

* * *

When at last the storm subsided, the women were exhausted. Jo and Annie washed in the basins provided then lay on their bunks and slept, ignoring the stench and conditions surrounding them. Later, still weak after their ordeal, they went on deck to ask for fresh blankets and to change their clothes. There was vomit everywhere as they sidestepped their way to their luggage. And it was days before they felt like eating.

'I thought we were going to die before we ever reached America,' Jo said.

In the days that followed, they joined their fellow passengers on deck for some fresh air and later ate their meals of potatoes, eggs, fish or stringy meat. As the days passed, they listened to the many stories of people fleeing their harsh poverty-stricken lives; some so desperate they were willing to risk anything in the hope of a better life.

They ran into more storms during the harrowing Atlantic crossing, each one milder than the one before until the women became less fearful. On these occasions, Jo and Annie stayed below deck groaning in the miseries of seasickness.

When, after three weeks, the ship sailed into New York Harbour, the stench from below deck was unbearable. Attendants came in with buckets of disinfectant and later helped some of the emigrants who were so weak from their long transatlantic journey. Jo and Annie climbed up from below deck to engrave on their minds their first glimpse of America; they managed to conjure up a relieved cheer as whistles blew to herald their safe arrival. Above them, the city's skyline loomed like a huge mountain range. The harbour teemed with activity and moving vessels, exhilarating their spirits. After the heat and stench, the air felt pure, and Jo breathed in deeply.

'Isn't it beautiful, Jo?' Annie's eyes misted when she saw the mute, but powerful, welcome of the Statue of Liberty.

'Yes, oh yes!' Jo cried, her hair blowing in the warm breeze. 'We've made it, Annie. Isn't it wonderful?' They hugged as excitement spread throughout the ship. 'Oh, look!' Jo pointed to a large red brick building on Ellis Island with its four towers. 'Soon we'll be on American soil.'

Disembarking was slow, and before they were allowed to leave the ship, they were given numbered tags to pin to their clothes. These indicated the manifest page and line number on which their names appeared.

'I feel like merchandise priced down at the sales,' Annie said, making Jo laugh.

All new arrivals had to pass through an inspection process. This was nerve-wracking. They queued in long lines stretching from the dock into the main building, winding their way up the stairways. Some who were too ill didn't make it that far.

Jo and Annie were jostled towards the echoing registry room, where doctors waited. Intimidating inspectors, wearing starched collars and heavy serge jackets, stood behind high desks watching for any signs of disabilities. Jo was astounded when an official lifted an exhausted child from its mother's arms to check that it could walk unaided, while a fatigued woman, helped by her husband – desperate to suppress a persistent cough – was taken aside by the officials.

The overpowering surge of so many nations desperate for access through the gates was, to Jo, a stark reminder of the Irish famine victims of eighty years ago, who had passed through here before them. After what seemed like hours, they were finally taken separately into a small cubicle and examined by a nurse. Jo's face reddened when asked if she'd ever been intimate with a man and if she'd ever had a baby. They examined her mouth and Jo felt the bile again rise in her throat.

The frightening possibility of exclusion remained with the two women as they passed along the line to be interrogated separately about their age, occupation, marital status, destination, and – most importantly as women – their means of supporting themselves.

After all that, they were left to sit around for ages while they waited to hear if they would be allowed through. Jo was beginning to despair. 'Annie, what if we don't–'

'Don't even think that. I'd never face that journey back.' There was a catch in her voice.

Jo swallowed. 'I never expected this. It looks like a dispensary for sick people. Do you think they'll pass us as fit?'

'I don't know, Jo. They've let very few go so far.'

Two hours later, Jo and Annie were taken away one at a time and asked to read a long passage. Having satisfied the officials, they were told they were free to enter. Overwhelmed with relief, both women wept.

CHAPTER TWENTY-EIGHT

Jo and Annie were directed to the railroad ticket office where they purchased two tickets to the Bronx. Exhausted but happy, they found themselves outside on the streets of New York caught up in the thrill and excitement of their new surroundings. Jo dropped her case at her feet, and stood craning her neck upwards at the tall skyscrapers, the likes of which she had never seen before.

'Gosh! Annie, can you believe this place? How insignificant we look against these tall buildings.' She circled her head, scanning the side streets to the right and to the left, where electric trolley trams trundled past at speed.

'Good God!' Annie shouted over the noise. 'It's positively dangerous to cross the street with all this traffic. Don't you go wandering off, Jo, I'd never find you again.' There were so many places advertising food and the various appetizing smells made their mouths water.

'Let's get something to eat, I'm wall falling.' Jo pointed to Beck's food and sandwich bar, and they carried their cases across the street and went inside. The place was already packed with people who had just come off the ship and it was noisy with nowhere to sit. They didn't stay long, just long enough to drink their tea and eat their ham sandwich.

Somewhat refreshed, they made their way to the train. The steam trains chugging and clanging their way along the banks of the east river to the various points around New York, left behind a pungent smell. The subway was crowded and they were jostled by workers intent on getting to their place of work unhindered by emigrants. When they emerged once more on the vibrant streets, they stopped to read Ned's directions.

'It's this way,' Annie pointed, as the latest automobiles roared past and prosperous faces stared out at them. Trams clanked along the busy streets and traffic rattled past them as they plodded their way along the sidewalk. After a few enquiries, they finally found the right direction. Fatigued, their gait slower, they moved along passing tenements four and five storeys high. Harsh sounds of familiar voices selling their wares alerted Jo, and her hand rushed to her face as young boys, holes in the seats of their breeches, ran ragged in the street.

'Please don't tell me that we've come all this way to *this*?' Jo almost cried. These streets were indeed a dismal sight in comparison to their earlier vision of New York.

'Of course not,' Annie retorted.

Jo, feeling hot and sticky, looked down at her own dishevelled appearance. 'God, Annie, don't we look a sight? I'd love a long soak in a real bath.' She put down her case and flexed her arm before picking it up again.

'Me too! It won't be much further now. Look, doesn't that say 134th Street, the next block up? All we have to do now is find number 209,' Annie said, forcing a smile. They moved faster now in their excitement to reach the lodging house.

They were shattered when they finally arrived at the three-storey boarding house of Mrs. Miller, and hobbled up the steps to the door, their sighs audible. Jo knocked and the door swung open to reveal the bustling, apron-clad figure of Mrs. Miller. She welcomed them with open arms and a cheery smile.

* * *

The following morning, Mrs. Miller – a chatty woman with a perm, and a large mole on her chin – placed a delicious cooked breakfast in front of them. The breakfast room was situated to the left of the tunnelled hallway and the parlour on the right. As they tucked in, Mrs. Miller asked, 'Is your employment far from here, Annie?' Her Irish accent was still strong after years of living in the Bronx.

'To be honest, I'm not too sure, Mrs. Miller.' Annie pulled a letter from her purse and passed it to her. It had Mr. Thomas's address printed on the top.

'Oh, not far, only a block away,' she lilted. 'That'll be grand for the two of yeh now. What have you got in mind, Jo? Sure, there's plenty of little jobs round and about.' Then she added, 'I'm always looking for help meself, if you get stuck.' She chuckled.

'Thanks, Mrs. Miller, I'd be very grateful for anything really.'

'What do yeh's think of the New World then? Isn't it just grand?' She sat down and poured the tea. 'Ned and Beanie loved it here. By the way, how's the pair of them?' she asked, placing mugs of tea in front of them.

'Oh Beanie's expecting their first baby,' Jo said.

'That's grand. Sure, they'll make good parents. Well, I'd better stop gassin'.' She piled the tray and went out swaying under its weight.

Jo liked Mrs. Miller and she could see why Ned had recommended her lodgings. Annie stayed at Mrs. Miller's a couple of days, before taking up her position as nanny to Mr. Thomas's children.

* * *

With Annie working only a block away, they could catch up with each other most evenings. And now it was Jo's turn to find a job. Domestic service was all she'd ever known, but right now she wasn't fussy, as long as it paid her board and lodgings. Meandering along the crowded sidewalks, it wasn't easy to figure out the lay of this vast place. She felt a new freedom in being here and the sun was warm on her face. The sights, sounds and smells challenged her at every turn. Fearful of losing her bearings, she walked a few blocks at first, but felt as though she had walked for miles.

The buzz of the city with its wide streets, department stores, and magazine and newspaper stands on every corner, fascinated her. She thought it would be impossible to find a country more deluged with newspapers. She picked one up and handed the man a few cents. 'Can you point me in the direction of the employment exchange, please?' she asked.

'First left, three blocks along on your right,' he bellowed above the roar of the trams trailing past.

Jo found the average New Yorker courteous and willing to divulge information. Turning left, she hadn't gone far when she came across a small music shop. A large piano took pride of place in the window, reminding her of Madame Colbert. The advertisement in the corner of the window caught her eye. '*Part-time evening shop assistant urgently wanted to start soon.*' Crossing her fingers, she went inside. When she came back out, she had a smile on her face. She had no need to go any further, and she rushed back to tell Mrs. Miller.

With a secure part-time job that paid well, Jo wrote letters making tentative enquiries at The American Academy of Music, Manhattan School of Music, and Julliard School of Music. Armed with prospectuses for all three, she pored over them in the evening with Mrs. Miller.

Jo found working at the music shop exciting. It was a popular place, selling large and small musical instruments, sheet music and records, and attracted people from all over New York. It provided her enough income to get by, but it would not be enough to pay for her music tuition, should she be lucky to get a place.

Jo dressed in a fashionable black skirt pleated from the hips down, and a white frilly blouse for work. She liked to look smart and was glad she had a reasonable wardrobe; from now on, she would have to budget carefully.

'Gosh! You could easily pass for a model with your figure, Jo. Wish I was slim like you,' Annie remarked one evening when she popped in to see Jo at the music shop.

'Don't be daft. You always look great,' Jo said, placing the records back in alphabetical order.

'Even so,' Annie sighed. 'I'd never fit into one of those new fashionable skirts.' She glanced down at her out-of-date one. 'We could go shopping at the weekend,' she said to Jo, as the shop began to fill up again.

People of all races and colours visited the shop, and Jo did her best to understand the different accents. Only occasionally did she have to call on her boss, Mr. O'Rourke, to help with an Italian or Chinese customer. She found the variety of customers who frequented the shop in the evenings exciting – many were artists and writers; most of them lived in Greenwich Village, an area of Manhattan.

While Jo waited to hear from one of her chosen schools, she spent time in libraries reading American history. She visited many churches and found the imposing structure of St. Patrick's awesome. Ned had been right when he'd said she would have no time to write. The weeks just flew past, and before they knew it, they had been in the Bronx a whole month.

* * *

It was Annie's day off and they'd arranged to meet in their favourite café in downtown Manhattan. 'Have you heard anything from the music schools yet?'

'No. Not yet.' Jo sighed.

'Did they say anything about grants?' Annie asked, curiously.

'No, but I'll make enquiries.' The summer sun had put a glow on her cheeks.

'You look well. Have you heard from home?'

'Ned's written and Madame Colbert's was just a short note.' She shrugged. 'Letters make me homesick. What about you?'

'My mother's written three letters. I miss her, but remember, we said we'd feel like this for a while. Everyone must feel this way when they leave home.'

Jo nodded. 'Do you still like working for Mr. Thomas? What are the children like?' Jo leaned on her elbow, her hand under her chin, watching Annie.

'Well,' she said slowly. 'Mr. Thomas is very American, and sports a moustache. He works in textiles.' She bit her lip. 'Now, the children are a bit precocious. Harvey is six and Ella is five. They both like their own way, especially Harvey. But I'll soon have them eating out of my hand, don't you worry.' She smiled good-humouredly.

'They're probably spoiled, losing their mother like that.'

'Umm…' Annie nodded. 'They also have a woman, Mrs. Jolly, who cooks and cleans, so it's nice really.' She sipped her coffee and ran her tongue around her top lip. 'Let's meet here every week on my day off, Jo. You can let me know how you're getting on.'

'Okay!'

'If you're lucky to get a place at one of the schools, you can study during the day and work in the evening. Most of the shops stay open late, you know.'

'I want a place so much, Annie. I don't care how hard I have to work. I'm determined to get my degree.'

Finishing their drinks, they went outside and took a leisurely stroll along the wide pavement, craning their necks to look up at the tall skyscrapers. Annie liked the tall Woolworth building with its Gothic-style detail, and Jo said that City Hall, with its French Renaissance detail, reminded her of Paris. New York had many movie palaces, and Annie treated Jo to a showing of the movie *The Jazz Singer*.

'Aren't the movies spectacular over here, Annie?' Jo remarked when they came outside again. 'I don't think I'd like to go back to my old life now, would you?'

'Not likely! But I do miss my mother. And you're missing Ned and Madame Colbert.' Annie's keen observation surprised Jo.

'Yes, I am.'

'What about Jean-Pierre?'

'I don't expect to hear from him. I've not left a forwarding address. It's best that way, Annie.' Then she smiled brightly, nudging her friend. 'Let's walk down and watch the lights twinkling on Brooklyn Bridge.' Manhattan at night was like a fairyland, a place they both said they would never tire of.

Before she returned to her lodgings, Jo picked up one of the many New York newspapers, determined to familiarise herself with the present government. Mrs. Miller was still up. She had just finished setting up the breakfast room for the morning.

'Oh hello, Jo,' she smiled pleasantly. 'Another newspaper! You'll ruin them lovely blue eyes of yours, with all that reading,' she said, as Jo spread the paper out on the coffee table.

'Look at this picture of President Coolidge,' Jo said, turning the paper round for her to see. 'He looks rather severe, don't you think? But his wife, Grace, has a pleasant smile.' When Jo got a disgruntled reply, she knew that Mrs. Miller – unlike Madame Colbert – had no time for politics. How she missed the old lady and their political debates.

Jo continued to read about the New Deals which Governor Alfred E. Smith was proposing, including an eight-hour working day. But what interested her most was a State Aid for health and education. How different it was to Ireland and the poor laws that existed over there. But then there was no comparison; America was a big country and rich, by all accounts. She thought herself very lucky to be here.

CHAPTER TWENTY-NINE

Turned down by two of the music schools, Jo was beginning to despair when the final letter arrived. She rushed into the kitchen, took a knife from the drawer, and slit open the envelope. It was, as she expected, from the Manhattan School of Music. Her heart beating fast, she quickly scanned down until she came to the word – accepted. She kissed the letter and let out a loud whoop of joy.

Mrs. Miller came running from the drawing room. 'Jo, what is it?' she frowned. 'Not another let-down?'

'I've had an acceptance from Manhattan School of Music. Isn't it wonderful, Mrs. Miller?'

'Congratulations! That's good news, Jo.' She glanced at the letter. 'It's expensive.'

'Yes, I'll have to get another job.' However, she couldn't wait to tell Annie her good news. Smiling, she dashed up to her room to get ready for her evening shift at the shop.

When she got home, a letter with an Irish stamp had been pushed underneath her door. She recognised Ned's handwriting.

Beanie had given birth to a baby boy and they had named him Joseph. Jo cried when she read that if it had been a girl, they would have named her Josephine. It was too late to wake Mrs. Miller and tell her the news of the new baby, so she slept happily, hugging the letter to her.

* * *

The building where Jo began her studies was impressive. It took her a whole week to find her way around, getting lost in the corridors, some days as she went from tutorials to lectures. But students and tutors were friendly and helped her settle in. She was an eager student determined to succeed.

Any free periods she spent studying or visiting the school's library. It was about this time that she began reading American authors. Theodore Dreisi's novels about the injustice of the social classes were of great interest to her, and she read both *Sister Carrie*, and *An American Tragedy*. She liked his writing and empathised with his characters. She read many others, including the poet and novelist Gertrude Stein. Her character study of three women in *Three Lives*, Jo read twice. These American writers covered most of the issues that fascinated her, and gave her a broader view of America and the American way of life.

When she discovered she would get no help with tuition fees, her heart sank. Mrs. Miller had been right – it wasn't cheap. Keen to succeed, she hadn't thought it out properly. How was she going to find the fees for the next semester? The funds she had come to America with had all but disappeared and, after she had paid her board and lodgings, she found herself struggling. The money she earned at the music shop wasn't going to be enough now, and it wouldn't be easy finding something with the hours to suit. Otherwise, how was she going to continue her studies? Mrs. Miller had offered to take her on at one stage, and Jo could see that her landlady was hard pushed at times, especially in the mornings. She'd ask her first, before looking elsewhere.

'Sure, I wouldn't say no to a bit of help in the mornin's,' Mrs. Miller said, pursing her lips. 'But I can't pay much, love,' she frowned, 'unless, you could help out during the day as well. Ah, but that would interfere with your studies.'

'I've two half days, and I could hurry home on the other days. Please, Mrs. Miller, I need the money.'

'Oh, go on then,' Mrs. Miller conceded, nodding her head. 'You can start in the mornin', but I can't see how you're going to pull it all in, Jo.' She was carrying a tray of breakfasts into the guests. The appetising smell reminded Jo of what she was missing, turning down a cooked breakfast, in favour of toast and marmalade to save money.

'Thanks, Mrs. Miller.' Grabbing her shoulder bag and textbooks, she left the house.

* * *

When Jo woke the following morning, there was a nip in the air. Autumn was well and truly upon them, or 'the fall' as Mrs. Miller called it. Jo tried to stay positive that with Mrs. Miller's help she would be able to afford to pay her college fees on time.

With only three other guests in the house besides herself and Mrs. Miller, she was surprised at the amount of work that needed doing throughout the day. The landlady tackled downstairs, and Jo was expected to clean the two upper floors. The bedrooms were hard work, and she hated the smell of Jeyes Fluid that Mrs. Miller insisted she pour down the toilets every morning. Some days she rushed through the work, fearing she would be late for her morning class and later for her evening job at the shop. If she skimped on the dusting, Mrs. Miller, who had eyes like a hawk, was sure to bring it to her attention. In between, she had to find time to study.

When Annie heard of Jo's predicament, she offered to sub her, but Jo wouldn't hear of it. 'I have to stand on my own feet. I'm going to have to do this for a few years if I'm to get my degree.'

'You'll run yourself ragged, so you will.' But when Annie saw that defiant look, she knew she would have to let Jo try. 'Well, if you change your mind.'

'Thanks, Annie.' Jo had had no idea it was going to be so tough, but she had no intentions of giving up. Some days she sat in the classroom taking notes, struggling to keep her eyes open. Even the students said, jokingly, that she should get more sleep. Some nights she stayed awake revising in her room, her back aching. Other nights, she drank black coffee to keep awake until Mrs. Miller complained about the light being on all night.

Weeks later, she arrived home to find a letter from Ned propped up on the hall table and took it up to her room.

Dear Jo,

I'm sorry to tell you that Larry passed away. He was in poor health, and died in the Sanatorium. Cissy is coping well. She did okay on her second baby. A little girl called Sarah-Jane. Larry doted on her.

Ma complains of pain in her joints all the time. Joseph is a bonny baby. Beanie sends her love. I hope you are well and happy in America.

From your loving brother, Ned

Poor Larry! She had been so fond of him, and he had always been kind to her. Poor Cissy, too, she thought, with a new baby. Collapsing onto her bed, she wept.

* * *

Jo's meetings with Annie were brief, snatched in between her two jobs. Her weekends were spent swotting for her exams. Some mornings she woke to find the light still on and sheets from her folder scattered on the floor. And Annie couldn't help but notice the tired look that hung over her young friend.

'I'm so sorry to hear about Larry, Jo.' She placed a supportive arm around her shoulders. 'Look, we've got time. Let's go down to Macy's store, buy something for Sarah-Jane, and send it to Cissy,' she said, hoping to cheer Jo up.

Jo hadn't the price of a cup of coffee, but she went anyway. They were both surprised at the choice of baby clothes, and she fingered a soft pink baby dress with matching booties. 'Aren't they sweet, Annie? I'll buy them when I get paid.'

'Let me buy them,' Annie offered. 'You can pay me back later, if it makes you feel better. Please, I really want to.'

'Annie, I can't pay you back. Every dime I earn gets swallowed up in books and fees,' she said, running her fingers through her shoulder-length hair.

'Why won't you let me help? You'd help me, I know you would.' Annie sighed. 'I've a good wage and live in.'

'Okay, but you must let me pay you back when I can. Cissy will be delighted.'

Smiling, Annie watched as the assistant gift-wrapped the baby clothes. Jo addressed the parcel, and Annie put enough American stamps on to ensure its safe delivery.

As they walked back from the post, Jo recalled how easy her life had been at Chateau Colbert, and Madame's kindness before Molly hid the precious pearls in her room. She was homesick for Ned, Cissy – and even her mother. She rarely thought about Jean-Pierre. Neither of them had written since she had emigrated. He could have sought her out through Ned or his grandmother if he'd wanted to. But she guessed he'd married some society lady with money and forgotten all about her. Jo wrote often to Madame Colbert, but hadn't heard anything from her for a couple of weeks.

'A penny for them!' Annie said, as they reached the tram.

'I was thinking of Ned, and Madame Colbert.'

'You're homesick. We must have a night out soon. Let me know when you're likely to have a free weekend.'

* * *

Some weeks later, a large brown envelope arrived from Dublin. It contained a portrait of her new niece, Sarah-Jane, wearing the American dress and booties. Jo thought her the most beautiful little girl in the world and she proudly showed the picture to Mrs. Miller.

'Ah, sure, she's a little dote,' she said, turning her head towards the kitchen clock. 'Have you seen the time, Jo? You better get a move on, or you'll be late for work.' Jo quickly put the photograph back into the envelope.

'Before you dash off,' Mrs. Miller said, a painful expression on her face. 'I'm afraid I'll have to let you go. It's me slack time.'

'What am I going to do?'

'I'm sorry, Jo, but when Mr. Coffee leaves for the Christmas vacation, and with Mrs. Canings gone already, it only leaves yourself and one other guest. I can hardly pay the bills as it is.' She sighed heavily. 'Couldn't you write to Ned? He's a good lad. He wouldn't see you stuck.'

'I couldn't do that, Mrs. Miller. He has his own family to support now.' Her eyes clouded. 'I'll think of something.'

That evening on her way to work, a cold wind blew around

her ankles. Even the trees were bare and the carpet of brown and golden leaves that only weeks ago covered the sidewalks, had disappeared. As soon as she arrived, she had a word with her boss, Mr. O'Rourke, who kindly agreed for her to come in an hour earlier each evening. It would be a rush to get there on time, but it more than made up for the few dollars she earned working at the lodging house.

* * *

The music shop was at its busiest in December and Jo hardly noticed the man patiently waiting for her attention. His thick black hair came down over his ears, and he peered over the top of his glasses. 'Excuse me, miss.'

'I'm sorry,' she said. 'It's one of those busy evenings again. Can I help you?'

'I'm looking for this month's *Jazz* magazine.' He straightened his glasses on the bridge of his nose. 'I've tried the other branch and they said you might have it here.' A hopeful expression crossed his unshaven face.

Jo reached behind and lifted a small pile of music books from the shelf, placing them down in front of him. 'The latest should be on top. Would you mind having a look through while I serve someone else?'

He mumbled his thanks, then he flicked through and picked out the one he wanted. When Jo returned, he was drawing a clean dollar bill from his wallet. 'Sorry, I have no change,' he said.

'That's all right. It's easier to count at the end of the night.' Smiling, she handed him his change. He thanked her and left.

The following evening, he called again. This time he didn't buy anything, but he passed Jo two complimentary tickets to a jazz concert at the weekend in Greenwich Village.

'Please try and come,' he called, as he rushed out. 'Bring a friend. We need a crowd.'

Nodding her thanks, she pushed the tickets into her handbag to examine later. She had heard the students talking about Greenwich Village. It was, according to them, an intriguing place where artists lived an unconventional lifestyle. Certainly not the kind of place Mrs. Miller would approve of, but Jo decided to ask Annie to go with her. What harm could it do? She deserved a night off.

Mrs. Miller told her that it wasn't a fit place for two Irish Catholic girls to be seen. 'What's wrong with the parish dances here in the Bronx?'

'I'm not a child, Mrs. Miller. Besides, I'm going to ask Annie to come with me.'

'Well! I thought she'd have more sense.'

'If it gets you away from studying for a few hours,' was Annie's reaction, 'it'll be worth it.'

'What's this fellow's name?'

'I don't know. We never got a chance to talk, but he looked different; happy-go-lucky, but nice.'

* * *

On Saturday night, Jo and Annie discovered a district of winding streets and old houses, restaurants and jazz clubs. It had a uniqueness all its own, and it was easy to forget they were surrounded by skyscrapers. They found the atmosphere convivial and carefree and it made a change from the hustle of city life.

Once they located the jazz club, they could hardly hear themselves speak above the chatter and the noise of the band. The smell of tobacco and cigarette smoke hung in the air. The man with the long hair smiled and beckoned them towards a table. 'Hello again.' He pulled over a chair for Annie and relinquished his own chair for Jo. 'Glad you could come. By the way, my name's Max, and these are my friends.'

A few people were sitting drinking soft drinks and iced teas. 'This is Jo and Annie,' he told them. There was a drum roll and Max's name was called over the microphone. 'Sorry, that's my queue. Mike, look after the ladies,' he said, and hurried off to join a group of musicians on the small stage.

'Hello!' Mike said, over the sound of Max's saxophone. When Jo shook his hand, she looked up into dark blue eyes. 'I don't know why we follow him around,' he said. 'He's a hopeless player really. Only joking!' He smiled and flicked the ash from his cigarette. 'What would you ladies like to drink? As liquor is still off limits, the choice is easy.'

Jo would have welcomed a glass of red wine – a taste acquired from her days at Chateau Colbert – but she settled for a Pepsi with a twist of lemon, while Annie asked for apple juice. Each time Max finished his number, he joined them. He played in a variety of clubs in Greenwich Village, and had acquired quite a following. Jo liked the laid back attitude of the folk who frequented the village. They all looked like they hadn't a care in the world. But she particularly felt drawn to the young Mike Pasiński, a tall athletic type with fair hair that flopped untidily over his eyes, and she found herself engrossed in his tales of the old village.

'Even today,' he was saying, 'people are attracted to the bohemian way of life that some artists enjoy.' Each time he turned his face to look at her, something strange happened that she couldn't explain. And she didn't want the night to end.

'I take it you're not a conformist, Mike?'

'Me! A conformist! I'd call myself a misfit, not sure where I fit in. But for now, I'm happy living here in Greenwich.' He laughed, tossing back his hair. Jo glanced across at Annie, gripped in a debate on the issue of birth control with Max and two women in the group.

'What do you do, Mike?' Jo asked, sipping her drink.

'I'm a struggling musician. I teach the violin and harp most mornings in my apartment. In the afternoons, if I'm inspired I compose music and make a shocking attempt at adding the appropriate lyrics.' He took a long drag on his cigarette, circled his lips and blew the smoke away. 'What about you, Jo? You have the looks and figure of a model.' She felt her colour rise. 'I'm sorry. I didn't mean to be personal. I was just speaking the truth.' He smiled. 'You have ambitions, I'm sure.' He leaned in closer.

'Yes,' she began, his nearness making her nervous. 'I'm a student at the Manhattan School of Music. I want to become a music teacher; piano mainly,' she paused. 'I also like writing lyrics and poems.'

'Well, I'm impressed,' he told her, shaking his head. 'You look like the kind of girl who will follow it through as well.'

'It's what I've always wanted to do.'

He flicked open a packet of Camel and offered her a cigarette. She raised her hand and shook her head. 'What do you think of the American way of life, Jo?'

'I'm still in awe of the place, and I'm fascinated by American politics. Do you think President Coolidge is doing a good job?' she said above the din.

'He doesn't say much, but I like him, he's a free thinker.' He smiled. 'Did you know that George Washington lived in one of these terraces in 1776 before he became President?'

'That's remarkable. Did anyone famous ever live in your apartment, Mike?'

'I don't know about the apartments, but Eugene O'Neill and Edgar Allen Poe had rooms here at one time. Both were passionate about social causes, from education reforms to birth control,' he said.

The lilt of his American accent fascinated her, and she listened intently, her elbow on the table, her chin cupped in her hand. Time flew and before they realised it, Jo and Annie were running towards the subway.

CHAPTER THIRTY

On a recently created mound in a Dublin suburb, the colourful bouquets, wreaths and flowers left at the graveside were coated in frost. Jean-Pierre stood motionless by the burial plot of his grandmother, now at rest alongside her beloved Louis. He removed his hat and held it in front of him. Numb and unable to function since her death, he had come to the graveside to grieve privately. His pain, coupled with Jo's move to America months before, was still raw.

He found little consolation here, or in the confines of Chateau Colbert that had, not so long ago, pulsated with life. He straightened his shoulders, blinking back tears, and pulled the collar of his black woollen coat up around his neck. He closed his eyes; his body swaying slightly. '*Grandmère. Ma chérie.*' Removing his glove, he reached into his inside pocket and pulled out a white silk handkerchief and held it to his face. His shoulders shook with emotion as memories of his grandmother tumbled into his head. Clearing his throat, he blew his nose.

From the age of sixteen, when a ski lift cable broke killing both his parents, his grandmother had been there for him. It was she who had made him the man he was today, encouraging him to focus on his studies; moving back and forth to Paris to be near his boarding school whenever he needed to see her. Even while grieving the loss of a devoted son, she had helped him to overcome his pain. On the many occasions when he had strayed down undesirable paths, she had guided him back with her gentle wisdom, always backing his many failed ventures. The thought of never seeing her again made his heart ache. How could he bear it?

Their special bond severed forever.

Foster stood by the car, clapping his gloved hands together to keep warm. Jean-Pierre had no idea how long he had been standing there until he felt the butler's light touch on his elbow.

'I think we should be getting back, sir. There's a heavy fog coming down.'

'Forgive me, Foster. Is that the time?' Jean-Pierre glanced at his watch, walked towards the car, slid onto the red leather upholstery and closed his eyes. As well as feeling bereft, he was missing Jo. He hadn't written to her, thinking he had in some way contributed to her abrupt departure to America. His grandmother had told him only that it had been the girl's dearest wish; that she had encouraged her to go, and that it was only right she should follow her dream. But he could tell from her letters that she missed Jo as much as he did. The whole business of her departure had puzzled him, and for months he had regretted disclosing his feelings, wishing he had been more thoughtful, more considerate towards hers.

On their return to the Chateau, Jean-Pierre nodded his thanks to the butler and withdrew once more into the depths of desolation. Almost a week since the funeral, when he had cried openly at the graveside, he had shut himself away from the rest of the household sending back most of his meals untouched; the staff left speculating their futures. Miss O'Breen had wanted to intervene.

'You must leave him to come to terms with his loss,' Foster told her.

When Jean-Pierre emerged from his grandmother's rooms, Miss O'Breen pitied him. He looked tired and drawn, much older than his thirty years. His dark hair was dishevelled, unlike the handsome gentleman that had once entertained his grandmother at Chateau Colbert. She instinctively wanted to put her arms round him, and tell him she understood. But, instead, she approached him with caution.

'*Bonjour*, Jean-Pierre.' She smiled up at him. 'Is there anything I can do for you?'

He stared down at her, his eyes revealing the depth of his grief. 'Thank you for everything you've done.' He forced a smile.

'Madame Colbert was a wonderful lady. We all miss her.' The housekeeper sighed and straightened her shoulders. 'I have strict instructions from Mrs. Quigley to inform her the moment you put in an appearance. You know what she's like. She will prepare something light for you. You need nourishment,' she said, as though encouraging a child.

'I can't eat now. At least not until I speak to you all on a very important matter. I must do it soon, or I will have yet another troubled night.'

'Can't it wait, sir?'

He shook his head, joined his hands and held them to his lips. 'I have spoken to my grandmother's solicitor.' He paused. 'I can no longer put this off. I'd like to see everyone in the drawing room. Can you see to it for me, Miss O'Breen, and please include James the gardener?' His manner was courteous and to the point, before retreating back to his grandmother's rooms.

Miss O'Breen and Foster remained professional, their private thoughts kept to themselves.

Mrs. Quigley dabbed the corner of her eyes. 'I've been working at Chateau Colbert since Madame was a bride. I know no other home.' The maids were thoughtful and the atmosphere unsettling as they lined up to hear their fate.

When Jean-Pierre walked into the drawing room, he coughed nervously. Mrs. Quigley sat anxiously, rubbing her hands together, the rest of the staff remained standing. He cleared his throat.

'Thank you all for your patience this past week or so. You probably know as well as I do how much dear *Grandmère* loved Chateau Colbert. But due to my work schedule and business interests in Paris, it would not be practical for me to reside here.' He stopped to clear his throat again. 'It grieves me to inform you all that the valuation officer is coming to-morrow and a sale is imminent.' Mrs. Quigley gasped, and her hand flew to her mouth.

'Some of you,' Jean-Pierre said, 'have served my grandparents a long time.' His French tones deflated, he directed his gaze towards the cook and the gardener. 'Your dedication will not go un-rewarded.'

Having delivered the news as sensitively as circumstances allowed, he apologised and left.

* * *

In the middle of the week, Jo was surprised to get another letter from Ned. She took it upstairs to read. It was dated end of December.

My Dear Jo,

I was delighted to hear that you received all my letters safely. Proud to hear you are doing so well at the School of Music. I never doubted you would.

I am sorry to tell you that Madame Colbert passed away peacefully at her home. I read it in the obituary column. I thought you'd like to know as you were close.

Everyone here is well and we hope you are too and that you are having a wonderful life in America. Write whenever you get time.

I remain,

Your loving brother, Ned

Tears sprung into her eyes and she tried to remember the last time she had written to Madame Colbert. Her former employer had been so good to her, unusually kind, and she would never forget her. She couldn't eat or sleep that night. First poor Larry, now Madame Colbert. Her first year in America was proving to be a very sad one indeed.

CHAPTER THIRTY-ONE

'Guess what, Jo?' Annie said as soon as they met. 'Mr. Thomas has asked me to go on summer vacation with the family. We're going to *Florida*!' she emphasised. 'Oh, I can't wait.'

'How grand, Annie. When are you going?'

'In two weeks time,' she sighed. 'I need you to come shopping with me; help me select some outfits for the trip. You being a follower of fashion, you know what would best suit an old spinster like me. You're always telling me to change my image.'

'Stop being silly, Annie. You're only twenty-seven. There's plenty of time to find a nice man and settle down.' Jokingly, she added. 'Who knows, maybe Mr. Thomas is your man?'

Annie nudged her and told her to stop matchmaking.

'You like him, don't you?' Jo persisted, as they boarded the tram that took them to Manhattan and the big department stores.

'Yes, I do like him. Now will you stop this nonsense and keep your mind on why we're shopping today.' As they stepped from the tram, she said, 'Your exams, Jo, is there any news?'

'I heard this morning. I've passed my first year and my grades will be posted up at school.'

'Why, that's wonderful.' Annie hugged her. 'We should celebrate.'

'I'd rather wait 'til I get my degree. I've a long way to go yet, Annie, but it's an incentive for the next semester in the autumn.'

'Well, congratulations!'

They reached Macy's, their favourite store, and searched every department until they found the most becoming outfits for Annie, settling on a dress of light summer material in powder blue with a white-laced collar, and a pretty green blouse and matching skirt that came to just above her ankles. It reminded Jo of happy times when Madame Colbert had treated her to new outfits at Brown Thomas's in Dublin. She hadn't bought herself any new clothes for a year and she was sorely tempted to spend money put by for textbooks.

When Annie came out of the dressing room, she did a twirl.

'Perfect,' Jo said, nodding her approval. The outfits were then completed with matching beads and accessories. 'Why not have your hair done at the same time?' Jo said. 'Your hair would look great with one of those new wavy perms. I'll browse around the book shops while you're having it done.'

'Umm,' Annie pushed back her shock of chestnut hair and glanced into the mirror. 'You're probably right,' she conceded. 'I'll pay for the clothes and then pop into one of the hair salons. We can meet up for a coffee later,' she said, and disappeared into the changing booth.

While she waited for Annie, Jo sauntered along the sidewalk. It was hot and humid, but even so she felt relief that the harsh winter was behind them. It had been a difficult time since her arrival in America, and she hoped things would get easier. New York was full of courting couples, some flashed past her in automobiles. The increase in motor transport in the past twelve months amazed her. It was rare now to see a pony and trap, or carriage on the streets of New York. She walked as far as the river and sat on a bench gazing out across the glistening waters towards the Statue of Liberty and Ellis Island. Memories flooded her mind. Never once, since that memorable first day, had she regretted coming to America. She might have been better off financially had she not decided to study for a degree. But she wouldn't have been happier. One day it would all be worthwhile, she told herself.

She thought about Annie and Mr. Thomas. She hadn't met him yet and wondered what he was really like. She had a feeling that Max liked Annie, but when Jo mentioned it, Annie – always the practical one – said she was looking for an exceptional male, one she admired as well as loved. At the time, Jo had laughed, telling her she was too fussy. She thought about Mike; wondered what he was doing, and if he had thought about her since their visit to Greenwich Village.

Glancing at her watch, she was surprised at how quickly the time had flown, and she wandered back to meet Annie. Jo almost passed her by outside the coffee shop. Gone were the auburn locks. Her hair now had a middle parting, set in waves close to her head, and covered her ears.

'God, Annie, you look just like Bee Jackson, the Charleston dancer. Peter will hardly recognise you.'

'It'll take some getting used to.' Annie ran her hand over her new hairdo. With no time for coffee, the two women – laden with bags – made their way home.

* * *

Over the next few months, Jo and Annie were frequent visitors to the Village and Jo looked forward to one night a week where she could relax. It was nothing like the den of debauchery Mrs. Miller had made it out to be, and the girls became part of a crowd.

They made fascinating friends within the group, and Max was always pleased to see them both. When Mike Pasiński presented himself, the evening had special meaning for Jo and a friendship sprung up between them. They shared many topics of interest, and coming from similar backgrounds gave scope to their conversations. As she gradually grew to know him, his Polish parentage and his struggle to make something of his life, it encouraged her to keep going and get her degree.

In spite of knowing nothing of how he regarded her in his affections, Jo's feelings for Mike grew stronger each time they met. And when she compared them to the way she had once felt about Jean-Pierre, she knew that this time she was falling in love. She kept her feelings to herself, telling no-one – not even Annie.

* * *

While Annie was away, Jo continued to frequent Greenwich Village. During prohibition, many were attracted to the area because of the secret speakeasy drinking houses.

'Come on,' Mike murmured, holding her hand and escorting her out of the jazz club. 'I know the landlord of a place where we can get a drink.' He winked. Like Jo, Mike had been working hard, and tonight she thought he looked older than his twenty-six years.

'Are you sure it's okay, Mike? Won't it be dangerous?'

'Yes, and no, but we can be alone, get to know one another better.'

His handsome face eased into a smile, and she felt as if she had known him all her life. He made her laugh; was good-natured; great company; witty; and he certainly livened up her evenings.

She glanced up at him, slightly hesitant.

'If I knock with a certain rhythm, the landlord will let us in. Lots of people do it, you know.'

The speakeasies in Greenwich Village were pleasant, quaint, if not quieter and less flashy than uptown drinking houses. Mike found a secluded corner where they chatted and enjoyed their drinks. People talked in whispers, looking over their shoulders. And every now and then, Jo jerked her head round when she heard a unique tap on the back door.

'Don't worry,' he told her, when he saw her frown. 'If we get raided, I'll save you first. But it won't happen.'

'I hope you're right.' She was beginning to wish she hadn't agreed to come.

'Trust me.' He lit up, drew in the smoke and let it escape through his nostrils. The place was filling up and she began to relax. Curtains were drawn across the small windows, making the place airless, and she could taste the thick tobacco smoke.

'Did I ever tell you that my mother was Irish?'

'Only that you were born of Irish and Polish parents.' She placed her elbows on the table.

'They met on the emigration ship in 1890. My mother was only eighteen, my father a young Polish boy in his twenties when they married, not long after they arrived in America.'

'It sounds romantic!'

'They may have thought so at the time, Jo, but it wasn't.' His expression was serious. 'They were poor and struggled to bring up a large family in the tenements of New York City.' He looked directly at her. 'I guess that's how it was. My eldest brother died in the war.' His face clouded and Jo, on impulse, reached across and gently stroked the side of his face, feeling the short spiky growth of his beard. He removed her hand and held it. 'I mean, it was a hard dismal life then. Being the youngest, I fared off best and learned the art of survival from my older siblings. My mother had six children in conditions too horrible to contemplate, and died young. I remember her crying, wishing she was back in Ireland. It broke my heart.'

She felt humbled by the way he had opened up to her. 'Like you,' he continued. 'I want to make something of my life, so I tried to be enterprising by scrimping and saving to put myself through college, and then through the American Academy of Dramatic Arts.' He paused and stubbed out his cigarette. 'I've never told anyone that before.'

'I'm glad it was me.' Her eyes misty from the smoke, she said, 'You've achieved so much against the odds, Mike. She glanced up at the clock. 'I have to go now if I'm to catch the early tram.' She got to her feet.

'I'll come with you.'

Outside, they walked hand-in-hand along the narrow sidewalk when Mike invited her over to his apartment. Without hesitating, she accepted. There was always the late electric tram that would take her back to the Bronx. She and Annie had had cause to use the service on a number of occasions. She longed to see where Mike lived and had often imagined what the rooms were like.

His apartment was situated on the West side of the Village, a couple of streets from the bustle of the night revellers. The cobbled streets and coloured slatted shutters on the windows were unique. And if it were not for the occasional clanging of bells and piercing sounds of the emergencies racing to answer calls, it was hard to imagine she was in the heart of New York City.

When Mike unlatched the door that led into his first floor

apartment, he stood back and Jo stepped inside. Then he bent his shoulders to allow his tall frame to enter. 'Please excuse the untidy mess,' he said. The room was surprisingly light, in spite of the late hour. The table was covered with music sheets, and books were scattered about on chairs. Two violins lay on a smaller table, and a harp and music stand graced a corner of the room. He was just about to clear a chair for her when she spotted the black wrought iron balcony and walked towards it.

'How exciting, do you use it?'

He was behind her now. Loosening the catch, he pushed open the window so they could step out onto the veranda, his arm around her slim waist, his closeness making her tremble.

'There's a pretty garden out there, too.' He smiled and moved back inside. 'I hope you get to see it in daylight.'

Was that an assumption? She wondered, gazing up at the clear night sky.

She could smell the exquisite scent of the rambling rose bush that wound its way up the wall. It was a warm night and as she turned back into the room, she removed her jacket and caught a glimpse of Mike in the bedroom, pulling the covers over his unmade bed. An ashtray overflowed. So this was what a bachelor's apartment looked like. She smiled to herself.

He came back holding a lighted red candle, made room on the table and placed it down. Jo watched, bemused, as he made another attempt to clear a pile of papers from the armchair and invited her to sit down. He opened a small cupboard and took out a secret bottle of wine and two glasses.

'For very special occasions.' He raised his eyebrows.

'If I didn't know you better, Mike Pasiński, I'd say that you were trying to get me tipsy.' Although she said it, she felt more afraid of her own feelings; if she drank more wine, she was sure to miss her tram.

'I would never do that.' He was standing before her holding two empty glasses. She shook her head. 'I'll make tea or coffee if you'd prefer,' he said, walking towards the small kitchen.

'I'll help you.' She followed him and they collided in the tiny space between the sink and the stove. Before she knew what was happening, she was in his arms; Mike kissed the tip of her nose. She lowered her head to hide her blushes. He raised her chin, brushing back strands of fair hair. She closed her eyes. He kissed her eyelids, face and neck. She trembled. Never before had she experienced such ripples of pleasure. His lips touched hers. She felt his hot breath against her ear.

'Stay with me tonight,' he murmured.

Her body tremulous, she pulled away, embarrassed to have responded to his advances so readily. Although she longed for love, she had no idea how Mike felt about her.

'I should never have asked you that.'

She felt foolish. She couldn't answer, recalling her Confirmation day, the year before her grandmother had died. After all this time, Sister Catherine's words came tumbling into her head. Remember young ladies that your body is a temple, not for fornicating.'"

A frown creased Mike's brow. 'I'm sorry, Jo. I never meant to offend you. I acted impulsively. I've wanted to kiss you from the first moment I saw you.' He took her in his arms again, but she shook herself free. Mike had awakened feelings in her that she never knew existed, and she was frightened to be alone with him.

She reached for her handbag, feeling a hot flush to her face. 'I have to go, Mike.'

'Please, Jo. Don't go like this.' He glanced at his watch. 'Stay a while longer.'

'No, I must go.' Tears of disappointment or anger – she wasn't sure which – rolled down her burning cheeks. There was her reputation to think of.

He swung her round. 'Jo, I love you. Don't you see? It beautifies everything. It's the greatest of heaven's blessings.' Gently, he pulled her close.

'But it's wrong.' She looked up into his eyes, searching for an answer to satisfy her conscience.

'To me, love is the most natural thing in the world, but I realise that everyone may not share my liberal views.' He looked down into her troubled face. He sat in the armchair and pulled her onto his knee. They kissed. He caressed her trembling lips, then they kissed again. She felt her pulse race and his heart beat against her chest. And when he carried her towards the bedroom, she felt powerless to resist. His kisses became intoxicating; his touch, gentle, skillful.

'Mike, we shouldn't be doing this, it's wrong,' she cried, as he began to undo the buttons of her blouse.

'How can it be wrong, Jo? I have never felt like this about anyone in my life,' he told her, his eyes searching hers. She was clutching her open blouse across her breasts.

'I love you, too, but I can't do this. It's against everything I believe in.'

Mike sat up, his body bronzed in the candlelit room. He laid his head in his hands. 'I'm sorry, Jo. I never meant to disregard your feelings. I, too, used to believe. I was an altar boy once, you know.' A wry smile creased his face. 'People live a lifetime and never find what we have. I think it's special, and I don't want to lose you.'

He looked down at her. Tears were welling in her eyes, and her hand covered her mouth. He gathered her into his arms again. She wanted him more than she'd ever wanted anyone.

'I love you and I believe you love me, too.' He kissed her tears, her eyes, her ears, her throat. Gradually, she felt her limbs relax, and with a will of their own, her arms fastened around his neck and pulled him to her. She felt his hot breath brush her lips as he murmured, 'My sweet Jo.'

She felt his bare skin touch hers as ecstatic waves of joy filled her being. All fear and doubt left her, and when it came, the arousal was so powerful it was impossible for them to stop.

CHAPTER THIRTY-TWO

When Jo awoke sunlight was peeping through the slatted windows. She looked down at Mike, his blond hair tousled on the pillow next to her. He was sleeping soundly. She felt shame for what she had allowed to happen. So this was what love was like, she thought; an inexplicable joy that left an intolerable pain of guilt. Her hands shaking, she pulled on her clothes that were scattered on the floor. Embarrassed to face Mike, she had to get away. She grabbed her jacket and handbag, and quietly crept from the apartment.

Outside, everything looked normal, but Jo felt anything but, as she hurried along the sidewalk towards the subway. A man smiled and winked, making her blush; she felt that everyone she passed knew what she had done.

It was quiet when she arrived back at the boarding house, and she was thankful not to have bumped into Mrs. Miller. She would tear a strip off her, and threaten to write to Ned about her staying out all night. And what excuse could she give?

'Oh. Dear God!' she cried. 'Everything's going wrong.' Inside her room, she felt miserable. The brown paint and fading pink flowered wallpaper depressed her. Was this what she'd come to America for? Homesickness and worry engulfed her. Unable to stem the tears stinging the backs of her eyes, she slumped down onto her bed, buried her face in her pillow and wept.

Her tears achieved nothing except red eyes. Everything felt different; her life had changed; she was changed, because she had gone against her beliefs. What would Annie think when she got back from Florida? How was she going to tell her friend that she had done such a thing? The more she thought, the worse she felt; her love for Mike her only excuse. What if she became pregnant? She could still smell the scent of him on her clothes, on her skin. She wished she were back in his arms. Nothing would ever compare to that first time with Mike as he gently brought her to fulfillment. The whole wonderful experience had overwhelmed her, awakened something inside her, and she knew she could never go back to the way they were before that night.

* * *

While Jo waited for Annie to return from vacation, she stayed away from Greenwich Village. But she couldn't get Mike Pasiński out of her head. In spite of having heard nothing from him, she thought about him all the time, at her music seminars, at work; he occupied her every waking hour. She thought about going to confession, but shame and fear kept her away. She knew what she had done was wrong, but God forgive her, she wasn't sure she felt sorry for loving Mike. Annie was the only other person she could possibly tell.

When, finally, Annie returned from vacation looking radiant, her suntan made Jo look pale in comparison. Anxious to see her, Jo was first to arrive at the coffee house and ordered their usual lunchtime snack, noting Annie's irrepressible smile. 'Gosh! Annie, you look fantastic. How was your vacation?'

'Oh, it was great, Jo. I don't know when I enjoyed myself more.' She ran her fingers through her wavy bob. 'The children were well behaved, and happy. Peter, I mean, Mr. Thomas, was very generous. Oh, Jo,' she said, 'I don't know where to start. The beach was warm and heavenly. If the sand had been put through a sieve it couldn't have been finer. It was hot underfoot, like walking on hot coals until you hit the water. I even swam in the sea. We all did.' She sighed and looked upwards.

'I never knew you could swim?'

'Well, I can a bit. I used to swim in Sandy Cove when I was little, but there's no comparison.' She shook her head.

'It all sounds wonderful. You must have had a grand time.'

'Oh, I did. But look at me going on,' she said, glancing at Jo's serious expression. 'What have you been up to, since I've been away? Have you been to the Village?'

She couldn't bear to spoil Annie's homecoming by telling her what had happened with Mike. 'I haven't been for ages,' she said. 'I've been waiting for you to get back.'

'You are silly! Why ever not? I thought you and Mike got on well?' When Jo shrugged, Annie became concerned. 'What's happened?'

'We had a slight disagreement, that's all. You don't want to hear my troubles.'

'What troubles?' Annie moved in closer. 'You're in love with him, aren't you?

'I think I am.'

'How does he feel about you?'

'I don't know really. He says he loves me, but...' Jo bit her lip.

'What? You don't think he's the marrying kind, is that it?'

Jo shook her head.

'Give him time, Jo. If he's the man I think he is, he won't be able to resist your charms for long.' She smiled, leaning one elbow on the table.

The moment had passed and Jo knew she'd become upset if she continued to talk about Mike. 'Tell me more about you and Mr. Thomas, Annie.'

Annie seemed eager to oblige. 'You know, when we were having breakfast one morning, Mr. Thomas said – in front of the children, mind – "Annie, I want you to call me Peter from now on". And on another occasion, while we were dining, he asked me a rather personal question. "Have you ever thought about marriage, Annie?" he said, just like that. It was quite unexpected, Jo, I was dumbfounded.' She laughed, and Jo's eyes widened.

'What did you say?'

'Well, after I'd recovered from the shock, I said that of course I had, but the right man hadn't surfaced in my life yet.'

'What happened then?'

'He went quiet, then apologised for asking the question. Can you believe it?' Annie shook her head. 'Men, they're not as bright as us, and sometimes you have to let them know how you feel.' They chatted on, and Jo went to work that evening still clinging to her guilty secret.

* * *

A week later, Jo's music classes resumed and she had less time to think about Mike. At least she wasn't pregnant, one less thing for her to worry about.

'Not hungry this morning, Jo? Would you like a light poached egg instead?' Mrs. Miller asked, looking down at Jo's untouched food.

'No thanks, Mrs. Miller, I'm meeting Annie after my lecture. I'll have something then.' She glanced at the clock, then pushed back her chair, said goodbye, and left. Her mind wasn't on the lecture, and she hoped that she would remember some of it. She couldn't afford to be slacking in this way after all her hard work. Now she couldn't wait to talk to Annie, whatever the consequences.

Later, as Annie gave the waitress their lunch order, Jo sat opposite, knowing she wouldn't eat a bite until she told her friend the truth. She had no idea how she might react. Would she be moralistic? She hoped not, because she desperately needed her support. It wouldn't seem quite so bad if she and Mike were committed to one another in some way, but she'd only known him a short time.

'You're quiet,' Annie said. 'Don't let your food go cold. This vegetable soup is quite tasty.'

'Sorry, Annie. I'm not very hungry after all.' She forced a smile.

'Oh, would you like something else?'

She nodded. 'This is fine.'

'Are we going to the Village on Saturday night then?'

'I can never go there again.' Jo pushed a strand of hair behind her ear and moved her soup to the side.

Annie stopped eating. "What's wrong, Jo? There's something you're not telling me.' She stood up and placed their food back onto a tray. 'We'll move across to that corner booth. It'll be more private and we can talk.' Annie's face was full of concern. 'Come on. What is it? Remember, we promised to tell each other everything, and there's something worrying you.'

Annie had helped her in so many ways back home when she was growing up. This was different. But who else could she trust?

'I…well…Mike and I…we slept together.' She hid her face in her hands.

Annie was speechless, her eyebrows arched in alarm. 'You mean, you actually…how? Where?'

'At his apartment.'

'You went to his place at night? Oh, Jo.'

'Don't hate me, Annie. I love him.' She wept quietly.

'I could never hate you, Jo. But I am concerned for you. Did he force you?'

'Oh no, it wasn't like that. We both knew what we were doing.'

'The swine!' Jo was shocked to hear Annie swear. 'He took advantage and I trusted him to look after you while I was away.' She reached out and touched Jo's hand. 'I never should have gone away and left you.'

'You're not responsible for me, Annie. It wasn't your fault, or even Mike's. It was mine for letting my feelings run away with me.' Her eyes clouded again.

'God! You're not pregnant, are you?'

Jo shook her head and noticed Annie's shoulders relax. 'Thank God! If this was to leak out, it could ruin your career. Have you thought of that? Not to mention your reputation. Do you think he's serious about you?'

'I hardly think so now.' She placed her head in her hands.

'Well, perhaps it's best you forget him. We won't go to Greenwich Village again. New York's a big place.'

Her chat with Annie had been a huge relief. She needed forgiveness, but from whom – God? Sister Catherine? She wasn't sure.

CHAPTER THIRTY-THREE

A week later, Jo woke late and came downstairs to find a letter addressed to her on the hall table. She slipped it inside her bag and, calling to Mrs. Miller that she had no time for breakfast, she left the boarding house. The tram was almost full when it got to Jo's stop and she was lucky to find a seat. Taking out the letter, she looked again at the handwriting. It was unknown to her. She ripped open the envelope, and read.

Dear Jo,

I had to write to you. I've hardly slept a wink since you walked out of my life.

I loved you, as one should, to excess, with folly, delight and now despair. Please come back to the Village. If I've erred, it was with my heart, and I'm suffering now. I was a fool to ruin things between us. Each Saturday I've waited for you in the vain hope that you, too, had felt something for me.

Not sure I got the zip code correct, but if you do get this letter, please meet me on Saturday evening at Claude's, the French restaurant in the village, at 8 o'clock.

Love,

Mike

Her hands shook as she folded the letter back in its creases and put it into the jagged envelope. Tears gathered in her eyes. How she had longed to hear from him. His declaration of love had eased her conscience somehow, but she had read enough books to know that one person's meaning of love might not necessarily be another's.

At intervals during the morning lesson, she re-read his letter.

191

She just had to see him again, if only to eliminate doubts about his sincerity. Would he understand how she felt? After all, they weren't engaged or anything. He may not believe in engagements. Not that she wanted to get married; not yet anyway.

The next few days dragged, and on Saturday, Annie had to babysit the children as Peter had an urgent appointment. It made Jo's decision to go to the Village easier. She wore a floral sundress and white cardigan around her shoulders and, when she arrived at Claude's, Mike was waiting. He wore a dark suit and a white open-necked shirt. Seeing him again made her realise just how much she loved him. He stood up, clearing his throat.

'I'm so glad you came. You look lovely.' His New York twang seemed more pronounced. He pulled out a chair and she sat down. The restaurant, popular with couples, had the right level of intimacy. The tables for two were covered in pink chequered cloths with lighted red candles. He held her gaze and she tried to stay focused in spite of the strong chemistry between them.

'Mike, I…we have to talk.'

He nodded, lifted the glass jug and poured her a glass of cordial. 'I've missed you. What have you been doing with yourself?'

'I've been busy.' She took a sip of her drink and the waiter passed them each a menu. 'I'm not very hungry. I'll have something light, please.' She glanced down the menu, then up at the waiter. 'Crepes, please.'

Smiling, the waiter nodded before turning towards Mike.

'Salad and smoked salmon.' Mike took a long drink from his glass and Jo was surprised that he hadn't smuggled in a bottle of wine. 'I meant everything I put in my letter, Jo. Why did you leave without a word?'

'Well, I…' She paused and glanced out of the window. The evenings were drawing in. She sighed.

'Why? Tell me, Jo. I've been out of my mind wondering.'

'I was embarrassed and ashamed.'

'But why?'

'I didn't think you'd understand.'

He reached for her hand. 'I do understand.'

Her heart raced at his touch. He kissed the back of her hand and she could smell nicotine on his fingers. 'Do you?' She forced a smile.

'I love you. God damn it, Jo. Surely you know that. Where's the shame in that?'

'It's not that simple, Mike. I need more than that!'

'What are you talking about?'

'Does your love come with a commitment?' Did she have to spell it out for him?

The waiter arrived with their food, and she could hear the chinking of glasses and soft romantic music playing in the background. Mike lowered his head and tucked in. 'Do try and eat something.'

Lifting her fork, she played with the strawberries with cream oozing from the middle of her pancake. She placed a little into her mouth. It was delicious, but she only managed to eat half. Her direct question had upset him, hit a nerve. Now she wouldn't rest until he had given her a straightforward answer.

She waited until he had finished eating, then she said. 'Mike, do you still think it was right for us to have—'

'Jo, listen.' He leant across the table. A tap on his shoulder with a walking cane interrupted him, and he turned round. 'Theodore!' Pushing back his chair, he got to his feet, grasping the man's hand in a warm handshake. 'Written any good books lately?'

'Written any good lyrics lately?' The older man had the appearance of someone about to embark on a country walk rather than dinner at a French restaurant.

'Aren't you going to introduce me to your beautiful companion?' The man glanced at a bemused Jo.

'Yes, of course. Miss Jo Kingsley, Mr. Theodore Dreises, one of America's greatest novelists.'

Jo immediately recognised the name and offered her hand. 'I'm very pleased to meet you. I have read most of your books,' she said with enthusiasm, 'and I have learnt so much about American life through reading them.'

'Thank you, young lady. It's kind of you to say so.'

'Won't you join us?' Mike offered.

'Thank you, but I'm with someone.' He clapped Mike on the back, running his other hand through his unruly mop of hair. 'It was lovely to meet you, Jo. See you around, Mike.' He walked away towards the back of the restaurant to join his lady companion.

'Was that really Theodore Dreises?' Jo asked in disbelief. 'What a wonderful stroke of luck, meeting him like that.'

Mike nodded. 'He's often around the Village. He's an interesting guy. I never knew you read Theodore's books, Jo.'

'There's a lot you don't know about me, Mike Pasiński, and what's more, things I don't know about you.'

He lit a cigarette and drew on it, then stubbed it out in the ashtray. 'Dance with me?' He leaned across and kissed her gently on the lips. 'I'll tell you anything, you know that.'

Placing his arm around her waist, he guided her onto the small dance floor.

'You haven't answered my question, Mike,' she whispered into his shoulder.

'The fact that I love you is all I'm sure of at the moment. I guess that's how it is, babe, and I don't feel we've done anything wrong in showing how we feel.' He held her tight in a slow foxtrot.

She could feel her heart beating. She'd never felt like this when she had dined out with Jean-Pierre in Dublin. Her heart had never fluttered like this either. The dance finished and they returned to their table.

'So, you want us to be irresponsible lovers?'

'I'm not against monogamy. But I don't feel any necessity for marriage. So I have no conscience about that.' His expression was determined.

'Are you saying you don't want to marry me?'

'Yes...no...It's not that? I'm a poor artist, still learning my skill. I've seen my mother struggle when my father was out of work, so you know, I can't put you through that. I won't. Please try and understand.'

Their values were worlds apart, she knew that now. 'This isn't going to work, Mike.' The words choked in her throat as she rose to her feet.

He touched her arm. 'I can't let you go again.' Scrambling to his feet, he dropped a few dollar notes onto the table and followed her to the door. 'Jo, please wait. At least, let me explain.' He was behind her now, his arm around her shoulders. She knew he was a free spirit and in a way she understood that. It was one of the things that at first attracted her to him. But the fact that he didn't want to marry her after what had happened between them, hurt and infuriated her.

'There's no need. I understand perfectly.' They were outside now.

'Oh, but there is.' On impulse, he took her in his arms. She struggled free, her voice shaking.

'Please, let me go.' Every fibre of her body wanted to stay with him, knowing that if she did, they would end up at his apartment. 'You're right, we both have a lot to learn. Please don't follow me.' And she ran to the subway and was lost in the crowd. As the train moved away, she turned her head towards the window, letting her tears run freely. She felt bitterly disappointed.

She arrived at her lodgings, surprised to find Mrs. Miller still up. 'I hope this isn't the start of more late nights, Jo. I feel responsible for you and I have to think of the other boarders.'

'I'm sorry, Mrs. Miller. It won't happen again,' she said, before rushing upstairs to her room to hide her distress. She lay fully dressed on top of her bed. Why, she asked herself, was she born with such strict values on morality? She thought about a book she had once read, set years into the future. A time when women were freer, rules relaxed, women on an equal par with men. She remembered thinking at the time it was very unlikely to ever happen. Now she wished it would come to pass, and that she was living in that time with Mike, free from guilt and recriminations.

'Oh, Mike,' she cried aloud. 'You're the only man I'll ever love, but I can't risk seeing you again.'

CHAPTER THIRTY-FOUR

Jo continued to receive letters from Mike, each one proclaiming his love, but no mention of marriage or even a compromise to their situation. Although her mind was consumed with thoughts of him, she replied to none. She pictured him lying in bed looking pensive, his hair falling across his eyes, his nicotine fingers holding a cigarette. At other times she could see his smile; his smouldering eyes gazing down at her telling her he loved her; the way he held her in his arms; his kisses making her whole body tingle. She missed him so much. At times, lonely with despair, she longed for him to suggest some kind of commitment. It wouldn't have taken much for her to relent and run back into his arms. If he really loved her, surely he would consider her reputation. And she wasn't prepared to sacrifice her principles.

Annie stopped relating snippets of gossip that filtered through from the Village and, to uplift Jo's flagging spirits, their Saturday evenings were spent at the theatre.

'It might help to talk, Jo.'

'There's nothing more to say, Annie. I just want to get on with my life, make money, and save for my future.'

'Max rang to say that Mike is longing to see you and, in spite of what you say, you are, too. Why won't you see him?' Annie asked.

'No, Annie. It won't change anything.' So with no choice but to respect her wishes, Annie never mentioned Mike again.

* * *

A month later, Annie called in at the music shop. Jo had just finished serving a customer and smiled towards her friend. She noticed that look of excitement in Annie's eye. It usually happened when she had some good news to impart.

'What is it?' Jo's asked.

'Peter's asked me to accompany him to see the musical *Oh, Kay!* on Broadway in November. I'm so excited.'

'That's wonderful, Annie.' Jo smiled. 'Look, I'm sorry for the way I've been lately. I've been so wrapped up with other things I never thought to ask how things were going with the two of you.'

'Oh, that's all right. I understand.'

Jo glanced at her watch. 'I'll be finishing soon. If you like, we can go somewhere for a catch-up.' Jo had yet to meet Peter, but it was obvious that he and Annie were becoming close. For the remainder of the evening, Annie talked about nothing else. And for the first time in ages, when Mike's name was mentioned, Jo didn't get upset.

* * *

During the coming months when cold winds swept in across the Hudson River, Jo missed Mike most. If only she had not given in to his desires, they might still be friends. The fact that he didn't want to commit wouldn't have come into question and she wouldn't have been left feeling tainted and ashamed. Max stopped calling at the music shop and Mike's letters had tailed off, too. His previous letters were locked away in her suitcase, and her memories of him locked away in her heart.

It was when Jo was in the last year at music school that she admitted to Annie her doubts of ever getting through her studies. If only she could go home to Ireland, but with so much still to do there was little chance of that.

'You can't give up now, Jo. You just need a break. One day you will be able to afford to go back to Ireland. You must stay focused.' Annie sighed. 'Why not come for dinner one evening? Meet Peter and the children. I'll arrange it.'

Mr. Thomas's house was similar to the lodging house, apart from a small basement where Annie said Mrs. Jolly, the cook, lived. The woman had prepared a delicious roast lamb dinner, leaving everything ready for Annie to serve up in the dining room.

Jo found Peter to be a pleasant hospitable man, forty-five, with a receding hairline. He wore a pinstriped business suit that accentuated his tall, lean stature.

'Lovely to meet you at last, Jo.' He smiled, shaking her hand.

'And you, too, Mr. Thomas. It was kind of you to invite me.'

'Oh, call me Peter. Please sit down.' He pulled out a chair. 'Some wine?'

Jo held up her glass. The last time she'd drunk wine was in Mike's apartment, and now it was a treat.

'It helps these days to have some in stock,' Peter said.

'It's lovely,' she said, sipping her drink.

The children were already seated, looking down the table at Annie as she placed the meat on their plates. 'Have you both said hello to our guest?' Peter said.

'Hello!' they said in unison.

Jo smiled. They were attractive, blond-haired children, a little reserved. They didn't look like they'd appreciate a hug, so she said, 'It's lovely to meet you both.' They gave her a guarded look before tucking into their meal.

'They're not good with strangers,' Annie whispered.

'Well, of course.' Jo had never known children like them. They looked like butter wouldn't melt beneath their austere expressions, but then she only had her own siblings back home to compare them to. She remembered Annie saying that they were hard work and it had taken her a while to gain their trust.

The meal was enjoyable, and afterwards the adults had apple turnover. Ella cried and kicked the table when Peter said she wasn't allowed more than one helping of jelly and ice-cream. The children, who finished first, got down from the table and, like Siamese twins, moved towards the door.

'Aren't you forgetting something?' Annie said.

'Goodnight!' Jo could hear them tramping upstairs like elephants, while Annie excused herself and followed.

'I'm sorry about the children, Jo,' Peter said, as they retired to the lounge.

'Oh, they're only children.'

'I'm afraid I've been a bit lenient.' He smiled and waved his arm towards the sofa. 'I only hope Annie can undo some of my bad habits.'

While they waited for Annie to put the children to bed and read their bedtime stories, Peter engaged Jo in conversation about his textile business and how he had put his money into stocks and shares. When Annie came back down, Peter had made a pot of coffee and later insisted on driving Jo back to her lodgings. Her break from constant study had done her good, and her chat with Peter had got her enthusiastic about investing in the stock market.

* * *

When, at last, Jo saw her name on the list of distinctions at the Manhattan School of Music, her joy was apparent. Her tutor, admitting to having reservations after she had missed a few tutorials, congratulated her by shaking her hand warmly.

'Well done, Miss Kingsley. You should be proud.'

Jo walked away with a smile on her face. She wrote to Ned and told him of her achievement, and Mrs. Miller couldn't stop telling the other boarders that they had a qualified music teacher in their midst.

It was now over a year since she'd seen Mike and she wondered if he knew about her success, what he was doing with his life, and if he ever thought about her. But from now on, she would be too busy working and saving for her own apartment to wonder about Mike Pasiński.

With no more studying, Jo was free to find a daytime job which, together with her job at the music shop, would increase her wage. It might take her a while, but she was determined to find a place of her own, and bid for a piano at the auction. Then she could think about taking on students. The thought excited her.

When she was offered a job as a waitress at an Italian restaurant in the Bronx, she couldn't have been happier. The boss, Mr. Coplo, was a fiery Italian who ate too much and shouted orders at his staff. Jo guessed he was stressed after the death of his wife and with no children to help with the business. The restaurant was popular, in spite of his offhand manner. The hours were long, starting early and finishing late afternoon, with just enough time for her to get to the music shop. Some days her legs ached and, as well as serving customers, she was expected to wash up.

'You're a glutton for punishment,' Annie told her.

Jo smiled. 'Don't worry, Annie. I'll be grand. The extra dollars will help me to get a place of my own sooner. I couldn't be happier.'

No matter how early Jo arrived at the restaurant, there was always someone waiting to be served. It was a fairly big place, with two plate glass windows that overlooked the sidewalk. And the inside was ostentatious, the walls decorated with Italian food and wine. A long, shiny, mahogany counter stretched almost the length of the restaurant. Some customers wandered in for a coffee, others a cooked breakfast. And throughout the day orders were taken over the phone, usually by Mr. Coplo, for the Italian evening meal. He spoke perfect English most of the time, but when anything annoyed him, the Italian in him exploded.

Jo and the other waitresses who worked shifts were allowed to sample the Italian breads and cheeses during their lunch breaks. That way, Mr. Coplo maintained they were able to recommend a variety of the produce to the customers.

By late afternoon, delicious aromatic scents wafted through the kitchen as the chef began to prepare the pre-booked evening meals. The strong flavours of oregano, saffron, spaghetti and pesto sauce, and chili peppers, almost made Jo's insides rumble with hunger.

One morning, when she had been working there a month, she was late arriving at the restaurant. Coplo gave her a stern look as she passed through to hang up her coat. She hoped he wouldn't start shouting. He was strict about most things, especially time keeping, and she didn't want to lose her job.

'I'd like a word later, Miss Kingsley. My office, after lunch.'

Nodding, she tied on her apron and hurried out to serve. Surely he wasn't going to sack her for one late, but then he was an unpredictable man. This job suited her fine, even if the work was hard; she was prepared to put up with it to get what she wanted.

That afternoon, Jo went upstairs to his office, a nervous knot curling in her stomach. She found him seated behind a mahogany desk. His office was quite grand, she thought, decorated in a similar manner to the restaurant. He leaned back in his leather chair and she was surprised to find everywhere tidy, just a few invoices in the in-tray. He smiled, showing perfect white teeth. Jo hadn't noticed before that, apart from being overweight, he was good looking, with brown eyes. This was the first time she'd seen his dark curly hair, as it was usually covered with a red chequered bandana.

He didn't invite her to sit so she remained standing, twiddling her thumbs.

'To be honest, Mr. Coplo, I was late this morning because I overslept.' She took a deep breath. 'So if you're going to let me go, I'll…'

'Let you go? Of course not, Miss Kingsley. You're one of my best waitresses. Please, sit down a moment.' He stood up and took a few paces, his hands clasped behind his back.

'How you like to live above restaurant?'

The question surprised her. 'I…well…I already have lodgings, besides,' she straightened her shoulders, 'I couldn't afford to live in this part of town.'

He sat down and smiled across at her. 'Don't worry. My rent not unreasonable, Miss Kingsley. I understand your struggle to get here on time. Think of convenience to yourself.'

The offer was tempting. She'd outgrown Mrs. Miller's and a place of her own away from her prying eyes was just what she needed. But not if it was going to cost her more money. She hadn't seen the flat but she felt sure it would be tasteful and expensive. 'Thank you, Mr. Coplo, but I'll have to think about it.'

'You do that, and in the meantime, here's the key. Take your time. But don't take too long.'

CHAPTER THIRTY-FIVE

Jo was surprised to find the rooms carpeted and furnished to the highest standard. The kitchen was small, but the living room was a good size and the bedroom had a double bed. Jo wondered if he had lived here at one time with his wife. There was also a bathroom. Jo had never seen such luxury. After she had finished looking round, she left, locking the door behind her. She felt foolish and annoyed with Mr. Coplo for offering her a place he knew she could never afford. Annie would laugh when she told her.

She went downstairs and returned the key.

'Well, what you think?'

'It's lovely, but I'm not sure it's for me.'

'Why you feel like that, Miss Kingsley? You not know how much rent is yet.'

'I can guess it's expensive.' She turned to leave. 'I'd better get back to work.'

'You pay me what you pay at your lodgings?' He threw his arms wide. 'What you say?'

She swirled round. 'I'd say you were mad.'

'No.' He gesticulated with his hands. 'The place is lying idle. I need someone I trust, like you, Miss Kingsley. Now, what you say?'

Frowning, she looked at him. 'I…'

He handed her back the key. 'Let me know by the end of the week.'

* * *

'It's a dream of a place, Annie.'

'It sounds too good to be true. Has he…you know…tried anything?'

'No!' But an ulterior motive had crossed her mind.

'Umm, he wants something, Jo. If you do decide to move there, lock your door.'

'I have until the end of the week to decide. Why don't you come over tonight and see it for yourself?'

When Annie saw the flat, she was bowled over. 'A double bed! I can stop over one night. He could get a lot more for it.' She walked from room to room and glanced out of the window onto the busy boulevard below. 'He stays open late, so watch he doesn't have you doing extra shifts.'

'In six months I'll have enough money to rent my own apartment and start teaching.'

'Well, in that case,' Annie laughed, 'I suppose it can't do any harm.'

A week later Jo moved in. When Mrs. Miller heard where she was going, she went on and on at her about Italians and especially one that had no wife to keep him in line.

'How can you afford a place like that? Ned trusted me to look out for you and I feel responsible.'

'You've no need to worry about me now, Mrs. Miller.' In the end, Jo was relieved to get away.

The first few weeks went well, and Jo had no reason to worry about her boss. In fact, at times she felt sorry to have harboured suspicions about his motives. She had been living above the restaurant for over a month when he knocked on her door. Inviting him inside, she offered him coffee.

'How you like the place, Miss Kingsley?'

'It's lovely, thank you.'

'Good!' He sipped his drink. 'Good coffee. Can you cook?'

'I've had plenty of practice back in Ireland.'

Smiling, he nodded. 'Why pretty girl like you don't have *ragazzo*?'

Jo frowned.

'No boyfriend.'

That surprised her, because he didn't like boyfriends hanging about the place and she'd heard him berating one of the waitresses when he saw her boyfriend hanging about outside. She laughed. 'No. I don't have time,' she said. 'I want to teach students to play the piano.'

Ignoring her statement, he placed his cup back in the saucer and turned towards her. 'What you think? You likea me, no? I mean, as a person?'

His question stunned her. She stood up, lifting her cup. 'Well… what do you mean?'

He swallowed and ran a fat finger over his thick set eyebrows. 'You grow to like me, yes?'

'Mr. Coplo, I don't feel I have to–'

'Please…please sit down. Just hear me out.'

She remained standing.

'You noticed I feel about you, no?'

'No, I can't say I have.' Unsure whether she should feel threatened, or feel sorry for him, she moved away towards the door.

'If you were to agree to marry me, you'd never want for anything. Half the business would be yours.' He smiled. 'I would, of course, expect bambinos – a son to carry on the business.'

Anger flushed her face. She took a deep breath. 'Marry you!' She tried to stay calm. So, this is what all this was about. 'Why, I couldn't possibly give you an answer without thinking it over. I hardly know you.'

His smile faded. 'Well, I'm Antonio and you are Jo, yes? It all makes perfect sense to me.'

What could she say? No-one had ever proposed marriage to her before. 'As I said, I need more time. It's been a shock. But if you'll excuse me now, I've an early shift in the morning.'

* * *

For the next couple of days, Jo avoided him as best she could. And each time he came within feet of her, she hurried off to serve a customer or clear tables. She didn't want to marry him, and nothing would entice her to marry a man she didn't love. She knew this Italian's temperament too well from working with him. An easy life was the last thing she would have married to Antonio Coplo. Besides, he was too old. He must be at least forty. How could she have been so gullible? This was America, for God's sake. Would she ever learn? After her experience with Mike, how could she settle for a loveless marriage?

Each time she went upstairs, she locked the door behind her. Ashamed to have misjudged the situation, she told no-one, least of all Annie. But when someone knocked on her door the following night, she switched off the light and feigned sleep.

'Jo, open up. It's Annie.' She had no choice but to relay the whole sorry tale to her.

'Surely you're not considering marrying the fiery Italian?'

'Are you coddin'? I'd be at his beck and call from morn' till night.' She sighed.

'What are you going to do?'

'I doubt Mrs. Miller would take me back.'

'Why not ask her? Once you refuse him, you won't be able to stay here.'

'I know. I'll give him notice and start looking for a room. Can I leave my stuff at Peter's until I find somewhere?'

'Course. I'll take some of your things with me now. You know,' Annie laughed. 'It's a shame really.' Annie walked over and flopped down onto the double bed, running her finger across the silky eider down. 'I was looking forward to staying over one night.'

Jo picked up one of the satin cushions and threw it at her. 'Why don't you stay tonight?'

'I can't, Jo. Peter's expecting me back.'

'I feel such a fool, Annie. I've lost a good job as well as somewhere to live.'

'Don't be silly. It's not your fault if pompous Italians fall at your feet. You'll soon find another job and somewhere to live.' Annie came over and placed an arm around her. 'Come on, put the kettle on. I'll have to be going soon.'

* * *

To say Mr. Coplo was upset when she turned him down, was an understatement. His face reddened and Jo thought he was going to burst a blood vessel. 'You can't just leave!' he ranted, hunching his shoulders and waving his arms in the air. 'Have you no gratitude?'

He was treating her as if she was already his wife. 'Look, one week's notice is all I'm entitled to give you.'

'What about the *appartamento*?'

She wished she could give him notice right now, but if she asked Mrs. Miller to take her back, she would only remind her that she'd told her so. 'I'll move out as soon as I find somewhere else.'

'I demand at least a month's notice for upstairs.'

'You can't expect me to stay here now. Besides, I've not signed any contract.'

'*Voi* ungrateful *ragazza*!' he yelled. 'I've had a lucky escape.'

'In that case, we both have.' The thought of being married to a man with a vile temper made her shudder.

* * *

When Jo met Annie the following day, she mentioned some newly-refurbished apartments a few blocks away. 'Peter saw the advertisement last week; leasehold, mind,' Annie said. 'What do you think?'

'Are they expensive?'

'I don't know, Jo. I didn't ask because you were so excited about the Italian's apartment. I'll ask Peter to check them out and then we can go and have a look. How much notice do you have to give whatshisname?'

'A week will be long enough, as far as I'm concerned.'

Two days later, Annie turned up at the restaurant, armed with information and advice from Peter, who said the rent was reasonable. They walked the few blocks and, from the outside, the apartments looked no different to many other residences in the Bronx; sturdy three-storey houses with sash windows. Peter arranged with the agent for them to view the apartment and return the key.

'According to Peter, there's only two left,' Annie said. 'Let's go inside.' Stone steps led up from the pavement to the hall door. 'This one's on the third floor. Peter says the view is spectacular,'

Annie said, as they climbed the stairs. Inside, the front room had a panoramic view, and in the distance Jo could see Brooklyn Bridge.

'Annie. Isn't it just grand?' she said, rushing from room to room. Their voices echoed in the empty building and there was a smell of new wood putty and paint. It reminded her of Ned, who never failed to write and sent her shamrock on St. Patrick's Day. She had never managed to get it to grow.

Annie smiled when she saw the spark return to Jo's eyes. 'It's just what you're looking for, Jo.' Then, as if reading her mind, added, 'you can always have a window box.'

Jo smiled.

'If you want to lease the property, and you're sure you can afford it, then snap it up while you've got the chance.'

It had one bedroom, bathroom, kitchenette, and the large front room that Jo had already fallen in love with. She did a twirl on the spacious floor. With an apartment of her own, she would feel beholden to no-one. 'I'm sure, Annie. Can you come with me to the Real Estate office?'

'What are we waiting for?' Annie laughed. 'You'll probably be the youngest music teacher with a place of her own, Jo. Can you imagine a woman leasing property back home?'

'That's one of the many good things about America.'

* * *

Jo survived with the minimum of furnishings and it was weeks before she could afford to take Annie with her in search of good second-hand furniture shops. They went to Macy's sale looking for fabrics, cushions, and bed linen. When it was all finished, Annie gave her a hug and said, 'I'm excited for you, Jo.'

'Thanks! I couldn't have done it without you. It's a shame they can't see it back home.' Her eyes clouded as she glanced around her. It had a cosy feel about the place and that was what she wanted.

'I see you're still trying to grow Ned's shamrock.' She glanced at the window box with the green sprig wilting between the red geraniums. 'They say it only grows in Ireland.'

Jo smiled wryly.

'Do you ever wish you could go back?' Annie asked in quizzical mood.

'Sometimes I do. But I want to get on my feet first,' she mused. Then she walked across to the window, drawing the thick green velvet curtain against the darkness outside, feeling the softness of the material between her fingers. 'It looks like it's going to be another hard winter, Annie,' she said, turning round to face her.

'I hate the winters here.' Annie gave a little shudder while running her finger along the bookshelves. Jo had quite a collection, including books on politics, and Irish/American history. 'Perhaps you should have taken up law?' Annie raised her shapely eyebrows.

'I doubt that. It was Madame Colbert, who sparked my interest in politics.' Her eyes clouded again. 'If only I'd had the opportunity of speaking to her again before she passed away, Annie.'

'It's best not to think about it.'

She crossed the room and sat down next to Annie on the comfy, beige, second-hand couch. 'I know,' she said, her face brightening. 'I'll mark the occasion with a small party. Bring Peter and the children. I'll invite one or two friends and Mrs. Miller. I'll get in sodas for the children. What do you think?'

'Good idea. It'll help you settle in.'

It was one way of thanking Annie and Peter for their patience and help while she had been struggling. After that, it became a weekly meeting place for Jo and Annie. On the occasions that Annie brought Peter with her, Jo noticed a real closeness developing between them and the glow on Annie's face was unmistakable. Seeing her friend happy reminded Jo of what she had lost, and her heart ached all the more.

The following weeks were busy for Jo. The hard work of advertising, interviewing and collating suitable clientele interested in learning to play the piano, proved more difficult that she had first thought.

'These things take time,' Annie told her. And Jo soon realised that her success would be built on trust and word of mouth. She had already bought a second-hand piano from a friend of Mrs. Miller. After having it tuned, it took pride of place in the front room.

It wasn't long before a steady stream of pupils, eager to learn the piano, were calling at the apartment, and her income increased substantially. Since her chat with Peter, she had a good insight into the stock market and she had no hesitation in investing her money in stocks and shares.

It had taken her years of hard work to achieve her dream and she was determined never to return to those dark, dismal days in Dublin when she had struggled to buy a loaf of bread.

CHAPTER THIRTY-SIX

It was a chilly afternoon in January, when Annie called at Jo's apartment. She was dressed warmly in a fur, hooded coat against the bitter wind that blew across from the Hudson River. As soon as she opened the door, Jo noticed something different about her; her green eyes shone with excitement.

'I hope I'm not interrupting a music lesson, Jo.'

'Not at all. Come in, it's great to see you. My next pupil's not due for another hour.'

Annie removed her coat and sat down.

'You've good news?' Jo asked.

'How'd you know?'

'I don't. I just know you too well, Annie O'Toole. Well, out with it, what's happened?'

Annie leaned forward on the couch and slipped off her gloves, placing them with her handbag on the table next to her. 'Peter's asked me to marry him.' Her cheeks, pink from the cold, flushed a bright red.

'Why, Annie! That's wonderful.' Jo sat down next to her. 'When did all this happen? Although, I'm not surprised! It was obvious that the two of you are in love,' she rattled on excitedly. 'Have you given him an answer?'

Annie gripped Jo's hand. 'Look, shut up and I'll tell you everything. Peter started to open up to me, telling me things he had found difficult to discuss before. His wife, Miriam, died on the birth of Ella, when Harvey was two years old. Miriam's death devastated him.' Annie paused.

'That's tragic!' Jo placed her hands in her lap. 'It must have been hard. How did he manage?'

'He took on a succession of nannies. All turned out to be unsuitable. For some time his family helped out, but for most of the time he looked after the children himself, until he feared for his business.' She paused again and looked at Jo. 'That's when I came in.' A smile broke across her face. 'I love the children, Jo. They've had a lot to contend with and they're beginning to trust me now.'

'That's understandable. But tell me about you and Peter.'

'Well,' Annie said, 'last night after I'd put the children to bed, Peter took hold of my hand. "Annie," he said, "will you do me the honour of becoming my wife." I was stunned, Jo, I needn't tell you. I had hoped, you know, from little things he'd said in the past.' She smiled again. 'But when he said he'd fallen in love with me, I told him I felt the same way.'

'I don't doubt it for one minute,' Jo said. 'I wish you both all the happiness in the world.' She reached across and hugged Annie; at the same time she felt a lump in her throat, and wondered if their relationship would change once Annie was married.

'Thanks, Jo, I'm sure we'll be happy. We're quite well suited.'

'When is it all to take place?'

'We're going to see the priest at St. Patrick's at the weekend to arrange a spring wedding. Will you be my bridesmaid?' She touched Jo's arm.

'Just you try asking anyone else, Annie O'Toole. I've never been a bridesmaid, not even for my sister's wedding.'

'That's settled then.' She sighed. 'So much has happened, Jo. Last night, I couldn't sleep a wink.'

'I'm not surprised. You were too excited.'

'Yes, that was one reason.' Her smile faded.

'What do you mean, Annie?'

'Well, you've heard the good news.' She paused. 'It's... there's something else, Jo... but please...'

'Oh, Annie, get on with it, you're making me nervous.' Jo began to fidget with the buttons on her cardigan.

'You remember me telling you that Peter's business interests had shifted to Brooklyn, well, there's a strong possibility we'll be moving there after we're married.' A moment of silence fell between them, then Annie continued. 'I'm so sorry, Jo. This won't be easy for me either.'

Jo, desperate to keep her emotions in check, couldn't bring herself to speak. The realisation of what Annie was saying was beginning to sink in, and a lonely feeling engulfed her. She had made acquaintances through the music shop and her teaching, but Annie was the only true friend she had ever had. And she couldn't imagine life without her. 'Oh, Annie,' she said at last, stifling a sob. 'It's silly, I know, but I'd never given any thought to us ever being separated.'

Annie reached out to her. 'Go on with you, a professional music teacher. You'll be too busy to miss me.'

'You don't really believe that, do you?'

'No, I don't. But we'll cope, we have to. Besides, we're not going a million miles away.' Then, smiling again, she said, 'You can come and stay with us as soon as we get settled. The textile trade is very lucrative in Brooklyn and Peter feels it would be a better place to expand the business.' She opened her coat to show Jo her powder blue jumper. 'It's one of the new season's.'

Jo felt the softness of the lambs' wool between her fingers. 'It's lovely, Annie. The colour suits you.' She bit her lip. 'I'll miss you.' Jo felt a tear sting the corner of her eyes.

'Oh, you'll be fine; before long, you'll meet someone and fall in love. I still can't believe it happened to me first. Somewhere out there you'll find your Mr. Right.'

'I might have already and let him slip through my fingers.'

'Well, in that case, only time will tell.' The clock in the room chimed out the hour and Annie jumped up. 'I must be off.' Easing on her gloves, she explained, 'I've the children to collect.'

She turned and gave Jo a hug. 'I'll need your help picking out my trousseau,' she called, as she hurried down the stairs.

When Annie had left, a sudden wave of homesickness swamped Jo. She thought about Ned, Beanie, and her family back in Dublin thousands of miles across the Atlantic, and wondered if she would ever see them again. She'd read that the boat fares had gone up again, a ploy to stop too many emigrants from coming in.

With no time to feel sorry for herself, Jo freshened up, straightened her shoulders, and opened the door with a smile to her next young client.

CHAPTER THIRTY-SEVEN

Annie and Peter's wedding in the spring of 1927 was a lovely affair, and Jo made an attractive bridesmaid. Annie's special day was momentous for Jo, but tinged with sadness and tears at their parting. If only it hadn't been so soon after the wedding, they both agreed. But Annie had stayed strong to the last minute in order to give strength to Jo, whom she felt she was abandoning.

Neither woman had envisaged the pain of separation, and they wept bitterly in each other's arms. Then Annie, suppressing her sadness, straightened her shoulders and forced a smile.

'Look! In a few weeks we'll be together in Brooklyn. We'll have a grand time, won't we, Peter?' She turned to her husband, who smiled and reassured them both. But Jo felt a funny feeling in her stomach, Annie had been a guiding influence for most of her formative years, and already she was feeling isolated and lonely as she waved goodbye to Annie and her new family.

Within days of the wedding, a letter arrived from Annie. It was filled with encouraging words, urging her to keep her dream alive. And a month later, Jo was on the ferry service across the East River to Brooklyn. She spent a wonderful week with Annie, Peter and the children in their beautiful new home. They went for days out, picnicked on sandy beaches, and visited the amusement parks on Coney Island.

All too soon it was time to go, and Peter walked with the two women towards the ferry. 'This is a beautiful place,' Jo said, as they sat watching the ferry come in. 'I can see it's better for the children.'

'There's plenty of beautiful parks, museums, colleges and

universities, and life here is every bit as exciting as it is in Manhattan,' Annie told her. 'I'm finding new places to see every day. The children are already making new friends at school.' She smiled. 'The world's a big place, Jo. You and I have seen more of it than our families back home ever will.'

Peter, previously engrossed in his morning newspaper, glanced across at the two women, both deep in thought. He stood up and walked towards them. 'Charles Lindbergh has just made the first non-stop Atlantic crossing from New York to Paris. Isn't that amazing?' he said.

Annie nodded. The news hardly raised interest.

'If Lindbergh can do it,' Peter continued, 'people will travel the world a lot faster in the future.'

Jo, who had so far managed to keep cheerful, glanced towards Annie, who had tears welling in her eyes. Saying goodbye again wasn't going to be easy. They had been through so much together and Jo felt totally alone without her dearest friend. People began moving forwards and boarding the ferry. 'Well, this is it,' she said, glancing up at Annie.

'You can visit us any time you want,' Peter said, shaking her hand warmly.

'Thank you for a lovely week. I feel so much better for it.' She had to bite her lip hard to prevent herself from crying.

'It's what friends are for,' he said, moving to the side to allow the two women to say their goodbyes in private.

* * *

In the summer of 1928, driven by ambition and loneliness, Jo received her master's degree. She had at last achieved her ambition, and her life changed. She had more bookings than she could handle. As well as giving piano lessons, she had invitations to play in concerts in and around the borough. She was invited to talk in schools and give lectures at seminars. And occasionally, she allowed herself to be pampered and escorted by a male colleague to the follies on Broadway. Some weeks, she hardly had time to miss Annie, or even think about Mike.

For now, she found her work fulfilling. Every dollar she earned over and above her expenditure, she invested in the stock market. She bought *The Wall Street Journal* most days to keep track. Peter had been right; her shares had doubled within weeks. It made everything she had worked for worthwhile.

Annie and Ned continued to send letters to Jo. She missed them, especially Annie, but with other interests to fill her time, the pain became less. They each said how proud they were to hear of her achievement. Ned sent photos of his children and of Cissy's children. Looking at them brought tears to her eyes. She could hardly wait to see them, especially her little niece Sarah Jane, who looked so like Larry with dark curly hair. Her collection of photographs had grown. She now had enough to fill a photo album. Two framed portraits hung on her apartment wall – one of her and Madame Colbert, taken by a photographer on the crossing to Cherbourg; the other of Annie and Peter taken on their wedding day. A happy couple, Jo thought, each time she looked at it.

The photographs gave her a sense of belonging. She hoped that one day she would find that special someone. But so far no-one had come close to Mike Pasiński.

American politics continued to intrigue her. She listened closely to the elections, wondering who would take the place of President Coolidge as his health declined. The newspapers declared he was suffering from chronic stomach pains. Jo had no reason to consider him an inefficient President, except that she had noticed how badly the farmers were doing lately, and it appeared they got little understanding from him in their plight. It was no surprise to her when he retired from office. Herbert Hoover was a strong candidate for the Republican Party, and his reputation as a humanitarian put him in good standing. Jo at first thought he would make a good President. He was Roman Catholic, struggling against a Protestant nation. She felt she should support him, but changed her mind when she discovered he was linked with New York City's Tammany Hall, a political organisation with a corrupt reputation. So it was with baited breath that Jo listened to the radio as the elections drew closer.

In November of the same year, Hoover won by a landslide, and by March of 1929 he was ceremoniously established as the new leader of the United States.

* * *

With more work commitments, Jo's plans to return to Ireland were shelved, but she was determined to make it home in the spring of 1930. She planned to inform her students well in advance; that way she would not be letting anyone down. Almost five years had passed since she and Annie had first arrived on America's shores. Jo could hardly believe it was that long ago.

So much had changed, particularly Jo. She now had the means of supporting herself, and the excitement of watching her hard earned dollars grow. She planned to sell some shares early the following year, knowing she would make a good return, and two months later sell some more. This would give her enough money to purchase a first class ticket from the shipping office, and buy some new clothes for herself when the new spring fashions appeared in the shops. She would pick up some fashionable clothes at Macy's for Liam and James, who were young working lads now. She missed them, and longed to see them again.

On nights too hot to sleep, she lay awake excitedly planning her return trip to Ireland. She thought about her mother and wondered how she was. Ned only mentioned her arthritic complaint occasionally. Good old Ned, he always replied to her letters. Her life would be lacking without him.

During the next six months, America's economy continued to prosper under Hoover and Jo had no reason to be concerned until she read that agriculture was still economically unsound, due to an increase in efficiency around the world. It was September, six months before her planned journey to Ireland. She was keeping a close eye on the stock market, wondering whether or not to sell before then.

Annie and Peter advised her to wait and get an even better return, but Jo wasn't so sure. She had always trusted Peter's judgement. Within a short space of time, because of the high rise in stocks, the demand to buy grew. And Jo became uneasy when she read that individuals were investing billions of dollars on the stock market, some borrowing from banks, re-mortgaging their homes and obtaining money by whatever means they could in order to buy. Realizing how risky that could be, she felt herself fortunate that the money she had invested was at least her own.

Again, she wondered if this was the right time for her to sell. Then one evening as she sat reading the newspaper in her apartment, she noted that industrial sales were beginning to slow down.

Everything changed as if overnight. And Jo began to panic when an urgent telegram arrived from Peter, advising her to sell immediately.

CHAPTER THIRTY-EIGHT

On arrival at Wall Street, Jo couldn't believe her eyes. She had to fight her way through the panic-stricken crowds before joining the growing queues outside the banks. It was a long hour of waiting before she eventually got inside. That was even worse – thronged with investors, haggling over price drops, intent on getting the best price. With a sinking feeling, she realised that it might already be too late; everything was happening so fast.

Frightened of the panic around her, she prayed, 'Dear God! Don't let me lose my savings.' The feverish buying had given way to desperate selling. Prices were dropping even as she queued up waiting her turn. Jo felt an anxious feeling in her stomach as the crowd pushed forward. People were shouting and yelling, waving their arms. She thought she would faint and be trampled on. In the charged atmosphere, she felt confused, wondering if she should wait. Would the prices go up again? She strained to see the notice displaying prices falling, rising a little, and falling even lower.

'Dear God,' she cried, holding her head. 'What shall I do?' She wished Peter and Annie were here. For all she knew, they could be somewhere in the massive crowd. Peter had so much more to lose. Chaos erupted around her. Police were called in to control the crowds. Men were shouting above the crowds.

When eventually her turn came, a battered and bruised Jo had no alternative but to accept what was offered – a very small fraction of her hard-earned investment, which had in past weeks trebled and at times quadrupled over the past two years. Tearful and exhausted, she heaved her way through the endless crowds until she was outside again, where she crouched down in a collapsed state on the sidewalk and wept. She was not alone. There were hundreds of people in the same predicament, but it was of little comfort to her. She felt totally devastated.

Burying her head in her hands, she rocked backwards and forwards, moaning as if she was demented. And she stayed there in a state of shock, unaware of the cold October winds that swirled around her shivering body, until she felt someone touch her arm. She glanced up into the tear-streaked face of Annie, Peter ashen-faced by her side, sobs choking his throat. Shakily, Jo stood up. Her feet and legs were numb. Cold and dazed, she wrapped her arms around Annie and they wept.

Then she looked towards Peter. 'Did you manage to save anything?' Both Peter and Annie shook their heads. Seeing the distress on their faces, Jo knew that they, too, had been left without a dime. Peter's investment in the stock market had given him remarkable profits over the years, with no reason to doubt his own judgement. He, like millions, was completely crushed by the suddenness of the fall. The two women looked on bewildered as he drew a white handkerchief from his pocket and held it to his face in a bid to hide the despair that threatened to engulf him. Annie was suddenly in his arms, comforting and soothing the man she loved.

'Oh, darling,' she was saying, stroking the back of his head. 'This has got to be a nightmare.'

'This is as real as you are standing here before me,' he said, his voice barely audible. Clinging to Annie, he sobbed, 'I'm sunk. We've lost everything.'

Listening to Peter, Jo thought her heart would break. 'Why? Oh, why?' she cried. Annie reached out and drew Jo into their circle. And they clung together, like a permanent fixture in the midst of hundreds. She could hear the sounds of devastation all around them as individuals learnt of their losses. Investors climbed onto the roofs of buildings, threatening to throw themselves off. Gangs of police with truncheons charged down Wall Street, and masses of dazed and shocked people were ushered from the area.

Police vehicles, their sirens shrill, closed in around the building, and riot police rushed inside. It looked as if all hell had broken loose, and Jo would never forget the cries of despair.

'It's time to move along now,' a policeman touched Peter's elbow, 'you could get hurt standing around here.' Slowly, the trio moved away.

The day had been one of extreme anxiety and hopelessness, which would be etched on their memories for a long time to come.

* * *

The world outside was blanketed by snow, and the weather became treacherous. The bleak winter did nothing to uplift the thousands who had lost all they had invested; many were completely ruined financially. Peter's sales went down and down, until he had no choice but to declare himself bankrupt. Annie still had her own bank account, which Peter had insisted she keep separate after they were married; with the children to look after, it saved them from the poverty line. But she told Jo that Peter was adamant things would improve, and they must hang onto that hope.

When Jo's parish priest told the congregation that they had no choice but to trust the President, she wanted to believe him. But when her clients could no longer afford to have music lessons, it threw her further into despair. With cutbacks everywhere, it appeared that the income she now depended upon was halved, and within weeks cut to a third. She felt impoverished and lonely, barely able to pay the lease on her apartment. Two of her neighbours had already moved out due to non-payment. What would she do if she lost the roof over her head? Would Mrs. Miller take her back rent-free? She doubted that very much. It was a case of do or die.

Determined to survive, she wrote poems and songs about love, which she surprisingly sold to publishers. It helped keep her afloat, bought her frugal meals, bread and cheap cuts of meat to make soup. Living with her mother years before had taught her how to survive on very little.

Her life was anything but easy, and if things hadn't gone so terribly wrong, she would now have been on a ship home to Ireland to be with her family. She lied when she told Cissy that the reason she wasn't coming was due to work commitments. In her letter to Ned, she told of the devastation the crash had caused, but never let on how destitute she was.

Jo, and millions like her, soon became disillusioned with President Hoover and longed for a re-election. Time dragged with no money and less work. On the odd occasion when she ventured downtown, she was appalled at the sickening queues of men looking for work. Thousands of people lined the sidewalks in New York every day, but few were hired.

After such a sight, she thought herself luckier than most. These men, with little hope of finding work, probably had wives and children waiting at home hungry.

Jo and Annie continued to support one another and visited each other whenever they could afford to. But Jo's loneliness increased. The economy's growth was slow and her hopes of returning to Ireland faded.

Hoover was blamed for not doing enough to divert the depression, and most people were keen for change. When Roosevelt won the election, Jo celebrated the results with her neighbours in the street. Like many other women, she warmed towards him, for he was the first President to appoint a woman, Frances Perkins, to his cabinet. Jo had great belief in the new reforms that he was proposing to deal with the depression, and she wrote him a special poem basing it on what he had achieved for women. His personal reply astounded her. He thanked her for sending it, said how much he'd enjoyed reading it, and would keep it always. Jo framed the letter and hung it up in her apartment. Once her friends and neighbours heard, it attracted many visitors to the apartment.

CHAPTER THIRTY-NINE

Spring of 1935

When Jo awoke, the sun was bursting through her bedroom window. The previous day, she'd had an enquiry from a client who wanted to resume their piano lessons. It had lifted her spirits and she felt the black cloud that had hidden the sun from her life for so long, beginning to lift. She scrambled from her bed and drew back the curtains. It was the first time in ages that she had bothered to look up at the sky. Today it was blue, and when she emerged from the bedroom, there was a spring in her step.

She decided to get some, much needed, sun on her pale face, and write her poems outdoors; years of frugal dieting had done nothing for her once smooth complexion. She bathed quickly and washed her hair, before making herself tea and toast. Afterwards, she ran her hand along the rail of dated dresses hanging in her wardrobe, choosing a bright yellow to match her mood. It was fresh, with a wide white belt, and reminded her of a day in Paris with Jean-Pierre, so long ago. With her weight loss, there was no problem about it still fitting her.

Lifting her long hair, in badly need of a trim, she pinned it up on top of her head. She was twenty-nine years old; it was time she stopped living in the past, and began looking towards the future. She had let herself go of late. But today, looking at her reflection in the cheval mirror, she felt satisfied with her appearance. She smiled. Both she and Annie had picked the mirror up in a second-hand furniture shop, because it reminded Jo of Madame Colbert. Placing a pen and notebook into her handbag, she slipped her feet into a pair of soft navy walking shoes, picked up her cardigan, and left the apartment.

She took the subway to Manhattan and walked towards Central Park, feeling the warm sun on her face. It seemed ages since she had gone there with Annie but the park hadn't changed. The fine weather had brought people out of doors, and the traffic was almost at gridlock. Automobiles lined the pavement along the entrance to the park.

Inhaling the fresh air, she walked through the gates. She had forgotten how much she loved this park, with its peaceful atmosphere and rocky hills and winding paths. It was the best place to be at this time of year. Its open woodlands stretched for miles, with beautiful gardens, lakes, and shady nooks, idyllic for peaceful contemplation or just relaxing. Annie had once said that Central Park was like a green oasis that appeared to have been dropped from the sky into the middle of Manhattan. How right she was.

With more people using their own transport, the park seemed noisier, but as she walked further into its interior, outside influences lessened and she felt more relaxed in the pleasant surroundings.

In normal times Jo had enjoyed free outdoor concerts and other events that took place here, but most things had come to a standstill during the harsh depressive years. She was gladdened to see it was still a haven for freelance artists, and aspiring writers who came hoping for inspiration. She came across an empty bench by a stone wall that curved into a recess, and sat down with just her thoughts, her notebook and pen. Here, it was easy to forget her worries and let her creative mind run free.

She closed her eyes, listening to a variety of sounds. Migrating birds had returned to the park to build nests. She could hear one rustling in the tree above her. Small sparrows twittered around her feet and small children laughed and played nearby. She wondered what her nieces and nephews were like now. When she opened her eyes, more people had entered the park and were sitting on the long benches, eating sandwiches. Birds swooped down to eat the crumbs. She found the average New Yorker friendly and willing to chat with a passing stranger, reminding her of Dublin in that way. Her notebook on her lap, she leaned her head backwards and closed her eyes once more, seeking inspiration to write one more verse to a poem she'd started earlier. Someone was calling her name.

'Jo! It is you!

Glancing up, she shaded her eyes with her hand. The sunlight dappled him in light and shadow. Stubble covered the lower part of his face, but there was no disguising those piercing blue eyes.

Her heart raced. 'Mike? Mike Pasiński?' He'd lost a substantial amount of weight and his tall frame bent slightly towards her.

He fingered the collar of his blue open neck shirt. 'May I?' he asked.

She moved along the bench. 'How've you been, Jo?' His smile, and the way he glanced towards her, brought the past flooding back. It had been a long time ago. He didn't look at all as she remembered him. She was so taken aback she didn't answer.

'I'm sorry,' he said. 'I've no right to ask.'

'That's all right. I'm grand,' she said.

'Congratulations on attaining your master's degree. I always knew you had it in you.'

'Thank you. How about you? Did the crash affect you much?' Her eyes moved across the strong lines of his thin face. He looked older than thirty-five.

He straightened his shoulders. 'I was lucky,' he said, 'I kept my money under the mattress.' She laughed. He still had his sense of humour. 'No, thank God, it didn't, Jo. I'd always invested my money in Chase National Bank, here in New York City. And although they, too, were lending thousands of dollars, the bank didn't fall in the crash.'

'Oh, so you weren't swayed by the stock market?'

'No, but I think we all lost something.' He ran his hand distractedly over his unshaven face. 'You know, if I'd had an inkling I was going to bump into you today, I'd have made more of an effort.'

'It's been a long time, Mike.' She lowered her eyes as old feelings surfaced. She had dreamt of this moment so often, and wondered if this too, was a dream. Was he really here, or was she hallucinating?

'Sure, eight years…and five months,' he said, 'I've thought of you often.' He tugged at the cuffs of his shirt. His fingers, once stained with nicotine, were white.

'You're not smoking?'

He looked pensive. 'Umm. No! That's one habit I managed to kick.' He knitted his fingers together. 'Why did you never answer my letters?'

She wanted to reach out to him, but for all she knew he could be married.

'I was young, confused by a love I didn't understand.'

'I'm sorry, Jo. I should have made my intentions clearer. I should never have rushed you. I never married. I suppose, I mean…' He glanced down at her hand. 'You didn't…'

She looked up at him. 'I never found anyone I loved.'

'Me neither.'

Shocked by the sudden turn of events, tears welled in her eyes and she fell silent.

Mike stood up, pulling her with him. He took both her hands in his and held her gaze. 'I never stopped loving you, Jo.' Then, on impulse, oblivious of the people around them, he put his arms around her and kissed her, gentle at first, then with the passion she remembered. She felt alive again for the first time in years.

* * *

Over the next few days, they met in various parks around New York. They walked and talked, confiding in one another. She told him of Annie and Peter's marriage, and their subsequent move to Brooklyn; her honoured and admired letter from the President; and how her aborted trip to Ireland had hit her badly.

'If only I'd known. If you'd just got in touch? Just a note would have been sufficient for me to come running. But you left me no choice but to keep away.'

'I'm sorry. It's in the past now, Mike. You, too, must have suffered, if not due to the crash. What else has been happening with you?' she asked. It was as though they had never been apart. But the Mike she remembered had been muscular, and she wondered if he'd been ill.

'About a month before the crash, I heard a rumour that Chase Bank was considering merging with Equity Trust. Fearing there might be a reason behind this, I withdrew enough capital to purchase a house in Camden, New Jersey.'

'So what are you doing in New York?'

'I've not entirely left the Village, Jo. For a long time I'd hoped...' He sighed. 'Besides, my business interests are here, and I'm in New York to finally let the apartment go.'

'So, you're moving away?' Thoughts of losing him again brought a lump to her throat.

He paused on the busy sidewalk and reached for her hand. 'Do you think you could ever love me again?' He was looking at her with adoration in his eyes.

Her heart raced. 'I don't think I ever stopped.'

'*Really!* Then marry me, Jo! And come with me to New Jersey. The house is in Fairview, in the historic district of Camden. It's a wonderful place to raise a family.'

'Oh, Mike, I thought you were against marriage?'

'That was back then. I was a fool. I'll make it up to you if you'll be my wife.'

'Are you sure?'

'I love you, and I'm never going to let you out of my sight again.'

'Well, in that case.' Laughing, she reached up and kissed him.

They stood on the pavement, arms circling each other, quite unaware of the smiling pedestrians hurrying past them.

CHAPTER FORTY

Jo and Mike were married in the Roman Catholic Church of Saint John the Baptist, in Fairview, N.J., in July, 1935, three months after their reunion. It was a fairly quiet affair with just Annie, Peter and the children, Max and a girlfriend. Annie was Jo's maid of honour, and Max was Mike's best man. Mrs. Miller, who had retired and gone to live in Queens with her sister, sent greetings of congratulations.

'It's like a dream come true,' Jo told Annie, her eyes filled with happiness, before she walked up the aisle a radiant bride on Peter's arm. She wore a white chiffon dress trimmed with lace that hung beautifully down the contours of her trim figure. Her fair hair framed her face and her skin had a healthy glow. She was aware of Mike's intake of breath as he turned to take her hand. Wearing a slate grey suit and white shirt, he looked every bit as handsome as when she had first set eyes on him in Greenwich Village. His fair hair was trimmed shorter than when she'd first known him.

He lifted her veil, and she looked up into his eyes. 'You look beautiful, Jo. I'm a lucky man,' he whispered, and squeezed her hand. Jo smiled. Their vows taken, Annie cried and congratulated her friend, along with the few guests and the small congregation that had gathered in the church at the sight of a wedding. Jo and Mike, deliriously happy and in love, only had eyes for each other.

They held a reception befitting their small party, at an established eating-house, where a quartet played romantic melodies especially for the newlyweds. Mike stood up in front of his wife. 'May I have the pleasure of this dance, Mrs. Pasínski?'

It had been so long since Jo had danced, but somehow she

found herself following her husband's every move as he guided her onto the small dance floor, followed later by Peter and Annie, Max and his friend. Mike nuzzled her neck. 'I'm glad you could make it. The party wouldn't have been the same without you.'

Jo reached up, cupped her hands around the back of his neck, and stroked the back of his head.

'That's nice,' he said, looking down into her eyes, his arms around her slim waist. They paused for a moment as if transfixed. Then they danced slowly across the floor, lost in a world of their own. The ban on alcoholic drinks during prohibition had just been lifted, which gave way to jolly merriment throughout the establishment, including the wedding party.

Because the recession was far from over, Jo and Mike spent their first night as a married couple in their own home which Jo had helped to furnish and decorate. She had fallen in love with it the moment she set eyes on it. At the time of their marriage, Fairview was sparsely populated, and their house and grounds – surrounded by a low white fence – took up a huge area of land. The outside of the house was also painted white, with dormer windows to the front overlooking a garden plot with well-established trees and shrubs. The branches of the trees overlapped each other, shading parts of the three bedroomed house from the hot sun. To Jo and Mike, it was the house of their dreams; their nearest neighbour was hardly visible through the thick lush greenery.

Mike carried her over the threshold and when they finally reached the bedroom, her cheeks were flushed. Still holding her tightly, he placed her down on the bed just as he had done all those years ago, her body trembling at his nearness. Unlike then, this time she had nothing to fear, no inhibitions. She was a mature woman of twenty-nine, intent on making her husband happy. When Mike lay next to her in their new bed, a surge of excitement rushed through her; his touch so gentle that when he reached for her, she melted in his arms. His lips were warm on her neck, and moved slowly down her slender body.

'Oh, Jo!' he whispered softly. 'I love you so much.'

'I love you, too,' she said, as another wave of excitement shot through her. Nothing mattered except their great need for each other, as they merged together in an endless night of passion. Later, as they lay spent in each other's arms, Mike turned towards her, resting on one elbow. 'Are you happy, Mrs. Pasìnski?'

'I'm very happy, Mr. Pasínski! You'll be the first to know if I'm not.' She smiled and snuggled close to him.

'I want to spend the rest of my life making up for the unhappiness I caused you,' he said. 'I'll make sure you never want for anything.'

Jo kissed his lips to stop him talking, and again they became entwined, reaching heights of passion she never knew existed.

* * *

The weeks passed blissfully. Jo's personal possessions, together with her piano, were ferried across the Hudson River to her new home in New Jersey. Jo couldn't have been happier and at times found it unbelievable that she and Mike had been reunited in such an unexpected way. She took nothing for granted, fearful that her newfound happiness would be snatched away.

Her life with Mike was bliss, and she wondered if all married couples were this happy. As they settled down in their idyllic surroundings, they found that by combining their talents they could achieve almost anything. Jo wrote powerful love poems that came from the heart, and introduced words of love into Mike's beautiful melodies. Publishers were keen to accept their work, and they were both surprised by their good luck. Their song, '*Honeymoon*', sold hundreds, then thousands, of copies and they fast became household names.

They were working long hours to meet deadlines, and Jo again worried about her husband's weight loss. She sat writing at the desk, delighted in her choice of words that perfectly matched his musical arrangement. But she could tell by the way he glanced across at her, something troubled him. She had tried to get him to see a doctor, but he flatly refused. In the few months since their marriage and becoming business partners, Jo and Mike had accumulated hundreds of dollars, which had given her a feeling of security. Their money remained in Chase National Bank, along with Mike's savings.

The gloom of the recession was still evident everywhere, and the economy had a long way to go before it could be said normality had returned. The busy period in their work schedule, however, showed no signs of waning. And Jo, mindful of the dark shadows that circled her husband's eyes, wondered if now might be the time for them to take their vacation. Mike had promised to take her to Ireland for a whole month after they were married. She thought this might be a good time to broach the subject.

'Would you be terribly disappointed, darling, if we postponed it for another while? The recession is still biting hard for some, and we can hardly turn work away,' Mike said.

'Umm...' She wrinkled her nose with disappointment, but had to agree.

'We should consider ourselves lucky to have so much work while others are still struggling to get on their feet.' He stretched his back and stood up.

'Well, as long as we don't put it off indefinitely.' She put her arms around him and kissed him.

'I'm sorry to be such a slave driver,' Mike said, picking up his jacket. 'We both deserve a night out. Come on, my love, I'm taking you out to dinner.'

* * *

It was as if their songs were giving joy to the American people during the depressing years, but as the months passed and the weather turned colder, Jo became aware of Mike's restlessness. He was edgy, unable to sleep at night, resulting in him snatching sleep during the day. Her heart ached for him. At times she caught him staring into space, a faraway look in his eyes.

'Mike. What is it? Talk to me! Tell me what's bothering you?'

'There's nothing for you to worry about, Jo, everything's fine.' Sighing, he stood up and went to the bathroom, leaving Jo feeling miserable and excluded. Another woman perhaps? But they hadn't been married a year yet, and Mike was so loving towards her, except when he shut her out. She felt frightened and lonely again. Their heavy workload left little time to talk during the day but she tried being patient, hoping he'd tell her when he felt ready.

Later, as they lay in bed, Jo suggested that they should ease up on work. 'We can afford to take on less. We'd manage, Mike, at least until you feel less stressed.'

'Why can't you leave me alone!' he snapped, then scrambled from the bed and went downstairs.

Jo was devastated, hurt by his tone of voice and his refusal to confide in her. Only a few months ago, he couldn't bear to have her out of his sight. She waited a while before going down to join him. He was sitting at the piano and glanced round as she came into the room. He opened his arms and she rushed into them. She saw tears in his eyes. He pulled her onto his knee and buried his face in her hair.

'I'm so sorry, darling, please forgive me.' He stroked her hair and Jo felt a lump form in her throat. After a moment, he said, 'We can't ease up just yet, Jo. I want to make sure you never want for anything ever again. That's why I work so hard. Memories of my mother's struggle still haunt me.'

Jo tried to understand his reasons and promised to fuss less. 'You know you're turning into a workaholic. But I intend to do something about that right now,' she said and closed the lid on the piano, put his sheets of music away, and led him over to the couch. But before they sat down, Mike swept her up into his arms and carried her back upstairs to bed.

CHAPTER FORTY-ONE

Winter turned to spring; Mike became less stressed as their bank account grew. It was a year since their reunion in Central Park and they decided to celebrate the occasion at home, as Mike rarely ate the food they ordered in a restaurant. When Jo returned home with the groceries, including a bottle of champagne to celebrate, she found Mike slumped over the typewriter, his face ghostly white, a half-typed letter to their publisher in the typewriter. She hadn't the heart to wake him, and busied herself making dinner for them both. She cooked only what she knew he would eat; his appetite was spasmodic.

Although they were now well known for their music and writing talents, no-one, no matter how well they were doing, could afford to stand still. The recession still raged in certain areas. If they couldn't deliver, there was always someone in the wings waiting to jump into their shoes. Annie wrote to say she had picked up one of their lyrics and song sheets in a music shop in Brooklyn, and how proud both she and Peter were to have friends who were famous.

Mike woke up as Jo brought in the food. He came over and sat at the table. 'You should have woken me, sweetheart,' he said, looking up at her.

'You seemed so tired, Mike, I didn't like to. Now might be a good time to take that holiday to Ireland. I'm so longing to see my family.' She added quickly, 'We could visit Tipperary, your mother's birthplace. What do you say?'

'Okay, it sounds good, sweetheart,' he said with interest. 'As it's close to our anniversary, it could be the honeymoon we didn't have.'

'That's wonderful, Mike. When can we book our tickets?'

'Tomorrow.'

'Oh, that's grand.' Relieved and excited at the same time, she had to suppress the tears that threatened. She busied herself serving the food as Mike filled their glasses with the champagne.

'We'll check our account at the bank. After that, we can call at the shipping office, make enquiries about shipping schedules.' Mike's growing enthusiasm delighted Jo.

'This salmon is delicious, Jo.' He put a forkful into his mouth. 'Get some more of this next time.'

'Oh, I will. Mr. Brown said he only buys in the best.' Thrilled to see her husband in such good spirits, Jo couldn't wait to get to the bank the following morning.

Mike was staggered at the amount of money they had accumulated. And on the way home, Jo couldn't help smiling at him as he glanced at every passing motor vehicle.

'Hey, Jo, it's time we had an automobile. After all, we've a reputation to maintain,' he joked, his old charm returning. 'With four children on order, we're going to need one big enough,' he chuckled. 'We'll look around when we get back from Ireland.' He squeezed her hand. She loved him so much. This was one of Mike's good days and she was all too aware that tomorrow might be a different story.

Later, as they checked through the sailing times for the next few weeks, Jo said, 'Oh Mike, I'm so excited about going home.' Her face flushed with excitement. 'We could be in Ireland for our first wedding anniversary.'

'Great. And once I've delivered my finished concerto to the publishers, I'm all yours.'

That afternoon they went back to work. Jo had hoped to talk to Mike about seeing a doctor before they sailed, but she did not want to spoil his happy mood so she decided that tomorrow would be soon enough.

* * *

When at last Mike's work was finished, Jo told him she would drop it into the publishers as she had shopping to do in town. That morning, Mike wasn't very hungry. She made scrambled eggs with lightly buttered toast; Mike's favourite.

'Try to eat a little,' she coaxed. But he moved the plate to one side, and sipped his tea. 'I'll call at the drug store on my way back, get you something to boost your appetite,' she said, clearing the breakfast things.

'Leave those, honey. I'll wash up, while you get off. They'll be pleased to have it a week earlier. When you get home, we'll go to the shipping office.' She kissed him and said she would be back in just over an hour.

On the subway across the city with the finished concerto, Jo's heart was full with thoughts of seeing her family again. But her husband's health worried her greatly. If only she knew what was wrong with him. He had told her he could sleep on rocks, and that the tiredness he felt was overwhelming. But what could she do if he refused to see a doctor?

At the publishers, Jo explained about their forthcoming vacation. They wished her *bon voyage*, and said they would be in touch in a couple of months' time. That sorted, Jo began to organise presents to take home. At the last count, there were three new additions to the family that she had yet to meet, and she couldn't wait for everyone to meet Mike. She had no doubt that they would find him very agreeable and charming.

At the drugstore, Jo had a word with the druggist behind the partition, explaining about the terrible tiredness and loss of appetite plaguing her husband's life.

'How long has he been like this?'

'Quite a few months now,' Jo answered.

'I'll give you these vitamin tablets which might help his tiredness. But,' he hesitated, 'if there's no improvement, get him to see a doctor. If you go across to the dispensary, ask for a tonic which should improve his appetite.' He smiled.

'Thank you.' Jo paid the required sum and collected the tonic before making her way to the subway. It was more crowded than earlier. Her heart was lighter now she had something to offer Mike. A light rain began to fall, and a cloudy mist hung about, making the air humid.

By the time she reached Fairview, her spirits were high, her thoughts positive. It wouldn't do for Mike to see her otherwise. When she went inside, he greeted her with a smile on his pale face, the dishes washed and the kettle whistling. He looked relaxed and was anxious to hear what the publishers' reaction had been to their forthcoming vacation. He sat down to listen to all the news, and examine the medicine that Jo had brought back from her trip to town.

Before bed, Mike helped her lift their cases down from the cupboard and put them in the spare bedroom, ready to be packed. The night was hot and sticky, making sleep difficult and too soon to know if the tonic and vitamins would relieve Mike's lethargy.

He was sleeping when Jo slipped from underneath the sheet. On Sunday, they usually had breakfast in bed. When she returned, she was surprised to find Mike's breathing laboured. Placing the tray with tea, milk and cereals on the bedside table, she asked, 'Are you all right, darling?' She propped an extra pillow under his head. He woke immediately, running his fingers down the outline of her face.

'I'm fine. Couldn't you sleep?' he whispered.

She lay down next to him. He held her close and in the warmth of his embrace, she drifted back to sleep along with him, ignoring the breakfast. When she awakened, the room was bathed in bright sunshine. It was midday. Shoving her feet into her slippers, she turned to Mike, who was still sleeping. There was a large lump under Mike's right jaw that she hadn't noticed earlier. She was gripped by fear and her gasp woke him.

'What is it, sweetheart?' he asked, alarm in his voice. His hand shot up to the discomfort he felt in his face.

'Something's wrong, Mike. Please don't shut me out any more.' Tears began to trickle down her face.

'Please don't cry. Come here.' His eyes were saying he loved her, but she could see he was too weak to raise his head.

'No, Mike, this has gone on long enough, I'm going to phone for a doctor.'

In spite of his protests, she continued to get dressed, glancing over her shoulder at her husband. 'I won't be long,' she said, and hurried downstairs.

CHAPTER FORTY-TWO

Since his admission to Our Lady of Lourdes Medical Centre in Camden, Mike had become withdrawn. He hadn't spoken about his feelings, not even to Jo. His head swirled with possibilities as to what his illness could be. Torn with guilt for marrying Jo and then having to burden her with the likelihood of a fatal illness, had plagued him ever since he first felt languid six months ago. Shutting his mind to it hadn't made it go away, and now he had to be brave for Jo's sake. He decided to ask his doctor; it would be better to know than stay in ignorance.

Doctor Nicol, who had carried out a number of tests on Mike, was looking after him. He specialised in anaemic disorders. That evening when the doctor stopped by his bed to ask how he was feeling, Mike got his opportunity.

'What exactly is wrong with me, Doctor Nicol?'

'I can't be sure without doing some more tests.' He smiled. 'We'll get them done straight away,' he said reassuringly.

'But you must have some idea what you're looking for?'

'I'm sorry. I know how this must feel, Mr. Pasiński. I'd prefer to wait for the results. Rest assured, I'll be perfectly frank once the tests are done. They'll be done this afternoon.' The physician moved away.

Alone in his room, Mike's mind raced. He knew something was wrong, he'd have to be stupid not to. Oh my darling wife. My sweet Jo, how can I bear to part from you; to leave you alone? He was shaking his head, thinking aloud. 'I'll fight it whatever it is, sweetheart, I promise.' An unexpected sob choked in his throat.

It was the first time he'd allowed his suspicions to run away with him, but his instincts told him that his illness was fatal. While Jo was out, he had read the medical encyclopaedia for knowledge of blood disorders, and he was convinced he had leukaemia. He felt remorse for the way he had treated Jo, but how could he share his morbid thoughts with her. He must protect her for as long as he could.

She had come every day to visit him. He recognised the sound of her high heels in the corridor before she reached his room. She had sat by his bedside until she was informed politely that it was time to go. He wished she could stay. How he missed her soft body next to his during the endless nights they were parted. He had never felt like this about anyone before, and he knew that, in Jo, he had found his life companion. But how much life had he left? The thought frightened him.

It was hours yet to visiting time and he couldn't wait to see Jo's lovely face, hold her close, and tell her how much he loved her.

* * *

The doctor treated Jo for mild exhaustion when she became weary travelling back and forth to Camden every day. But she couldn't stay away. After a month of tests and blood transfusions, which appeared to have given Mike a new lease of life, Jo was no wiser as to the cause of his illness.

She found the house lonely, and she couldn't bear to sleep in their bed without Mike to wrap his arms around her, and tell her that everything would be all right. There was no-one she could immediately confide in. Her nearest neighbour – a midwife – lived half a mile away, and Jo had only spoken to her a few times. She missed Ned, Annie and Peter, especially this last month, and had to content herself with letters. In one letter, Annie said that they were lucky to be in America where Mike would get the best possible treatment, and how pleased she was to hear that the blood transfusions were showing results. She told Jo to stay positive, and that she would be in touch again soon.

When Jo read the Medical Journal herself, and discovered that Doctor Nicol was one of the Medical Association's top physicians, who specialised in radiation therapy in the treatment of blood disorders, it only increased her anxieties. She remembered a woman at the Manhattan School of Music who had suffered with anaemia. Her doctor had treated her condition with an iron tonic and she soon improved. All Jo wanted was for Mike to return home to her, and their happy life to continue.

Each time she visited Mike he was in fine spirits, banishing her fears and worries to the back of her mind. He joked and laughed with the other patients, leaving her in no doubt that he was improving. 'Look at me, sweetheart,' he said, when Jo entered the room. He drew himself up tall, stretching his arms wide to show how strong he was, before gathering her into his arms. 'The doctor said I can go home in a couple of days.'

'That's wonderful news, Mike.' A smile lifted her face. All her negative thoughts vanished when Mike kissed her in a passionate embrace. They moved apart when Doctor Nicol knocked and walked in.

'Hello, Mrs. Pasiński. Your husband never stops talking about you.'

'Oh,' Jo said. 'He's been telling you all my faults, has he?' She laughed and glanced sideways at Mike.

'On the contrary,' the doctor said, winking at Mike. 'He was singing your praises. I'm sure you'll be pleased to have Mike home. He's feeling much better at the moment.' Then he was called away and he hurried out leaving them alone.

'What did he mean, Mike? Has he told you anything? What caused you to feel so exhausted in the first place?'

'Nothing, honey, there's nothing for him to tell me. It was probably only anaemia. I'm fine now.'

'Just the same, Mike, you should ask him some questions when he comes round tomorrow.'

The following evening as Jo was leaving the hospital, the receptionist called her over. 'Doctor Nicol would like to see you, Mrs. Pasiński. He's in his office.' Her heart skipped a beat and she wondered if Mike had questioned him about his illness.

'Please sit down, Mrs. Pasiński. Jo, isn't it?'

She nodded.

He squared his shoulders. 'I have the final results from your husband's tests.' He cleared his throat.

'Is it…serious?' She could hear the tremor in her voice.

'I'm so sorry, but your husband is very sick.'

'Can't you make him better?' She became agitated, rubbing her hands together.

The doctor looked uncomfortable and, lowering his head, he coughed into his handkerchief.

'Have you spoken to him? Does he know?'

'No. If you tell him, he could become depressed with the medication he's on. You need to be very brave, Jo.'

'But…but he hasn't looked so well in ages. What's wrong with him?'

Dr Nicol sighed. 'He looks well because he's had a transfusion. I'm afraid he has a fatal blood disease. I'm so sorry, but there's nothing more I can do. He is in the advanced stages of the disease.' The doctor rested both his elbows on his desk, lowered his face into his hands and rubbed his brow.

Tears welled in her eyes. She was speechless. Her mind grappled to make sense of what she'd just heard. The doctor was consoling her, but his words were incoherent. Her mind became confused, until his voice sounded muffled. She started to shake uncontrollably. This was not what she had expected to hear. She tried to speak, but the words stuck in her throat. Her whole world had been turned upside-down.

'I believe you have only been married a year.'

She tried again to speak, but she was unable to form the words. She couldn't move. She sat in a trance. It felt like she and everyone around her were frozen in time. Her mind buzzed with questions she was incapable of asking. She could hear a gentle voice. But were they speaking to her? She wasn't sure.

She felt an arm go around her shoulder, and she let herself be guided out of the office. She stopped to glance down the long corridor. Mike was outside his room, his back turned away from her, chatting to another patient. He wore the blue silk dressing gown she had bought him for Christmas. She wanted to run to him, cling to him, never let him go,

but instead she turned away and continued to walk out of the hospital. She felt dead inside. She tried to speak and cry out, but the words formed in her mind and stayed there.

God wouldn't be so cruel, not when they loved each other so much. What had they done to deserve such a fate? Please don't let it be true. Don't let this be happening to us.

She arrived home with no recollection of getting there, with no-one to console her, and no-one to tell her troubles to. She dropped down on the sofa, and when her tears came there was no way of suppressing them.

CHAPTER FORTY-THREE

When Jo wrote to Annie and Peter telling them what she had discovered, their reply was almost instant, offering their support. It was arranged that Annie would come to New Jersey to be with Jo when she needed her.

Mike was overjoyed to leave the medical centre. He looked pale after his spell in hospital, and when the fresh air hit him, Jo realised he was weaker than he had first thought.

But once they were home a few days, it was obvious how much he had missed her. Mike loved her with a passion and afterwards, as they lay together, it was hard to believe her husband was ill.

'Let's go out for a meal this weekend to celebrate,' he said.

Jo agreed and tried to match his enthusiasm, but found the strain not to weep overpowering; it was so difficult to keep smiling when part of her had died. In spite of her relief at having Mike home, thoughts of losing him hung heavily. Keeping what she knew a secret felt wrong; it was the hardest thing she had ever had to do.

On good days, Jo could almost believe that Mike was going to get better, yet there were other times when she almost told him the truth. But when the mood passed, she was glad she had stayed silent.

When Jo informed her family of their postponed trip, she told them that Mike had been ill but was now in recovery. So when a letter arrived from Ned to say he would be over to see them in a couple of months once he had time to book his passage, Mike said, 'Well, we certainly have the space. It'll be good to meet Ned at last.'

'You and he will get on well, I know you will,' she smiled. A visit from Ned was just what she needed to keep her focused. And she could see Mike was already looking forward to meeting her brother.

They were only taking in a third of the work since before Mike took sick, and even then his energy at times appeared drained. His tablets, renewed monthly by their local medic Doctor Merrick, appeared to do little but give Mike a bloated appearance. Some days she noticed how he would suddenly stop what he was doing and gaze into space. She wondered what was going through his mind. Other days, her heart weary, she watched him reading medical books about anaemia. She listened as he questioned why he was still feeling weak, and it took all her strength to stay focused on getting through the day.

'Do you think my illness has any bearing on you not conceiving, sweetheart?' he asked one night, as they lay in bed.

'I don't know, Mike! Perhaps it's me wanting a baby so much.' She sighed. Mike pulled himself up on one elbow and looked into her eyes.

'Please try not to worry, Jo. I know it's hard for you. Some days I feel so well I could climb a mountain.' He lowered his voice. 'It's frustrating, honey. But I won't give in.'

Jo stretched out her arms and pulled him down to her. 'I know.' She gently kissed his lips.

'I don't know how you put up with me.'

'I love you.' She swallowed the lump forming in her throat.

'You need cheering up. I'm going to take you to Manhattan for the day!'

'Mike, you don't have to, we can–' But he interrupted her before she could finish.

'I want to. We'll climb to the top of the Empire State Building. I'll point out all our favourite places – where we first met, and where we were re-united.' He kissed the tears cascading down her face. It was almost one hundred miles across the river to New York.

'Whatever's the matter, Jo? Have I said something to upset

you?' he asked, an anxious look on his pale face.

'No, Mike. They're tears of happiness.'

'Come here.' He wrapped his arms around her. 'Now that I'm on the mend, you can stop worrying, okay?' He kissed her, and all her fears drifted away as he made love to her as he had done before he went into the clinic. For some reason, maybe because their relationship was close, Jo had the strangest feeling that Mike knew more about his illness than he was letting on. But, like her, he couldn't bear to discuss the finality of death.

It was over a year since Jo had been to Manhattan Island; since she'd married Mike, she'd had no reason to go there. They dressed in warm coats and scarves for the journey, and the ferry crossing was good for September. Jo was in a pensive mood as Mike dozed on and off.

He woke and stood up, pulling her with him. He placed his arm around her shoulder and they looked out across the water. 'They say,' Mike told her, 'every month something changes in New York; a new skyscraper appears from nowhere.' His blond hair lay lank across his forehead.

Later, they strolled hand-in-hand along the sidewalks. It was obvious to anyone who bothered to look their way that they were in love. After their quiet rural life in Fairview, Jo found Manhattan polluted and noisy in comparison. The vast increase in motorcars and public transport surprised her. New York was a hectic, busy place, and it was lovely to be here again with Mike, but she would never want to live here again.

They arrived outside the Empire State Building. A small crowd was beginning to form so they tagged onto the end of the queue. When they eventually took the lift to the top, the view was breathtaking. Jo had been up before with Annie, but this time she would never forget, because she was with the man she loved. They were together and she never wanted to come back down. The panoramic view swept across the whole of Manhattan Island, taking in the Chrysler building, hailed the tallest skyscraper in New York until the Empire State surpassed it in 1931. They could clearly see the Statue of Liberty, and the Hudson River where cargo ships and moving traffic below them became mere toys. Jo and Mike stood together, their arms linked, gazing out at the world above and below them.

Later, with Mike showing no signs of slowing down, they browsed old bookstores and music shops, where they picked up copies of their own music.

'How are you feeling, Mike? We don't have to shop if you'd like to sit awhile.'

'Aren't you enjoying it, darling?'

'Absolutely!' She beamed at him.

'One more thing before we go to the Village.' Taking her hand, he took her into a small out of the way shop, where Mike bought Jo an Irish sweater. And it wasn't until they were enjoying a meal in Greenwich Village, that Jo noticed how tired he looked. She knew the signs well and it brought her down to earth with a bump. Although one or two nodded towards Mike, Jo recognised none of the new crowd. 'I wonder where Max is?'

'Oh, didn't I tell you? The last I heard, he fell for a Polish girl and they went to live in Krakow.'

'Really! I never knew he was Polish?'

'He's a true New Yorker.'

'Well, I hope they're as happy as we are.'

Mike pushed his half eaten meal to the side and finished his coffee.

Jo, trying not to show concern, said, 'I've had a lovely day, Mike, but to tell you the truth I'm feeling a bit weary. What do you say we catch the earlier ferry home?'

He looked up at her with love in his eyes. 'I'm ready whenever you are, Mrs. Pasiński.'

She reached for his hand. 'Wherever we go in the future, whether it's Ireland or somewhere else, I'll treasure today when we stood together at the top of the tallest building in New York.'

Leaning across the table, he kissed her. Then he stood up, and hand-in-hand, they took a slow walk back to the ferry.

CHAPTER FORTY-FOUR

Mike became weaker until he was no longer able to work. Jo did her best to carry on but she missed the working relationship they had shared. She thought about teaching the piano again, but decided against it. Mike needed peace and quiet, and she felt fortunate to have been offered part-time freelance work with a publisher. Their bank account was healthy, but Jo needed the distraction of work to help her cope with the situation she now found herself in. Working from home enabled her to care for Mike and to see to his needs at any time throughout the day. She rarely left the house, except for provisions and to renew Mike's medication.

It was warm and sunny and Mike was sitting in a wheelchair, shaded by the large oak tree. The garden was at its best, a blaze of colour, and she could hear the sound of a cricket through the open window. Mike was reading the morning newspaper and she gave him a cheery wave. In half an hour she would bring him inside and try and tempt him with one of the dainty sandwiches she had made with the crust removed.

The secret she had been entrusted with by Dr. Nicol was still locked inside her heart. Each morning she woke, she expected to find her beloved husband dead beside her. Distracted from her work, she recalled how her dear grandmother had died. This past week Mike appeared to have shut her out again, and she wondered if he, too, had secret worries he longed to discuss with her but daren't. 'Oh Mike, why?' She felt a tear trickle down her face and dashed it away with her hand. She wished she could get inside his head, but when he was like this there was nothing she could do except wait until he was ready to tell her his worries.

* * *

Mike treasured his life with Jo, since the day they had been reunited in Central Park. Now he guessed too much happiness wasn't allowed. The garden was special to them both and showed the love and care they had put into it. Jo had contributed the colours that surrounded him today. His sense of smell had waned, but he caught a slight whiff of the hyacinths growing nearby.

Today, the beauty of the garden did little to console him. His mind was in turmoil. He agonised over his illness and how Jo would react if he told her he wasn't going to improve. He knew by the way she looked at him what must surely be going through her head. But to come out and hit her with such thoughts would be cruel. She needed his support just as much as he needed hers.

He hated himself for not being a proper husband to her. He could hardly bear to have her out of his sight, with so little time left. He'd speak with her today; it couldn't be worse than it already was. When he raised his head, he saw her walking towards him. But once inside, Mike felt exhausted, and after a cool drink and small amount of food, he slept.

* * *

A week later, Jo went to see Doctor Merrick. It was now three months since the specialist at the centre had divulged to her the true nature of Mike's illness. And no matter how she tried to fool herself that he wasn't going to die, she knew it was inevitable.

The doctor appeared pleased to see her and pointed to a chair in front of his large desk. 'How are you, Jo? Are you coping?' he asked, looking across at her tired face, her eyes clouded and anxious.

'Why does life have to be so sad, Doctor?' She sighed, and tears began to form in her eyes.

They had only known Doctor Merrick for a short time, but even so, she could see the compassion in his eyes. 'It might be time to send for your friend,' he said. 'Annie, is it?'

Jo nodded.

'You've been very brave, Mrs. Pasiński.'

'How long, Doctor?'

'It's hard to say...but...' He coughed to clear his throat. 'Perhaps to the end of the summer...maybe longer,' he added.

'I'm so sorry.'

Her fears had been confirmed. She was going to lose Mike, the only man she would ever love. She wanted to scream or shout, get it all out of her system. But who was to blame? Not Doctor Merrick. Oh, dear God. She stood up and felt herself sway. When she came to, the doctor and a nurse were leaning over her. The nurse was holding smelling salts in front of her nose.

'What happened?' She placed her hand to her head.

'Here, take a sip of water. You're not eating properly. You must take better care of yourself, Mrs. Pasiński. You have a grim task ahead of you. If this happens again, promise me you'll come back and see me.' Doctor Merrick helped her to her feet.

* * *

Annie arrived in October, and having her around was a great source of comfort and support to Jo. Looking radiant after nearly nine years of wedded bliss, Annie quickly spotted her friend's anxiety and weight loss. 'If only you'd told me how bad things were, Jo, I'd have come sooner.'

Mike's gone downhill over the past few weeks.' She reached out and hugged her friend. 'I'm so grateful you could come, Annie.'

'Well from now on you can leave the practical tasks around the house to me, while you spent as much time as you can with Mike.'

'Do you think I should tell him the truth?'

'I don't know, Jo. But if you feel it would help. It's been a terrible burden for you to carry. I really don't see why they didn't tell him in the first place. It's caused untold grief for you both.'

That night as she went upstairs to bed, she heard the most piercing scream penetrate the windows. 'Oh no. Not the Banshee!' With the realisation that it was a fire engine and she was no longer in Ireland, Jo let out a slow sigh. 'Dear God, what is happening to me?' She sat on the stairs and wept.

A few nights later, as Mike lay languid in bed beside her, she knew she had to tell him what she knew. 'Mike darling, I have something to tell you. Please…forgive me for…for keeping it from you…I…'

'It's all right, sweetheart.' He pulled her closer so that her back was to him, his arms around her. 'Jo, my sweet, I think I'm going to die. Thinking about it tortures me. I can't bear to leave you alone.'

She tried to turn towards him, desperate to comfort him and be comforted, but his hold tightened. She heard a sob catch the back of his throat and he buried his head in her long hair.

'Oh Mike, darling Mike,' she cried.

He loosened his grip and Jo turned and wrapped her arms around him. Emotions hidden for so long spilt over. Then, as the strain of protecting each other from the terrible truth became apparent, Jo felt renewed strength. Together they would face whatever came. That night, neither of them slept. Emotionally drained, Jo and Mike spent most of the night talking of private matters.

* * *

Mike passed away in the early hours of a cold December, just days before his thirty-seventh birthday. Jo was inconsolable. In those last distressing weeks, Annie's presence had done wonders for Jo. Just having a shoulder to cry on when things got too much, kept her focused.

When Father Kelly came to administer the Last Rites, Jo's emotions were all over the place. 'Can you tell me why good people die while He allows the wicked to live on?'

The priest sighed deeply. He had become fond of this young couple since they had joined his parish. 'Ah sure, God works in mysterious ways, child.' He stood up to go. 'You know where to reach me, should you need to talk at any time, day or night.' He nodded towards Jo.

She felt grief-stricken at the injustice of it all and like a defiant child, hurt and distressed, she lashed out. 'I doubt I'll do that, Father. In fact, don't expect to see me inside your church again. If God can rob me of the only man I've ever loved…' Her voice trailed away. The old priest shook his head slowly, lowering his head.

Jo, sobs choking her, passed the priest his hat.

'I'll pray for you, my child.'

Jo remained silent.

'I'll see myself out.' He made his way slowly down the stairs.

Her mind in turmoil, she flopped down into the large armchair next to the bed, the pain of loss unbearable. She buried her face in her hands and let her tears come.

After thanking Father Kelly for coming, Annie went back upstairs. Rushing to Jo's side, she placed her arm gently around her friend's shaking shoulders. 'Come downstairs for a bit. It will do you no good to stop up here.'

'Oh poor Mike, Annie. Poor Mike, who never did anyone an ounce of harm,' Jo cried, locking and unlocking her fingers.

'He's at peace now, no longer suffering, Jo. Take comfort from that.' A tear trickled down Annie's face. Knowing Jo as she did, Annie knew that comfort was a long way off. The trauma of losing Mike had affected her judgement, otherwise she would never have spoken to the priest in that manner. But grief affected people differently and after all Jo had been through, Annie thought it was rotten luck.

'I don't know how to go forward without him, Annie. Not sure I want to. I still remember how lonely I felt living with my mother; at times it was unbearable. I used to look up at the stars and say to myself, one day I will change my life. I knew in spite of everything I had to come to America. Oh Mike, Mike,' she wailed, and flung herself down onto the bed next to his corpse, soothing his brow, talking to him.

Darkness fell across the room, but Annie could not persuade Jo to come downstairs.

She sat in silence, staring into space while Annie struggled to keep her eyes from closing. Just after dawn, a knock on the front door alerted Annie. Wearily, she dragged herself downstairs, undid the latch and threw open the door. The cold air rushed at her face, refreshing her, and a thick frost had formed on the front garden. She looked into the face of a man wearing a peaked cap, a brilliant smile, and a twinkle in his eye.

'Oh, I'm sorry,' he said, taken aback. 'I'm looking for my sister, Jo, Mrs. Pasiński.'

'Oh, do forgive me. You must be Ned, Jo's brother,' Annie said, rubbing her hand across her brow and straightening her hair. 'Please come in.' She held open the door.

A frown took the place of his smile and he glanced at Annie. 'I don't understand. Has something happened? Where's Jo?' he asked, looking around the hall.

Annie felt her throat tighten and she guided him through to the kitchen. 'We can talk in here.' Offering her hand, she said, 'I'm Annie Thomas, Jo's friend. We made the crossing together.'

'Of course,' Ned said. 'I remember. It's been a long time.' He shook her hand warmly. 'It's nice to meet yeah again, Annie.'

'I hate to be the bearer of bad news, Ned, but Mike passed away this morning, and Jo's in a state of shock.'

'Glory b' to God! Where is she?' He threw down his bags. 'I must see her.'

'You'll find her changed. She's been through a rough time. To tell you the truth, I'm glad you're here, Ned, because I'm really worried about her state of mind. We need to get her out of that room, before the undertakers arrive.'

Annie led him upstairs to where Jo sat staring at the dead body in front of her. Ned called her name a couple of times before she turned round. He opened his arms and she went to him. Deeply moved, he held her, soothing her and telling her he was here now and would look after things.

'Why didn't you tell me things were this bad?' With no response, Ned glanced at Annie. 'I had no idea he was that ill,' he said. His arm around Jo, he drew her toward the open door. 'Was that the real reason you cancelled your vacation in July?'

Annie answered. 'She didn't want you to worry.'

With Jo downstairs, a warm blanket around her shoulders, her eyelids closed.

'She's exhausted.' Annie raised the lace curtain, willing the undertakers to get here before Jo woke again. She and Ned were sitting quietly sipping hot drinks when they arrived. 'She'll no doubt be upset we didn't wake her.'

'Do you have Jo's doctor's number, Annie? I think it might be wise to get him to call,' Ned said.

When Doctor Merrick arrived, he found Jo upstairs hugging Mike's pillow. And when he came downstairs, Ned and Annie were waiting. Ned rushed forward. 'Well! Will she be all right?'

'She'll sleep soundly now. God knows she needs some. She knew for some time, but it's still a shock when it comes.' He nodded his sympathy.

'It's going to take time and patience, Mr. Kingsley. How long can you stay?'

'I'll stay as long as I have to.'

CHAPTER FORTY-FIVE

Mike's funeral mass took place at the church where, just eighteen months before, they had taken their marriage vows. Jo's dark clothes accentuated her white face and red eyes. Ned and Peter flanked her on either side as she followed her husband's casket out of the church. And she watched silently as Mike's body was lowered into the ground at the nearby cemetery. The frost had hardened over the newly-dug earth and, as Jo dropped a single red rose on top of the casket and stepped back, giddiness caused her to sway. Ned reached out to steady her.

'It'll be over soon, pet,' he murmured, putting a firm arm around her thin shoulders.

Afterwards, at the small restaurant, a fire crackled in the grate, giving a glow to the room. The heat and the food warmed her and a spark of colour returned to her face. In spite of well meaning mourners genuinely sorry for her trouble, Jo couldn't respond. Once she did that, it would be like accepting it had happened. And she didn't want to believe it. Ned thanked the many friends and neighbours who had come to comfort and show their support.

After the funeral, Annie and Peter returned home. Ned, determined to see his sister through her terrible loss, stayed on to care for her. Doctor Merrick called in regularly to check on her progress but there were days when Jo could barely function and hardly spoke a word to Ned; other days she cried on his shoulder.

'Talk to me, Jo, please. At least try,' Ned pleaded, but she continued to stare into space. When awake, she was barely aware of her surroundings. All she knew was, Mike was dead and she could not pull herself up from the depths of despair. How could anyone understand that?

'He loved you as much as you loved him,' Ned was saying. 'He had no choice, but you...you have, Jo.' He sighed. 'If you can bring yourself to talk about how you feel...' He paused and took her hand, hoping for some reaction. She glanced round at him, her eyes big and pitiful. Hoping he had awakened something in her, he continued to gently coax and encourage, wary of overdoing it or saying the wrong thing. Ideally, he wanted to take her back to Ireland with him. But as things stood, she wasn't strong enough, and any thought of leaving her here alone caused him anxiety.

* * *

Ned had been in Fairview, New Jersey, a month when Jo showed signs of recovery. He was reading the *New York Post* when she called his name. He rushed to her side.

'What is it, pet?'

'Oh Ned, I'm so sorry. I don't know how long you've been here,' she sobbed.

'Shush now. It's all right. You've been in shock.'

'Half of me died with Mike.' And when she allowed herself to cry, it came as an outpouring of grief. Ned held her until her tears subsided.

'Don't stop talking, Jo. Let it all out.'

'How can I live with only half my soul, Ned? Can you possibly understand?'

'I can try. Please let me try.' And he listened for as long as she needed him to. Each day Ned learned more about his sister's life with Mike Pásinskí. Each telling proved to be a huge step forward in Jo's recovery.

One morning, as they breakfasted together, Ned said, 'I'll have to go back soon, Jo. Come with me?' He smiled. 'What do you say? There's nothing here for you now.'

'My husband's buried here.'

'Wherever you are, he'll be in your heart. Come home, Jo. You'll love the kids, and Beanie would welcome you.' As he spoke, he saw the determination in her eyes and knew he couldn't win.

'I'm sorry, Ned. I'm not ready to leave yet.' She bit down on her bottom lip. 'I'm so grateful for all you've done. If it weren't for you and Annie…' She broke off. Her life was here now where she felt close to Mike.

Ned's disappointment showed in his downcast face. 'Please don't worry about me, Ned. Annie will be back in a couple of weeks.'

After he left, Jo cried and missed him terribly. She felt guilty for the days she had hardly known he was around. When they parted, it had taken all her willpower not to beg him to stay. She'd kept him away from his family long enough.

Just when she was wondering how she would face the lonely night without Ned in the next room, Annie telephoned to say she would be over the following day and that the two of them were going shopping. She hadn't been shopping for ages, and the doctor had recommended she get out more. Dear Annie, she thought, what would she do without her? Only a true friend would have given up so much of her time to help her. And she was truly grateful to her and Peter for their patience.

* * *

When Jo stepped into Doctor Merrick's office, he was pleased to see her looking so well. 'Ah, it's nice to see you, Mrs. Pasiński. No more dizzy spells, I take it?' he smiled.

'I'm grand, Doctor Merrick. In fact, I'm thinking of teaching the piano again and writing songs. It won't be easy without Mike, but I'd like to try.'

'That's wonderful. Work gets us through the bad times.' His smile reassured her. She liked this elderly man who had been so kind to them both when Mike took ill, and always had time for a chat. As they talked about how she was coping without Mike, she mentioned how she had been feeling nauseous, and wondered if it might be the medicine he had prescribed her. A few questions later and a quick examination of her tummy confirmed that Jo was pregnant. Mixed emotions overwhelmed her and tears gathered in her eyes.

'A baby!' she exclaimed, surprise lighting up her face. 'I never gave it a thought,' she cried, and her hand rushed to her mouth. When she'd missed her period for a second time, she had attributed it to her miserable state. Why had she not realised? She was elated and crying at the same time.

'Congratulations,' Doctor Merrick said. 'I'm very pleased for you.' 'You're around ten weeks, I guess. You've been through some of the critical weeks and I'd like you to take things easy.'

'Ten weeks. I can't believe it. This is just what I need to get my life back on track. Thank you, Doctor Merrick.'

'I'm glad to be the bearer of good news for a change.' Smiling, he opened the door for her. And as she walked down the street, a smile lit up her face.

'Oh, Mike,' she whispered. 'We're going to have a baby.' With new life surging through her, she felt alive again. She wanted the world to know, and she could hardly wait to tell Annie.

That weekend, Annie arrived to take her shopping and Jo couldn't wait to tell her the news. 'Well, that's great news, Jo! It's grand to see the colour return to your cheeks,' Annie remarked.

'Can you believe it, Annie?' Jo was exuberant and Annie wept with joy for her friend.

'Life is stranger than we know,' Annie told her as they headed out.

Jo found it impossible to pass a baby shop without stopping. 'Aah! Annie, will you look at this,' she'd say, picking up a little pink matinee coat with matching booties. 'Oh, aren't they lovely?' Jo brushed her hand over the soft baby wool.

'If you want my advice, buy everything in white. That way you won't be tempting fate,' Annie said excitedly. 'You can always buy blue or pink after it's born.'

And in the days that followed, they rarely went anywhere without buying something for the baby. The two women, well wrapped up against the cold February wind blowing across the river, arrived home laden with baby clothes.

'Phew!!' Annie said, whipping off her gloves. 'That wind cuts through to the marrow.' She laughed, 'Hey, Jo! This time next year you'll be pushing a pram.'

Jo agreed. 'It will be nice to have a summer baby.' She heated a tin of Heinz Mulligatawny soup and as she carried it to the table, Annie was pondering, her hand underneath her chin. 'What are you thinking about?'

'I just wondered if you've given any thought to where you'll bring up the baby?'

'What do you mean?' She placed a bowl in front of Annie. 'Get this down you, it will take the chill from your bones.'

'Are you planning to stay in New Jersey? This is nice,' Annie said, sipping her soup. 'What's it called?'

'Mullega…something. I've thrown the tin in the trashcan. To tell the truth, Annie, I haven't thought about what I want to do. But now that you've brought it up. Part of me wants to stay here near Mike, where I've been happiest. But I miss my family – it's been so long now. Maybe when the baby's born, I'll take it back to show everyone.' She smiled, tilting her head. Her hair fell across her shoulders, giving her a girlish look. At thirty-one, Jo still looked stunning with a figure about to blossom with signs of pregnancy.

'I won't get the chance to play aunty then,' Annie remarked.

'Oh Annie, of course you will.' She shrugged. 'I'm not thinking of staying in Ireland, at least not yet.'

'Ned will be so pleased. Have you written to tell him?'

'As soon as I found out, I wrote Ned a long letter,' she chuckled. 'I feel reborn, knowing that a part of Mike is growing inside me. I thought I'd lost everything when he died, Annie. Isn't it amazing how the human spirit bounces back?' She reached across the table and squeezed Annie's hand.

'I couldn't be happier for you, Jo.' Annie, who never had a baby of her own, said it was God's will. Now that Peter's children had grown up, she was longing to play mother again, but she was resigned to the fact that it might never happen.

In Annie, Jo had the best friend a girl could wish for, always around when she needed her; leaving her husband and family to be with her. She was a real treasure. Jo guessed she could never repay that kind of friendship.

'I bet Peter will be glad when I get myself together again, so he can have his wife back,' Jo told her friend.

'He's a good kind man, Jo, and I wish you no less in the future, when you're over Mike,' Annie said before they parted company.

As the weeks passed, Jo became engrossed in preparation for Mike's baby. She decorated one of four bedrooms in lemon and white. Neighbours, frightened of intruding before, came across to visit, delighting in her joy. The midwife left Jo her telephone number in case she needed advice. With Mike sick, Jo hadn't had time to get to know the neighbours. How kind they now were, offering their help when they observed her carrying home large tins of paint, paste and wallpaper.

Jo experienced a new kind of contentment. Mike had left her comfortably off, but she continued to teach the piano. Sometimes she imagined she could see herself and Mike sitting together by their piano, writing and composing their favourite music and lyrics. With their baby growing inside her, she felt happy. God was good, after all.

CHAPTER FORTY-SIX

It was towards the end of her fourth month that Jo woke in the middle of the night. Crushing pain raced like waves around her back and abdomen. Instinctively, she knew what was happening. She crawled from bed to the bathroom and, weak from loss of blood, she staggered to the telephone and managed to call her neighbour, the midwife, before collapsing.

When Jo awoke drowsily, at first she had no idea where she was. A feeling of despair rushed through her. The expression on the nurse's face as she walked towards her bed told her what she now suspected.

'Are you sure? Have I definitely lost my baby?' Tears stung her eyes as she searched the nurse's face for some sign of hope.

The nurse sadly shook her head and tried to explain that it wasn't to be. Jo turned on her side and wept.

'Oh God, how can you be so cruel? Have I been so bad that you must punish me so harshly?' she sobbed bitterly.

When Father Kelly called at the hospital to see her, he asked her to pray, but she told him she had nothing to pray for and no-one to pray to, because she no longer believed in a merciful God.

The loss of Jo's baby brought Annie rushing back to her side. It was too much to bear so soon after the death of her husband. Annie was broken-hearted and grieved with her friend over the baby, but there was no consoling Jo.

'If only I'd known the hardship and heartache you were to endure,' Annie cried, 'I'd never have asked you to come to America. Oh Jo, I'd change places with you if I could.' Annie, who could hardly bear to see the pain in Jo's eyes, prayed for her recovery. Would her music be enough to sustain her and pull her through? After such a loss, Annie had doubts. What would become of her dearest friend? Nothing anyone could say or do made any difference, as Jo plunged into the depths of depression.

Doctor Merrick suggested to Annie that a short vacation to Florida might help Jo's recovery, and asked if it was possible for her to accompany her. But Jo refused to even consider the idea, saying that no matter where she was, the pain would never go away. When Annie had to return home, she was relieved when Jo agreed to go to Brooklyn with her.

Annie and Peter were kindness itself, but even so, Jo retreated into herself. Some days she rarely stirred outside her room while Annie kept a watchful eye. At night, while Jo slept, Annie cried in Peter's arms. 'Dear God, Peter. Poor Jo.' And Peter agreed with his wife that life had dealt her friend a cruel blow.

Spring was again beginning to show signs of new life, and under protest Jo accompanied Annie to a nearby park. They fed the ducks and Annie saw a slight smile crease Jo's lips as she watched them squabble over the bread. A mother pushing her baby around the duck pond brought stinging tears to Jo's eyes.

'It's bound to affect you,' Annie consoled. 'It's early days yet.' Linking her arm through Jo's, she guided her in the opposite direction. But inside, Jo felt dead, unable to come to terms with the tragedy of losing the man she loved and their precious baby.

'Was I such a bad person, Annie?' she asked, her eyes pleading.

'Of course not. Tragedy happens to good people, too. Nothing in life is evenly distributed, you know that, Jo,' Annie reassured her. 'You mustn't think like that.' Annie knew only too well Jo's character, her strong principles, her caring nature, and her determination to finish what she set out to do. She felt an overwhelming admiration and affection for her friend. But fearful of losing control and upsetting Jo, Annie kept her emotions in check until she was alone.

The healing process was doubly painful for Jo and as each agonising day ended, she began to dread the next. Annie and Peter did all they could to help her through her grief, but she appeared to have lost the will to live.

'If only she would get angry,' Annie told Peter. 'It might help.'

'She's too sad for anger, Annie. But it'll come.'

In the quiet of her room, Jo poured out her grief in letters to Ned and Cissy. Their replies were a comfort to her. Ned's arrived first by airmail. She had hoped her mother would send a word of support in her loss, but then she had never written to her, not in all the years Jo had been in America. Her sister hinted more than once that she should come home, and Ned pleaded with her to seriously reconsider her decision to stay in America.

'What will you do?' Annie wanted to know, when Jo came down that evening.

'I don't know.'

'God alone knows why this has happened, Jo. But hard as it is, I know you'll find a way through it.'

'I wish I had your faith, Annie. Do you know?' she said, shaking her head. 'A week before I lost the baby, I was contemplating going to see Father Kelly to apologise for my behaviour, you know, when he came to administer the Last Rites to Mike. I hoped he'd understand, even forgive me,' she laughed bitterly. 'I was going to ask him to baptise the baby when it was born.' A sob engulfed her, and Annie put a comforting arm around her shoulders.

After a fortnight with Annie and Peter, Jo – still numb – returned home to Fairview. It took many more visits back and forth to Annie and Peter's before they saw any sign of her returning to a normal life. She began writing and teaching music again, throwing herself into her work, even working into the early hours.

Doctor Merrick gave her tablets to help her sleep and was very encouraging. 'You're doing fine, and you'll get over this. You have a great reserve from which to draw upon.' He smiled warmly.

She wanted to believe him, and was aware she would need every ounce of strength to carry on living here alone.

She found Doctor Merrick to be an exceptional doctor, caring and kind; Jo had known him to drive miles in the middle of the night to help his patients. And now, two months after Jo's miscarriage, he still called on her regularly to make sure she was coping. It was on such a visit, after Jo had opened her heart to the kindly doctor, that she made her decision.

With the arrival of spring and Annie's visit to Fairview, Jo delivered the surprise news of her imminent return to Ireland. They were sitting in Jo's kitchen sipping tea and eating American pecan pie with cream. Annie had just finished a forkful of pie. Her eyes widened. 'Are you sure, Jo? Is that what you want?' she asked, concerned.

'Yes, I've been thinking about it since Ned went back, and you know how persuasive he can be.' She smiled and sipped her tea. 'Ned said he can sort me out somewhere to live. But,' she swallowed, 'I'll miss you, Annie.'

'Me too! I'd probably do the same in your situation, Jo.' Annie put her arm around her. 'But that's life. With the children away at college, the house seems empty.'

'But you still have Peter.'

'Oh yes, he's a gem, and you mustn't worry. Besides, I've made friends through the children and Peter's business. When were you thinking of going?' Annie asked. 'Because you can't go without a party.'

A farewell gathering was the last thing on her mind, but she owed it to Annie and Peter and the kind friends she'd made since she and Mike moved to New Jersey. 'Well, there's the house to sell, and odds and ends to wind up first,' she said, in a sad voice.

'What is it, Jo?' Annie asked. 'What's worrying you?'

'After all you've done for me already, I hate to impose on you further.' Jo paused, a lump forming in her throat.

'What? Tell me?'

'There's no-one else I can trust to do this.' Lifting the cups and plates, she placed them on the draining board.

'What do you want me to do, Jo?'

'Will you look after the grave? I know it's a lot to ask, especially as you have to come over from Brooklyn, but I'd be so grateful.' Jo bit her lip.

'Consider it done. Peter and I will see that it is well cared for. You can rest assured of that, Jo. What are best friends for anyway?'

Annie pulled a handkerchief from her bag and held it to her face. Their embrace was warm and unhurried. And when they pulled apart, both were choked with tears.

CHAPTER FORTY-SEVEN

In May of 1937, Jo boarded the ship for her journey back across the Atlantic. She felt a great sadness saying goodbye to her husband and baby, knowing that nothing on God's earth could bring them back. Her travels had brought her first hardship, then love, sorrow, and finally wisdom. And the love she had known with Mike would live forever in her heart. With these thoughts, she made her way on deck to wave a last goodbye to Annie and Peter, who were waving white handkerchiefs amongst the crowd at Ellis Island. Leaving behind all that had become familiar to her, as well as two wonderful friends, added to her sadness. Both women had found the parting difficult until Peter lightened the mood with his promise to take Annie on vacation to Ireland at the first opportunity.

Jo stayed on deck until the figures on the shoreline became smaller, and Manhattan and its tall skyscrapers faded from view. Heartbroken and choking back tears, she made her way to her cabin. The first class self-contained cabin she occupied was a far cry from how she and Annie had travelled on their trip across the Atlantic. She shuddered now to think of it. There was no overcrowding on the return journey; most Irish emigrants could never afford to return, and she felt fortunate in that respect. Without Annie, she found the voyage uneventful and spent her time between wandering the deck when the weather was fair, to staying huddled below in her cabin when storms raged. When the long, lonely voyage was finally over, she felt exhausted.

She went on deck to see the Irish coastline slowly coming into view, and a lump formed in her throat to see again the land of her birth. Seagulls squawked and swooped overhead and smoke billowed from the ship's black funnels heralding their arrival.

It was a clear dry day as the ship docked and anchored in the Bay. Only a few people waited waving and cheering, anxious for relatives and friends to disembark after their long voyage home. Jo craned her neck for a glimpse of her brother, but when she didn't immediately see him, her heart sank. She descended the gangplank; excited passengers pushed forward and were greeted enthusiastically.

Then Ned was beside her, his smiling face before her, scooping her up like a child. He swung her round before putting her down again.

'Oh Ned, you'll never know how good it is to see you,' she cried, throwing her arms around him.

'Sure, you're a sight for sore eyes. It's grand to see you.' Straightening his cap, he picked up her cases. 'Come on. Let's get you home.'

The streets of Dublin appeared quiet for the time of day. 'What's it been like here, Ned? I've lost touch. Have things quietened down?'

'There'll never be true peace in this land of ours, Jo. There's murder in Belfast. Sure, only the other day a publican and his sons were shot dead. It's crazy, but life goes on,' he sighed. 'But don't you worry your head. You've enough to think about.'

'No change then,' she smiled. As they entered the street, Jo thought it unusually quiet; no curious neighbours peering through their small casement windows, no children playing in the street. 'What's happened, Ned? Where've all the tenants gone?'

'They've been re-housed. I'll tell you all about it later.' He ushered her inside their grandmother's house where a delighted Beanie welcomed her with a hug.

'It's grand to have you home, Jo. Come in, sit yourself down.' Jo removed her coat and Beanie hung it up.

'I'll pop your cases upstairs,' Ned said, leaving them alone.

Jo hardly recognised the old place. The table was set for breakfast and the kitchen now fitted with modern appliances.

'The place looks grand, Beanie.'

'Ned did all the work, but I had to butter him up.' Beanie was just as Jo remembered; her lips painted red even at this time of the day. 'The kettle's almost boiled.' She crossed to the stove where bacon rashers and sausages sizzled.

'It's a bit early for your mother.' As she turned towards Jo, a loose strand of ginger hair fell over her face and she hooked it behind her ear.

'How's she?'

'Oh, you know, there's none of us getting any younger.' Beanie shrugged. 'You must be jaded after the journey. How was the crossing?'

'Rough at times. At other times I was comfortable, but I missed Annie.'

'I'm sure you did. You were brave to come alone. Well, you can rest and enjoy the bit of peace and quiet for a few hours, until the children come home from school.'

'I can't wait to see them.'

Ned came back down and Beanie brought the breakfast to the table. He put an arm around his wife's waist. 'She nags me all the time, Jo,' he laughed, 'but she certainly knows the way to a man's heart.' Rubbing his hands, he inhaled the appetizing smells of the cooked breakfast. And silence descended as they tucked into rashers, eggs, sausages, black and white pudding, and fried bread. Jo had forgotten what a good Irish breakfast tasted like.

Despite her tiredness, she relished the food. 'That was lovely, Beanie,' she said, sitting back in her chair.

'Sure, you're welcome, Jo. I was sorry to hear what happened, you know,' Beanie said. 'I was shocked when Ned told me. But things will get easier now you're home. They say time is a great healer.'

Jo nodded. Beanie was a good sort and she meant well, but Jo didn't want to talk about the past, so she steered the conversation in another direction. 'How are Cissy and the children?'

'Umm, she's much the same, Jo. Larry's death, so soon after you went to New York, hit her badly.' Ned sighed. 'Patrick has a job working at the Gas Co. He's a good lad. Comes and helps me for a few pennies on his day off.'

'I can't wait to see them,' she smiled. 'By the way, what's been happening round here? Why are the cottages empty, Ned? I don't remember you saying so in your letters.'

'No, there was no point in worrying you when you were so far away.' He took a deep breath and poured himself another mug of tea. Beanie took the plates to the sink and poured hot water from the kettle into a bowl.

'Here, let me help,' Jo stood up, but Beanie pressed her to sit back down.

'I wouldn't hear of it, after your long journey. Sit and talk to Ned. I'll finish these and then pop out and get us something nice for dinner.'

'I'm not used to the streets being so quiet,' Jo said, looking out through the lace curtains.

'Oh, you wouldn't say that when the kids are here,' Ned laughed.

Jo sat down again. 'Where did everyone go, Ned?'

'The Corporation rehoused the families in different areas. Sure, the cottages have been condemned this long time, Jo. We struggled for a bit until I'd saved enough to buy a couple of cottages to rent out in Ringsend. They weren't in bad order.' He smiled. 'Better than me poor grandmother's were, God rest her soul! And not so much maintenance either.'

Jo stifled a yawn. She could hardly keep her eyes open.

'Look, you're weary after the crossing and I've got work to do. Get yourself upstairs and don't worry about Ma, she'll sleep a while longer. We'll have plenty of time for catching up later.' He kissed her cheek, grabbed his jacket from the back of the chair and left.

As Jo went upstairs, she was reminded of the unhappy times she spent living here with her mother. As she reached the landing, Kate came out of one of the bedrooms. She looked older, vulnerable, and Jo was taken aback to see how slow her movements were.

'Ma, it's great to see you. How have you been?' She kissed her cheek.

'Who are you and where's Ned?'

'It's Jo Jo, Ma! Don't you remember me? Didn't Ned tell you I was coming home?'

Her mother gripped her arm. 'Jo-Jo, is it really you?' she said, peering into her face. 'Where on earth have you been this long time?'

Jo was shocked by her mother's aged appearance and the strange look in her eyes. Just then Beanie came running upstairs. 'It's all right, Jo. You get your head down, I'll see to your mother.' And, gently guiding Kate downstairs, she said, 'I'll make you a nice pot of tea.'

It was just like Ned to keep their mother's state of mind from her, and as she closed the bedroom door behind her, she remembered how neglected her younger brothers had been when they slept here. Removing her boots, she slipped off her skirt and sat on the edge of the bed. Her eyes moved slowly around the room, now tastefully painted in pastel shades as opposed to the crumbling distempered walls she remembered. There was even a second-hand dressing table with a mirror. The windows sparkled. Getting to her feet, she drew the pretty floral patterned curtains against the sunlight. Wondering what her grandmother would think of it all, she slipped beneath the pink cosy eiderdown. Her eyelids heavy, she slept.

The next thing she heard was the children's chatter as they arrived home from school. Dressing quickly, she tidied herself in the mirror, opened her suitcase and took out the small toys she'd brought from America, and hurried downstairs. Kate wasn't in the room and the children glanced up as Jo walked in. Tears sprung in her eyes when she saw them. Joseph had Ned's dark curls and cheeky grin, and Bella had ginger hair like Beanie. They were happy children, fun to be around just like Ned and Beanie.

She hugged them affectionately and then put her hands behind her back, asking them to choose a present each. They ripped the paper from their spinning tops, and thanked her in turn with a kiss. 'These are grand, so they are, Aunty Jo.' They rushed outside to play with them, when Ned burst in through the door. The children rushed to his side, and he swung them up in the air, one on each arm, making them laugh out loud.

'Ned Kingsley, you'll never grow up,' Jo smiled.

'It's like having three children in the house instead of two,' Beanie said, and laughed. This happy family reminded Jo of what she had lost.

CHAPTER FORTY-EIGHT

Jo saw a changed Dublin from the one she had left behind. She had to keep reminding herself that Sackville Street was now O'Connell Street. And many other street names had been changed since the South's independence.

The city stores were thriving once more, but poverty was still rife, with young women and children begging on the streets. Many men were still jobless, and there wasn't a lot of work to be had.

She stood on O'Connell Bridge, savouring the sights and sounds of the city, but the pungent smell drifting upwards from the River Liffey forced her to move swiftly on.

The leisurely pace of life was just what she needed after her demanding lifestyle in America. As she strolled around the city, stopping to glance in shop windows – especially estate agents – she noted many properties offered for lease. It was then that the idea struck her. Ned had made his money in property development, so maybe that would be something she should consider.

With that in mind, she caught the tram back, getting off a few stops from home to call on Annie's mother to deliver small gifts and a letter. Mrs. O'Toole welcomed her with open arms. 'Jo, it's a sight for sore eyes you are.' And as they sat chatting, she sympathised with Jo over her loss, and thanked her for finding the time to pay her a visit.

'Annie writes letters regularly, but it's nice to hear about everything first hand,' she said, offering Jo tea and homemade soda bread before she took her leave.

When she arrived back, Beanie greeted her warmly. 'Did you enjoy your afternoon, Jo?'

'Yes, I did thanks.'

Ned was at the kitchen sink, scrubbing the hard plaster from his hands. That familiar smell of putty made her feel comfortable.

He turned and smiled, dried his hands on a towel and removed his cap before coming and sitting next to her, kissing her cheek.

'What did you think of Dublin then, Jo? Noticed a few changes, I expect.'

'Indeed I did. The traffic has increased and there seems to be lots of properties for lease.'

'Ah, you've noticed, have you?' Ned said, as Beanie brought the meat pie with plenty of vegetables to the table.

'We can eat in peace tonight,' she said. 'Joseph is at football and Bella is at her Irish dancing class.'

How different their lives were to the way she and Ned had been brought up. During their meal, she talked with Ned and Beanie about the property market.

'If you're keen, come with me tomorrow,' Ned said. 'Take a look at what's on offer in the Ringsend area. You can drop in on Cissy while I'm working,' he suggested.

* * *

After looking over Ned's cottages that he was still repairing, Jo walked the short distance to Cissy's. There were tears of rejoicing as they embraced.

'It's good to see you, Jo. You did the right thing to come home.' Cissy glanced down. 'It takes time to get over something like that. I know!' She shook her head. Cissy's ample figure made Jo's look skeletal. 'You're not thinking of going back, I hope?'

'I don't think so. With Annie married and living in Brooklyn, it can get a bit lonely.'

'I don't know how you stayed in America on your own, Jo.' Cissy was manoeuvring around the small scullery, making tea for them both. 'When Larry passed on, I was glad to be around family and friends.'

'I know what you mean, Cissy. There's no fun in cooking for one.'

'There's not a pick on you, but I see he left you comfortable,' she remarked, glancing at Jo's fashionable clothes. 'That's more than I can say for me own fella.' She clicked her tongue; her hair had a sprinkling of grey, and her plump figure swayed from side to side as she carried in the tray of tea and homemade scones.

'Money isn't everything, Cissy. I'd give anything to have Mike back.' At the mention of his name, she felt a stab of pain. 'When will the children be home?'

'Sarah-Jane's at school, and Patrick, well, he's working now,' Cissy beamed.

'How old is Sarah-Jane now? I can never remember if she's eleven or twelve.'

'She's eleven, Jo. Larry was so ill at the time of her birth.' She took a deep breath. 'She's the spit of him, he would have spoilt her rotten,' Cissy chuckled good-humouredly. 'But you have your own troubles, you don't want to listen to mine,' she said, offering Jo another scone.

'What time does Patrick get home?'

'The siren goes at six, but he won't be long getting home on his bike,' she added. 'He'll be that pleased to see you, so he will. You will wait, won't you?'

'Of course! I'm looking forward to seeing them both.'

'You've brought back a slight American accent, Jo.'

'Have I really? I hadn't noticed.' She laughed. 'Well, after so many years, I'm bound to have picked up traces.'

With so much to talk about, time slipped past and before long Sarah-Jane arrived home from school. She was a lovely child and Jo warmed towards her.

'Aunty Jo,' the child squealed and planted a kiss on Jo's cheek. After a light meal of milk and biscuits, the girl rushed off to her piano lessons.

Jo was so impressed by her enthusiasm that she told Cissy, 'She can have free lessons from now on.'

'Thanks, sis. That'll save me a few bob.'

When Patrick arrived home, his eyes widened when he saw Jo. He shook her hand warmly and sat down opposite her.

'How's the job going, Patrick?' she asked with interest.

'Ah, it's all right,' he shrugged. 'I'm working me way. It'll get better after I serve me time.'

He had Larry's hazel eyes, and now he was a young working man bringing home a wage to his mother. Jo remembered bouncing him on her knee as a baby. How she had doted on him. Patrick sympathised with Jo on her loss and then bombarded her with questions about America.

'That's where I'm going some day, Aunty Jo.'

'There's nothing to stop you, if you save your money,' Jo said, as his mother brought in his meal.

'What have I told you about sitting down without, first, washing your hands, Patrick?'

'Sorry, Ma, I was hungry.'

As Patrick ate hungrily, the two sisters chatted.

'The cottage must get crowded, now that the children are older.'

'Ah, at times, and with that tall lank.' Cissy nodded towards Patrick. 'But I like it here.' Her shoulders sagged. 'The neighbours are a jolly lot. We get by.'

Jo had found Cissy to be more amiable than she remembered, more at peace with herself and her lot.

CHAPTER FORTY-NINE

June was a glorious month, and Jo woke to the smell of night-scented stock floating upwards towards the open bedroom window that overlooked her grandmother's back garden.

'You've done wonders with the garden, Beanie,' she remarked when she arrived downstairs. 'You must have green fingers.'

'Thanks, Jo.' Beanie's red lips parted in a satisfied grin. 'I like to do a bit when I get the time. It's very relaxing, you know! Enjoy your breakfast. I'll see you when I get back.'

'Bye, Aunty Jo,' the children called. Jo smiled, she liked being called aunty. It gave her a sense of belonging. She had found solace here with Ned, Beanie and their family, while she planned her own future.

That evening they discussed properties again over dinner.

'What I'm after, Ned, is a substantial property, big enough to let on different levels. I want to take rooms there myself and get my business back on track,' she told him.

'A woman of means!' he teased.

'My money's as good as any man's.'

'This is little old Ireland you're in now, not America. It can be pretty hard for a woman buying property and living alone, Jo. Have you thought of that?' he looked gravely at her.

'I won't be deterred, Ned Kingsley. I want to buy a large property and let off rooms. So you see, I'm not planning on living entirely alone.'

He nodded his head and pondered a while, rubbing his chin before continuing. 'I know a reputable land and property office in Baggot Street. If you like, we'll go over there, see what he has on his books.'

'Give me the address and I'll meet you there tomorrow at lunch time.'

'Okay!' He gave her a wink and scribbled the details on a corner of the newspaper. 'Get off the bus at the bridge and walk down. You can't miss it.'

* * *

Ned was glancing in the property window when she arrived. 'Spotted anything interesting?' she asked.

He pointed out two or three houses, but when Jo screwed up her face, he removed his cap and scratched his head. 'Why do women have to be so picky about everything?'

'Maybe that's because I can be.' Jo laughed.

'Let's go inside,' Ned said. 'I've done business with Mr. Dugan before.'

The man must have seen them browsing the window and, eager to help, he showed them a property in Sandymount, overlooking the sea.

He glanced down at Jo's wedding ring and assumed them to be husband and wife. 'It's a very prestigious property, Mr. Kingsley.' He addressed Ned over the rim of his glasses, and they discussed the characteristics of the property as if she wasn't there.

'Excuse me! But I'm the one interested in buying this property,' Jo said.

Ned placed his arm around her, laughing at her indignation. 'Sorry, sis, I'm still an old-fashioned man at heart.'

Mr. Dugan's mouth dropped and he looked from Jo to Ned. 'I'm sorry, Mrs…'

'Mrs. Pasiński!' she replied. 'I'm interested in buying this particular property.' She pointed to a different picture. 'It's just what I'm looking for.'

'Are you willing to vouch for the young lady, Mr. Kingsley? Be her guarantor, so to speak?' He eyed them curiously, clearly unused to dealing with a woman and eager to tread cautiously.

Jo was furious and had to remind herself that she wasn't in America. 'So, my money isn't good enough, is that it?'

'Certainly not, Mrs. Pasiński. It's just highly unusual.' The little man's face reddened. 'At the moment it's only on lease. The owners don't want to sell.' He glanced at Ned as if looking for reassurance, but Ned – his elbow on the counter, his fist underneath his chin – appeared to be enjoying the performance.

'Dear me. That's a shame,' she said.

Fearing he might lose the opportunity to do business with this forceful woman, he reached under the counter, picking up details of two other properties that were for sale. After a quick glance at the details, Jo's interest returned to the leasehold property.

Ned glanced over her shoulder. 'You can't seriously be thinking of leasing, Jo?'

'Yes, Ned, listen. I want to buy this property, if not now, later,' she said, looking up into his puzzled face.

'But it's foolish to lease when you can buy another property,' he remonstrated.

'This is the house I want, Ned. Surely it's negotiable.' She already pictured herself living on the ground floor, and letting off the upper floors. She could spend her days writing music and walking along the beach for inspiration.

'What if it's non-negotiable, sis? Are you still going to throw your money away leasing something that will never be yours?' But when Jo gave him that determined glare, he threw his hands up in defeat.

Mr. Dugan, who was eavesdropping, moved closer, rubbing his hands. 'If you like it, may I suggest a small holding fee, Mrs. Pasiński?' He smiled. 'People like yourself can be disappointed.'

'Just one more question. Will there be the possibility of purchasing the property at some stage?' Her question left both Mr. Dugan and Ned in no doubt of her determination to have this property by whichever means.

'I'm not sure,' the man said. 'It only came into the office this morning. I could find out for you,' he said, glancing sideways at Ned, who was rubbing his fingers over his chin. Mr. Dugan disappeared to the back of the shop to make a phone call.

Ned lifted his cap and scratched his head. 'I think you're the first woman he's dealt with in the property stakes, Jo,' he whispered, a huge grin spreading across his face.

'Hmm, let's hope I'm not the last,' she said, as the man returned.

'Well?' Jo asked impatiently. 'Will the owners consider selling the house? I'm quite keen to buy.'

'Their instructions are quite specific,' he informed her. 'They are not prepared to sell at this moment in time. The leasehold is to continue for twelve months, after which time they would consider renewing the contract. I'm afraid that's all I know,' he said, fumbling with his hands.

Her face fell.

'But,' he said, 'if you'd care to take a look around the property tomorrow, I could meet you there at midday.'

'Thank you, Mr. Dugan. I think I can manage to do that.' She smiled, opened her purse and handed him the small holding fee. He quickly wrote out a receipt and handed it to her.

'Thank you.' A smile lit up her face. Before offering her his hand, the agent wiped it down the side of his trouser leg. Ned tipped the side of his cap and they left the shop. Once outside, he threw back his head rippling with laughter. 'He's a funny little chap, and you got him all flustered, Jo.'

Jo found herself laughing along with him until she was holding her sides. She couldn't remember when she had laughed so much. Being with Ned today made her realise how much she had missed her brother.

'Will you still go ahead with this property, if you can't buy, Jo?' He frowned.

'Yes. I'll take in lodgers until such time as they decide to sell.' She was smiling, and he couldn't bear to disillusion her. He had experienced disappointment over property before and would hate that to happen to Jo.

'I wonder what the asking price will be, Ned?'

'I'm guessing anything upwards of eight hundred guineas.'

'You'll look it over for me, won't you?' she said, linking her arm through his as they strode off towards the tram.

'I have a job on tomorrow, but I'll postpone it just for you.' He grinned down at her.

CHAPTER FIFTY

It was an excited Jo who went with her brother to look round the house. She wore a fashionable navy suit and a white short-sleeved frilly blouse. The air was humid and she pinned up her long hair to keep cool. Her tummy fluttered with nervous anticipation as she entered the property with Ned and the agent. The gate and railings needed painting, and the front door paint was peeling. The garden was unkempt and neglected. The house was completely empty and their voices echoed down the long hallway.

Two large rooms led off the hall on either side. The large casement windows to the front of the house, which reminded her of Chateau Colbert, overlooked the street and sea front. Ned left her to wander while he did a maintenance check, and she could hear the sound of his boots treading the bare boards as he went from room to room. The house had five bedrooms, all in need of redecorating. Jo loved it and could hardly wait to start putting her own stamp on the place. Carried away with it all, she went downstairs to find Mr. Dugan.

Ned was coming in from the back of the house. 'Well! It looks as sound as a bell to me, Jo. If you're that interested, you'd best see a solicitor soon, and sign the leasing agreement.'

Delighted with Ned's report, Jo turned to the agent. 'Do you know who lived here?'

He shook his head. 'It's a gentleman who's leasing the property.' He shifted nervously, perhaps fearful that she might change her mind. 'I have the name of a solicitor when you're ready to sign, Mrs. Pasiński?' He bent his head to open his briefcase and his glasses fell off his nose.

Jo turned away fearing he would see her giggle, and Ned made things worse by pulling funny faces behind his back. He could be childish sometimes, but she loved him for it.

'I'd like to take another look around first, if that's okay?' Jo said, turning back to face the agent. He was holding his glasses to his face, his briefcase open and resting on the window ledge.

'Take as much time as you like,' he said, and began talking to Ned about various aspects of the property.

Downstairs, Jo went from room to room feeling that the house belonged to her already; she wanted to leave the shutters open and let the light in. Upstairs, she walked along the landing, looking again into the bedrooms. She was pleased with their size. The fifth and smallest bedroom at the back of the house had thick velvet curtains drawn across the window. It reminded her of her bedroom when she worked at Chateau Colbert, and when she drew back the curtain, it overlooked a long neglected garden. How happy she had been working there, until that terrible day when she had been incriminated in Madame Colbert's missing pearls. But there was no point in looking back. It all seemed a long time ago now.

'Are you quite happy to take on the lease of the property?' Mr. Dugan asked when she came downstairs. 'Only there are one or two minor details to discuss,' he smiled, holding his glasses to the bridge of his nose with his forefinger.

Once the technicalities of the lease were considered, he passed her a card with the solicitor's name. 'I'll leave the rest to you,' he said, and shook her hand.

Outside, he bid them both a good day, then rushed off clutching his briefcase. Jo lingered awhile and looked up at the house. 'I've not felt this happy since, well, before Mike took sick, Ned.'

'I'm happy for you, so,' he smiled.

'How are you fixed for time, Ned? Look at the blue sky.' She glanced upwards. 'There's not a cloud in sight. We could walk back along the sea front. It's much too warm to sit on a tram.'

'I'm easy. We can talk as we walk,' Ned said, in nonchalant mood.

'Is there something on your mind, Ned?'

'Are you sure you want to move so soon?' A serious look creased his face. 'You're quite welcome to stay with us until you're sure, you know.'

They stopped walking and she glanced sideways at him. 'I've got to do it sooner or later, Ned. I'm stronger than you might think. Besides, it's what Mike would have wanted me to do.'

'Living alone, you'll be vulnerable, Jo.'

'I won't be alone, Ned. I'm taking in lodgers, remember!' She released her long hair and let the sea breeze blow it around her face. Smiling, she slipped her arm through his. Anyone passing would have taken them for a courting couple.

'It's great to have you smiling again, but if you do change your mind,' he said, turning his head towards her and winking, 'I might be interested in it myself.' He removed his cap, whipped out his handkerchief, and wiped the sweat from his brow.

'My mind's made up, Ned. I won't change it. Unless,' she said, pursing her lips, 'the price is too high in the sale.'

'Just prospecting, sis,' he said, holding his head to one side. 'But,' he continued, 'if it comes on the market, would you let me buy a share as a sleeping partner, so to speak? For me it would only be a vested interest.' He looked down at her. 'But only if you want me to.'

They strolled in silence, while Jo was thinking about Ned's proposal. It sounded good, and understandable that he should find it an interesting venture; after all, he was in the property business. Going into partnership with Ned, if the house came on the market, would increase her chances of securing it. 'I like the idea, Ned. Let's mention it to the solicitor when I go to sign the lease.'

* * *

Jo was as disappointed as Ned was when their solicitor pointed out the pitfalls that could result from entering into such a proposal on an assumption. 'I'd strongly oppose any such notion. Families,' he shook his head, 'are their own worst enemies when it comes to untangling money and property. A year's a long time. Things change, people change their minds,' he smiled across at them.

'Surely there must be a way around it,' Ned said. 'It's just a business deal.' He was holding his cap in his hand, a deflated look on his face.

'You say you're in the property business, Mr. Kingsley. I'm sure you've seen the consequences of people doing deals on the assumption that a sale will follow. The house could go for auction,' the solicitor said, pursing his lips.

'So, once we know for sure what's happening, we could try again?' Jo asked, as she signed the lease.

'Yes, if you still think it's a good idea.'

The excitement drained from Ned's face. 'Ruddy solicitors,' he grumbled, once they were outside. He was agitated and Jo hadn't seen him in such a state since he had been forced to evict the bad payers from the cottages years ago.

'Ned, let's go for a drink. Celebrate me signing the lease.'

'No, I can't. I have to get back to work. I'll see you back at the house.' And he walked away, leaving Jo to meander back to Beanie's in her own time.

CHAPTER FIFTY-ONE

Ned appeared preoccupied at dinner, and it dampened her mood. She hadn't realised how much he had been looking forward to buying a share in the house. But it was early days yet, there was still time. Maybe Ned's coolness had nothing at all to do with the house. He could have worries that he would never admit to. Beanie, on the other hand, told her that the new property would be the making of her.

'You'll be so busy settling in, Jo, that you won't have time to dwell on the past,' she said, then nudged her husband when she saw her mother-in-law standing in the doorway.

Jo rushed to her aid, and Kate looked up at her, a bewildered expression on her face. 'You're kind,' she said, then turned to Ned. 'Is she family?'

'It's Jo, Ma. She's home from America,' Ned told her, like he did most days.

Jo tried many times to jog her mother's memory of things that happened a long time ago. Sometimes she appeared to remember, patting her on the hand, 'Yer're a good girl, Jo-Jo.' But other times she would sit and stare at Jo, a puzzled look in her eyes, asking over and over, 'Who are yeh, girl?'

The doctor wanted to put her into a home, but Ned refused, telling him that his mother had a home with him. Beanie did a great job looking after her. Her mother could be cantankerous and many times Jo offered to take over, but Beanie insisted that it would only confuse her. The two women had always got on well, from the time Ned had brought Beanie home from New York as his wife. Jo felt a tinge of sadness that she had never been able to share any kind of closeness with her mother.

'I suppose you're missing the old neighbours, Ma,' Jo said, guiding her towards the table.

'What's she saying, Beanie? Who is she?'

'It's Jo, Kate. Now here's a nice cup of tea for you.'

'Couldn't you take her to see Aggie Murphy, Ned?' Jo asked.

Ned sighed. 'Aggie's dead. You don't understand, she gets confused. Besides, she could never get on and off the trams,' he said, and buried his head in his newspaper.

Jo wished she'd thought of that before she spoke. She felt stupid for suggesting it now, and felt a lump rise in her throat. What on earth was the matter with Ned? She hoped that this business with the house wasn't going to be a bone of contention between them.

* * *

It was September before the final details of the lease were sorted and Jo could eventually move into the property. Ned and Patrick helped with the decorating. Although Jo had never cleared the air with Ned about his moodiness, he had happily started the work on the house. So she put it down to her sensitive imagination.

Beanie, who was good with interior design, helped Jo with the refurbishing. They selected bright coloured curtains and light pastel shades for the walls.

Under the leasing agreement, there was little Ned could do to alter the structure of the house except modernise the kitchen, putting in new worktops and cupboards.

'It has to be a communal kitchen: your tenants, when they arrive, will share it along with yourself,' he reminded her. Ned was right, and she was grateful for all the work he had done for her, working in the evenings and doing his own work during the day.

When at last Jo's furniture arrived from New Jersey, the rooms she had chosen for herself on the ground floor began to look homely. Her piano took pride of place by the front window, having arrived unscathed all the way from America. She felt excited when she unwrapped the newspaper from around the knick-knacks which she and Mike had bought together, and some wedding presents from Annie and Peter, friends and neighbours. Handling them again gave her a strange kind of comfort.

Cissy helped her to arrange the furniture upstairs and place ornaments around the place for a homely effect. And she encouraged Jo when she felt low. 'Come on now, enough o' that, we have work to do,' she said and tutted.

Jo admired her courage, how she had coped on her own with two children since Larry's death. Underneath Cissy's austere image, Jo sensed an underlying sadness that she never showed.

Sub-letting the property was relatively easy, and she was pleased with her choice of tenants. They paid their rent on time, unlike the poor tenants her grandmother had had to contend with years ago. But this was the grander south side of Dublin. Her tenants were influential people who had money, or good jobs.

The Miss Higgins' – two elderly retired spinsters – took two rooms on the first floor. They were the most expensive rooms, commanding good views front and back. They kept mostly to themselves, only knocking on Jo's door to pay their monthly cheque. Jo thought them a little eccentric, but they were very polite as they passed in and out, and always bid her good morning or evening. Ned called them the Siamese twins, because they went everywhere together arm-in-arm. Dressed in identical winter coats, one wore a brown beret on her head and the other sister a brown hat with a feather. Only occasionally did they use the kitchen, sometimes bringing food home in the black shopping bag that went everywhere with them. But Jo paid them no heed, once they were paying their rent.

Mr. Hill, another of Jo's tenants, worked at the National Library in Kildare Street. A man, she could tell, dedicated to punctuality. She observed him each morning, dressed smartly in a suit, raincoat, and fashionable trilby, as he stopped at the gate, took out his chain watch, noted the time then walked hastily down the Strand Road towards the tram. Apart from his cheery good mornings, he never stopped to speak to Jo, except when he called to pay his rent. Then he took tea with her, and they discussed books and topics of interest to them both; she looked forward to his visits. The last tenant to take up residency was a young woman called Maisey, from Waterford. In her softly spoken voice, she told Jo of her delight to have landed a shop assistant's job in Cleary's department store.

'I feel bad about leaving my parents,' she said meekly. 'But they wanted to keep me tied to their apron strings.' Her shoulders sagged.

'We all have to leave home some time. Life is too short for regrets.' Jo smiled, remembering how guilty she had felt years ago when she left her family to work at Chateau Colbert.

'I'm enjoying meself for the first time in me life,' Maisey said. 'I've never been to Dublin before.' Her eyes shone with excitement. In her thirty years, she had never been to the city! Jo was shocked – saddened, too – but said nothing. She thought of all the places she had visited and the different lifestyles she had experienced in her own thirty-two years. She watched the woman rush off to work, her head bent low, and thought that could have been her if she hadn't gone away. She liked Maisey and it was nice having someone her own age around the house.

Here in the front room of her new home, Jo regained her love of creative music. She worked hard to re-create the style that had made her and Mike household names in America, and during the process it brought back painful memories. She sent her work overseas to the American publishers who knew and liked her style. When her songs were quickly accepted, it was the boost she needed to get herself back on track.

November brought rain and strong gales that swept along the Strand. Blustering winds could quickly whip up a storm, creating high waves that lashed up against the sea wall. Jo kept a fire burning in the grate most of the day while she worked. She enjoyed having the house to herself during the day, and looked forward to her tenants' return in the evening. She wrote often to Annie, telling of her therapeutic life by the sea.

Ned never mentioned buying into the property again. Although he was always happy to help whenever she needed him, by replacing light bulbs and unblocking drains, he rarely joked with her anymore; something had changed him, and it bothered her. She mentioned it to Cissy.

'He's got work on his mind, and besides, he worries himself sick about Ma. God knows why? But that's Ned for you,' she said. 'Now she has you and me doing her bidding as well, after she left us as children,' Cissy grumbled. Their relationship had never fully recovered from their battles of years ago.

'But why won't he talk to me about it? He doesn't seem close any more.'

'He's probably got his eye on some property deal or other. He's just as off with me,' her sister chuckled. 'If you're that bothered, why don't you ask him?'

CHAPTER FIFTY-TWO

It was a cold December morning when Ned took his mother a cup of tea and found she had passed away in her sleep. He cried bitter tears by her bed. Beanie said it was a blessing that she had gone. But she hadn't expected her death to hit Ned so hard. Cissy remained aloof, dealing only with the practical arrangements. Jo wept with her brother at their mother's funeral.

Weeks later, Jo was surprised when Beanie revealed her anxiety over Ned. 'I can't get a word of sense out of him, since Kate died.'

'Are you sure that that's the reason, Beanie? I found him a little subdued before Ma died. There's something on his mind.'

'Well, whatever it is, Jo, he won't tell me. It's not like him.'

Jo called most days to see Ned, but he remained quiet, miles away, deep in thought. She recalled how patient he had been with her when she could not bring herself to speak to anyone. How could she forget how he had given up his time to come to New Jersey when she couldn't raise herself to speak to him? He was the best of brothers and she felt a great sadness seeing him like this. Ned had been her mother's favourite, the only person she would listen to.

Jo could see the sadness etched on his face. Ned had always been strong and this was out of character. Was he ill, or suffering from depression? In spite of their mother's rejection when they were children, Ned's heart had been big enough to forgive her. He had cared for her and financed her all his life.

'Ned, please, can't you tell me what's wrong? Have I done something to offend you?'

'Oh, I'm sorry, Jo. No, no, it's not that.' He sighed. 'It's nothing for you to worry about.'

'Is it Ma's death?'

'No. Look can you leave it alone, Jo. Why can't people leave me be?'

Jo felt tears sting her eyes. Never before had Ned been so abrupt with her.

'I've things to sort out, that's all.' He stood up and stared out of the window.

'Please tell me what it is, Ned?'

He turned back into the room. 'It's not just Ma dying. I've had a terrible disappointment with a block of flats I put money into. I thought I had it in the bag that day we went to look at the house. I couldn't say anything before,' he sighed. 'Not a word of this to Beanie, mind, I don't want her to worry. Promise?'

'I promise, Ned. Is there anything I can do?'

'No thanks, Jo, I've a few ideas of my own that I'm hoping will solve things.' He gave her a half smile. She knew the discussion regarding his financial problem was over when he said, 'You know, Jo, that all through Ma's illness, her forgetfulness, she always knew who I was. Isn't that amazing?' His face clouded.

'Yes, it is, Ned. I wish she had been aware that I was home from America, though,' Jo sighed. 'No matter how much time I spent with her, she never really knew who I was.'

Ned put his arm around her shoulders. 'You were away a long time, Jo, but there were times I caught her smiling across the table at you.' He straightened his shoulders. 'Well, she's gone now, and life goes on.' He glanced at his watch. 'I've a fella to see. When Beanie gets back, tell her I won't be long.'

* * *

Months passed pleasantly for Jo, and with her sister's family within walking distance she was never short of visitors. Ned's mood improved as his business deals took off. And Patrick's appetite for information about America became insatiable; he called often on Jo to discuss the possibility of going there. She was concerned at being the cause of influencing him away from his home, telling him he had plenty of time to think about travelling. 'Besides,' she stated. 'You're too young yet to be considering such a huge step.'

'You took the plunge, Aunty Jo,' he retorted. 'And you're a woman!'

'I went with a good friend, who never deserted me once we arrived in New York. We had somewhere to stay and Annie had a job to go to.' Patrick could be hot-headed and stubborn when he wanted his own way, not unlike his mother. Jo plucked a book from her bookshelf and handed it to him. 'If you're that determined to go to America,' she told him, 'you had better learn something about the country and its history. And remember, it can be difficult when you're miles away from home, with no-one to turn to.' She hoped she had succeeded in putting him off for a while yet.

The year was almost up and Jo had received no word from her solicitor regarding a sale of the property or a renewal of the lease. So what was going on? She already felt that the house was hers. Although she had made little profit in the first year, she had made no losses either. Ned advised her to cancel the lease now while she had the chance. But she had grown accustomed to her tenants and would miss them terribly if the contract had to change. She knew Ned wouldn't be pleased.

'You're throwing good money after bad by leasing when you could be putting your money into another property,' he said. 'I could find you a good property tomorrow. You've paid out hundreds of pounds already, for what?' he asked. 'If they're not willing to sell, then for God's sake look for something else. There's no shortage of fine houses for sale.'

'I know it makes sense to buy, Ned, but...' She shrugged. 'I like it here. I'll wait another while.'

* * *

A week later, Jo was sitting by the window working on a new lyric, when the postman walked up Strand Road. He stopped outside her gate, extracted a letter from the small pile in his hand, tipped his hat towards her where she sat in the window, and dropped the envelope through her letterbox. She rushed into the hall and picked it up. It was from her solicitor. Hurrying back to her desk, she found the letter opener and sliced the envelope open.

Dear Mrs. Pasiński,

I hereby inform you that instructions have been received in this office regarding the sale next week of the above property. If you are still interested in acquiring this property, I will be pleased to arrange an appointment to our mutual convenience.

Yours faithfully,

C.Ranken

She sat for ages mulling over the content of the letter. A sale! This was what she had been hoping for. There would be plenty of interest in a property of this size, and a house by the sea was always sought after. Her chances would surely be higher as a sitting tenant. Excitement bubbling, she could hardly wait to tell Ned. He knew all about this kind of thing. Although his financial situation had improved, she doubted that he would want to invest anything in this house. She would keep her tenants, of course. They had been a Godsend this past year, taking the emptiness out of the house and brightening her life.

On a sunny morning in September, Jo and Ned emerged from the solicitor's office after Jo had signed an agreement to buy the house in Sandymount. Ned was happy to opt out this time and delighted at Jo's success in acquiring the property, in spite of the interest shown in the sale. She still had money left thanks to the careful providence of Mike's money. Her tenants were happy for her, pleased they wouldn't have to look for alternative accommodation.

Jo settled down to a busy work schedule. It gave her great satisfaction, and between the house and her work, she laboured away, leaving no time for a private life except the odd night out to the Abbey Theatre with Maisey.

But as the months passed and in spite of what she'd achieved, her heart longed to love and be loved; to have Mike back in her arms. There were times when she wept just thinking about him and his sad demise, just when they had found each other again; their baby that never had a chance of life, and what might have been.

CHAPTER FIFTY-THREE

Jo yawned and stretched before getting out of bed. She drew back the curtains. The early morning drizzle had given way to a glorious sunny May day. She had planned a trip to the city with Sarah Jane, now an attractive young lady of thirteen. Pushing open the window, she breathed in the scent of the rose bush she had planted over a year ago.

She dressed in a blue frilly blouse and a floral print skirt. Tying her hair up under her sunbonnet, she twirled in front of her mirror. At thirty-three, she had gained only a couple of inches around her waist. The sunshine and the thought of a shopping trip with her niece had put her in a happy mood. It was some time since she had indulged herself in a new outfit; she was always careful, frightened of becoming destitute again. But today she would forget all that, and treat herself and Sarah-Jane.

It was late afternoon when she returned to Strand Road, having taken her niece home. She was hanging her new outfit – a pink laced blouse and a calf-length black skirt – in her wardrobe, when she heard the urgent knock. It was too early for any of her tenants, she thought, and went to open the door.

Ned rushed past her into the hallway, a look of astonishment on his face. 'Have you seen this afternoon's paper?' He had that expectant look in his eye.

'The paperboy hasn't been yet. Why?' She smiled. She hadn't seen him get excited like this in ages. He showed her the newspaper, the notice he wanted her to see circled in red ink. 'Is this true, Ned? Is Chateau Colbert going up for auction?'

She sat down to take in the news. She had called around there once since her return to Ireland, hoping to see Mrs. Quigley, but found the place empty and the garden overgrown. It had made her feel sad to see it so neglected and she had never gone back again.

She glanced up at Ned, reading his mind. 'No, Ned, I can't get involved in this, it's too big. Besides, it would only make me sad.'

'But you were happy there?' He looked at her, his cap in his hand.

'Of course I was, but you know, Madame Colbert dying there and everything.'

'Well, you can't live in the past, Jo. How about it?' Ned could be persuasive when he wanted to. 'Just think, sis! Chateau Colbert. We could expand our leasing business in a well-sought after area. We'd have no trouble finding clients to fill it.' He was eyeing her, willing her to go along with his plan.

She was mulling the idea over in her head. 'But an auction, Ned. What chance would we have bidding against people with more money than us? Property magnates would scoop it from under our noses.'

Like a dog with a bone, Ned knew all about auctions and had been to plenty. Jo could see determination on his face, excitement in his eyes. 'Come on, Jo! Where's your adventurous spirit?' He tilted her chin. 'There's no harm in trying now, is there?'

'Let me sleep on it. I'll let you know tomorrow.'

* * *

The more Jo thought about Chateau Colbert, the more the idea of making a bid for it appealed to her. Besides, she was curious to hear about the property, and who had bought it after the death of Madame Colbert? She knew Ned would be around first thing to cajole her some more into making a bid for the property. She slipped into the front room and was about to start work when she saw her brother walk briskly up Strand Road. He raised his cap to her tenants as they passed down the path on their way to work. Jo shook her head and smiled. Apart from a couple of bad deals, Ned had made a success as a property dealer and she trusted his judgement. But since losing all she had in the Wall Street crash, she was ever mindful of risking large amounts of Mike's money.

Ned was jubilant when he heard that she was prepared to make a joint bid for Chateau Colbert, swinging her round until she felt light-headed.

'Ned Kingsley, will you ever grow up?' Jo chided, sitting down at the table.

'Never! Grow up and life becomes boring.' He laughed and joined her at the table. 'I've worked out a few figures I'd like you to look over.' He rubbed the stubble growing on his chin, his gaze sweeping over her face as she studied the notes in front of her, a frown creasing her forehead.

'You're sure about this, Ned?'

'Yes, of course I am.'

'Do you really think it will go as high as fifteen hundred guineas?'

'Without a doubt, Jo. It could go for a little as nine hundred guineas. It could even go way over the fifteen hundred guineas. Shall we agree on seven hundred and fifty guineas each – and be prepared to stop there. We have everything to gain if we acquire the property, and nothing to lose if we fail.'

Jo felt excitement bubbling inside her. Who would have thought it? Jo Pasiński, the girl who had come from nowhere, contemplating bidding for Chateau Colbert. A tear stung the corner of her eye.

'That isn't a tear of regret, is it, Jo?'

'No. I find it hard to believe what we're about to do, that's all.'

'Good, because my advice is this,' Ned explained. 'We get there early, and sit near the front. That way we won't be distracted by who is bidding against us. Let someone bid the opening price, then follow it up with small increments.' He gave her a wink. 'Now don't worry,' he said. 'You'll enjoy it. I know you will. Everything will be fine.'

'Won't you be there?'

'Of course.'

'Like you said, Ned, we have nothing to lose.'

'Nothing at all.'

* * *

On the morning of the auction, Jo rose early. The month of June was warm but overcast. Wondering what to wear, she put on a white cotton calf-length dress, with a large navy collar. Her navy court shoes drew attention to her slender ankles encased in fine denier nylons. She was carrying a matching handbag and an umbrella, in case of a shower. With a navy linen jacket over her arm, she was about to leave when one of Ned's workmen came hurrying up the path to her door. The message was brusque. He told Jo that a business proposition had come up which her brother could not afford to miss. He would explain later, but his instructions were that she should go along without him.

Crushed and disappointed with Ned for letting her down at the last minute, she sat down to ponder her predicament. What was he thinking, asking her to go alone?. It was too late to ask Patrick to come along. Anger bubbled inside her; after all, it had been his idea.

He'd kept on about it until she'd agreed. What could be more important to him than this? How dare he do this to her? She had never been to an auction before. And she had been so looking forward to going with him. Now she felt deflated, not sure how she felt about the whole thing. The more she thought about it, the angrier she became. In a furious mood, she stood up and glanced towards the clock. What was she afraid of? She'd show him.

CHAPTER FIFTY-FOUR

She arrived late. The auction room was packed, and she was glad to see a few women amongst the hordes of men. She sat at the back, trying not to disturb or draw attention to herself. She felt uncomfortable for what seemed like an eternity before the auctioneer came to the sale of Chateau Colbert. He tapped the table with his wooden gavel and Jo took a deep intake of breath. She swallowed, feeling quite trembly. The palms of her hands were moist and she wiped them with her handkerchief.

He described Chateau Colbert, detailing its many excellent features, on the south side of the city, in the sought-after residential area of Rathgar. Jo felt an overwhelming desire to see the place again, to walk around the rooms that had given her sanctuary years before.

The bidding started enthusiastically, and Jo soon got into the rhythm, aware of the bids coming fast and furious all around her. Pleased that she had listened to Ned on the ways of auctions, she was now nodding her head as professionally as the rest of the silent bidders. Some contenders dropped out as the price rose. Jo was still holding her own, along with one or two strong bids coming from the front of the room. You could hear a pin drop as the atmosphere grew tense. The bidding was getting dangerously close to the price she had agreed with Ned, and she realised the chances of acquiring the Chateau were slim, so she dropped out. She kept her gaze on the auctioneer. The bids were rising steeply way over two thousand guineas and still rising. She stayed put, curious to hear the final bid. Her heart raced when the bidding came to an abrupt stop.

She heard the thud of the auctioneer's gavel as he announced, 'Going, going and sold, to the gentleman in the front row, for the sum of two thousand, seven hundred and fifty guineas.'

It was all over. Jo blew out her pink lips and sighed with relief. It had been a silly idea of Ned's, but now she felt curious. She craned her neck, but failed to get a look at the new owner of Chateau Colbert, too many people were milling around the cashier's desk. Others were cramming the doorway to exit the stuffy auction rooms.

Jo moved outside along with the crowd. Her annoyance with Ned had now subsided. She wondered where he'd had to rush to at such short notice. She wondered, too, if he would be disappointed about the sale. Well, it served him right for changing his mind. But he had been right about one thing – it was exciting, and she had enjoyed it, in spite of feeling nervous.

Outside, she gulped in fresh air, her head tilted upwards. It was still warm and humid, with no break in the heavy grey sky. She was pondering the idea of taking a tram to Rathgar, curious to have one last look at the Chateau, when someone called out her name. Jo swung round. She frowned, not sure who the gentleman was walking towards her. Then her eyes widened and a lump rose in her throat. 'Jean-Pierre!' she cried. 'Is it really you?'

'Jo. Jo, *ma chérie*. Am I dreaming?' A smile creased his thin face. His dark tired eyes searched her face.

'You're not dreaming, Jean-Pierre. But what are you doing in Dublin?'

'I came here for the auction. And you?' he asked. Lightly touching her elbow, he guided her to a wooden bench at the side of the pavement and they sat down.

'Jean-Pierre! I don't understand. Were you bidding for Chateau Colbert? Are you the...'

'Yes, *chérie*, I am the new owner,' he declared. He was wearing a summer weight gabardine that hung on his thin frame. 'Were you?' He smiled. 'Oh Jo, were you really making a bid?'

'Yes, I was. Ned was supposed to meet me here, but he got called away and I went in out of curiosity,' she told him. 'But how did you hear about the auction?'

'*Grandmere's* solicitor sent me a telegram as soon as he found out about the forthcoming auction. He knew I'd regretted selling Chateau Colbert years ago when I returned to Paris.' He paused, his dark eyes sad. 'I flew over immediately. It is incredible that you, my beautiful Jo, are here, too,' He spoke perfect English, mingled with the silken tones of his French accent. 'Where are you staying?'

'I live here, in Dublin. Have done for two years.'

'Two years! If only I'd known.' He glanced down at her hands folded in her lap. 'You're married?' He sounded disappointed.

She began to play with her wedding ring. 'I…'

Jean-Pierre stood up, interrupting her flow. His dark hair, showing a sprinkling of grey, fell across his eyes. 'Forgive me, I should have known someone like you, as lovely as you…' He broke off, and took a deep breath. 'You don't have to explain.' He smiled broadly.

She stood up to join him and they walked in silence. The day had turned out to be incredible, and Ned letting her down seemed insignificant now. How good it felt to see an old familiar face.

'Would it be proper for us to have a drink together?' he asked tentatively, breaking into her thoughts.

'Yes, that would be just grand,' she replied.

They strolled on, comfortable as ever in each other's company, and caught a tram to the city, alighting at Trinity College. Then they walked along Grafton Street towards St Stephen's Green, where they found a quaint restaurant that suited their needs. It was contemporary in comparison to the lavish Premiers French restaurant where they had wined and dined so long ago now. They ordered two Caesar salads with fresh rustic crusty bread, and red wine.

Jo was aware of Jean-Pierre gazing at her across the table, his hands resting on the table in front of him. Poor man, she thought. He looked like he had suffered as much as she had. But it was too soon to ask personal questions.

She leant over and gently touched his hand. 'Now that Chateau

Colbert is yours, what do you intend doing with it?' Her smile wrinkled the corners of her eyes.

'I have no idea at this moment, Jo.' Jean-Pierre looked older than his forty-three years, his once tanned face now pale. He was wearing a grey suit, white shirt and light grey tie. And the toes of his black lace-ups shone. She couldn't now, or even back then, find fault with his impeccable dress sense. And Jo was delighted that she had taken care over her own appearance before heading to the auction that morning.

Their food was served and they tucked in, relaxing in their old familiar style. They reminisced of happy times, each avoiding anything too painful.

'So, you have no plans to develop it, or perhaps use it as a home again?'

He smiled. 'What a lovely idea.' He paused. 'I just felt the need to own it again.'

'Do you still live in Paris, Jean-Pierre?' Jo asked, with both hands underneath her chin.

'Yes, at my apartment on the Champs-Elysees.' A sad look crossed his face as he straightened his shoulders. He was looking at her now as he did years before, when he first told her that he loved her. She recalled how young she had been, how she had blushed at his advances, and how devastated he had been when she had turned him down on the River Seine. In lonely times, she had missed him and his grandmother so much; missed their intellectual company, discussions on the arts, music and politics.

'What are you thinking about, Jo?' He raised the bottle of claret, but she declined, covering the top of her glass with her hand.

'I was thinking about the evenings we spent in Paris with your grandmother.'

Jean-Pierre leaned forward. 'Where did you go, after you went to America? Please tell me. I want to know everything that happened to you since our last correspondence. That is, of course, if you feel it is appropriate to tell me.'

Jo put a finger over his lips. 'Let's just enjoy being together, Jean-Pierre.'

She had no idea how long he was planning to remain in Dublin, but she hoped he would be staying a bit longer. If that was the case, there would be plenty of time for him to hear about her sad life, and for her to hear about his.

CHAPTER FIFTY-FIVE

The following morning, Ned called on Jo, his expression serious. He removed his cap and followed her into the front room, making no attempt to apologise for his shoddy treatment of her the previous day.

'If you've come here with another of your prospecting ideas, Ned Kingsley, you can forget it.'

'No. I just want to know if you went to the sale yesterday.'

'Yes, but no thanks to you.'

He was smiling now. 'And did you enjoy it? Tell me you enjoyed it, Jo.'

'What is the matter with you, Ned?' Her eyes flashed. He was playing games. 'I've got work to be getting on with. If that's all you've come for, you can go.'

'I thought you'd be full of joy this morning.' He scratched his head. 'Things didn't go that well then?' He pursed his lips.

'What do you mean? Don't you want to know how much it went for?'

'I'll come clean, Jo. In the first place, I knew that Chateau Colbert was out of our reach. and also that I wouldn't be able to come.'

'What! You knew we didn't have a chance and yet you went to such lengths to make sure that I went. Why?'

He sat down next to her. 'Can't you guess, sis? Meet anyone interesting?' He was eyeing her closely and she punched him in the arm. She could never stay mad with him for long.

'You knew all along, didn't you, you rascal?' She was laughing now. 'How? How did you know he would be there, Ned?'

'I have my ways.' He touched the side of his nose with his forefinger. 'Word got round that a certain Frenchman was interested in the property, and I guessed it had to be Jean-Pierre. I had to make sure you'd attend the auction. I wanted you to be surprised and find out if there was still a spark between the two of you. So, was there?'

'You were playing Cupid? But why didn't you come with me, Ned?'

'If I'd been with you, Jean-Pierre might not have spoken to you. Besides, I had a notice from the Corporation, saying that Grandma's house is to be condemned. I had to go and talk to them, see how long we had like, before they start redeveloping the street. It was best you didn't know.'

'Oh Ned!' she cried, and embraced him. 'That's awful news!' She felt terrible now for the thoughts she had harboured against him.

'Well, it's not for a couple of months yet. We'll just have to find somewhere else.' He smiled good-humouredly. 'But tell me, Jo. Did Jean-Pierre bid for Chateau Colbert? What did it go for?' And over a tray of tea and biscuits, Jo told her brother all about the auction, including Jean-Pierre's outrageous bid, his changed appearance, and how they had lunched together afterwards.

'What do you think he plans to do with it?'

Jo shrugged. 'I don't think he knows himself yet.'

'Will you be seeing him again?'

'Oh, yes, I hope so, Ned.'

'In that case,' he said, pulling a bundle of letters from his pocket, 'You'd better have these. She turned the letters over in her hand and recognised Jean-Pierre's handwriting. Some were quite recent and others yellow with age.

'And you kept them all this time. Why?'

'I couldn't give them to you before, not once you were happily married to Mike.' He chuckled. 'It never does to burn all your bridges.'

She reached up and kissed him tenderly on the cheek. 'Thanks, Ned.'

'Aren't you going to read them?'

'No, not yet. Sometime perhaps,' she said, and locked them in a drawer.

* * *

Jean-Pierre stayed at the Gresham Hotel overlooking O'Connell Street, and a few days later, he arranged to meet Jo in the foyer with its elegant furnishings. It was here, seated on the *chaise longue* in a quiet corner of the lobby, that Jo told Pierre about her life since leaving his grandmother's employment. Jo felt at ease with Jean-Pierre, and within days of being in his company, the sparkle returned to her blue eyes. His spontaneity of affection was just what she needed right now, bringing excitement back into her life. A week later, when he slipped his arm around her waist, she didn't object. In fact, she felt a faint stirring of desire.

In time, she related the sad and happy times of her life in Manhattan, about her life with Mike, including his untimely death. Some of the memories were so sad to recall – her joy when she discovered she was pregnant, and her distress when she lost the baby; how Annie and Peter had been her most loyal and trusted friends through all the bad times, even when they, too, had lost everything in the Wall Street crash; and finally, her struggle to sell up and return to Ireland. It was impossible to avoid tears trickling down her face as she spoke.

Jean-Pierre listened without interruption until she was finished. 'Oh my poor darling. If only I'd known.' His hand caressed her hair. 'Isn't life strange?' he mused. 'It took all that pain and sorrow to bring you back to me.'

This was where she hoped he would fill her in on his own life. The last time she had heard from Pierre, Ned had forwarded his letter saying that he was married and that his wife, Francesca, was expecting a child. She had stopped communicating after that.

'And you, Jean-Pierre?'

He reached for her hand. 'I, too, had tragedy in my life, Jo. When Francesca told me about the baby, I felt a sense of duty towards my unborn child. When my son, Francis was born, I was besotted with him.' He gave a wry smile. 'We were happy for a while, Jo,' he confessed, nodding his head.

'Where are they now?' She had to ask, yet she was terrified of the answer.

He took a deep breath and leant back in the *chaise longue*. Jo saw pain etched across his brow and lowered her head. He was still holding her hand. She knew only too well how difficult it was to relate a painful past.

'In the winter of 1930,' he began, 'my wife decided to take Francis, then only three years old, to visit her parents in Bordeaux.' He paused. 'They went alone. I couldn't get away.' He ran his finger across his top lip, a habit developed from when he sported a moustache. 'They were killed in an automobile accident. It was instant, I was told. I felt overwhelmed with guilt because I wasn't there with them.' Pain creased his face, and Jo's hand rushed to her mouth.

'Oh Jean- Pierre!' she gasped.

'I'm sorry, *chérie*. I'm making you sad, forgive me.' His eyes clouded. 'You have suffered so much already and now to hear all this…' he said, trying to mask his grief.

'What did you do then?' She wanted to know. 'Did you stay on in Paris?

'Oh Jo,' he sighed. 'I don't want to talk about the past. I want to talk of our future.' He paused. 'All through my unhappy marriage, you were never far from my thoughts. But to answer your question, I travelled all over Europe, but it did little to deaden my pain. Then I went to America with the sole purpose of finding you. As I journeyed from one place to the next, the image of your lovely face was always before me.' He sighed. 'I hoped and prayed that one day I would find you again, Jo.' His voice was full with emotion. 'I never stopped loving you.' He raised her hand to his lips, kissed it, and held it there.

'Dearest Jean-Pierre,' she cried. Was it possible, she wondered, for her to love again? And when Jean-Pierre looked at her with renewed hope in his eyes, she knew it was time to put her ghosts to rest. Then, like two solitary birds moving slowly towards each other, they finally embraced.

'My beautiful Jo, will you marry me?' Before she could utter a word, he gently placed his forefinger over her lips. 'I want you to know that whatever your answer will be, I will always love you. And if your answer is yes, I will devote the rest of my life to making you happy.' She knew he was sincere.

He sat close to her, his arm around her shoulder waiting for her reply.

Jo choked back tears, unable to speak. She felt staggered by the suddenness of everything that had happened. There was nothing to stop her loving this sensitive, wonderful man, who had loved her before and still loved her now. They were great friends and could talk, laugh and cry together. They had the same tastes and interests. There was no need for hesitation.

As soon as she could stem the tears running down her face, smudging her mascara, she took a deep breath. 'Yes, I will marry you, Jean-Pierre. I love you. I know that now.' And turning towards him, she kissed him.

Pulling her to her feet, he kissed her forehead, her nose, her tear-stained face, and finally kissed her passionately on the lips. When they pulled apart, he said, 'You can decide where we will live after we're married.'

'Could we possibly restore Chateau Colbert to its former glory? It's always been my safe haven, Jean-Pierre, and the place I've been happiest.' Then a thought flashed across her mind. 'What about my tenants? I can't desert them.'

Pierre cupped her face in both his hands. 'Why not take them with you. If it suits them, they can rent rooms at the Chateau, until we fill it with beautiful children,' he said, taking her in his arms. He kissed her till she felt breathless, returning his kisses eagerly as she felt the strong chemistry between them.

In the spring of 1938, when Chateau Colbert had been restored to its former glory and Jo's tenants were in residence, she was ready to marry the man she now loved. She was disappointed when she discovered that Annie and Peter could not make the wedding, but were planning their vacation in Ireland. It was arranged that they would spend it at Chateau Colbert with Jo and Pierre.

Pierre called at the small country cottage which he had bought for Mrs. Quigley's retirement, ensuring that she was an honoured guest at their wedding.

The happy couple were married in the church just a short walk from their beautiful home. Jo, in love, looked every bit as radiant as she did when she married Mike.

This time, a happy Ned gave her away, Cissy was maid of honour, and Sarah-Jane and Maisey were bridesmaids. Mr. Hill was Pierre's best man. They celebrated the union in style, with a magnificent banquet for friends and family afterwards.

While they honeymooned in the romantic city of Venice, Jo knew with certainty that she had again found love; a love that they both knew would withstand the test of time.

ABOUT CATHY MANSELL

Cathy Mansell writes romantic fiction. Her recently written family sagas are set in her home country of Ireland. One of these sagas closely explores her affinities with Dublin and Leicester. Her children's stories are frequently broadcast on local radio and she also writes newspaper and magazine articles. Cathy has lived in Leicester for fifty years. She belongs to Leicester Writers' Club and edited an Arts Council-funded anthology of work by Lutterworth Writers, of which she is president.

GET IN TOUCH WITH CATHY MANSELL

Cathy Mansell
www.cathymansell.com

Facebook
www.facebook.com/cathy.mansell4

Twitter
twitter.com/ashbymagna

Tirgearr Publishing
www.tirgearrpublishing.com/authors/Mansell_Cathy

* * *

Thank you for reading Where the Shamrocks Grow

Please log into Tirgearr Publishing
www.tirgearrpublishing.com
and Cathy Mansell's website for upcoming releases.

OTHER BOOKS BY CATHY MANSELL

SHADOW ACROSS THE LIFFEY
Released: February 2013
ISBN: 9781301231720

Life is hard for widow, Oona Quinn. She's grief-stricken by the tragic deaths of her husband and five-year-old daughter. While struggling to survive, she meets charismatic Jack Walsh at the shipping office where she works.

Vinnie Kelly, her son's biological father, just out of jail, sets out to destroy both Oona and all she holds dear. Haunted by her past, she has to fight for her future and the safety of her son, Sean. But Vinnie has revenge on his mind . . .

HER FATHER'S DAUGHTER
Released: July 2014
ISBN: 9781301256402

Set in 1950s Ireland, twenty-year-old Sarah Nolan leaves her Dublin home after a series of arguments. She's taken a job in Cork City with The Gazette, a move her parents strongly oppose. With her limited budget, she is forced to take unsavory accommodations where the landlord can't be trusted. Soon after she settles in, Sarah befriends sixteen-year-old Lucy who has been left abandoned and pregnant.

Dan Madden is a charming and flirtatious journalist who wins Sarah's heart. He promises to end his engagement with Ruth, but can Sarah trust him to keep his word?

It's when her employer asks to see her birth certificate that Sarah discovers some long-hidden secrets. Her parents' behaviour continue to baffle her and her problems with Dan and Lucy multiply.

Will Dan stand by Sarah in her time of need? Will Sarah be able to help Lucy keep her baby? Or will the secrets destroy Sarah and everything she dreams of for her future?

GALWAY GIRL
Released: June 2015
ISBN: 9781310901614

Feisty Irish gypsy girl, Tamara Redmond is just sixteen when she overhears her parents planning her wedding to the powerful and hated Jake Travis. In desperation, she leaves Galway, a place she loves, and stows away on a ship with disastrous consequences. On her release from a cell in Liverpool, she takes refuge in a travelling circus and falls in love with Kit Trevlyn, a trapeze artist.

Accused of stealing, she is thrown out. She sleeps rough in Covent Garden where her fear of Jake Travis finding her dominates her waking hours. When he kidnaps her and keeps her captive, her life spirals downwards. Then Tamara hears a truth, a truth that will change her life and her very existence forever.

Lightning Source UK Ltd.
Milton Keynes UK
UKHW021807270519
343403UK00011B/170/P